Beautifully Unbroken

D. M. Brittle

Beautifully Unbroken

Copyright © Beautifully Unbroken

Dedication

For my Dad, I wish that you were here to see this.

1

I felt nervous as I boarded the plane to New York to begin the new chapter in my life just over a year ago. Moving my life to New York was always going to be the biggest decision in both my life and my career, but making that decision had been easy. I needed out, I needed new, I needed unfamiliar, a place where for now no one would know me, no one would care. I wouldn't be followed or harassed and would be free to eat where I wanted, shop where I wanted, and do what I wanted without it being headline news. New York was going to be that place, and despite the nerves, I couldn't wait.

Aside from my parents, whom I loved deeply, there was nothing in London that could convince me to stay. Work had been steady for the past couple of years, and I was slowly becoming stuck in a rut. I didn't go out any more, unless it was for work. I needed a new start, a new chapter, a new life.

My parents had helped me get through the hardest time of my life, so when the opportunity arose for me to build a fresh life in New York, they were adamant that I should take it.

Michael was my ex; my dad had wanted to kill him on numerous occasions. He would show me with his hands exactly how he would strangle the man until he took his last breath. I loved my dad so much; he was my rock. I would miss him so much, but as he told me time and time again, I was only a seven-hour flight away, that was all. I'm not sure it was me he was trying to convince, though, and not himself.

I had dated Michael for twelve months before my life changed.

Michael Robinson took away any trust I had ever had in men. He ripped my heart right out of my chest and stamped on it until it was beyond repair. The man who promised me the world had given me only hell. At twenty-one I thought I loved him; I was besotted yet failed to see the real Michael, the man behind the mask who would destroy me and take away any faith I ever had in love and in happiness.

Michael was very talented footballer playing for one of London's top clubs; I was a TV and film actress. Together we were a paparazzi dream, especially when things weren't going well; the media, of course, loved that. The man who I thought loved me and would do anything for me turned out to be a horny, fame-hungry vile specimen of a man whose treatment of me would steer me clear of loving another man for the rest of my life.

Then into my life walked Blake Mackenzie.

I had spent my four years since leaving Michael building a perimeter around myself, keeping out any man who ever thought he had a chance. No man would ever be allowed to break down the barrier and let me fall helplessly in love with him before he then decided it wasn't what he really wanted and threw me head first into the lion's den. No way.

But there was something about Blake. He had the ability to break me down. He already had; I had fallen hook, line, and complete sinker in love with him and no matter how hard I tried, there would be no escape. I would close my eyes, he would be there; I would dream … only about him; I would open my eyes, and my first thought would be to wonder what he was doing. I read once that the first person who is on your mind the moment you open your eyes after a long sleep is the reason for either your happiness or your pain. Blake was my reason for both.

I had built up a strong belief that with happiness came pain. There was always a price to pay for being happy. I was yet to have this theory proved wrong, and I doubted that I ever would.

Blake and I had been working together on a new romantic comedy for the past six months; filming had finished only nine days prior. I missed him already – which was ridiculous, but I did – so much so that I had gone out of my way to see him a couple of times.

I had it bad, and I tried to resist; I really did. But with Blake that was impossible.

I hadn't told Blake about my feelings for him. I couldn't tell him for fear of what would happen. My being an actress came in very useful, yet I'm not one hundred per cent convinced he didn't see behind it all. There were times with Blake when I sensed that not only did he see how

I felt but also that he felt it too. Maybe I just wanted to believe that he liked me, and maybe just imagining it would be for the best. After all, I had issues. I couldn't trust that everything that happened to me four years before wouldn't happen again, and if it did, what then? Move to another country to escape?

But the more I thought about Blake, the more I wanted him. I wanted the image I had every night while I was sleeping to become reality and not fantasy. I wanted his hands all over my body. I wanted to taste him, to be tasted by him. I wanted him above me, inside me. I wanted every single part of him, but I wasn't sure that I could handle it.

Damn you, Michael Robinson and your playboy lifestyle, for making me this way. I wish I'd hated you this much when we first met, instead of falling for your charm. In fact, I wish we had never laid eyes on each other in the first place. My life would have been so much easier that way.

Casey is my roommate. I didn't know Casey before I moved to New York, however sharing my new agent had put us in contact. She was rattling around in an apartment which looked out over Central Park West. It was the perfect escape for me.

Casey and I hit it off immediately. She too had left her family for a new life in New York, albeit her family was still here in the US; but they were in Florida, so the two of us would prove to be good for each other.

One of the things I loved most about Casey was that she dated Blake's best friend, Alex. It was as if fate had intervened and Blake and I were destined to keep bumping into each other.

When Casey arrived in New York, she was alone. She had no idea of where to go or whom to contact. While drinking in one of Alex's many bars one night, she and Alex had got to chatting, one thing led to another, and they became inseparable. Alex then introduced Casey to Blake, who Casey said took her under his wing and helped kick her career off. She said that fate took her to that bar that evening; I wonder if fate brought me to New York?

That night, we were all going to be attending a party to celebrate the end of filming. I had been waiting eagerly for this party for the past nine days. Just to see him; to be near him; to hear his voice – his deep, raspy, sexy voice; to look into those piercing blue eyes that glistened like diamonds against the sun; and to see his smile – his perfect, dazzling smile. My heart rate increased at the thought of it all. I wanted him so badly, yet I knew I was probably going to end up broken again – broken and alone. Yet something inside me was pushing me closer and closer to him, and I was willingly going, whether I wanted to or not.

My mind wandered back to the last time I saw him, two days before.

I stumbled into my apartment overloaded with shopping. Just as I made it into the kitchen, one bag slipped and crashed to the floor.

"Shit!" I cursed as I watched everything head off in different directions.

"Here, let me help you," he said with a hint of amusement, obviously laughing at my lack of coordination while carrying shopping. Looking up, I noticed Blake standing above me. He was here. Why was he here?

"Blake … hi," I said. "What are you … um … why are you here?"

He smiled his winning smile as he crouched next to me, retrieving food that had strayed to every corner of the kitchen.

"Alex and I are off to the game; he's running late as usual."

"Do you two not live in the same building?" I asked, confused.

"Yeah, we do," he answered simply before a small grin tugged at the side of his mouth.

Realizing I was staring, I stood up quickly and placed the rest of the items on the worktop.

"So," Blake said as he stood and walked over next to me. I inhaled his scent; he smelt of soap and the aftershave that he had worn every day on set. He smelt clean and beautiful; just his scent made my legs feel weak and the area between my thighs throb with want.

Trying not to appear too obvious, I turned and started putting the groceries away.

"Are you looking forward to Friday?" he asked.

"Friday?"

"The party," he replied.

"Oh, yes." was all I managed.

I sensed the smile in his reply but couldn't bring myself to turn to look at him for fear that he would be able to read me easier than a book. I felt my skin heat; it was written all over my face.

I saw him from the corner of my eye; he gently leaned against the unit, his eyes burning into me. "Do you have a date?" he asked.

My heart sped up; I could feel it beating hard without even placing my hand on my chest.

"I'm taking Casey," I replied shakily. Turning to face him, I noticed he was studying me. A small smile graced the corner of his mouth. "You?" I asked, trying to sound casual.

"I'm going alone," he said as he started tossing an apple continually into the air.

Good, he was no longer staring, so he wouldn't have noticed the obvious relief that flooded my face.

Placing the apple in the bowl, he turned and faced me once more. "Look, Jo, I was wondering—"

"Ready, Blake?" Alex appeared, dressed and ready to go.

I didn't miss the sound of Blake sighing at the interruption. Without taking his eyes off me, he smiled. "Yeah, I'm ready." As he passed me and headed to the door, he leaned in towards me. "I'll see you Friday, Jo."

The feel of his cool breath on my neck sent goose pimples over the whole of my body. I was unable to answer and watched as he left without another word.

I couldn't have imagined what had just happened. He liked me – he must? I had this feeling in the pit of my stomach that I couldn't shake; something was going to happen between Blake and me, and I wasn't even near strong enough to do anything about it.

"Jo! Come on already, we're gonna be late!"

Casey was yelling at me from outside the bathroom, where I had spent the past three hours doing everything that I could do to make myself look irresistible. I had left my brown curly hair loose; Blake had made one tiny comment once – just once – about how nice my hair was, and I was wearing it loose at the time. I shook my head in disgust at myself for the way I was acting – the way I had sworn I would never act around a male ever again for as long as I lived. And yet here I was doing it all, the whole kit and caboodle. I felt ashamed of myself, yet there was no denying the excitement that I could feel bubbling up inside me at the thought of being near him again.

After taking a few deep, cleansing breaths, I headed into the lounge where Casey stood waiting eagerly.

"Holy shit, Batman," she said with a smirk. "Who in God's name are you trying to impress!"

Trying my hardest to look innocent, I glanced down at my dress and back at Casey. "Too much?" I asked.

"Definitely." She nodded with a huge grin on her face. "You look amazing! Who is he?" She pushed her hip out to the side and rested her hand there as she waited for my reply.

"He is no one," I sighed. I walked past her, grabbing my bag, and headed for the door.

"Not such a good actress when it comes to lying about a man, Jo!" she teased as she caught up with me. She then whispered, "I'm watching you," before breaking out into a laugh.

Shaking my head, I smiled at her. "Now you're gonna make us late; come on."

She headed past me and out of the door. I had told Casey everything about Michael one night over a few cocktails. She knew my feelings about men and trust, but she also knew me well enough now to know that yes, I was trying to impress someone, and that that someone was only a ten-minute cab ride away.

Peter was head of security in our building; he spoke with a very traditional English accent, which always made me feel at home. He held the door open for us as we stepped out onto the hot streets of New York. "Enjoy your evening, ladies," he said with a smile.

"Don't wait up!" Casey yelled.

"So," Casey said in mock disgust, "we're all dressed up and off the Plaza, yet we're getting in a cab."

"Come on," I teased. "Where's your sense of adventure?"

"I must've left it back in the apartment with my fear of being murdered by a loony," she replied dryly.

"Yellow cabs are an icon; I love them," I replied as a cab pulled up beside us.

"So are limos and champagne," Casey said sarcastically as she climbed into the cab. Casey was stunning; her golden hair was long and completely straight, and she had legs that went on forever and a figure to die for. She was confident, which I envied immensely. She had taken knock-backs quite often but was always professional and carried on regardless. I vowed to train myself to be more like her.

It felt like the longest drive ever to the Plaza Hotel; my heart had begun a steady increase in the strength of its beats until it was actually beating so hard I swear I could actually see it pulsing against my skin. The thought of what the night would bring made me feel exited yet anxious.

Casey talked non-stop, and I would throw in the odd yes, no, or maybe answer when prompted, but I had no idea what she was talking about. My mind was focused on one thing and one thing only.

"Are you okay over there?" Casey asked, pulling me from my Blake dream.

"Yes," I answered, forcing a smile.

"You seem … fidgety," she observed.

"It's just the heat, that's all; it's so bloody hot." I waved my hand in front of my face as if cooling myself down.

"Well, if we had hired a limo, you wouldn't be suffering now and we could have cooled off with some ice-cold champagne," she complained.

I shot her a glare to which she held her hands up in defeat. "Just saying."

I hurried us both through the waiting media as quickly as I could. Even though shots of us filming had hit some gossip sites over the past few months, I was still managing to keep myself quite anonymous, and I wanted to keep it that way for as long as was possible. I was enjoying the new found freedom that New York had given me, and as much as Casey hated the yellow cabs, I loved them. I loved that I could go anywhere and do anything and no one seemed to care. That was one thing that was so different in England. Back home I couldn't even pop to a chemist for a box of aspirin without it being misinterpreted as me being there for a pregnancy test. I had yet to experience anything like that over here; New York was fast becoming my new home. I was happier here than I had been for a long time back in London.

Casey and I entered the room where most of the cast and crew, including guests, were already gathered. The room was breathtaking; it was as if we had stepped out of 2014 and straight back into the 1920s.it was huge, with enormous chandeliers that hung around the centre of the room.

Every table boasted a gigantic flower arrangement made up of white calla lilies and perfect pink roses; the room both looked and smelt delicious.

We were both handed a glass of champagne by a passing waiter, and I immediately took a large glug which sizzled warmly as it settled in my stomach. It tasted divine, and it was helping to settle my ever-growing nerves.

Casey headed off into the crowd to mingle, but I found myself frozen to the spot, my brain failing to send any signal to my feet to enable me to move.

My eyes immediately started to scan the growing crowd of people. I could feel Blake's presence somewhere in this room. I knew he was here, but I couldn't see him anywhere.

"Looking for anyone in particular?"

I felt a soft, warm breath on the back of my neck which made my skin tingle. I gasped and turned to face him; our eyes locked immediately.

"Blake," I whispered with a smile.

"Jo," he replied softly.

"Hi." I smiled.

"Hi yourself," he replied with a smile before taking a sip of his champagne. I took a moment to drink him in; he was the definition of beautiful. His body was toned in all of the right places, and his face was chiseled to perfection. He wore light stubble that I always imagined rubbing against my skin. His hair was dark and just long enough to grab hold of; I wanted to grab it and hold it so tightly between my fingers.

"You look beautiful, Jo," he said in the velvet tone that made the area between my thighs ache with want.

"Thank you, so do you." I immediately regretted adding that last bit, and I felt my face blush.

Blake obviously noticed, as he smiled knowingly. "Thank you." His fingers brushed my arm, stroking from my shoulder all the way down to my wrist. His fingers then linked with mine as he brushed his thumb over the palm of my hand.

"You're shaking," he observed. "Are you nervous?" I managed a nod as I took another large gulp of champagne. "Can I be honest with you?"

"Of course," I said quietly.

"I'm nervous too," he said slightly amusedly, causing me to laugh.

"Listen, the other day, at your apartment"—my eyes shot up to his immediately—"what I was about to say before Alex and his ability to spoil any moment walked in"—Blake rolled his eyes—"was if maybe I could take you out to dinner sometime … maybe?"

"Yes, maybe you could." I smiled.

"I could?"

"Maybe." I nodded with a smile.

"Okay then." Blake nodded. "Maybe I will." His mouth curled up into the most gorgeous smile I had ever seen grace his face. I felt my body begin to relax.

"You've stopped shaking," Blake observed as he began moving his fingers up the length of my arm.

"Maybe I'm not so nervous anymore," I said, feeling my body tingle from just the slightest touch of his fingers.

We stood for a long moment just watching each other, visibly trying to read each other's minds. The more I watched him, the more beautiful he seemed to become.

"Ah, Blake, there you are." An elderly gentleman whom I hadn't seen before was approaching us, pulling us both swiftly from the moment we were sharing. Blake's hand moved from my arm as he stood straight. "Now, this man here is officially the oldest man in New York," Blake whispered, causing me to laugh. "Franklin, it's good to see you." Blake nodded as he greeted him.

"Blake, my boy, it's good to see you too," the man said, sounding every bit like one of the Mafiosos from the *Godfather* films. "There is someone here who I insist you meet; come with me." He beckoned.

"Sure, Franklin, I'll be right there." Blake smiled before turning back to me.

"So," he said.

"So," I replied.

"I'll call you."

"I look forward to it," I replied honestly.

My heart began to race even quicker as Blake turned on his heel and followed Franklin across the ballroom, I had convinced myself that maybe I had imagined Blake's feelings for me, but the way he had looked at me, the way he had spoken, the way he had gently stroked my arm – it all confirmed that something was going to happen between us. And for the first time in four years, I could not wait.

I quickly pulled myself together, grabbed another glass of champagne from a passing waiter, and headed off to where I could see Casey chatting happily with a group of people.

One of the people Casey was chatting to was Sara McDonnell; Sara had starred alongside Blake and me in the film. She was stunning; her long red hair fell in waves almost to the bottom of her back, and she was tall and very slim. I felt quite intimidated by her and hadn't really bonded with her while we were either on set or off; there was something about her that I didn't trust. She had never done anything to offend me, but something about her made it hard for me to connect to her.

"Hey, Jo!" Casey said a bit too enthusiastically, "Sara is trying out for that same part as you are next week for that new series on USA network!"

I found myself forcing a smile. "Oh, good luck."

"It's no biggie." She shrugged. "I do know the casting director, however, but he's strictly professional, so you shouldn't have anything to worry about." She winked, and I could sense the sarcasm. Yes, I actually did dislike this woman.

"So, I saw you and Blake," she said, eyeing me carefully. "I didn't realize there was anything between the two of you."

"There isn't" was all I said before I felt my phone vibrating in my clutch bag. Refusing to give anything more to Sara, I grabbed my phone, noticing it was my mum calling.

Panic set in. London was five hours ahead of New York, meaning that my mum was calling me at 2.00 a.m.

"I need to take this," I said quickly as I hurried out of the ballroom into the lobby.

"Mum?" I answered quickly.

"Josephine, oh Josephine." She was sobbing; my mum never cried or showed any emotion. Unlike me, my mum was made of steel, inside and out. Being a national treasure on British TV had done that to her. Years of bad reviews and press had made my mum invincible to any form of emotion.

"Mum, what is it? Are you okay? Is it Dad?" I felt my throat starting to constrict as if someone had cut off my air supply.

"Your father has had a heart attack," she sobbed. "Josephine. They … they don't …" She continued to sob.

"They don't think he is going to be okay, do they?" I said quietly as Mum continued to sob uncontrollably.

2

My stomach sank and my hands became clammy and shaky, my dad had had a heart attack, and they didn't know whether he was going to survive. I needed to get there. I needed to be with him as soon as I could. The only problem was the huge sea of water that separated us. *Seven hours, it's just seven hours,* I kept repeating in my head to myself. *I can be there not much longer than that; it's just seven hours.*

"Can you come home?" my mum asked gently.

"Yes. God, Mum, of course. I'm going to book a flight, and I will be there with you as soon as I can, I promise. Just do something for me, will you, Mum?" I scrunched my eyes tightly shut; trying to relieve some of the pain I was now feeling. "Give Dad a big kiss from me, and you tell him I'm coming and tell him" – I sucked in a deep breath as my voice started to shake – "please tell him I love him to the moon and back." My voice cracked towards the end, and I closed my eyes momentarily while I tried to process everything that had happened in the past few minutes.

"I love you, Josephine."

I love you too, Mum."

I let my hand slip down to my side. Suddenly it felt as though the whole room was closing in on me. I needed to go; I needed to pack a bag and get on a plane.

I rushed back into the room, my eyes frantically scanning every inch. I couldn't see Casey anywhere. My eyes finally found Sara. She was going to have to do; I couldn't waste a single second more trying to find Casey.

Sara's face dropped when she saw I was crying. "Jo, what is it? What's wrong?"

"The call," I said. "My dad, he's …" Tears started rushing down my cheek as reality hit home, "He's had a heart attack. I need to go; he needs me."

Sara reached forward and placed her hand on my shoulder. "You go. I'll make sure Casey knows; he will be okay, Jo." Her expression was of genuine concern; maybe I'd misread her all along.

"Thank you," I said quietly as I turned and rushed for the door, running straight into Cooper.

"Hey, where's the fire!" His smile faded quickly when he noticed I was in a hurry. Cooper had been a good friend to me while filming. He had not only been another co-star, but he had also taken it upon himself to show me a few of New York's best features. We had become good friends; he had been like the brother that I had never had. I felt grateful that now, in this moment, I had run into him.

"What's happened?" he said as he took my hand. I explained quickly about my dad and how I needed to be there as quickly as possible. "Okay, let's go," he said, taking my hand.

"No, no, you should stay; I'll be okay."

"Look," he said, "truth is, I don't even like these events. Give me a club and a bunch of hot chicks any night of the week – but this?" He shook his head. "Not my scene. You're a damsel in distress; I'm gonna be your knight in shining armour." He smiled. "Now come, we need to get you on a plane."

"Are you sure?" I sobbed.

"What are friends for?"

I threw my arms around his neck in gratitude. "Thank you so much, Cooper," I said before placing a quick peck on his cheek.

We hurried quickly out of the hotel and to Cooper's car. There were a couple of photographers hanging around, but Cooper got us to his car quickly enough that I think we missed any attention. I was thankful for the tinted windows as I climbed into Cooper's Porsche 911.

"Let's show you how appropriately fast this car can be." Cooper winked at me before pulling swiftly out of the spot and speeding off through the busy streets of New York.

We sat in silence on the short ride to the apartment. My mind wandered to Blake. I wished I had seen him before I left, but I needed to get out of there as soon as possible. Maybe he would call once he knew about Dad; I hoped so, anyway.

"How are you doing over there?" Cooper said, breaking the

silence.

I sighed. "I just wish I wasn't so far away; he needs me, and I'm so far away."

Cooper squeezed my knee gently. "You will be there by morning; he's not gonna go anywhere, Jo, I promise."

I wanted to believe him, I really did, but no one knew the truth; no one knew whether he would make it. I sat silently praying to God to protect him, to keep him safe for me, to get me to him before he could get any worse.

Cooper insisted on helping as much as he could. While I threw some random clothes into a small case, he called the airline and booked me a flight which was due to leave in three hours. As much as an extra three hours was going to be a traumatic wait, I would still be in London as soon as I could be. I was grateful for everything Cooper had done for me; I couldn't have done it all alone. My mind was all over the place, and having someone there to help had taken a massive weight off my mind.

"Thank you for everything this evening, Cooper; you have no idea how much I appreciate it." I lifted onto my toes and gave him a quick kiss on his cheek.

He smiled. "I'm just glad I was in the right place at the right time."

"When I get back from London, I'm taking you out."

"It's a date."

"It's a thank you," I confirmed.

"A thank-you date?" he teased. I shook my head and smiled for the first time since I had spoken to my mum.

"You have been such a good friend to me, Cooper; I'll never forget that."

"That's what friends are for, Jo. Take care and call me if you need anything – a chat, a shoulder. I'm here, okay?"

"Thank you," I said, placing a quick kiss on his cheek.

Picking up my bag, I turned and headed for the departure gate. This was going to be one hell of a long, worrisome flight with no communication from my mum until I landed, but I was also now even closer to being there with my parents, where I was needed and where I wanted to be.

I finally landed at London's Heathrow airport at twelve thirty British time. I switched my phone on at the earliest convenience. There were no missed calls, just one text from my mum informing me that my dad's twin brother, Uncle Anthony, would be there waiting when I came through arrivals.

As soon as I spotted him, my legs found the strength to hurry towards him. It was hard to make out his expression.

"Please tell me he's okay," I said as I threw myself into his arms.

He held me so tight against him. "No change, sweetheart," he breathed into my hair.

"Is that a good thing?" I said between sobs.

"I'd like to think so," he replied.

"Take me to him please."

Uncle Anthony released me but kept hold of one of my hands while picking up my luggage in the other. "Let's go," he replied.

I was dreading the sight that was going to greet me. The last time I had seen my dad, he was so full of life. He was healthy and happy as he stood waving me off to start my new life. I remember seeing a single tear fall from his eyes as I walked away, but he continued to smile and wave at me and wish me good luck. He was so proud of me and everything that I had achieved, and now he was lying in a hospital bed, unaware of his surroundings and what lay ahead.

London was still the same; nothing had changed. It was a warm day, yet not so humid as the heat in New York. Thinking of New York reminded me of Blake; I wondered whether he knew yet that I had had to leave.

It felt like such a long drive to the hospital. Being a Saturday, the streets were swarmed with shoppers and tourists, and all I wanted was to get to my dad.

We pulled up at the hospital an hour later, and as I had suspected, there were reporters gathered near the entrance. "Fuck sake,"

I muttered under my breath. Uncle Anthony shot me a surprised look. "Sorry," I said, realizing I had just sworn for the first time in my life in front of him. "It's just" – I gestured towards the greedy reporters – "they thrive on this. Look at them, waiting for a fu ... flipping exclusive."

"Shall I see about another entrance?"

"No, it's okay; I just want to get in there. I need to see him." I hopped out of the car quickly and dashed towards the entrance while Uncle Anthony went on to park the car.

It didn't take long for one of the pack to notice me, and then it began.

"Miss Summers, how's your father?"

"Miss Summers! Is it true your father's heart attack is a result of his losing the Dixon case?"

"Miss Summers! *Miss Summers!*"

"Jo! This way! Jo, can you tell us how he is?"

I proceeded to ignore the constant screams and made it through the entrance unscathed. I was taken immediately to the room where my dad lay fighting for his life. I paused for a moment before entering the room.

After taking a few deep breaths, I opened the door to find my mum curled up in a chair next to my dad's bed. She was sleeping but had a firm grip on his hand. Then there was my dad. My breath caught at the sight of him; he looked completely different to how I remembered him. He had lost weight since I last saw him – a lot of weight. His face was gaunt and grey. He had tubes and pipes attached to his mouth and arms, and numerous machines were beeping and pumping. It was all so hard to take in. He looked lifeless.

Mum stirred, and her eyes locked with mine.

"Josephine! Oh, my darling, you are here." I saw the relief in her face as she sighed heavily. "Come here," she sobbed. Loosing Dad's hands, she leaped from the chair and took me in her arms. We stood for what felt like an eternity, holding each other and crying; I didn't realize how much I had missed either of them until this moment – the familiarity of being with them, the safe feeling I felt just knowing they were close by. I had missed them more than I could ever explain. I didn't want to let Mum go; she had needed me since the night before, but I was too far away to help her. But now I was here, I would do everything I could to help her and to help my dad. They needed me now: it was now my turn to look after them.

Mum stepped back and held my face in her hands. "Look at you." She smiled slightly. "You have grown into such a beautiful young lady. Just look at you." She used her thumbs to wipe away my tears before turning to my dad. "She's here, John; she's back. Look, our beautiful girl is here." Mum sat back down, taking one of his hands in hers once more. I stepped closely and perched myself on the edge of his bed, taking his other hand in mine.

"Talk to him," Mum said quietly, not taking her eyes from him. "They think he can hear us," she said, nodding to the nurse who was hovering outside the door.

"Really?" I asked.

Mum nodded.

"Hey," I choked out, "look at you with all the ladies running around after you." I tried to smile, to sound positive, but it was hurting so bad. I looked to Mum, unsure of what I should say. She just smiled and nodded for me to continue.

"Could you open your eyes for me, Daddy, please?" The beeping and pumping of the machines seemed to get more intense the more I sat there and begged him to wake up.

"Why won't you wake up, Daddy? Just stop it now and wake up!" I couldn't help the rise in the tone as I begged him, causing my mum to flinch slightly. "Please," I whispered, "please don't you dare die." The dams broke and the tears flew freely down my face. Mum stood and wrapped her arms around my shoulders, comforting me while she was the one who could potentially lose the man who had been her rock for the past thirty-five years. She held me so tightly as she too sobbed. I realized that I needed to be strong; it was killing me seeing Dad lying there helpless and hanging on for dear life, but Mum needed me now. I needed to be her rock. She had been my mother for twenty-five years and had looked after me through every page of my life; it was time now for me to return her the favour.

Sucking in numerous deep breaths, I turned to Mum. "He's going to be okay. He *is* going to be okay, Mum, I promise."

The minutes felt like hours; the hours like days. We just sat, watched, and waited. Nurses came and went, checking OBS and jotting down numbers on his chart. He wasn't improving, but he also wasn't getting any worse. I kept telling us both that that was a good sign; no news was always good news. Always.

Placing my head against the coolness of the glass window, I watched as life outside carried on as normal. Shoppers and tourists went about their business as normal. Some people rushed as though the apocalypse were about to arrive, and others dawdled as if they had all the time in the world. Old couples sat hand in hand on benches, eating ice creams and drinking coffee.

It wasn't until this moment, here and now, as I stood looking out of a hospital window, that I realized just how cruel life was. We would breeze through it as if nothing mattered, not noticing tiny milestones yet worrying about things that in the long run would mean nothing, and for what? Life should be lived, enjoyed, remembered, yet we only remember this when it becomes too late, when we're standing at our father's bedside while he fights for his life. Yes, life was cruel.

"Were you with him?" I said, breaking the silence that had formed in the room. I turned away from the outside world and walked back to Mum and Dad. "Please tell me he wasn't alone."

Mum never took her eyes away from Dad as she spoke. "I was there."

I felt relief knowing he wasn't alone when it happened.

"You know he lost the Dixon case?" Mum said.

Closing my eyes, I sighed. Dad was a high-class solicitor, and over the years he had won some very high-profile cases. He had built up such a reputation that celebrities from every walk of life were now looking to him for help. Work had taken over Dad's life when I was just eleven. Before that, he would work a normal day, come home, and spend every minute of his evenings with me. We were inseparable; I was well and truly a daddy's girl. I would wait at the window for him every night without fail. And no matter what sort of day he had had, he would never bring it home. He was happy; we were all happy. But that would all change as he became better and better at what he did best.

Eventually we ended up moving from our family home in Kent to Kensington so as Dad could be closer to work. He was spending every waking minute on cases and was hardly home, so moving closer to London pulled the family closer before we started drifting away.

"He's never lost a case before," I replied.

"I've never seen him so … I don't know … he was just devastated," Mum recalled. "It was late. He came walking in, and for the first time in thirty-five years, he wasn't smiling. He was sweating. His face was so pale; he looked terrible. I didn't know what to do or what to say." She shrugged. "What do you say to someone who had been invincible until that day?

"I did the only thing I knew to do. I kissed him, hugged him, and told him everything was going to be okay. I told him to sit while I got him something to eat, but he kept insisting that he wasn't hungry and to just stay and hold him for a while." She sniffed. "Eventually I loosed him and headed to the kitchen. And then" – she let out a loud sob – "I heard him. He cried out in pain, and then I heard this heavy, horrific thud."

Mum was now crying uncontrollably. I wrapped my arms around her. "Shh, it's okay," I choked out. "He is going to be okay. We're going to get him better, Mum, I promise."

"You need to get some rest," Mum said, looking up at me warily.

"No, I need to be here with you and Dad."

"You must be exhausted, Josephine; you haven't slept for so long, and the flight over. Go home and get some rest, please."

"Mum, you haven't rested either. If anyone needs rest, it's you."

Mum let out a tired laugh. "You know I don't sleep anyway, Josephine; this chair is good enough for me. Please, go home, have a couple of hours. I'll call you if I need to, I promise."

I didn't want to leave them, and even though I was exhausted, there was no way I was going anywhere.

"Please, Josephine. I know you want to stay, but you are going to end up dropping. I need you strong. Here, call Uncle Anthony; he will come and get you." she handed me her mobile phone.

"No," I said, handing her phone back to her. "I just need coffee. Can I get you some?"

"No," Mum said with a smile, placing her phone back into her pocket. "I've drank enough tea and coffee to sink a ship this past twenty-four hours."

"I will be down in the cafe. My phone is on; if you need me, you call me," I said firmly.

She smiled. "Of course."

I gave Dad a long kiss and told him to have those eyes wide open by the time I arrived back. As I approached the café, my phone buzzed. Immediately thinking of Blake, I dug into my handbag and removed it.

It was Casey calling, and even though I felt a slight disappointment, I was grateful.

"Hello," I answered as I sank into one of the uncomfortable plastic seats in the cafe.

"Jo" – I heard her exhale – "how is he? How's your dad? I'm so sorry, I only just found out."

Thinking that Casey must have had one too many champagnes the night before to remember Sara had told her, I replied, "No change. I'm so scared, Casey. He's going to die; I just know he is." I tried to hold back the tears, but it was impossible.

"Oh, Jo, I wish there was something I could do to help you," she said sympathetically.

"Just talking to you means so much," I replied.

"I miss you," Casey said. "We all do."

"I miss you too," I said, sucking in a sob.

"You call me, okay?" she said with emotion in her voice. "Any time; day or night, I may be thousands of miles away, but I love you."

"I love you too," I replied.

Mum was reading sections of the *Financial Times* out to Dad when I walked back into the room. She looked up at me and smiled.

"You weren't gone long."

"I didn't like being away from him," I replied. I walked over and kissed her on the cheek before then going to Dad and doing the same. "Any change?"

Mum shook her head slightly as she looked at him. "They're not really saying anything; they come in and out all of the time but don't tell me anything."

"That's good though, surely?"

Mum didn't reply; she just carried on looking at Dad. I could see all of the emotions running through her; I could see her love for him, the need she had for him – it was all there to see.

"Mum?"

"Yes dear?"

"I think I'm in love," I said quietly.

Mum gasped in surprise and turned her full attention to me. Even though her eyes looked so heavy and desperate, she wanted to hear about Blake.

"Tell me everything. How did you meet? What does he do? Does he feel the same?"

Shaking my head as I smiled at her, I said simply, "It's Blake."

"Your co-star?" she said with a hint of amusement.

I nodded.

"And does Blake know?"

"Yes. Well, I think so. He wants to take me out to dinner."

"Oh, darling, it's about time," she teased.

"I'm scared, Mum," I admitted.

Mum took my hand in hers. "He's not Michael, Josephine."

"I know." I nodded in agreement but frowned.

"What is it?"

"It's been so long, Mum; I'm scared of letting him in, getting close and …"

"And?"

"What if it happens again?"

"Darling" – Mum wrapped her arms around me and kissed my head – "you can't live your life worrying about what ifs. There are no guarantees in life, but what happened to you" – Mum paused, deciding on her next words – "what happened was …"

"I know what you are trying to say, Mum, I do. But—"

"Ah." Mum placed a finger to my lips. "No buts. Do you know how long your father and I have waited for you to find someone who can give as much love as you can give to them?"

Smiling, I removed her finger from my mouth. "You don't even know him, Mum."

"No," she admitted, "but you do, and after four years it was going to take a good man to break you down." She smirked and sat back down in the chair she had become so used to.

I shook my head in disbelief at the conversation I was having with my mum. "Every single man that I have ever dated cheated on me, Mum; who is to say he won't do the same?"

"There are no guarantees in life, Jo. Sometimes we have to just take a chance. So when your dad gets better and you go back off to your new life, you go get him, you hear me?" She picked the newspaper back up and continued telling my dad about the world and its problems.

I laughed for the first time in days. She was such an old romantic at times.

It started to become easy sitting and talking to Dad as though he could hear me. The constant beeping and pumping sounds were beginning to fade now. I had become so used to them that I barely noticed they were there without looking directly at them. It was my turn to read to Dad now, so I took the sports pages in hand and read Dad the main stories. There were plenty of stories because the World Cup was about to start, and that was one tournament that Dad loved.

I was in the middle of telling him about an incident that was being reported regarding a scuffle between some fans when I felt his hand tighten around mine.

I froze; unable to breathe for fear that I had imagined it. He squeezed again.

Mum was dozing in her chair. "Mum," I said in a hushed tone. "Mum, he can hear me; he's squeezing my hand! Mum!"

Mum shot quickly out of the chair. "Can you hear us, John?" she said desperately. "It's me, Diana, and look, our baby girl is here too! Darling, press for the nurses; get them in here!"

Suddenly there was hope. He was wriggling, and even though his eyes were still closed, I had felt it, I had felt him with me, and now I could see that he was trying desperately to come back to us.

He let out a groan.

"Come on, Daddy, open those eyes," I pleaded, holding his hand tightly in mine.

He groaned again. This time it was more of a strangled moan. "What's wrong with him? Why can't he open his eyes? He's trying. Look, look at him." I said as a couple of nurses came rushing in.

"Can you step out of the room, please?" one of the nurses said firmly before pressing another buzzer.

"What's going on?" my mum pleaded before turning to me. "Josephine?"

"Please, come with me, Diana." Another nurse had wrapped her arms around my mum and was tugging her to leave the room. "They're doing everything they can, but they need you both out of the way." she said, even more insistent.

"What do you mean, 'doing everything'? He was waking up!" I yelled.

But then I saw it.

The machine that was monitoring his heart rate was no longer giving out its steady rhythm of a beat, but instead there was one constant beep, a droll, deep noise. There were no lines bouncing up and down, indicating a heartbeat; no numbers … nothing.

"Mum," I said, panicked. "Mum, what's happening to him?"

A nurse gently took us both out of the room, where we both stood watching; screaming for him to come back, yelling at them to help him, to please help him.

People were coming from everywhere and rushing into the room. Every so often we would hear the word "clear" followed by a loud popping noise that made my stomach churn.

"Come on, Daddy, come on. Don't you do this; don't you dare give up," I whispered under my breath over and over as if he would somehow hear me and come back to us.

Eventually the door opened, and out stepped the doctor.

"I'm sorry," he said sympathetically. "We did everything we could."

3

My dad had passed away four days ago.

Nothing felt real.

Mum and I hadn't left the house. We were being looked after by Uncle Anthony and his wife, Elizabeth, who were also grieving their loss. My cousin Jemma was around a lot, which also helped; we had grown up together and had been inseparable until I moved to New York. She was the closest thing I had to a sister; we even looked alike, only Jemma's hair was bright blonde. Our facial features were like those of sisters. Her eyes were brown just like mine, and she was slim, too, but slightly taller. It was nice having her close again, even under such strained circumstance.

Something in my mind wouldn't let me accept that my dad was never coming home. Every time the door would open, for a split second I would think it was him, home from another day fighting off baddies.

But he was never coming home. I couldn't accept it.

I saw my mum falling apart around us all, and yet I had no idea how I could help her, or even if I had the strength to. For thirty-five years her whole life had revolved around my father. She would wake every morning next to him, and they spent every minute of their lives loving each other. She cooked for him and cared for him, and suddenly everything that she knew as routine had gone and left her, leaving behind only memories. That was all she had now – all any of us had – memories.

We were living a real-life nightmare, only this time there was no waking up from it, no escaping. We would live through this nightmare now for the rest of our lives. I wasn't sure either I or my mum was even capable of that.

Funeral arrangements had begun. I couldn't even bear to think about it. I listened to what was being planned, but I couldn't process that we were going to be burying my dad. I couldn't accept it, and neither could my mum.

She was breaking, slowly, into millions of pieces. She was putting on such a brave face, but I could see the real Diana Summers behind the mask she was wearing. I had heard her every minute of every night since we lost him; she would sob uncontrollably in their marital bed, where he should have been lying next to her. Each night, I would go to her and comfort her. Eventually she would doze off to sleep, but then she would start crying again. Her heart lay with my dad, and it was slowly beginning to shatter. How could you ever get over losing the man who you had loved unconditionally for the majority of your life? How do people ever get over that? I don't think I could, and I certainly couldn't imagine that my mum was going to either.

With that in mind, I decided that New York was now a chapter in my life that I had loved but I would not be going back to. My life was back here with my mum; she needed me, and I needed her. I couldn't even think about leaving her, not now, not after the death of the man that had kept us all glued together.

It would be selfish of me to ever think that Mum would be okay alone.

Leaving New York behind also meant leaving Blake behind too. But after seeing the pain that Mum was suffering, I knew I needed to do it. I couldn't be strong enough to cope if the man I loved suddenly left me. I would rebuild a new life here in London; I needed to.

My theory about happiness always coming with pain was becoming more and more apparent. I had allowed myself to feel happy about Blake; I had let down the barrier and had been about to let him in. With that happiness came the phone call about my dad, the pain. Would I ever be shown that happiness doesn't always go hand in hand with pain? I doubted it very much.

We buried Dad ten days after he passed away. It was the hardest day of our lives. I clung to Mum as we mourned our loss together in a church that was overflowing with friends and family.

You never truly realize how many people's lives someone has touched until he or she is gone. There were people who I had never seen before crying for my dad, telling me and my mum later what connection they had had to him. It was comforting to know that he was loved and known by so many people. He had touched so many lives and all of them in a good way.

I wouldn't say things became easier in the following days, but they certainly became more acceptable.

Every now and then I would lose all track of thought and forget that Dad had gone. Especially when I would hear a car pull up outside, I would momentarily think he was back from work, but as quick as I would think it, the reality would pop up and remind me that he wasn't home, and never would be.

It was the strangest feeling.

Mum and I started to spend each evening looking through old photos and family videos. There would be tears followed by laughter followed by yet more tears. But it was helping us both; we were becoming more accepting of our loss, and the grieving process was helping us both come to terms with everything that had happened so suddenly. Mum would tell me stories every night about how she and my dad had met, where they had spent their first date, and how my grandfather had taken a while to warm to my dad's charms. The latter story reminded me so much of my own dad; I had always been petrified to tell him that I was dating. I had always been his little girl. The only man in my life had always been my dad; he hated me growing up and finding the real world and, worst of all, boys.

Mum beamed with pride when she told me about how exited he was when they found out Mum was expecting.

They had been trying to conceive for over five years with no luck and were eventually told by a doctor that they had little chance of becoming pregnant, owing to a problem with Mum's fallopian tubes. They decided to stop trying, but it became unbearable when Aunty Elizabeth found out she was pregnant with her first baby, but by the next month, as if not trying had had the reverse effect, Mum became pregnant too.

Dad had wrapped her up in cotton wool, as she put it, looking after her every second of every day until I made my appearance nine months later.

Talking about Dad helped, and listening to mom's stories also helped.

It all helped.

It also helped me make my choice to stay in London with Mum easy. This was home; this was where I had made most of my happy memories while growing up. I couldn't leave her again. I would tell her

Beautifully Unbroken

the following day that I was coming home to stay.

I felt nervous as I stood and chopped the vegetables in the kitchen.

"You're not going to be hungry, darling, if you keep chewing those lips of yours," Mum laughed. "Is there something on your mind dear?"

My eyes shot up to meet Mum's as she looked at me with a waiting glare.

"Just want to get this right. It's been a long time since I've cooked for you," I lied.

"You sure that's it? You have been distracted all day." Mum handed me a glass of wine from which I took a massive glug.

"I'm fine." I forced a smile and continued looking down at the vegetables as I chopped.

"Have you decided when you are heading back to New York yet?"

Mum's question took me by surprise. The knife slipped, and I sliced my finger instead of the potato.

"Shit!" I cursed as I quickly put the finger into my mouth. "I mean shoot," I said with a smirk when I noticed Mum snarling at my choice of words.

"Let me see." Mum pulled my finger from my mouth to examine the cut. "You'll survive." She smiled. "Let's run it under the tap." Mum walked me over to the sink and held my finger for me while the cold water washed away the blood. I felt like a child again; she had done this many times when I was growing up, mostly when I would graze my knees and hands falling from the tree swing that Dad and Uncle Anthony had built at the bottom of the garden.

Mum was deep in thought watching my finger as the water lashed off it.

"I'm not going back to New York, Mum; I'm staying here, with you."

Mum let out a hard laugh. "Oh no," She shook her head. "You most certainly are not staying here; I don't need a babysitter, Josephine."

"I know that, but—"

"Your life is in New York now, not here."

Her eyes never lifted from my finger, so it was hard to read her expression.

"I don't want to go back, Mum; I want to stay here with you, and Dad would want that too." I said quietly whilst trying to gauge her reaction.

"Your father would want what is right for you, and staying here isn't." I opened my mouth to protest but was quickly stopped when Mum continued. "Do you have any idea how proud your father was when you got the call for New York?" She shut off the tap and placed a piece of tissue around my finger before lifting her eyes to meet mine. "He would want you to go back there, not waste your life here, where you became too afraid to even leave the house. New York has changed you." Mum gently brushed my face with her hand. "You're no longer the timid girl who left; you're strong now, confident and happy, and I want to see you continue to grow, I don't want to see you revert back to the girl who left here 18 months ago." She smiled.

"I don't want to leave you, Mum, it will kill me to leave you here alone."

Mum left me and headed back to finish chopping the vegetables. "I am far from alone, Josephine. You have seen this house recently; it's like Piccadilly Circus most days." She smiled slightly.

"And how about when it all dies down and people stop coming around so much, what then?"

"You know our family, darling. That is never going to happen." She laughed once and shook her head.

I shrugged. "It's decided anyway. I called my agent yesterday; he's going to cancel all meetings and auditions that I had lined up."

"Yes, dear, I know you did. I heard the call you made." She started to smirk. "And while you were in the shower, I called him back and made sure that he didn't follow any instruction that you had given him."

My mouth fell open.

"Oh, close your mouth, dear; you will catch flies like that."

"You called Max?" I asked in shock.

"Don't ever underestimate my abilities to make sure you do the right thing in your life, Josephine. You may be twenty-five years old" – she waggled the knife in the air – "but I'm still your mother, dear, and as the saying goes, 'Mother knows best.'"

"I can't believe you called him."

"Oh," she said, stopping mid-step to the oven before turning to face me, "and if you don't go back to New York, I may be forced to call that man you are in love with too. Blake, wasn't it?" She was smirking and mocking me. I hadn't seen Mum smile or play like this for so long. My chest hurt from the love I was feeling for her in that moment.

She turned and carried on over to the oven.

"You wouldn't."

"Oh, I would."

"You don't even have his number." I stated matter-of-factly.

"Oh, I do. I took it from your phone just in case I got this reaction from you."

"You … you …" I was speechless and struggling to put two words together.

"Look." Mum placed the roasting tin in the oven and turned back to me. "I know why you want to stay; I do. And I understand. I love you, and that is never going to change, but if you want to do something for me, then go. If things don't work out, then of course you can come home. This will always be your home, but I want you to go; I want you to make your Dad even prouder of you than he already was, please."

I sighed and closed the distance between Mum and me. "But I'm really going to miss you."

Mum wrapped her arms around me and breathed deeply. "And I

will miss you too, but I need you to do this, for me and for your father."

I sat in front of Dad's grave surrounded by the many flowers and wreaths that people had sent on the day of the funeral. Even now, almost two weeks after we had buried him, they continued to blossom. Some of the cards were fading, but I could still make out messages and condolences that had been sent.

The whole thing still felt so surreal.

Coming here to speak to my dad felt strange, yet comforting. I had felt his presence a lot over the past few days while I toyed with going back to New York. I suppose all I really wanted was some sort of sign from him, something from Dad that would tell me that going and leaving Mum here was what he wanted. I hated the thought that going could upset him; I needed his answer somehow, just a sign, just something that would ease the pain.

I took a deep breath and began to talk. "Daddy," My voice seemed to echo around me. I was alone except for an old couple in the far distance. I felt my eyes well up before the first tear escaped.

"I wish I could have hugged you one last time, Dad. I wish I could have told you just how much I loved you. I know we talked to you in hospital, but not knowing whether you heard me just makes it so much harder. I really hope that you can hear me now. In fact, I truly believe that you can hear me now, can't you."

I wiped my eyes on the back of my sleeve and took another deep breath.

"Why did you have to leave us? Why couldn't you have stayed, why you and no one else? You are the most amazing person I have ever known. You were the first man that I ever loved and I will always love you Daddy, always. No man that I will ever meet will ever compare to you, ever." I took a deep breath and wiped my eyes yet again.

"I don't want to go back to New York, Daddy; I don't feel that it's the right thing to do. How can I leave Mum here alone? I feel like I'm abandoning her. It's wrong; it's just insane." My voice was getting louder, and the more I thought about it, the more selfish I felt leaving her would be, whether she wanted me to or not.

"But you know what she's like." I rolled my eyes and smiled. "She's the boss, eh Dad? But I need to know what you want me to do. I want to do the right thing, Daddy, but I need you to somehow tell me what that is." I looked up to the sky, waiting for some sort of sign from him.

Looking back down to where his grave lay, I sighed.

"I will never, ever forget you, Daddy. I've loved you from the moment I laid my eyes on you. You were the best daddy any girl could ever wish for. I hope that if I ever do get married and have children, that their dad can be even just half the dad you were. That would be perfection. And I will make sure I make you proud; I will do everything I can to make that happen."

I sucked in a deep, shaky breath. "And I'm sorry too. I'm sorry for not listening to you about Michael; you did always know what was best for me, and I ignored you. If I could go back now, I would have no option other than to listen to you. I'm so sorry that I didn't." I sighed, unsure of what to do or say next.

After a couple moments of silence, I stood and looked down to Dad's grave.

"Please tell me what to do, Daddy. Should I go or should I stay? Please tell me. Somehow, I need to know." I took a deep breath and wiped my eyes. "I love you to the moon and back. Always have. Always will."

I blew Dad a kiss and turned and headed back to the car.

"Hi Jo."

A familiar voice startled me. My head immediately shot up to find Michael leaning against the driver's door of my car. He had his arms folded defensively across his chest; his expression was wary.

"What the hell are you doing here? I thought you were in Italy?"

"Season's finished I'm visiting Mum and Dad for a while before heading off to Brazil."

He had obviously made the squad for the World Cup; however, he wouldn't be getting my congratulations.

"Move away from the car, Michael." I stopped just a couple of feet away from him. I hadn't been near Michael since he visited me in hospital, practically begging me to lie to the police about what had happened, scared for himself more than me.

"I'm sorry about your dad."

"He hated you," I spat out.

He nodded and pushed away from the car but still stood too close for me to be able to open the door.

"I deserved that," he sighed. "But I'm still sorry."

I started looking for my keys, trying my best to ignore that the man who ruined me was standing only a few inches away.

"How's New York? You look good."

"None of your business," I replied in a harsh tone. "Ruined any more of your girlfriends' lives yet?"

"I deserved that too." He nodded.

"Damn right you deserved it. You deserve a damn sight more, too. You ruined my life, Michael; you reduced me into a shell of who I was. And what about poor Imogen? Do you ever think about her and what became of her because of you?" He attempted to answer, but I hadn't quite finished. "How dare you stand here now and tell me how sorry you are about my dad and think you can speak to me as if nothing ever happened."

"I've changed, Jo; I'm not that person any more, I swear."

I let out a hard laugh and shook my head.

"It's true, Jo. I'm sorry, truly sorry, for everything."

I stepped around him, and as I moved to open the door, his hand grabbed my wrist.

"Get your hands off me now," I said angrily. My heart started to bang hard against my chest. I didn't fear him; I feared the memories.

"I've never got over you, Jo. I was young, I was foolish. The fame, the money – it all got into me. But what happened – it was a wake-up call. I wasn't in control then, but I am now, I swear."

I looked up into his eyes; he was a lot taller than I was, but he had lowered his head towards me. He was still as good looking as I remembered, and I still found myself attracted to him, but the good looks were just a mask, covering up the person that he truly was underneath.

"Someone died because of us, Michael," I choked out.

"Don't you think I know that? Every minute of every fucking day I know that."

"I loved you," I choked out. "I fell out with my parents because of you." I took a deep, shaky breath. "And then I ended up in hospital" – I swallowed hard – "because of you."

I could see the regret in his eyes, but there would never be any turning back.

"I still love you," he said as I opened the door and went to step in.

Laughing, I shook my head in disbelief.

"You don't have a single clue what love is, Michael."

I slammed the door shut and started the engine.

"Don't go back to New York." He was leaning against the door again, poking his head in through the open window. "We could try again. I'll do it all properly this time, I swear. I'll treat you how I should have before. We were good together, Jo, and I can tell you still have feelings for me. Please, stay."

"Sorry, Michael." A small smiled tugged at my lips despite the pain I was feeling inside. "My life is in New York now. The past is exactly that; it's the past." I shrugged. "It's gone. I've started a new chapter in my life now. New friends, new jobs, and I love it there. I wouldn't give you a second chance if the apocalypse struck now and we were the only two humans left standing."

He stepped back, stunned at my words.

"Oh and when you do finally meet someone, and they fall for your spell, Do the right thing. Be a man, a real man, and love her – like you should have loved me. Goodbye, Michael."

Before he had a chance to answer, I put the car into gear and sped away. I didn't even look back. My mind was made up; I was going back to New York. "Thanks, Daddy," I said, smiling.

4

It had taken every ounce of my strength to peel myself from Mum's arms as I headed through Departures at Heathrow Airport.

The last time I had been here was to jet off to my new life. Things had changed considerably since that day. But thanks to what I considered to be a sign from Dad, I was heading back to continue what I had left just over three weeks ago in New York.

"Don't you waste a single second when you get back, do you hear me? You tell that boy exactly how you feel. Don't let him slip away, darling; you deserve to be happy." I smiled, remembering Mum's words. She was such a romantic.

Leaving her had been tough, but both Mum and my uncle had reassured me that Mum would never be alone, and again the old saying "You're only seven hours away" was used constantly to squash my doubts.

I was shattered; everything that had happened over the past three weeks had really taken it out of me. The plane hadn't even made it to thirty thousand feet when I felt the heaviness take over my eyes. I slept the whole way back to New York.

I stepped out of the airport and waited patiently for a cab. I hadn't told Casey I was travelling back today. I didn't want a fuss or a welcome-back committee; I just wanted to slip back into my apartment and start a fresh life here the next day.

The heat was a killer. July was here now, and even though it was late evening, my clothes clung to me as though I had just stepped out of the shower. I'd forgotten just how humid summer in New York was. I'd also forgotten how much I loved it here. The familiarity as we drove through the busy streets made me feel like I had come home – the smell of the food carts, the honking of car horns, the crammed pavements, even at this time of the night. It all felt like home.

I stepped into our apartment building and was greeting immediately by Peter. "Miss Summers, how lovely to have you back."

He smiled.

"It's good to be back," I replied as I headed to the lift.

I had so many things going through my mind on the ride up to our fifteenth-floor apartment. Mostly, what I would be saying to Blake the following day. The more I thought about him, the more exited I became. The explosion of butterflies was back in the pit of my stomach. I couldn't wait to see him, even though I was equally as nervous. I had really missed seeing him around.

I hoped that Casey would be staying the night at Alex's apartment, enabling me to sneak in unnoticed and get a good night's rest, but when I opened the door and heard her laughter bouncing from the walls, it made me smile. I had really missed her.

I left my case in the hallway and stepped into the kitchen. Casey and Alex were loading the dishwasher while enjoying a private joke. Their laughter continued as I cleared my throat.

"Hi," I interrupted.

Casey swung around first; her mouth fell open at the sight of me standing there. "Oh my God, you're home!" Within two big leaps, she had me in her arms, holding me so tightly I could barely breathe. "Why didn't you say you were coming; we could have come and gotten you," she said, still clinging to me tightly.

"It was a bit last minute."

Casey released me and held me at arm's length, studying my face.

"How are you?"

I nodded but didn't know what to reply. "I'm getting there."

"Hey, Jo, I'm sorry about your father." Alex stepped forward and hugged me briefly

"Thank you."

"We've just eaten, but shall I make you something? You must be hungry," Casey asked.

"I'm okay, thank you. I'm just going to grab a shower and go to bed; I'm exhausted."

"I bet." Casey smiled sweetly. "How about I bring you a nice cup of tea instead then?"

I smiled. "Perfect, thank you."

"It's really good to have you back, Jo; I've missed you so much," Casey said before hugging me once more.

"It's good to be back," I said before releasing Casey and turning to head to the bedroom. "I'll see you both in the morning." Just as I turned, I was greeted with the most unexpected sight. "Blake," I gasped. "Hi."

He smiled. "Jo, you're back." His smile widened as he held out his arms to welcome me.

Immediately I walked to him and wrapped my arms around his neck. His hands wrapped around my waist tightly. He was breathing deeply into my hair, breathing me in. I responded to his touch; my whole body began to tingle, and the area between my thighs throbbed with want. God, I had missed him, even more than I imagined I had. Being out of his presence had made my mind forget just how good he felt – his scent, his warmth, the comfort I felt from just being around him. It had all come flooding back, and if it was possible, I wanted him even more now than when I had left him at the party.

I heard Alex clear his throat, clearly confused by what was happening. I stepped back and smiled up at Blake.

"It's good to see you," I said.

He smiled back. "You too, I'm sorry about your father; it must have been awful for you all." His smile faded, and concern etched his face. I nodded and was about to respond when Blake's phone started to buzz. Casey and Alex broke out into a mixture of amusement and annoyance. Casey started growling, while Alex just laughed hysterically.

"Just answer the damn thing, Blake!" Casey yelled. "That's what, the thirtieth time tonight? She's obviously got it bad."

"Don't do it, Blake; you need to change the damn number, not answer it," Alex laughed.

I looked from Casey and Alex to Blake. "Who's she?" Blake was messing with his phone; he shrugged slightly but kept his eyes down on the screen.

"Who is she?" I tried again, this time turning my attention to Casey.

"Sara," she replied, completely unamused.

"You're seeing Sara?" I asked, turning back to Blake.

"No," he replied.

"Yes he is," Casey said as she turned and continued cleaning the kitchen units.

"More like as and when you feel like it, eh, Blake?" Alex gave a smirk which soon faded when Casey gave him a punch to the arm. "Ouch." he mouthed.

Blake and I stood looking at each other for a long moment, my eyes searching his for answers, just anything that he could tell me that meant I was imagining it all. If someone had run up to me in that moment and punched me in the stomach, the pain would feel like nothing compared to the pain in my chest that had formed in the past few minutes. His eyes were full of emotion, yet he never once offered an explanation. Not that I needed one. He was sleeping with Sara; that much I knew was true. I had left him at the party to fly home to be with my dying father. I had left him there only minutes after he made his feelings for me obvious, and then he had slept with Sara.

The room fell silent. Casey and Alex had no idea what had happened between Blake and me before I left. Well, at least I knew Casey hadn't any idea, and judging by Alex's outbursts of laughter every few seconds, I imagine he had no idea either.

"Everything okay Jo?" I heard Casey ask, concerned.

I forced a smile and turned to face them both. "Yes, everything is fine. I'm tired; it's been the worst few weeks of my life," I said, turning my attention to Blake for a brief moment. "So I'm going to say goodnight to you all. I'll see you tomorrow." I walked straight past Blake without a second glance.

I had believed in him. For the first time ever, I had believed that there was someone different out there for me. Someone who would treat me right, someone who would love me, be there for me when I needed him. I had believed that that person was Blake. I was wrong. He was no different; no one was. Every man I had ever met only ever thought with one thing – his dick. It appeared that Blake was no different, and yet again the happiness of seeing him on my return had been quickly matched with the pain of finding out he was sleeping with Sara.

Sleep had betrayed me all night. My body was working on London time, and my mind was focused only on Blake. My last glance at the clock had told me it was a quarter to six, so giving up on sleep; I climbed out of bed, got changed, and decided on a jog. I desperately needed to release the pent-up anger that Blake had placed into my mind the night before. His face when Casey had told me he was seeing Sara was cemented into my memory; his eyes were heavy and full of regret that I should find out how I had, yet he hadn't apologized or offered any form of an explanation.

Running faster wasn't helping to rid me his face. I decided to give up just as I felt my lungs were about to burst. Placing my hands on my thighs, I leaned forward, forcing myself to take deep breaths. Slowly my breath steadied. Deep breaths became easier to take, and my lungs finally felt as though someone had loosened the death grip that was keeping me from breathing. But the anger was still there, bubbling at the surface.

"You're back!" I heard someone pant as they approached. I looked up slightly to see a pair of long, tanned, muscular legs heading my way. Standing myself up straight, my eyes met with Cooper just as he slowed to a stop in front of me. For the first time since the previous night, I smiled a happy, genuine smile.

"Cooper." I walked into his open arms gladly, hugging him tightly. He had been an amazing friend the night I left for London, which I couldn't forget. He too was breathing hard, but his warmth surrounded me; he felt comfortable.

"It's so good to see you," he said quietly before releasing his grip on me and smiling down on me.

His dirty blonde hair was drenched with sweat, and stubble graced his chin, but he looked good. In fact, I had never noticed just how good looking he was; I had been too wrapped up in Blake.

"I'm sorry I haven't been in touch," I explained. "It's been a bit of a crazy few weeks." I frowned.

"I was so sorry to hear about your dad." He smiled sympathetically as he stroked my arm.

I smiled back. "Thank you; and thank you for everything you did for me too; I'll never forget that."

"Speaking of which," he said, straightening up and crossing his arms over his chest, "I do believe, Miss Summers, that you owe me a date." He grinned widely.

"I owe you a thank-you dinner, not a date," I replied, tapping him on his bulging bicep.

"Dinner? Date? Dinner date." He shrugged with a smile.

"Dinner," I replied.

"You could really dent a guy's pride, Miss Summers," he said, tilting his head.

"Cooper," I replied with a heavy sigh, "you are one of my closest friends. Dating you would just be weird." I shuddered. "You are, however, the best-looking friend I have, but that's as far as it goes I'm afraid. So" – I smiled – "when can I say thank you by buying you dinner?"

Copper smiled widely at me. "I'm free tonight."

I thought for a moment before replying, "Then tonight I will buy you your thank-you dinner."

"It's a date," he said before briefly stretching his legs and arms and heading off in the direction he had just come from.

"It's not a date!" I yelled back, laughing.

Cooper turned and started running backwards. "I'll call you!"

For a brief moment, I had forgotten about Blake and Sara as I realized that I could have a life here, without Blake being a part of it. As much as that pained me, that would be how my future was destined to go.

The smell of bacon hit me instantly as I walked back into the apartment.

Casey was busy in the kitchen, cooking for what looked like an army.

"We have guests coming?" I asked before grabbing a bottle of water from the fridge and emptying the entire contents.

"Nope," She shook her head. "It's just you and me and the truth about what's going on between you and Blake." She placed the bacon onto two plates before turning to grab some scrambled eggs.

I rolled my eyes and sat at the breakfast bar. "There is and never was anything going on between Blake and I."

"Bullshit!" she yelled. "I saw the way you both were last night; that was not 'nothing'," she said, emphasizing the last word with her fingers. "Something has happened between you two, and I want to know what – and how the hell I knew nothing about it."

Casey placed my plate in front of me, and as good as it smelled, I wasn't hungry at all.

"Eat," she demanded.

"You know I don't do breakfast."

"Well, technically you're still on London time, so this is lunch. Now eat and talk."

She placed her plate next to mine and sat waiting patiently.

I placed a forkful of egg into my mouth. "Mmm, this is good," I said appreciatively.

"Have you slept with Blake?" she said, straight to the point.

I coughed as I almost choked on the egg. "No. I haven't." I replied.

"But you want to," she stated matter-of-factly.

"Yes. Yes I do." I turned to look at her, her mouth wide open. "I've fallen in love with him," I said sadly.

"Oh, Jo, why didn't you say something?" she asked concernedly.

I shrugged. "I was scared, you know, after everything with Michael and the fact that I can't ever hold on to a man because I have some sort of repellent that tells them they are allowed to sleep with other people behind my back."

"Blake isn't like that, Jo; you know that."

"He slept with Sara," I said sadly.

"But the two of you weren't seeing each other, were you?" she asked, confused.

"No," I sighed, "but he knew how I felt. We had spoken at the party; he asked me out to dinner. But then he got called away, and I found you and Sara just as I got the call. I couldn't wait and find him, Casey; I needed to get home as soon as possible. I caught Sara on the way out and asked her to tell you. So you can imagine that when I heard about him and Sara last night, it was just—"

"Wait a minute," Casey interrupted, putting her hand up to stop me. "You asked Sara to tell me what?"

"About my dad," I confirmed, confused. "I told her to tell you about the call and that I had to go."

Casey sighed and sat back on her stool.

"What?" I asked, feeling more and more concerned as the conversation continued.

"She didn't tell me." Casey let out a big breath. "When I got back from the bathroom, Blake was standing next to Sara. He seemed distracted, angry even. I asked had they seen you, and Sara said they had seen you in Cooper's arms before leaving the party." Casey shook her head in disgust. "Blake saw you leave with Cooper, but Sara obviously hadn't told him where you were going and why."

"And she didn't tell you either?" I asked, feeling anger once again building.

"Nope." Casey shook her head. "I had no idea where you were until Cooper rang me on the Saturday afternoon to ask whether I had heard from you."

"What!"

"Blake got wasted – I mean, forget-your-own-name kind of wasted," she said, wide eyed. "I have never seen him in such a state." She reached over and took my hand. "Everyone saw him leave with Sara."

I was struggling to process everything. Sara had known that my dad was dying. She knew, yet she didn't tell anyone? Instead she waited for Blake to get wasted and took him home. I felt sick.

"So are they seeing each other? Are they a couple?" I asked, not sure I wanted to know the answer.

Casey shook her head. "No, it was just that one time. She has a habit of turning up wherever he is and making out like they're together, but I know he wouldn't lie to Alex, and he said it was just that one time."

I looked over at Casey, who seemed to be remembering something. "What is it?"

"The day after the party, I overheard him in Alex's apartment. I walked in after I had spoken to you on the phone, and he was telling Alex about the night before. He was saying how much he regretted it because he had fallen for someone else and that even though he wasn't sure she felt exactly the same, he couldn't stop thinking about her. He said he felt as though he had betrayed this someone else even though they weren't actually together." Realization dawned on Casey's face. "It's obvious now that he was talking about you." She shook her head. "I walked over and told them both that I had just gotten off the phone to you and that you had taken the call about your father at the party. Thinking back now, it was obvious. He got up off the sofa and seemed agitated; he obviously realized that Cooper had just helped you. He stormed out, and Alex found him later at Sugar Lounge; he was wasted yet again, completely out of it."

"Oh God," I said quietly.

"He feels terrible, Jo," Casey said carefully. "You do know he doesn't do relationships, don't you?"

"I know. I should have realized he was no different just from the fact that he doesn't date. I just felt he was different." I frowned.

"He has changed, Jo; how he feels for you has changed him. He wants you."

"It's too late. Thank God I found out what he's like before I fell into that trap again."

"It's not his fault," Casey stressed. "Sara knew about your father and didn't say anything. What kind of a person does that?"

"He still jumped straight into bed with her," I said sadly.

"You need to talk to him, Jo."

"I don't think so," I laughed as I stood and went to empty my plate into the bin.

"Tonight, at Alex's birthday meal, he will be there."

I had completely forgotten what date it was. This had been arranged for a while now; Alex was thirty today. Casey had arranged a meal at his favourite Italian restaurant, and then we were heading back to one of Alex's clubs for a private party.

"Casey, I'm so sorry; I kind of have plans already tonight."

"How? You only got back last night." she said in disbelief.

"I ran into Cooper this morning. I promised him a thank-you dinner for being a good friend to me the night I had to go back to London."

Casey smiled. "Perfect. Bring him along. Show Blake what he's missing out on." Casey rubbed her palms together in excitement.

"I'm not going to use Cooper to get to Blake, Casey; that's not fair."

"You won't be using him; you will be thanking him for what he did. And Blake would be seeing what a dick he has been by hopping into bed with Sara at the first opportunity."

"I don't like it; it's not right," I replied.

"And Blake sleeping with Sara was?"

"Blake and I were never official; he can sleep with who he wants, you as good as said that only one minute ago."

"Well, I've changed my mind," she shrugged "It's Alex's birthday, and I insist you be there whether you bring Cooper or not." She winked.

I picked up my phone with a deep sigh and dialed Cooper's number. I explained that I had double booked and asked whether he would like to come to Alex's meal. He agreed and said he would pick me up at eight.

"Sorted," I said to Casey before heading to the bathroom for a shower.

"Oh!" Casey yelled, "Just one more thing that I may have

forgotten to mention."

I turned and headed back to the kitchen, dreading what she was about to say.

"Sara kind of invited herself along to tonight's events too. Sorry, I forgot to mention that." Casey gave me a guilty lopsided grin. I growled and stormed off to the bathroom. Tonight I would make the most effort I ever had; I would make myself look irresistible.

At 7.59 I opened the door to a stunned Cooper.

"Close your mouth, Cooper; you will catch flies like that," I laughed, using my mum's line from only a few nights before. I had spoken to Mum that afternoon but had told her I had yet to see Blake. I didn't want to tell her that he was actually no different to any of my previous boyfriends. I didn't actually want to believe it myself.

"You look" – his eyes scanned my body up and down a few times, settling on my boobs for a little longer than felt comfortable. I smacked him with my clutch bag to remove him from the trance he was in. I had gone for a strapless knee-length black dress that clung a little too eagerly around my breasts. I had decided at some point whilst getting changed that I did actually want to show Blake what he was missing. "You look stunning," Cooper finally said as his eyes met mine for the first time since I opened the door.

"Thank you," I replied.

"Shall we?" He held his arm out for me to take; I placed my arm in his.

"Let's date," he joked as we headed to the lift.

The restaurant was already buzzing with laughter and chat as we entered. The waiter offered us each a glass of champagne before showing us to the table we would be seated at. The restaurant was small and intimate. Casey had hired the complete restaurant out, seating all fifty guests comfortably. It also gave us a lot of privacy – no onlookers, no photos being snapped. It was perfect.

"I'm just going to use the bathroom, I won't be a minute," I said to Cooper, who, being a true gentleman stood as I left the table. That made me smile.

I stood looking at myself in the mirror, taking deep breaths.

"You can do this, Jo; you *can* do this." I repeated that mantra over and over to myself as my reflection stared back, knowing that I probably couldn't do this.

Blake would be here any minute, and so would Sara. Would they arrive together? Why would they if he didn't want anything to do with her? This was all such a big mess, and I found myself once again getting wound up by a man, great. I wasn't feeling as brave now as I had felt while getting ready for this evening. In theory, I would be showing him what he was missing, yet in reality it would be me that would be seeing what I was missing.

I picked myself up and headed back out to the waiting guests.

The party was in full swing, everyone was drinking and laughing – especially Casey, who already appeared to have had her full quota of champagne. But that didn't matter; she was happy and in love. I couldn't help but feel a knot of envy for her.

Cooper was smiling when I returned. He stood and pulled out my chair for me. "Will you quit with this dating nonsense?" I laughed.

He winked. "Just being a gentleman."

"Cooper, Jo," Blake greeted us as we sat laughing.

"Hey, Blake, what's up, dude?" Cooper stood and shook his hand before sitting back down and turning back to me, but I hadn't yet looked away from him. He had smiled tightly at Cooper's greeting, and his eyes burned into me.

I said the first thing I thought of. "No Sara?" I took my champagne in my shaky hand and polished it off. Blake sighed as he sat down. I turned to Cooper in order to keep my mind from wandering. I was thanking Cooper for being such a good friend; he deserved my full attention.

Cooper grabbed a bottle of champagne and refilled my glass.

"Are you trying to get me drunk, MR Henderson?" I teased before taking a large sip again.

"Maybe I am," he teased in return as he sat back in his chair and placed one arm on the back of my shoulders.

I raised my eyebrows to him, to which he replied with a smile and a wink.

I heard Blake clear his throat, but as much as my neck was trying to control my every movement, I refused to turn and give into him. The champagne was now definitely helping to make him see what he was missing, and I was enjoying doing it.

I heard Sara approach before I saw her. The loud clicking of her heels seemed to echo around the restaurant. Champagne in hand, she pulled out the chair next to Blake and dropped her bag onto the table with a thud. "Where were you? I waited for you to come pick me up," I heard her whisper harshly to Blake.

He didn't reply. Instead he let out a long, hard breath. I could see from the corner of my eye he was still watching me.

I turned to Sara. "Trouble in paradise?" I asked, forcing a smile.

"Jo, I didn't know you were back. When did you … um … Blake, did you know Jo was back?" She turned to Blake, looking nervous.

Blake took a sip of champagne before replying simply, "Yes. I did."

"I got back late last night," I stated. "Blake was at my apartment. Weren't you, Blake?" He nodded. "Mind you, seems he didn't actually know that I had gone, for a while, did you Blake?"

Before giving either of them any time to respond, I turned back to Cooper, who was watching me intently.

"What are you doing?" he asked, quietly leaning in so as only I could hear.

"Nothing," I smiled innocently. "I'll be right back; I need the bathroom," I said.

"You only went like five minutes ago," Cooper replied,

confused.

"It's the champagne," I lied. The truth was I needed a breather. It was killing me seeing them both sitting so close to each other knowing that he had lay naked above her or below her as she rode him over and over, while he filled her insides with his dick. He had kissed her skin, caressed her. The more I thought about it, the more my skin crawled with hate for her, the more I wanted to smash her perfect teeth out of her lying, vile mouth. But the more I thought about it, the more I found myself wanting Blake, the more I wanted to be the one lying underneath him while he rocked into me, the more I wanted to taste him, hold him, and breathe in his scent. Yes, I needed a breather.

I hurried to the bathroom, this time locking the door behind me. I rushed over to the sink, turned the taps on full, and splashed the water against my face. I began to sweat. I was shaking as my heart pounded hard against my chest. I was about to experience my first panic attack since arriving in New York. My breathing become shallower with each breath; each gasp was a struggle to control. Forcing myself to focus in the mirror, I repeated to myself, "Stop it, stop this now, calm down. Come on, Jo, calm down, breathe … Just breathe …" I finally managed to calm myself. My breathing returned to normal, and my heartbeat finally steadied.

"Just breathe," I whispered one last time before deciding to head back to the table.

I opened the door to find Blake leaning against the wall opposite. He was waiting for me.

"Blake, you startled me," I gasped.

He pushed away from the wall. "Can we talk?" he pleaded as he closed the distance between us.

I looked up at him. He was standing so close that it was hard to concentrate on anything other than Blake.

"There's nothing to say, Blake," I said quietly. I took a step forward, trying to walk away from him, but before I could get past, he took my wrist in his hand and turned me back to face him.

"Don't, Blake, please. Just let go."

"I'm sorry," he said, his voice laced with hurt. "You have no idea just how sorry I am and how much I wish I could go back and change everything that happened that night, to rewrite it all. Please, Jo, just give me two minutes; that's all I ask for, and then you are free to just walk away – for good if that is what you want. I just need two minutes, please," he pleaded.

Part of me wanted to pull my arm from his grip and walk away, yet the other part of me kept my feet planted flat to the floor, unable to move.

"What is there to say?" I choked out. "You have been sleeping with Sara, Blake; what could you possibly have to say that would make it worth listening?"

"It was only once, Jo, I swear."

"Is that supposed to make me feel better?"

We stood in silence, looking into each other's eyes, searching for … what? I just didn't know. But it was impossible for me to walk away from him. His fingers loosened the grip on my wrist. Instead they moved down and knitted with my fingers. A spark of electricity shot through my body; every single limb tingled with want.

"I can tell that you feel that too. Tell me you don't feel that and I'll walk away myself right now." His voice was barely audible, but I could tell he too was choking back his emotions.

It was hard to say no to him. My body yearned for him, and as much as I wanted to walk away and not look back, I couldn't do it.

"Two minutes," I whispered.

Blake breathed a sigh of relief; quickly he shot a glance over my shoulder before leading us back into the bathroom that I had just exited, locking the door behind us.

I stepped into the bathroom placing distance between us immediately. If I became too close, I wouldn't be able to be as strong as I needed to be.

"I've missed you, Jo; I've missed you so much," he said.

"You slept with Sara the moment my back was turned," I choked out. "Why?"

"I was drunk. It didn't mean anything, Jo, I swear. She means nothing to me, nothing at all."

"How can you say that?" I asked, disgusted. "Is it really that easy for a man to just jump into bed with someone that actually means nothing to them? You're all the same. I actually thought that you were different, but no, you are no different to any of the idiots I have dated in the past. I'm actually thankful that I found out now, before I too made the mistake of jumping into bed with you only to get tossed aside when you felt like you had had enough."

"It wasn't like that, Jo," he replied sadly. "That's not how I feel about you, and you know that."

"Then why did you sleep with her!" I yelled.

"Because I saw you leave the party with Cooper!" he yelled back before calming his breathing with a few deep breaths. "I was coming back to find you. You had been all I could think about for days, and after I had spoken to you, I knew that you felt the same way as I did. I wanted to come find you and take you away somewhere, just the two of us, especially because I knew, I knew that you felt the same way as I did. Then I saw Cooper with his arms around you, and before I could even register what was happening, you were gone. It hurt, Jo; it really, really hurt." He clutched his chest. "I thought that after everything you had said to me, I was the one being used."

"Yeah, well, you imagine how that felt," I said, moving closer to him. "You imagine that feeling that you had right there" – I poked my finger into his chest – "and you imagine that that's exactly how I feel now, only a million times worse! I thought I could trust you. I sat at my dying dad's bedside and told my mum that I had fallen for you! And all along, you were sleeping with someone else!"

"I'm sorry!" he yelled. "Please, tell me what I can do to make it better. Please, Jo, I want you; nothing has changed."

"Everything changed the night you got into bed with Sara Blake," I said quietly.

Blake reached for my face and wiped my tears away with his thumb. "I hate that I did this to you. I hate myself so fucking much for making you feel like this, but I am not the person that you think I am, Jo; I'm not. I am petrified, do you know that? Scared to death at how I feel about you. I have never wanted a relationship with anyone. There hasn't been one single person that I have wanted to share my life with, until I met you," Blake moved his body until it was flush with mine, his hands remained on my face, "I felt it you know; when we were filming and we would kiss? I knew that you weren't acting, and neither was I, I had wanted to say something so many times but I could see that for some reason you were guarding yourself from me, why? I don't know, but now, I wish I had just told you because now I hate myself for messing up any chance that we ever had of being happy together."

"I want to hate you," I whispered. "I really want to hate you Blake, but I ..."

Blake slowly leaned forward and brushed his lips against mine. "Tell me to stop, Jo," he said against my mouth. "Tell me to stop, and I will." His lips brushed mine again. This time I opened my mouth slightly and gave him better access. His hands cupped my face gently as his lips brushed so slowly against mine over and over again.

"I've missed you," he whispered against my lips between kisses. "I'm so sorry," he said over and over.

"Stop," I said almost silently. I couldn't let him do this to me. "Just stop. Please." Blake pulled away slightly as his eyes searched mine. "I can't do this."

"It's okay," he whispered before leaning in for another kiss.

"No. No, Blake, it's not okay. Every time I look at you, I see her. I see you and her in bed together. I know we weren't exclusive and it shouldn't bother me, but it does, and it makes me feel physically sick thinking of the two of you together ... like that." I stepped out of his hold and unlocked the door before turning back to face him

"I can't do this. You have no idea how hard it was for me to let you in, Blake. You have no idea at all."

"Then tell me; tell me what to do," he said firmly.

"There is nothing that you can do," I replied simply before unlocking the door. I stepped out of the bathroom before turning once more to Blake. "Oh and by the way, Sara knew why I had left the party with Cooper, you do know that don't you?" His eyebrows knitted together in confusion. "No ... I didn't think so," I replied before walking away from him.

Cooper's smile soon turned to a frown when he saw that I had been crying. He stood and made his way over to me. "Everything okay?" he asked.

"Can you take me home please? I don't feel too good," I lied.

"Sure." he stood and placed his suit jacket over his arm and took my hand without asking any questions.

I didn't look back to see whether Blake had followed me out of the bathroom. I had just made a massive mistake by letting him get close, and now the more that I remembered his lips on mine, the more I wanted him, and the more I could feel myself craving his touch. I needed to get the hell out of there.

Cooper was quiet on the ride back to my apartment, he knew something was wrong, but he never pressed me for any details.

"I'm sorry about tonight," I said as we pulled into the underground parking at the apartment building.

He shut off the engine, removed his seatbelt and turned to me in his seat. "It's okay, maybe we can try again another night soon, when you're feeling up to it?" he asked.

"Definitely," I agreed, removing my seat belt.

"Jo?"

"Yes?"

Cooper was looking at me; there was something he wanted to say, but I could tell he was wondering whether to say it or not.

He blinked a few times and seemed to bring himself out of his thoughts for a moment, shaking his head.

"I just want you to know I'm always here for you." His hand reached over and took mine. "Any time you ever need to talk, or feel like heading out for a jog" – he smiled – "call me, okay?"

I nodded. "Thank you. That means a lot. You have been a really good friend, Cooper; I'll always remember that." I smiled, and he smiled back, but the smile never reached his eyes.

"You're okay though, right?" he asked.

"I will be." I nodded. "I didn't sleep last night, I've been busy all day, my body clock thinks it's breakfast time, yet I've skipped sleep again." We both chuckled. "I'll call you," I said.

"Do you want me to walk you up to your apartment?" he offered.

I smiled. "No, that's okay; I'll manage."

"I didn't mean—"

"I know," I said before he could finish, and he smiled softly at me.

"I'll see you soon then, Jo."

"See you soon," I replied before leaning towards him and placing my lips to his cheek.

I don't know what possessed me. Cooper had been so kind to me, and I had made it clear time and time again to him that we were friends and friends only; that nothing more was ever going to happen between us. But something sparked inside my body as my lips left his cheek and moved across to his mouth. His eyes opened wide with shock at first; he hadn't expected it just as much as I hadn't intended it.

"Sorry," I whispered against his mouth.

"Don't be," he whispered back before claiming my mouth with his.

He was a rough kisser, but his lips felt good against mine. His hands moved up, and he placed one around my neck, pulling me closer to him while his other gripped my back. Our tongues invaded each other's mouths over and over; only the sound of our heavy breathing filled the car. His body towered above me as we slid down onto the cool leather seat. I felt his hand slide slowly up my thigh, but something was missing; there were no butterflies in the pit of my stomach, no tingling in my limbs, no want for anything more to come from this than just a kiss. I realized it was wrong, it was all so wrong what I was doing, and the reason why was just too wrong. I pulled back and opened my eyes. It wasn't the person who I had wanted it to be staring back at me.

"I'm sorry," I panted as I pushed Cooper from me and straightened up in my seat.

"Well, I certainly wasn't expecting it." I turned to see his shocked expression.

God, I felt awful. I had done exactly what I had said I wouldn't do. I wanted Cooper and me to remain friends, good friends, and I had gone and led him on, for nothing.

I lifted my hand and wiped traces of my lipstick from his mouth. He noticed I wasn't smiling, and his face fell into a frown.

"That kiss wasn't meant for me, was it?"

"I'm sorry," I replied rubbing my brow frantically.

"It was meant for Blake, wasn't it?"

I didn't agree with him, but I also didn't deny it. "I'm all over the place at the moment," I said, refusing to meet his gaze.

"Isn't Blake seeing Sara?" I looked up as his eyes widened "Tell me you're not seeing him too, Jo? That's just wrong." He shook his head.

"I'm not," I answered quickly. "You know I'm not that sort of person. I would never do that. It's just … complicated."

"Don't use me, Jo,"

"I'm not," I replied instantly. "I would never do that; you know that, don't you?"

Cooper turned his attention to outside, refusing to answer me.

"Cooper, please, I'm sorry. Can we still be friends?" I asked nervously.

Cooper's face softened as he turned back to face me. "I will always be here for you, Jo; you know that; just don't ever do that again unless it's me that you actually want."

I nodded slowly. "So this won't be awkward?"

"It won't be awkward." He smiled.

"Good."

"Good," he agreed.

"Good night, Cooper," I said before hopping out of his car and heading into the building and straight for the lift. I couldn't believe what I had done to Cooper, the one man here in New York who had always treated me so well. I had used him, and I was thankful he had understood. I just hoped that we could continue with our friendship the same from now on without any awkwardness. Only time would tell.

5

I had slept for nine solid hours. I don't know how I had managed to switch off after the previous night's events. I had lay in bed thinking about Blake and Cooper and the mess that I had created around myself, whilst wondering what the days ahead would bring. My mind had gone into overdrive, but somehow sleep had won me over and shut off my overactive mind.

When I woke I decided to go for a jog, partly hoping to run into Cooper to check things were still okay between us, but there was no sign of him. The track that he took every morning was almost deserted. I couldn't help the disappointment that I felt; I really wanted to know that we were okay. I decided I would call him in the next few hours.

Running alone gave me plenty of time to think about Blake. As much as I wanted him, and as much as my chest hurt just thinking about how good his lips felt against mine the night before, I decided that I needed to forget about him and move on. Only a few weeks ago I had been prepared to stay in London. Had I stayed there, I would have had no choice but to forget about him; I could apply the same to New York. Yes, I would be closer to him, but in order for me to avoid getting hurt yet again, I would make myself move on. Today would mark the start of my "move on and forget about Blake" plan. I just hoped I was strong enough to get through it unscathed.

I was thankful for the busy week ahead that I had planned. The following week, I would be auditioning for a small part in one of NBC's most popular comedy shows, *Perfect Alibi*.

Perfect Alibi was filmed in front of a live studio audience, and I had never filmed in front of a live audience before, so I was both excited and nervous, but I desperately wanted to nail my audition. I needed my new life here to be successful.

Later that afternoon, I would be receiving scripts to run through before meeting with the casting director and main star of the show, Marcus Hardy, the following week. I was going to be the perfect student; I wanted this job, and the distraction that came with it.

Casey crawled back into the apartment late in the afternoon

sporting dark sunglasses and an obvious hangover.

I couldn't help but laugh. When Casey celebrated, she would do it in style and would always spend the whole next day regretting it. She would always vow "never again", and of course that vow was broken by the next time a celebration came around.

She slumped down onto the sofa opposite and swung her legs up onto the chair. "Urrggh never. Ever. Again."

"Are you only just getting back?" I asked, shocked.

"No, but I've only had a couple of hours sleep; Alex has his family over, and I can't deal with them on a good day, let alone a day when I'm dying of alcohol poisoning," she sighed.

I laughed. "No consideration for a hung-over Casey? Tut tut.."

"Yeah well, never again I tell you."

"Yes, okay," I laughed before turning my attention back to the TV. I was watching as many episodes of *Perfect Alibi* as I could fit in, getting an idea of how it worked and the storylines that they used. We didn't get this show in the UK, so it was all completely new to me.

"You want me to get you anything?" I asked, amused. "Coffee? Water? An aspirin maybe? Hair of the dog even?" I laughed out loud as Casey swung a pillow straight for me; it skimmed my head and landed behind the sofa.

"Why do you look so fresh and awake?" she asked curiously.

"Maybe because I didn't drink two magnums of champagne," I laughed.

"Urgh," Casey heaved. "Don't say that word." She threw her head back on the sofa and sat there groaning.

"You really were drunk," I laughed. "I left before the food even came out."

Casey shot up in her seat. "Oh yeah, you went to the bathroom for, like, ages." She waved her hand in the air. "And so did Blake." She smirked.

"You can wipe that smirk off your face; nothing happened between Blake and me and today is the first day in my 'forget all about Blake and move on' plan, and as much as so far today, I can't stop wondering what he's doing, who he is with, or how he is feeling about me. I just need to try, try to forget him. So let's change the subject. Please." I turned my attention back to the TV.

"Something happened in the bathroom." She practically sang the sentence. "Tell me tell me now!" she demanded.

"Let it go, Casey; I don't want to think about him, remember? That means you can't talk about him."

"Something happened in that bathroom, and I want to know what!" she demanded with a smile.

"I'm going to make a cup of tea." I stood and headed to the kitchen, intent on avoiding the looming interrogation.

I heard Casey scramble off the sofa and follow me close behind. "You are having a strong black coffee," I said without turning around.

"Please tell me what happened," she pleaded as she sat at a breakfast stool, studying me closely from behind her dark shades. "Tell me everything."

I sighed and proceeded to place the tea bag into one cup and coffee in another, ignoring the fact that Casey was pressing for detail.

"Blake will tell Alex, you know. Then I'll know. So you may as well just tell me."

I let out a low growl as I placed her coffee in front of her and took a sip from my tea.

"We kind of kissed a little. Nothing major, that was all." I shrugged.

"So why did you leave? He gave you what you wanted."

"What I wanted was to come back from London and have him be waiting for me – no other woman, no Sara," I said quietly.

"So after you kissed, you just left him?"

I nodded.

"So that would explain why he came back to the table just after you, grabbed his coat, and stormed out," she recalled.

"He left?"

She smiled. "Yep."

"And Sara?"

"Oh, she followed, but he had told her not to. He seemed angry with her. Did you tell him what she did at the party?"

"Of course I did," I said simply. "Has Alex heard from him since then?"

"No." Casey shook her head sympathetically.

"Well, they probably rowed about me and then fucked." I winced at my own words.

"Josephine Summers! What has gotten into you!" Casey yelled in amusement.

I sank onto a stool next to Casey and placed my cup on the breakfast bar. I pouted. "Blake has, that's what. I want to hate him; he has done the one thing that I despise in a man." I took a deep breath. "But the more I want to hate him, the further in love with him I fall. He seems to have me under some sort of spell that I can't escape from. I feel like I need him, only him. It's as if I can't function without him; is that weird?"

Casey placed her arm around me, and I dropped my head onto her shoulders.

"No, it's not weird. You have fallen for him big time, but he never meant to hurt you, you know. He thought you had slept with Cooper; I think he wanted to hurt you like how he was hurting."

"I know. But I can't let that go."

We sat in silence for a moment. Casey comforted me, and I just sat thinking.

"I know what you need."

"Blake is what I need," I replied.

"Vegas is what you need," she stated, nodding excitedly.

"Vegas?" I asked confusedly, lifting my head from her shoulder.

"Vegas. Alex and I are flying out this Friday for a couple of days. There's a club there that he's interested in, right on the main strip. It's perfect, and he's really excited about it. Come with us; you can keep me company while he talks business and shit."

I stood and grabbed my cup of tea, heading back to the lounge. "I can't. I have my audition Tuesday. I need this job, and I want to get it right."

"You need a break."

"I do; you're right. But I also need to do what I came here to do, and Tuesday's audition is big for me. Thanks for the offer, but you go. Enjoy yourself; just don't do anything stupid like getting married without me, okay?" I forced a smile.

"I'm sorry you're hurting; I hate to see you so sad."

"He's just a man." I waved her off, smiling sadly. "I'll survive. The past four years have been a breeze; I'm sure I can manage the next forty."

"Let's have a day out tomorrow, just the two of us. We will hit some shops, get a massage and maybe a facial, grab some lunch – what do you say?"

"I don't need babysitting, Casey; really, I'm okay."

"That's not why I'm doing it." She thought for a moment. "Well, it's not the only reason." She smirked. "What do you say?"

"Okay. But any mention of Blake, and I'm coming home."

"You will have forgotten all about him by this time tomorrow, I promise."

I hoped she was right; I couldn't bear the ache in my chest any more that had formed when I learnt about him and Sara. I needed to forget him and move on as quickly as possible.

We had spent most of the day shopping. I hated shopping for clothes. Shoes I adored – a lady can never own enough pairs of shoes – but clothes shopping I detested.

I wasn't comfortable enough in my own skin to try on an outfit and think I looked good, unless it was black, which most of my wardrobe was. Casey found it hilarious that everything I bought was black, with very few exceptions.

Casey, on the other hand, was bold. I don't think she owned a dark item of clothing. She loved bright and tight; that was her thing. But being five feet eleven and slim with perfect straight blonde hair that travelled to her waist, she could wear anything and look good.

We finally sat down to a late lunch in our favourite bistro overlooking the Hudson River. My feet were killing me, but we had had the perfect day.

"Cocktail time," Casey announced as she browsed the drinks menu.

"What happened to never again?" I teased.

"Did I really say that?" Her eyes twinkled as she peered over the top of the menu.

"Think I'll have a screwdriver," she announced to the waiter.

"Make that two," I added.

The waiter retreated as Casey leaned forward and started studying my face. "Well, that was a fun day."

"Just what the doctor ordered," I replied while my eyes scanned the menu. I was starving; I hadn't eaten yet. In fact, I hadn't eaten since the previous morning; I was in the habit of eating only when I felt I needed to. I always worried about gaining weight, so eating only when I was hungry had always seemed right. Casey didn't agree. She would hate it if I skipped breakfast, but I didn't see the point in eating unless I felt I needed to.

"Tell me this isn't the first you're eating today," Casey said, as if she had read my mind.

"I haven't felt hungry." I refused to look up.

"Well, you'd better order plenty, then; you will be wasting away."

"Chance would be a fine thing," I muttered under my breath.

I had hoped I could get through the day without thinking about

Blake, but the truth was that every single second of this day he had been at the forefront of my mind. Casey had behaved and hadn't once mentioned anything that could be remotely related to him, but it didn't make it any easier. Where was he? Was he with her? Or had he really finished things completely with her? Why hadn't he been in touch? Maybe because I had told him it was finished. What a mess.

"Are you even listening to me, or are you on a different planet over there?" I realized Casey was talking to me. I hadn't heard a word that she had said. She sat back in her chair and crossed her arms over her chest, a massive grin spread across her face. "Out with it," she demanded.

"What?" I replied defensively. "I'm just stuck between the cobbler and the steak, that's all."

"Liar."

I let out the breath I had been holding and placed my menu down on the table. "Has Alex heard from Blake?"

"Yes, he called him late last night."

The waiter appeared and placed our drinks in front of us.

"What did he say?" I must have sounded desperate.

"I thought we weren't talking about Blake today," Casey replied amusedly as she lifted her cocktail and took a long drag through the straw, her eyes trained on me the whole time.

"We weren't, but now we are. I made the rule; I'm changing it. What did he say?"

She shrugged. "Not much. Oh, but things are definitely one hundred per cent over with Sara."

"Did he say anything about me?"

"He asked how you were, yes."

"And?"

"And that's it."

"What did Alex say about me?"

"Why do you care? You said it was over between you before it even started." I could see she was loving every minute of this, and I was hating it. I shouldn't have cared, but I did; I needed to know everything.

The waiter returned and took our orders before again retreating to the kitchen.

"I just … I don't know," I said, deflated.

"Look. I know he did wrong to you, but he regrets it. I mean he *really* regrets it. Talk to him."

I shook my head. "There's no way I'm going to go running to him after everything that has happened."

"Well, for someone who doesn't care, you certainly seem to be asking a lot of questions."

I spent the better part of Friday morning listening to Casey's constant panic. She had so far that day lost her favourite bikini, her hair straighteners, and her iPod, and Alex was due here to pick her up in the next ten minutes.

"How can I go to Vegas without my iPod? I just can't!" she yelled. "It's okay; I've found it," she yelled again before I had a chance to reply.

"Maybe if you looked after your things, you wouldn't be in such a panic now."

"Okay, Mom," she replied as she pulled her huge case through to the lounge, causing me to burst out laughing.

"You're only going for two nights; what the hell is in that case?"

"Essentials," she answered excitedly.

On cue, Alex entered the apartment and called out to Casey before spotting her in the lounge.

"Travelling light?" he said, eying her case with wide eyes. She walked over and wrapped her arms around his neck, giving him a massive, long kiss.

"Hey there," Alex said sounding like a love-struck teenager.

"Hey there yourself," Casey replied.

"Uurrgghh. Get out of here, you two, before I throw up," I

mocked.

"Hey Jo," Alex greeted me shyly.

I loved Alex. He was nothing like the way he appeared on the outside. To look at him you would imagine the toughest man on the earth, with his bulging biceps and buzz cut, but he was one of the most caring, sensitive men I had ever met.

"Are you gonna be okay? I hate leaving you like this," Casey said.

I looked down at my clothes. "Would you rather I dressed up to wave you off?"

"You know what I mean." She tilted her head sympathetically.

"Look, I have a bubble bath with my name on it waiting in there. I then intend to indulge in a box set of zombie films whilst drinking wine and eating my meal for one. I'm going to be just fine. Now get out of here before I have you physically removed by Peter."

I headed past them both and opened the door.

"See you Sunday." Casey wrapped her arms around me and whispered into my ear, "Call him."

I loosed her and narrowed my eyes at her. "Don't go getting drunk, okay?"

"Am I ever gonna live that down?"

I scrunched my nose and thought for a moment. "Doubt it."

It was actually nice to have the apartment to myself. I enjoyed a long soak in the bath, surrounded by candles as Ellie Goulding's voice floated through the apartment. I had also by now almost memorized every line of the practice scripts that had been sent to me only a few days prior. For the first time in a while, I felt relaxed and peaceful, and I had managed to not think about Blake for at least the past ten minutes.

The phone rang just as I stepped out of the bath, and I was surprised to see Mum's name pop up, as it was after midnight back home.

"Mum?"

"Don't panic, Josephine; everything is fine." Her voice sounded calm and smooth for the first time in so long.

"Why are you still awake? It's late." I grabbed my robe and quickly tied it at the side before making my way to the kitchen and pouring myself a large glass of wine.

"You know I don't sleep much, and I knew you were alone. Just wanted to see how you were doing."

"You're checking up on me." I smiled as I took a large gulp of wine. It tingled in my belly as it went down.

"Well, with Casey away …" She trailed off.

I smiled. "I'm a big girl now, Mum."

"But to me you will always be my baby girl."

My heart tightened with love for my mum in that moment; she was the bravest person I knew, and yet she spent her whole life worrying about everyone else. "I miss you so much, Mum." I sucked in a deep breath to stop the tears from flowing; I didn't want to show Mum I was upset when I was so far away from her.

"I miss you too, darling."

"Is everyone looking after you?" I knew Uncle Anthony had promised me that Mum would never be alone, but I wanted to hear her tell me.

"They won't leave me be, dear." She said this so quietly, as though they could all hear every word she was saying. I giggled.

"Ah and I have some wonderful news. Well, two lots actually."

"I love good news." I smiled, poking a fork into the plastic wrapper on my meal for one.

"Are you having one of those horrid microwave meals for your dinner?" I could hear the disgust in her voice. "You need to eat properly, darling; those meals are no good for you whatsoever." I rolled my eyes. "And don't roll your eyes at me."

"How did you—"

"Mother knows everything, dear." I heard the amusement in her voice, and we both chuckled.

"Come on, then, tell me the good news."

"Your cousin Jemma called earlier; they are expecting a baby in December."

"Wow, that's amazing! I'll have to call her; they've kept that quiet."

"They wanted to make sure all was okay. She said they have been trying for a few years now. They almost gave up, bless them."

"That's fantastic. I couldn't be happier for them. Now, how is the second news going to top that?"

"I've decided to go back to work next week."

"What! Mum, it is way too soon for that; don't you dare."

"Darling, it is driving me insane being cooped up here. I need normality, I need to be around different people, I need to get lost in character, give my mind a rest from thinking. You understand that, don't you?"

I did. Getting back into acting was helping me forget everything in the real world. Even for just those few moments, it definitely helped.

"I understand, Mum. But if it gets too much—"

"I know," she interrupted, "if it gets too much, I'll step back. Don't you worry about me. Now, have you seen that boy of yours yet?"

"Yep, and don't get excited because things are over before they even started."

"Oh darling, why?"

"It's just … complicated."

"You have gone and pushed him away, haven't you." I heard her sigh. "Josephine, the way you spoke to me about him, I thought he could have been the best thing to happen to you in so long."

"Yes, well, things are never as they seem, are they."

Mum started speaking – actually nagging me – about Blake and my insecurities, but a knock at the door interrupted my telling off. "Just a second, Mum, there's someone at the door."

She continued, however, to rant about how I will end up old and alone if I continue to push those away who want to be with me. I listened and rolled my eyes at her as I made my way to the door.

My chin almost hit the floor as I opened the door to Blake.

"Hi," he said nervously as he stood in the hallway, hands in his pockets, rocking back and forth on his heels.

"Mum, I'm going to have to call you back," I said.

I heard Mum gasp. "He's there, isn't he?" I couldn't reply. "Don't you go messing this up, darling; don't you keep pushing him away, do you hear me?"

"I'll call you tomorrow, Mum; I love you." I hung up the phone without taking my eyes from Blake. He was here, standing in the hallway outside my apartment.

"Is your mom okay?" He removed his hands from his pockets and looked at his watch. "It's late in London."

"She doesn't sleep much and likes to keep an eye on me." I realized I was standing there in only my robe. I pulled it closer together and tightened the belt. "Especially with Casey and Alex away."

"Of course. Vegas."

An awkward silence quickly formed as I realized that Blake was still standing on the outside of the apartment.

"Can we talk, please?"

"Did we not say everything we had to say on Monday?"

"I didn't," he said carefully. With each word he spoke, I felt my heart breaking just a little more. God, he was beautiful; I could never forget just how much, but every time he stood in front of me, I would notice it even more.

"Come in." I stepped back to give him access to the apartment. His scent hit me as he passed by, sending shockwaves straight between my thighs. How did he always manage that with just his scent? It had always taken at least a good kiss from someone to really get me going, but with Blake, just his presence, his voice, and even just his scent could drive me crazy and make me want to rip his clothes off and make love to him over and over again.

I closed the door, realizing I had been standing there drooling over him while he had made his way through to the kitchen. I quickly followed behind.

"I'm not interrupting anything, am I?"

I smiled nervously. "No, nothing." I swept past him and placed my box meal back into the fridge. "Can I get you a glass of wine?" I offered without turning to face him.

"Wine would be good, thank you."

I poured Blake a glass of wine and handed it to him before taking a longer-than-necessary sip from mine.

The silence was back again. Blake leaned casually against the counter as I stood across from him leaning against the breakfast bar, more so to stop my legs from giving in and falling from beneath me.

"It's all over with Sara," Blake announced.

"I thought there was nothing there to even finish." I placed my glass down beside me before looking back to him. My whole body had started to shake and I didn't want to be picking up broken glass right now.

"There wasn't. But she seemed to be oblivious to that fact. Now she knows that there is nothing, there never was, and never will be, just one stupid reckless night that will haunt me for the rest of my life because it stopped me from getting what I really wanted, and what I needed … you."

My heart began to pound against my chest. Every time he spoke, the throb between my thighs thickened. I wanted so hard to resist him, but I too really wanted him and needed him.

He placed his glass down and closed the gap between us but was careful not to touch me. I wanted him to touch me, desperately. But he wouldn't; I could tell that he was being wary of my reactions to him. He seemed scared that at any minute I would tell him to get the hell out of there and leave me alone.

"I am never going to be able to show you how sorry I truly am for what I did. There are no excuses and no reason that any of it could ever be justified as acceptable. But every single minute of every single day since sleeping with Sara has been torture. I wish that somehow I could make it all go away, I wish that you had found me at the party, I wish that I had been the one who was there for you, not him," he said with a hint of venom.

"His name is Cooper," I replied "and at the moment I am thankful that I have someone like him in my life; he has been my rock, Blake, my friend. Don't blame him for any of this; don't you dare." I stood up straight, my legs working hard to support me.

Blake ran a hand through his wavy dark hair and turned away from me for a moment before his eyes rested again on mine. "What do I need to do to make this all okay?"

"The damage is done, Blake. How could I ever trust that you wouldn't go running off to someone for meaningless sex when things got tough between us? I can't trust you, and one thing I do need in a relationship is trust." My voice was barely audible as tears welled in my eyes.

"You can trust me, Jo; it was a mistake. People make mistakes all the time, and yes I've made one. I made the biggest mistake of my life the night I got into bed with Sara." He closed the gap between us, and his hands cupped my face. "I have never felt for anyone the way that I feel about you." his thumbs stroked my cheeks gently. "I have never wanted to be loved by anyone the way I want to be loved by you. I don't think I am capable of walking away from you again, Jo; you are the first thing that I think about the very moment I open my eyes every single morning, and the last thing that I think about before I finally go to sleep. Please don't ask me to walk away again. Please." He rested his head against mine, his cool breath the only thing that separated our mouths.

"I want to believe you," I whispered, "and I want to trust you too." I choked back a sob.

"I will make you believe me, and I will earn your trust; somehow I will, I swear. Please, Jo, I know that you're scared. Believe me, I am petrified. I have never done this before; I don't do relationships. I don't know how to do this. But one thing that I do know is that I feel something for you that I know is worth fighting for."

"I'm so scared," I whispered as my lips brushed his slightly. "Please, Blake, please don't ever hurt me."

Relief flooded his face as a smile tugged on his lips; it was as though I had taken the weight from his shoulders and given him the world.

I, on the other hand, felt flooded with fear. I had held my barrier in place for so long now and had vowed that no man would ever break it down. However, not only was I unable to stop Blake from tearing every last strip from me, but I was also unable to ever try to keep away. He was a drug, and I needed him to help me function. And as much as I found it hard to trust a man again, he had drawn me in like a moth to the flame, irresistible to resist. Even though I knew I could end up burning to the ground, I no longer cared.

This moment right now was what I had wanted for so long, and I was in too deep now to ever walk away.

6

It felt as though the whole world had stopped turning and the only thing that existed was Blake and me.

As his lips touched mine, I felt the earth disappear beneath my feet. I was floating. The only thing I could feel was Blake's lips as they crashed against mine with ultimate force. Weeks of want and need spilled out from us both as our mouths fought to get more, to taste more, trying to get closer to each other than was humanly possible.

With one tug of my belt, my robe was gone, leaving me naked and vulnerable. But I didn't care. Needing to feel his skin against mine, I worked on his belt with shaky fingers, stumbling to rid him of his clothes as quickly as possible. His hands moved down and intervened; in one fell swoop his boxers and trousers were pooled at his feet. I grabbed his shirt in both hands and tore it from him, revealing his hard abs under my fingers.

For a second our lips parted as his eyes took in my naked flesh in front of him. "You're so beautiful," he murmured before once again claiming my mouth with his.

He lifted me roughly and we stumbled until I was pressed firmly against the wall in the hallway. My fingernails dug so far into his shoulders I was sure I could draw blood, but I didn't care, and neither did Blake. In that moment we couldn't get any closer to each other, yet it wasn't enough; we both needed more, so much more. His fingers gripped my thighs, pulling me higher, closer, and with one hard thrust he was in me, filling me deeply, feeding the ache that was becoming more and more unbearable with every thrust that pounded into me.

His mouth moved to my neck and then my breasts as he sucked hard and hungrily. He was everything I had imagined and more. I was addicted, and I needed his fix, yet I don't think it could ever ease the craving.

Our bodies became slick with sweat as we ground hard against each other. "You're so tight," he growled. "So fucking tight, you feel amazing." He panted roughly against my neck. I could feel myself building, every pump of his cock taking me further and further towards orgasm. "Fuck, Jo ... ah fuck yes."

His words sent me spiraling over the edge. I gripped him tight around his neck as the first wave of my orgasm hit, screaming his name over and over as my body exploded with pure pleasure. "Jo," he panted, "we need to stop ... I can't ... I can't hold on." I wrapped my legs tighter around his waist and pulled his further into me. "Jo ... please, I'm gonna come ... Ah ... Jo!" Two more thrusts and Blake began filling into me, the warmth from his come pumping over and over again inside me. "Fuck! Ah!"

Wow.

I had never experienced anything like it in my life. I had also never wanted sex again straight after an orgasm, until now. I needed to feel him again, his long, hard cock inside me; I needed it.

We stood pressed against the wall, still wrapped around each other panting hard. Blake trailed slow kisses across my throat, his hot breath slowing steadily as we came back down to earth from what was, for me, the best sex I had ever had.

Finally his eyes lifted to mine and he smiled. "Hi."

"Hi," I replied shyly.

"About what just happened ..." he started.

I knew exactly what he was about to say.

"I'm on the pill," I replied, slightly embarrassed.

Blake smirked. "Thank God."

With his cock still rock hard, I felt him move inside me. "That was ..."

"Unexpected," I panted.

"Amazing," he answered.

"Very," I whispered as I reached up and ran my fingers across his short stubble.

"And knowing that I can do that again to you with no consequences is just making me harder and harder." He took one of my breasts in his mouth, sucking hard as his hand kneaded and teased it.

"Take me to bed," I panted.

Blake's tired eyes looked up at me through his long lashes. "I couldn't resist that offer even if I tried."

I released my legs from his waist and took his hand. We raced to my room with urgency. I turned to face Blake just as he grabbed my waist and flung me onto the bed. Climbing over me, he whispered in my ear, "I hope you have plenty of energy; this is going to be one very long night."

Oh my.

Where sex with Blake was concerned, I had energy boxed up and ready to go. This was one night that I never wanted to end.

I woke to a soothing voice singing along to the radio in the kitchen. I smiled instantly. It hadn't all been a dream; Blake really was here, in my apartment, singing in my kitchen.

I heard a crash, and then Blake cursed at something. Giggling to myself, I stretched my body, making me aware of exactly how long the night had been and how amazing he had made me feel.

Blake awoke every sense in my body the night before. He did things to me that I had only read about in books. I never thought it was possible to orgasm as many times as I had; each one more powerful and satisfying than the last.

My robe was hung on the back of my bedroom door when I got up out of bed. It had been sprawled on the kitchen floor during the night, and Blake had obviously brought it back in for me for when I woke.

Wrapping it around me, I headed to the kitchen to find the most beautiful sight possible. Blake stood at the stove, cooking in just his boxers. I leaned against the door frame, drinking in the sight of him. He was beautiful, and he was mine. Finally, the man who I had fallen so hard for was mine. Realizing I was drooling, I pulled myself out of my fantasy and walked over to where he stood, wrapping my arms around his waist and pressing my face against his back.

I heard Blake place a pan back on the stove before he turned to face me, wrapping me in his arms.

"Good morning, beautiful," he said, pressing his face to my hair.

"You're still here," I said with relief. Blake shifted and lifted my chin with his fingers until our eyes met.

"Of course I'm still here," he said as his eyebrows pulled together in confusion. "I meant every single word that I said to you last night, Jo. I won't be walking away from you – not now, not ever." I forced a smile and placed my head to his chest "Well," he said, "Apart from later – I have a meeting. But then I'm gonna come back, I'm gonna bring food, and then we're gonna carry on where we left off." his lips pressed against my head as I tightened my grip around his waist.

"Can't we carry on right now," I asked, feeling Blake's chest vibrate with laughter against me.

"Breakfast first," he said before releasing me and turning his attention back to the stove.

I gasped as I hopped up onto a breakfast stool. I was aching in places that I didn't know existed, but it was a good feeling. It reminded me of everything that Blake and I had done the previous night, the places that he had touched me first with his fingers, then with his lips, his tongue. I crossed my legs, trying desperately to ease the ache that was constantly present around Blake.

Everything felt too surreal. Blake stood almost naked in my kitchen cooking me breakfast after what had been the most amazing night of my life. I was convinced that at any moment I was about to wake up and realize that the whole thing had been a dream – a damn good one too. But after finally allowing myself to feel happy came the fear that something would soon come along and tear that happiness away from me.

My mind wandered briefly to Sara. I wondered how she would react if she knew that Blake and I had spent the night together. Part of me didn't want to care, but after what had happened four years ago, I felt I needed to care – more for Sara than myself. But for now I just wanted to create a bubble around the two of us and completely block out the outside world and everything that came with it.

"Coffee?" Blake asked, pulling me from my daydream.

"Do you know how to make tea?" I asked.

"Nope."

"Then coffee is fine," I smiled.

Blake placed two plates next to each other on the breakfast bar along with two cups of coffee and two glasses of fresh orange juice, before placing a lingering kiss on my lips and sitting down next to me.

"This looks incredible," I said, lifting my fork. "I don't really do breakfast, though – you know, for future reference."

"How can you not eat breakfast?" he replied, shocked. "It's the most important meal of the day."

His reaction mirrored someone who had just been told that breakfast was to be banned under some new law.

"I only eat when I'm hungry." I shrugged, poking at my breakfast with the fork.

"Well, if you're not hungry this morning," he said huskily as he leaned into my ear, "there's something that I didn't do right last night." He smiled before placing a forkful of scrambled eggs into his mouth. "Are you feeling sore?"

"A little," I admitted. "It's been a while."

"How long?"

"Four years." I nodded, keeping my eyes on my breakfast. "Maybe four and a half." I added.

"What!" Blake replied. "How is that even possible?"

Turning my head towards him, I felt my face glow with embarrassment. "Oh, it's possible; believe me."

"What I mean is" – he placed his fork down and rubbed his stubble frantically – "you're stunning. I mean look at you."

"You don't sleep with people just because they look good, Blake." My eyes widened. "Do you?"

"What? No!" he replied. "I just find it hard to believe that you haven't met anyone in that amount of time, that's all."

"I came out of a bad relationship," I said quickly. "Something happened, and it frightened me so much that I decided I would never date again. Before that relationship, every single man I had ever dated cheated on me, every single one. So relationships were already doomed for me, and then four years ago, not only did I get cheated on—" I stopped, realizing I was about to spill my entire history to Blake already. I wasn't ready for that just yet. "—let's just say that over the years I discovered a theory that I am yet to have proved wrong."

"And that theory is?" Blake asked carefully.

Turning to face him, I said, "There is no such thing as happiness without pain."

"That's deep," he said quietly.

"It's also true," I said, standing and heading over to the bin with my breakfast.

"Have I upset you?" Blake asked carefully.

"No," I said, turning back to Blake. "I just try not to let myself feel too happy, because as soon as I do, something happens to take that happiness away."

"Well, I will make it my mission to prove you wrong," he said, as though it were the easiest thing in the world.

"It's already happened twice since I met you, Blake," I admitted.

Blake stood and walked over to me and wrapped his arms around my waist. "When?"

"At the party," I said. "I was so happy when you asked me out to dinner, but then I got the phone call from my mum, happiness and then pain." Blake attempted to speak, but I cut him off. "And then when I came back from London and you were standing right there" – I nodded to the hallway – "I was so, so happy. Then your phone rang and I found out about Sara happiness, followed by pain again. Do you see?"

"I can see how you would associate the two, yes," he admitted.

"I'm petrified, Blake, because right now I am happy – happier than I have been in a long time. I'm on tenterhooks, just waiting for the pain."

Blake pulled my mouth to his and kissed me gently, slowly stroking his tongue against mine over and over before pulling away and looking deep into my eyes.

"How about if I make you the promise that I will make sure you get that happiness and there will be no pain."

I smiled. "You want to prove my theory wrong?"

"I *will* prove your theory wrong," he said, placing his lips to my nose.

"I hope so," I replied quietly.

My audition had managed to slip my mind. With Blake gone for a few hours, I ran through my lines again but found it impossible to think of anything other than Blake. So, giving up, I decided to call Mum.

Without divulging too much information about how we had spent our night, I told Mum that Blake and I were now together. She understood that I felt nervous but assured me that Blake could help me feel complete again.

It made me smile; she didn't even know him.

I then tried to call Cooper. He hadn't been jogging all week; nor had he returned any of my calls or messages. He had obviously only been acting polite to me when he said our kiss would cause no awkwardness between us. That was one mistake I needed to rectify at some point.

Blake arrived back at the apartment at eight o'clock carrying a brown bag filled with French food. I didn't tell him that I had never tried French cuisine before. I had always been put off by the type of food they ate – frogs' legs and snails had never appealed to me – so I had always steered well clear of anything French.

We sat facing each other, cross-legged on the rug in the middle of the living room. The food was actually delicious. I wasn't sure what it was, but it didn't look like it had anything to do with frogs and snails – at least I hoped it didn't anyway. I hadn't actually noticed just how hungry I was until the first mouthful made my mouth water for even more.

Ellie Goulding sang in the background with only candlelight around us. It felt perfect. It felt like a dream, it was so damn perfect. I just hoped that I would never wake up.

Blake talked excitedly about his new season and how they were going to be filming some scenes in Miami in a few weeks' time. We had decided that as long as my schedule didn't interrupt, I would join him there for the duration. It would be our first vacation, as he called it. I didn't care where we were, as long as we were together. The thought of him being there without me brought out a little of my jealous streak, so yes, being with him would be the best option.

"Can I ask you something?"

He smiled. "You can ask me anything beautiful."

"Have you dated anyone that you currently work with?"

He smirked. "No."

"But you date a lot of women you work with," I stated matter-of-factly. "Should that worry me?"

Blake leaned his arm on the sofa behind him and studied me. "Do you think it should?" he asked carefully, but his eyes were full of amusement.

I shrugged. "I don't know. That's why I asked."

Blake smirked, but he didn't reply. Instead he leaned forward and placed another forkful of food into his mouth.

"What has been the longest relationship that you have had?"

Blake seemed to think about it for a short moment. "Probably this one," he finally answered.

"Don't be ridiculous," I laughed.

Blake moved, and before I knew it we were both flat on the floor with Blake towering above me. He had both my hands pinned above my head with one hand while his other hand moved under my T-shirt and up to my breast as he nipped my neck gently. "I'm being totally serious," he said. He lifted his head and held my gaze; his face was impassive. "I've told you before; I have never met anyone who I wanted to be with, like this, until you."

He released my hands, and I immediately took his head in my

hands and guided him to my mouth, letting my legs fall open. He slid between my thighs, pressing his erection firmly against me.

"Any more questions?" he asked against my mouth.

"Yes, the one you didn't answer. Should I be worried?"

"No, you shouldn't," he answered seriously.

"Okay," I panted. "You haven't dated many brunettes. Why?"

"Are you serious?"

"Deadly," I replied, trying to pull him closer to me as I squirmed beneath him.

"I don't have a type," he replied, "so that question is void. Now, have you finished with your twenty questions?"

"For now," I panted, pulling him closer, but he held his head up and stared down at me.

He smirked. "Good, now it's my turn."

"First things first – where did you get all this information about me from?"

"Google," I answered simply.

"Google, of course." He shook his head in amusement as he laughed.

"Should I be worried that you only seem to date sport stars?" Once again his hand started to travel up my T-shirt. He took my nipple between his fingers, gently tugging and twisting as his eyes remained firmly on mine.

"They're better looking than the actors in England," I mocked, and he tugged my nipple harder. It was only slightly painful, but it sent shockwaves through my entire body.

"Witty, Miss Summers, I like that." He smirked and kissed me yet again. "And they all seem to have the same look," he said, pulling away from my mouth. "Clean-cut blondes fresh from college."

"Well, if you do the maths, you will see that they probably were fresh from college." He tugged my nipped again, harder. I liked it, but I gasped out loud.

"Do you know what your witty mouth is doing to me?" he nudged his ever-growing erection against me again.

"Is that one of your twenty questions, MR Mackenzie?" His hand left my breast, and he tugged my T-shirt roughly over my head before removing his shirt too and lying back down on top of me. His skin felt hot against my breasts. I desperately wanted him inside me, but he was teasing me, leading me on, seeing how far he could take me before I would give in and rip the remains of his clothes from him.

"Should I be worried that you only date sport stars?"

"You've already asked me that question?"

"And you dodged the answer. Should I be worried?"

"We will see when I meet your father," I laughed. Blake's dad had been one of the New York Yankees' most famous players; it was very well documented that in his day, he was as good at baseball as David Beckham was at football.

Blake gasped sharply and tugged at my jeans, unbuttoning them and practically dragging them from my thighs.

"I think your witty mouth is my new favourite form of foreplay, Miss Summers," he said as he worked at ridding himself of the rest of his clothes. "I have one more question." He turned serious as he lay back down on me and swept his hand down past my waist, resting it gently on the scar that sat just above my left hip. "Does this have anything to do with how you feel about happiness?"

I swallowed hard past the lump that had formed in my throat. "Yes."

"Do you want to talk about it?"

"Not right now, no. I just want to forget about it. I want to forget about everything that has ever happened to me, even if just for tonight," I said as I linked my fingers behind Blake's head.

"I am gonna show you how sorry I am for everything that happened with Sara. I will. And I am going to prove to you that there is no price to pay for feeling happy. Okay?" I nodded. "I'm going to make it all better, Jo, I promise." His mouth took mine again, this time gentler, more loving. He was reassuring me that he meant every single word that he had just said. As he pulled his mouth away from mine, our eyes locked as he pushed his hard cock inside me. Watching me closely, he rocked forward and back slowly, carefully, his eyes never leaving mine, no words leaving his mouth or mine, just eyes, mesmerized, trying desperately to read each other. I reached up and stroked his face as my legs tightened around his waist. My body was building towards the pleasure that I believed only Blake would ever be capable of. And in this moment, I believed that he could help me, that he could rebuild my broken body, and that only he could help me to be happy again, only Blake.

Blake collapsed on top of me, burying his head in my neck as we both came down from another earth-shattering orgasm. "Only you, Jo," he said against my skin before lifting his head and looking into my eyes. "There will only ever be you, forever." He took my hand and placed it over his heart. "This is all yours now; take care of it."

7

Waking up in Blake's arms as the sun was rising felt amazing. Waking up together after spending the whole day making love felt even better.

We barely made it out of bed on Sunday without ending up back there completely tangled up in each other's bodies. It definitely had been the best weekend of my life, bar none.

"Hey, sleepy," Blake said quietly as he pressed his lips to my temple.

"Hi," I replied quietly, wrapping my arm around his waist and moving closer to him.

"As much as I don't want us to, we had better get up soon. Casey and Alex are due back later, and this will take some explaining," he chuckled.

"Oh." I couldn't hide my obvious disappointment.

I felt Blake's body tremor as he laughed. "That's how I felt when I realized." His lips gently grazed my temple again. "We've been caught up in our own little bubble this weekend, haven't we?"

I pushed up and leaned on my arm as I pouted while looking down into Blake's bright blue eyes. "I like our bubble."

"Me too," Blake reached up and pushed the stray hairs from my face. "This weekend has been …"

I was searching for the right word when Blake replied, "Perfect."

"Yes, perfect."

Blake inhaled a deep breath and brushed his thumb over my bottom lip. "You know, I was so nervous when I turned up here on Friday. I thought you would slam the door in my face."

I lowered my gaze to where I was tracing the line of his collarbone with my fingers. "I never stopped thinking about you all week. I would wake wondering what you were doing and" – I sucked in a deep breath – "who you were with." I lifted my eyes back to his.

"I'm sorry I screwed up."

I managed a sad smile, unable to tell him it was okay. But I was beginning to see why he had done what he did that night at the party. There was never going to be a good excuse, but I could at least understand. I had, after all, kissed Cooper because of Blake. What he did was a million times worse, but I was beginning to understand.

"Is this your father?"

He reached for the photo of Dad and me that sat on my bedside table. In the picture, we had just finished building a giant snowman in the garden of our old house. It was my favourite photo of Dad and me; it held so many memories from that one day – my smile in it showed that.

"Yes, that's my dad." I smiled, reaching up and stroking the glass that framed the picture.

"You look just like him."

"Everyone always said that I was a miniature version of my dad. He would beam with pride when someone would say it."

"How old are you in this picture?"

"That was taken on my seventh birthday."

"It snowed on your birthday? What a gift."

"We thought so too," I laughed. "Mum, on the other hand, was not impressed. They had spent a fortune on me, yet all I wanted to play with was the snow." I felt Blake giggle.

"Of course."

"I was supposed to be having a big party at the house that afternoon. Mum had paid for caterers, children's entertainers, the lot. But that house was inaccessible in the snow, so everything had to be cancelled. I think Mum was more upset than I was. I remember that I didn't mind. Neither did Dad; we spent the whole day on that snowman. Look at him; he was brilliant." My smile faded a little. I was talking about one of my favourite memories of my dad when I realized that there would be no new memories any more, but I had a lifetime of them stacked up. I was thankful for that. Blake's arm tightened around me before he placed the picture back down.

"I loved that house. It was everything a family home should be. Dad and Uncle Anthony even built me my own tree house. It was huge. I would spend hours in there playing, and then reading as I became older. I wonder if it's still there." Blake's fingers stroked the length of my back as I recalled my memories.

"Then there was the tree swing. I must have fell off it over a hundred times over the years. The last time I fell off, I broke my arm. I have never been on a swing since then," I laughed.

"You have some wonderful memories."

"I do. It was the perfect house to bring up children. When I have kids, I want a house just like it, in the country, away from all the hustle and smoke. I want that house."

"That sounds perfect. Your dad was a lawyer wasn't he?"

I looked up at Blake and smirked. "Google?"

"Google," he confirmed with a wink.

Shaking my head with amusement, I placed my cheek back onto Blake's chest. "Dad was the best in the business," I recalled. "He wasn't always so high profile, not until he represented an MP. I can't remember much about it, but he won a case that was against all odds. Then, as if it happened overnight, the demand for him was instant. Celebrities from all walks of life wanted him; they would pay way over the odds for him, but he was very professional and would only take on their cases if he knew they were suffering an injustice. I really respected him for that. It took a toll on us, though; he was hardly home, and the travelling was too much, so that's when we moved closer to London. I think it saved us all, to be honest."

We sat in silence for a moment. I had really opened up to Blake, and it felt so good to share. I could tell that Blake was happy to have sat and listened too.

"I really miss him, Blake." A tear rolled down my face, and before I could stop it, it became a constant flow.

Blake turned to face me, wrapping both of his arms tightly around my waist as he buried his head in my hair.

"When he died, I decided I wasn't coming back to New York." I sniffed. "But Mum insisted and said it was what Dad would have wanted. I sat at his graveside and asked him; he gave me the sign to come back," I said quietly.

"I'm glad that he did," he whispered into my hair, placing gentle kisses between whispers.

"I wish he had known you," I sobbed. "He would have been so happy to see me happy."

"He knows, beautiful; he knows how happy you are, I promise."

I wiped the tears and looked up at Blake. "Sorry," I said.

"Don't you ever apologize for showing your emotion." He wiped the last few tears from my face. "I'm sorry that you had to face it all alone; I'd have gotten on that plane with you if I'd known. But once I found out where you had gone, and why, I was too ashamed to even contact you; I felt dirty, horrible." He held my gaze. "So don't you ever say sorry for being sad, or for anything. You have done nothing to apologize for, do you hear me?"

My heart melted. I had fallen so fast and so hard for Blake it was frightening.

"Blake?"

"Hmm?"

"You know what I said about being happy?"

I felt his head nod against mine.

"I've never felt this happy in my life. It scares me."

"Well, maybe now it's time to face that fear and conquer it," he said gently. "This time, your happiness is going to last, I promise."

"What happened to you that made you so guarded?"

"I told you, a bad relationship."

"Did he cheat on you? Is that why you keep yourself so guarded?" I felt my body begin to tense, I wasn't even near enough ready to talk about it yet, especially after the weekend that we had just spent together.

"I'm not ready to talk about the past, not yet anyway. Do you think Sara is okay?"

I felt Blake's grip tighten on me. "Forget about her; she's the part of my past that I never want to think about ever again. Let's concentrate on the future, our future."

The truth was, I couldn't forget about Sara. What she did that night at the party was unforgivable, but I couldn't help wonder how she was feeling now, and how she felt about me. She would see me as the one who took her happiness; I just hoped she didn't think there was a score to settle for it.

"Where are you going?" Blake complained, moving his hands and holding out his arms for me as I climbed off the bed.

"Casey and Alex, remember?"

Blake shot up quickly and leaped off the bed quickly; grabbing me by the waist and pulling me back down. "Blake!" I complained with laughter.

"We still have a couple of hours," he said as he removed my nightgown yet again and quickly placed his mouth around my nipple. Once again I forgot everything else that mattered in life; I was lost yet again in the power of Blake Mackenzie, and at this precise moment in time, I never wanted to be found.

Casey's laughter filtered through the apartment. We had fallen asleep again after making love for at least the tenth time that day. I shot out of bed quickly, noting that every muscle in my body ached from all of the pleasure, quickly grabbing a T-shirt and jogging bottoms out of my drawer. "Blake," I whispered loudly. "Blake, get up; they're here!"

Blake slowly opened his eyes as a lazy smile graced his lips "Why are you panicking? They're not gonna be shocked by us being together."

"Get dressed." I threw his shirt at him with force before quickly tying my hair in a loose ponytail and walking innocently out of the room.

Casey and Alex were laughing in the kitchen when I walked in. "Hello, you two, have a good time?" I asked as if Blake weren't lying naked and alone in my bed.

Casey went to answer, but she frowned instead. "Are you okay? You look flushed." She went to place her hand on my brow, which I dodged. I headed to the fridge for a bottle of water.

"How was Vegas? You married now?" I joked, taking a long swig from the bottle.

"Not quite yet, no," Casey grinned widely as she held up her left hand, flashing me a massive diamond ring.

I gasped loudly. "Congratulations!" I hugged Casey hard before releasing her and taking her hand in mine for a closer inspection "Wow, just wow! I was not expecting this!"

"You and me both." Casey hopped from foot to foot before walking over to Alex and wrapping her arms around his neck, planting a lingering kiss on his lips.

"You weren't expecting what?" Blake filled the doorway wearing only the suit trousers he had come over wearing the day before. I closed my eyes and sighed.

"Oh … my … God" I heard Casey say before she burst out in loud laughter. "You sly devil, you." She nudged me as I opened my eyes to see her staring at Blake.

"Put your tongue away, Casey; you are engaged now. And Blake, I thought I told you to get dressed." I rubbed my brow frantically, the embarrassment creeping in slowly.

"You did it, then," Blake said. He headed over to Alex, completely ignoring what I had just said to him. Alex was smirking as he looked from Blake to me and then back again. "Congrats, dude." They did the typical man celebration, with a shake of hands and a few good slaps to each other's backs. "And the club?"

"All official, I now own my very own slice of Vegas!" he said cheerily.

Blake let out a low whistle through his teeth. "I smell a Vegas bachelor party then."

"I'll second that." Alex nodded and grabbed two beers from the fridge for him and Blake.

"Okay, can we stop avoiding the obvious now," Casey

screeched; her eyes wide as she stood straight with her arms folded over her chest. "When did this happen?" She released her arms and waved her fingers between Blake and me. Blake walked up behind me and wrapped his arms around my waist, pulling me into his body.

"Friday," I answered.

"I couldn't stay away any longer. I took the chance, and I'm glad I did." Blake placed his lips to my temple gently.

"Finally!" Casey said excitedly. "So this is a triple celebration! I know it's late, but let's go out, just to Sugar Lounge. You know, just invite a select few and celebrate. What do you think?"

I could tell that Blake sensed my dislike for us going out and he gave me a reassuring squeeze.

"I'm not sure; it is quite late, and I really could do with having a clear head tomorrow in preparation for my audition Tuesday," I said.

"Please!" Casey placed her hands together as if begging me.

"It'll give me the chance to make sure the club is still standing," Alex said looking up from whatever he was reading on his phone. "I'll get the VIP area roped off, keep it private."

Sugar Lounge was one of Alex's many bars. They were scattered all over New York, with Sugar being the most upmarket and most popular amongst the rich and famous. It was also where Casey and Alex had met for the first time, so it held a special meaning for them.

"It's entirely up to you," Blake said quietly into my ear.

"Okay," I replied, trying not to sound disappointed. Blake squeezed me once more.

Casey bounced excitedly. "Yay!"

"I'm gonna need some fresh clothes; I'll head home and meet you there," Blake said, loosening his grip on me.

"I'll come with you," Alex said, placing his phone back in his pocket before tossing Casey his car keys. "Take the car, no cabs," he demanded.

"Got it," Casey said as she caught the keys.

"Jo?" Blake tilted his head towards the hall as he walked away. I quickly followed, closing the bedroom door behind us as we entered.

"You okay?" his arms snaked around my waist, pulling me to him.

"I suppose I just didn't want this weekend to end."

"We don't have to go," he suggested.

"We do; they're our friends. Celebrating their engagement." I shook my head in disbelief "How mad is that?"

"Crazy," he said as his mouth touched the corner of mine.

"Well," I said, pulling away, "It's time to pop the bubble. I'll see you there, I guess."

"I guess you will." Blake smiled before leaving the room.

Casey had grilled me to a crisp on the drive over to Sugar, wanting to know every single detail of every minute that Blake and I had spent together over the weekend. I had left a lot of the detail out for obvious reasons, but I could feel myself beaming as I told her about him turning up and making me feel too weak to resist.

She was pleased that I finally seemed happy, but she also understood my insecurities.

By the time we arrived at Sugar, I had managed to sway the conversation away from me and onto her upcoming nuptials.

They had decided that because of Casey's work schedule and the opening of Alex's new bar in Vegas, they would be planning a summer wedding for the following year, happening here in New York. That gave them twelve months to plan their perfect wedding.

Sugar was quieter than normal for this time on a Sunday evening, but it suited me better. I would've been happier staying at home anyway, with Blake, in bed. And the more I thought about that, the more I wanted to be home, with Blake, in bed.

Blake was sitting talking to Alex's sister when we walked in. I had only met her a handful of times, and she seemed nice enough. She was older than Alex and Blake but was still single. She was stunning; they must have had a really good gene pool in Alex's family. Even though she wasn't much taller than I was, her legs were long and super slim, her hair was blonde with bouncy curls, and her eyes were bright blue like Blake's. Casey wasn't overly keen on Christina. They got on well now, but when Alex and Casey first met, Christina had accused Casey of being with him for his money. Alex had been engaged prior to Casey, but it ended badly when he walked in on his former fiancée in bed with a mutual friend. After kicking her out of the apartment they shared, she repaid him by saying she was only in it for his money. So when Casey came along, and wasn't too dissimilar to Alex's ex, she had to endure the treatment from Christina that she didn't deserve.

Seeing Alex happy gave me faith. We were not all that different to each other where our pasts were concerned, and he had overcome trust issues to enable him to see a future with Casey. That gave me faith.

Blake looked stunning. He had changed into a black Ralph Lauren suit with a white shirt underneath, open at the collar. He had shaved, but there was still a tiny bit of stubble showing, which I was glad about; I loved the feel of his rough chin on my body. And his hair was styled to perfection. My mind drifted to me messing that up at the first opportunity.

Blake stood as I approached. "Christina, this is my girlfriend, Jo; Jo, this is Christina."

"Hello," I said, giving her my hand. She shook it, closely studying me.

"I thought you were dating Sara?" she said to Blake, keeping her eyes locked on me.

"No, I have not been dating Sara," Blake said in annoyance.

"Oh," she said, clutching her chest with embarrassment, "I'm so sorry, Jo; I shouldn't have said that." She shook her head in shame. "It's lovely to meet you properly, Casey has told me so much about you."

"Likewise," I replied, sensing my own annoyance.

"Can I get you a drink?" she asked.

"Thanks, Christina, but we're gonna mingle; there are people I want Jo to meet," said Blake.

She nodded. "Sure. Maybe we can do lunch or something. Get

Casey to let me know."

"Will do." I nodded, forcing a smile.

"Sorry about that," Blake said as we entered the hallway, away from the noise of the VIP area.

"She was obviously just saying what everyone else is thinking; I saw the way they all looked at me."

"You're being paranoid," he said as we stopped outside Alex's office.

"Sorry," I said. "It's just, the first person you introduce me to and that's what she said to me."

"Are you mad at me?" he asked as his eyebrows knitted together in concern.

"No," I sighed, placing my hand to his chin, feeling the rough stubble below my fingers I leaned up onto my tiptoes and kissed the corner of his mouth. "You have never dated Christina, have you?"

"Are you gonna ask me that every time you meet a woman I know?" Blake asked, amused.

"Maybe," I replied.

"I have it very bad for you, you know." He swept his nose against mine, taking a deep breath. His erection pressed against my hip as our mouths invaded each other. We were in a hallway in a busy club, but at that moment, I didn't care who could see us. I couldn't stop where Blake was concerned.

A door slammed to the right of us, causing us both to jump. Blake stepped back and immediately adjusted his jacket with a smile on his face. "It was just the wind," he said.

"Someone could have seen us," I panted.

"I was kissing my girlfriend; no law against that." He smirked as he held out his hand for me to take.

"Can we go soon?" I moaned, placing my hand in his.

"Definitely. Let's mingle, and then we will slip away unnoticed."

His eyes twinkled with excitement before he leaned in and kissed me firmly, hungrily even, before releasing me and leading me back to Casey and Alex's friends and family.

Every time we would try to get away, it was as if fate had other ideas, and somehow we would end up getting dragged back in. By the time three a.m. rolled around, there were only a handful of guests left, including Blake and me. He would throw me an apologetic look every now and then and mouth the words "I'm sorry," but it wasn't his fault. It was as if the whole club were against us leaving early.

Casey had got herself into a complete drunken stupor, and Alex was trying to sort out staffing issues after being forced to fire his current manager after witnessing him snorting cocaine in the office. It had been a good evening up until then.

Blake and I offered to take Casey home and watch her until Alex could get away. We wouldn't get to spend what was left of the night as we had hoped. I felt disappointed, but I had no doubt we would make up for it at the first opportunity.

Casey flaked out on the sofa shortly after we got home, but before I could let her drift off to sleep I made her drink two strong black coffees and a pint of water. She mumbled over and over about how much she loved Alex and couldn't live without him; then she cried. Then she laughed about crying. She was crazy, but I loved her to bits.

Blake stood in the kitchen, leaning against the counter. He was watching me with a smile as I walked back in after checking that Casey was sleeping safely with a bowl next to her on the sofa. He smiled. "You're gonna make a brilliant mommy someday."

"I wouldn't be this calm if that was my child lying there that drunk," I laughed as I lifted my cup of tea to take a sip.

"I'm sorry about how tonight has turned out," he said.

"This is how it's going to be now, I suppose. The bubble has well and truly popped." I frowned, and Blake's smile dropped. "Once you start filming again next week, and if I get my job, we will probably hardly see each other."

"But the sex will be amazing," he said huskily as he walked over and took my cup from my hand, placing it on the counter.

"Is that all I am to you, MR Mackenzie, a sex toy?" I ran my hand down the front of his trousers, feeling his hard length growing under my palm.

He seemed to think hard before replying with a smirk, "It's a good trait."

I closed my hand gently around his cock and gave it a little squeeze. "You want to say that again?" I teased.

"Ouch! I'm kidding, I'm kidding; let the fella go." He held his hands up in defeat.

The door to the apartment opened, and in walked Alex.

"What a fucking night," he moaned.

"Yeah, sorry man," Blake said as he walking over to pat Alex on the back. "Everything sorted now?"

"Kind of," he replied as he took three tumblers from the cupboard above and filled them all with brandy. He offered one to Blake, which he took. I shook my head. It was five a.m., and I was barley functioning as it was. "I mean, right under my fucking nose. Who knows how long that shit's been going on or who else is fucking doing it. That bastard could have gotten me shut down." He polished off the brandy and refilled the glass. "I've called a staff meeting for nine this morning; heads are gonna fucking roll."

A firm knock at the door interrupted us, and we all looked to each other in confusion. It was five a.m., and everyone who would have been knocking was inside the apartment.

"Who the hell could that be?" Blake said.

"Probably someone from the fucking club," Alex moaned. "I'll go."

He pushed away from the counter and sighed as he headed into the hall.

"You can't just walk the fuck in here; get out!" I heard Alex shout just as Sara walked into the kitchen.

"Sara," I whispered. The tightest knot appeared in the pit of my stomach. I had to swallow continuously to stem the sick feeling that had formed in my throat.

Blake immediately stood defensively in front of me, keeping her at a distance from whatever she was here to do. I tilted my head around Blake's shoulder in order to see her. She was a mess. Her hair was thrown up in a messy bun, and the usually flawless skin on her face was free from make-up and instead filled with red blotches under her eyes and her cheeks. She looked dreadful; she looked a shadow of the Sara that I knew and disliked.

"I knew it," she said angrily.

"I tried to stop her, but I can't manhandle no woman no matter who the bitch is; sorry, guys," Alex said as he appeared behind her and folded his arms across his chest.

"It's fine," Blake said, placing his hands out in front of him in a calming gesture. "Sara obviously has something she needs to say; let's hear her out, and if we need to, we will get security to remove her. Okay Sara?" He spoke calmly in order not to anger her more than she already appeared to be.

"How could you do this to me, Blake? How? We had something, something special, until *she* came back and ruined everything." Her words were shaky as her anger was visibly rising.

"We had nothing, Sara," Blake said, trying to remain calm. "It was just one drunken, stupid mistake that you instigated; there never would have been anything at all if you hadn't lied through your teeth in the first place. That was sick. What you did was sick, Sara; do you hear me?"

"I wanted you, Blake; I always have. I wasn't thinking straight; I just … wanted you."

"You kept something important from me." His voice was now slightly raised; the anger was bubbling inside him. "You did it to hurt Jo, and by doing that, you hurt me too. I never wanted you, Sara; I was angry – angry with Jo because you lied about her. God, she was going through the worst time of her life, and you did that. You disgust me."

"I know you don't mean that, Blake. I can tell that you felt something for me; you still do," she said sadly.

"You are delusional. You need help, and I mean professional help; you're a mess," he said angrily.

"There's only one thing I need, Blake. Please, I need you. If you don't leave with me now and come home with me, I'll finish it this time. I'll be alone in my apartment, and I'll do it. I'm not afraid; you know I'm not. You know that I'll do it."

"What is she talking about, Blake? What is she going to do?" I asked quietly, not taking my eyes from her.

She lifted the sleeves from her jumper, revealing two bandages, one around each wrist. It was obvious what she was telling me; she had tried to take her own life. I closed my eyes as my past came back to haunt me. "Fuck no."

"You!" she yelled at me. "You made me do this! You! I knew that night at the restaurant; I knew what the fuck you two were doing in that bathroom, behind my back!"

"Nothing happened in the bathroom; we only talked," I said shakily. "And it wouldn't have been behind your back; you weren't together, Sara."

"Is that what he told you?" She let out a sad laugh. "Did you tell her we were nothing?" she said, turning her attention to Blake.

"We *were* nothing!" he yelled. "I made one mistake – one big, huge mistake – and then you wouldn't leave me the fuck alone!"

My body started to physically shake. It was as though I were reliving the worst night of my life all over again. I needed to breathe. I could feel the whole world slowly slipping away as my mind struggled to process what was happening in front of me.

"And as for your wrists, you did that to yourself for attention, Sara; it's got nothing to do with Jo or me," Blake spat out. "It's you; you're nothing but a crazy fucking bitch."

Sara's eyes saddened even more. "But you helped me, Blake; you cared for me. If you felt nothing for me, you wouldn't have done that; you would have let me carry on until I killed myself."

Her words hit me like a slap in the face. "Did you know she did this?" I asked shakily.

"I didn't want to feel any responsibility for your stupid actions,

Sara; of course I wouldn't have let you kill yourself," he stated. "You need help serious help."

"I need you," she sobbed.

I could see Casey rouse from her drunken state on the couch. She stood up, slowly rubbing her head before heading into the kitchen. Her eyes caught mine, and I shook my head in warning to her, but she gave me a look of confusion before turning her eyes to Sara.

"What the fuck are you doing in my apartment? Get out now!"

"Casey," Sara said desperately, "tell Jo; tell her what Blake and I were, please. You know; you know what was going on between us. Tell her, please."

"You were a mistake," she said firmly. "Now get out of my home before I kick your skanky ass out myself."

"I'm not leaving without Blake."

"Go, Sara, now," Blake demanded. "There never was and there never will be anything between us. If I could go back and erase every single memory I have of you, believe me, I would do it right now. You were a mistake. Do you hear me? A mistake!"

"She has done this to you; I know she has!" she yelled. "I hate you! You have ruined my life, and I hate you! You will pay; you will fucking pay!" she shouted to me.

"Enough!" Blake yelled.

Sara sank to the floor, sobbing into her hands. She was a woman broken. She had believed that she and Blake could be something; she had believed that she meant more to him than she really did. I knew the signs; I had seen it all before. And as much as I was falling in love with Blake so quickly and so hard, I wasn't sure I could go through this again. I wasn't strong enough physically and mentally to deal with another woman who was in love with the same man as I was.

Tears started rolling down my cheeks as I saw her sobbing, desperate to be loved. I stepped around Blake, ignoring his hand that he held out for me. "She needs help," I said shakily as I stared down at her. "Don't just throw her out onto the street; she could do something stupid." I sniffed. "She's not well enough to be alone."

I looked up at Blake. He was watching me carefully. "Are you okay?" he asked, but I couldn't answer him. I couldn't tell him that he, too, needed to go. In that moment I realized that I loved him so much, but that wouldn't be enough to get through all of this. I had lived my life in fear in London for so long that New York had felt like my safe haven. I couldn't go through it all again, no matter how much it was going to hurt to say goodbye to Blake, no matter how happy I had felt over the past few days and how much I knew Blake was right for me, I couldn't go through it again; I needed to let him go.

I stepped around Sara and headed down the hall and into my bedroom.

After closing the door quietly behind me, I fell onto my bed and sobbed uncontrollably. I could hear voices in the hallway, and I was pretty sure that Sara was still in the kitchen.

My mind tried to process everything that had happened over the past few days. I had opened the door to Blake on Friday and had ended up spending the most wonderful weekend with him. I had seen my future with him. I had seen that I could be happy again. I had fallen in love with him. I had felt wanted. I felt through his kiss alone how much he felt for me. And then Sara had turned up and reminded me of the reality. While we had spent time in our bubble, everything was perfect. Things were never that simple in the outside world, and this episode had proved that.

I couldn't have a relationship with Blake for fear of what could happen. As much as I loved him, it would be easier to say goodbye to him now than to face a future full of fear and dread.

My door opened, and after a few seconds, I felt the bed dip beside me. Blake's gentle hand reached over and wrapped around me. I turned over to face him and buried my head into his chest. He held me so tightly, no words, no actions. We just lay together, and he held me until I had cried so much that I could cry no more. He never spoke; he never once told me everything would be okay. He just let me cry the tears that I needed to release.

Eventually I looked up at him. His eyes were full of sadness and regret.

"I'm so sorry," he whispered, sweeping my hair away from my face, but his eyes remained on mine.

"Were you really there when she cut herself?" I asked.

He nodded slowly.

"When?"

"She called me Tuesday threatening to do it. I didn't believe her at first, but I couldn't risk that she wouldn't. When I got to the apartment, there was blood everywhere."

I nodded and placed my head back down on his chest.

"Where is she now?"

"Casey called her mom; she's driving up from Washington to get her. She's agreed that she needs help, and her mom has said she will help her too. They've taken her back to her apartment while they wait."

I nodded before lifting my eyes to Blake's. "Blake," I said quietly just as a tear escaped.

He knew what I was about to say to him. "Don't do this; please, Jo, don't."

I leaned in and placed my lips against him. I could taste the salt from my tears against his mouth.

Our lips stayed locked together. I felt Blake's body shudder before I felt a tear from his eyes too against our lips. I pulled away slowly.

"This weekend has been—"

"Don't." He placed his finger to my lips and shook his head. "It's over. She's gonna get help. Don't let her do this."

"I have to," I said unconvincingly.

"We can't just throw everything away that we have found this weekend, Jo. You know yourself. What we have … it's more … much more. You have my heart now. I gave you my heart; please don't break it … please."

The thought of breaking his heart was killing me. I wasn't only breaking his heart, but I was shattering mine too. But I had to walk away now; I had no choice.

"Something happened to me four years ago; Sara just brought it all back tonight. I can't do this. I shouldn't have allowed myself to get close to you in the first place, Blake, but I did, and now I have to pay the price. We can't be together; I will ruin us, I will ruin you. I can't take that chance."

Blake's lips pressed against mine firmly, and then he was above me, kissing me deep, hard, and frantically. His hands held my face, his fingers gripping to my hair, not wanting to let me go.

He pulled his lips away and looked down at me, breathing hard. "I love you. I know you probably don't believe me right now, but I do, Jo; I fucking love you with every bone in my body. And I am begging you; don't do this to me, to us. Please, Jo, don't."

My breath caught as my heart slammed hard against my chest. I managed to push Blake from above me, and I climbed quickly off the bed. "I need you to go," I sobbed.

Blake scrambled off the bed, and I backed away. "Don't. Please, Blake, you don't understand. I need you to go; we can't carry on like this – not now."

"I know you love me too, Jo; I can feel it. You were going to tell me only yesterday as we lay in that bed; I know you were, but you thought it was too soon, so you stopped yourself. I know that you love me, Jo, and you know that I love you too, so doing this makes no sense."

"It makes sense to me!" I yelled.

"Then tell me!" he yelled back. "Tell me what it is that's making you do this! You are breaking me, Jo; you are going to break me if you make me walk out of your life. *I love you!*"

"Stop! Stop. Just please stop!" I placed my head into my hands. "I'm no good for you; you will see that. You will be glad I stopped this before it got too far. You will see."

"It's already too far." I looked up to see Blake pacing the room, running his hands frantically through his hair. "I'm crazy about you, Jo; I have never felt like this about anyone, and I know I never will again. This isn't just about this weekend; I have loved you from the first moment I laid my eyes on you. I always knew that you were hiding your feelings, why? I don't know, but I want to know, I want to know so as I can fix this."

"I told you I feared happiness. Do you see why now?"

"I can make this better, Jo; I can fix this. Please, just tell me, tell me what made you feel this way."

"I need you to go," I said firmly.

"Tell me why. Tell me why I need to go, and I will walk out of here and not bother you again. Just tell me, please," he begged.

"No" was my simple answer.

We stood silent for a few moments, both breathing hard, our eyes silently talking as he begged me not to do this and I told him I needed to even though I didn't want to.

"Look," Blake said, breaking the silence, "I'm sorry that you have been messed around in the past. I'm sorry that because of it, you feel the need to push me away. But I am not the past; I'm your here, your now, your future. I can fix it if you just tell me what happened. I promise you I will fix it; I will fix you."

"You can't fix it, Blake, no one can. That's what happens when you get broken one too many times."

Blake grabbed his jacket off the bottom of the bed. His heavy eyes stayed focused on the floor beneath him. "When you decide you want to talk, I'll be there. This isn't the end, Jo." his eyes slowly lifted back to me "There is no end for us." With that he walked out – out of my room and out of my life. I sank to the floor, and if it was possible, I cried more tears than I had ever cried before.

8

Stepping out of my audition onto the hot streets of New York, I should have felt elated. I should have been shouting from the rooftops that I had just nailed a two-episode part in one of America's most popular sitcoms. But all I felt was empty and alone.

I had made the effort and finally got out of bed twenty-nine hours after I had told Blake to walk out of my life. Well, when I say I had made the effort, I had been practically dragged from my bed and forced out by Casey.

After offering me the job, Marcus had bombarded me with information about filming and a night out that was planned which would be a great way for me to break the ice with the rest of the crew. I had listened and nodded, but nothing that he had told me had imprinted into my memory.

My phone buzzed to inform me of an incoming message. I scrambled into my bag and dug it out to see Blake's name on the screen.

I can't stop thinking about you. I hope the audition went well. I miss you. Call me please. xx

Immediately I was overcome with the emotion that I had managed to mask during my morning with Marcus, but desperate not to cry in a crowded street, I dropped my phone back into my bag, took a deep breath, and began dragging my tired, restless legs in the direction home. I would wait until I was at least back in the comfort of my apartment before I could cry as much as I wanted into the pillow that smelt so much like Blake.

"Jo!" I heard the familiar voice calling me from across the busy street. I lifted my heavy eyes, and they connected immediately with Cooper, who was walking with meaning towards me.

His smile lilted as he approached me and saw my obvious state.

"Don't tell me you didn't get the job," he said, stopping just in front of me.

"I got the job."

"Then what's happened?" his voice was soothing and sympathetic.

Unable to hold them back any longer, I let my tears fall. Cooper placed his arms around me, and as my head touched his chest, every bit of emotion I was feeling came spilling out uncontrollably.

"Do you want to talk about it?" he said quietly against my hair. I nodded and pulled myself away from him, quickly wiping my eyes.

"I could really do with a friend right now," I said.

"Have you eaten?" he asked.

"No."

"Come on, I know the perfect place. Let's see if I can bring back that gorgeous smile of yours." He smiled slightly and took my hand in his. The warmth I felt was comforting; it seemed that Cooper had a habit of turning up at the right moment, and he always managed to make things look better than they actually were.

Cooper drove us to a quaint little restaurant near Little Italy that was owned by his aunt. We sat in a corner booth, away from any prying eyes on onlookers. Cooper ordered us a bottle of their finest champagne as a celebration and two of their specialty burgers with extra jalapeño, even though I had told Cooper I wasn't hungry. He had insisted on making me eat. Cooper was doing his best to cheer me up, and it was exactly what I needed right now.

"I've been trying to call you since last week; have you been avoiding me?" I asked as Cooper poured us both a glass of champagne.

"No," he said quickly. "No, I er … I've had a few personal issues to deal with." His eyes scanned to me quickly before resting back on the bubbles in the glass that he was watching so intently.

"Nothing too serious, I hope?"

"Nothing I can't handle." Still his gaze remained fixed on the glass as he twiddled the stem between his fingers.

"I haven't seen you out jogging either," I said before taking a long sip of the champagne. The bubbles warmed my belly, and immediately I felt my body begin to relax.

"Sorry," he said, finally looking at me. "It does look like I've been avoiding you, doesn't it? But trust me, I haven't." He smiled. "Maybe we can start meeting up for a jog; what do you say?"

"Sounds good, I'm going to need the distraction," I admitted.

"Anyway," he sighed as he sat back into his chair, "why the sad face when you've just landed the role you had been dreaming of?"

I took another swig of champagne. "Blake," I answered simply.

"Ah, Blake." Cooper nodded. "What's he done this time?"

I shrugged. "It's not so much him."

Cooper straightened in his seat, resting his chin in his hands. "I'm listening."

"First of all, he slept with Sara," I said.

"Well, you weren't together."

"No," I answered, "but we had kind of made our feelings for each other clear. He had asked me out for dinner, I had said yes, and then I got the call from my mum."

"So he slept with Sara knowing you were going to London?"

"No. He didn't know about my dad. He saw me leave with you and thought that we were …" I nodded to Cooper, who smiled knowingly. "The thing is, Sara knew why I had left, but she didn't tell him."

Cooper's mouth formed into an *O*.

"He slept with her because he thought that me and you …" I let out a heavy sigh. "Anyway, we got past that, and I have just spent the most amazing weekend with him."

"And that's made you cry?"

I polished off the champagne and reached for the bottle to refill my glass. "Sara turned up at my apartment on Sunday night. She was a mess, Cooper; I felt so sorry for her. She had tried to kill herself. Blake knew, and he hadn't told me. If I'd known she had tried to take her own life over him, I would never have allowed myself to get close to him."

"None of this is your fault, Jo," Cooper said, reaching over and taking my hand.

"Then why do I feel so responsible?"

"Because you're you," he said simply. "You're kind, you're thoughtful, and you care way too much about other people. You didn't make Sara do what she did. She did that all by herself." Cooper released my hand just as our burgers arrived. "Now eat up; I know how much you like those jalapeños."

"The hotter the better," I said as I picked up the burger and took a small bite.

He winked. "Just like the lady sitting across from me."

"*Cooper,*" I said as a small smile touched my lips.

"There you go," he said, pleased with himself. "I knew I could get you to show me that gorgeous smile of yours."

As I entered the apartment, the strong smell of flowers hit the back of my nose. As I stepped into the kitchen, my breath caught at the sight of the most beautiful flower arrangement I had ever seen.

"They came just after you left this morning," Casey said as she stood against the counter drinking coffee, watching me carefully.

I walked over and took the card from the centre. "I don't even need to open this, do I?" I said quietly as I rubbed my thumb over the envelope.

"He misses you, Jo; you should call him."

"I can't." More tears filled my eyes. It seemed impossible to release the amount of tears that I had since Blake walked out, but they kept on coming.

Casey placed her mug down and walked over to me, wrapping her arms around me tightly.

"I'm so sorry that this has happened," she said into my hair.

"I shouldn't have let myself get close to him. I knew I could never be happy. I just thought it was going to be different with Blake, and now we're both suffering because of me." I stepped out of Casey's hold and wiped my eyes dry of the tears.

"This isn't your fault, Jo."

I shook my head in disagreement. "It's all my fault, and now Sara is in a clinic. That's my fault too." My eyes never left the flowers; they were truly beautiful.

"Did you get the job?"

I nodded. "Filming takes place next month."

"Well, that's good. Can I congratulate you?"

I gave her a weak smile. "Yes. Thank you."

"And Blake? What happens between the two of you now?"

I sucked in a deep breath. "I need to get on with my life and try my hardest to forget him."

"Do you think that's even possible?" Casey said carefully.

"I need to try." I took the huge box of flowers and headed to my room.

My body shuddered as I walked in and noticed that Blake's scent still filled the room. I needed to forget him. I had to remember this; I would have to change the sheets first in order to void my memory of exactly how good he smelt. But for now, I placed my flowers down on my bedside table, buried my nose into the scent on the pillow, and opened the card.

To the only woman who will ever complete me.
Tell me what to do to fix us, please. I love you. xx

The writing on the card was Blake's. He had written it himself from the heart. The pain in my chest worsened. "I need to forget you, Blake," I whispered, placing the card under my pillow.

I reached for my phone and reread his text over and over until my finger hit delete. I switched off my phone and placed in it a drawer next to the bed. The morning would mark the start of phase two in my "get over Blake and move on" plan, which I already knew was going to be impossible because now I knew exactly how good he really did feel. But for now, I allowed myself to inhale his scent until my eyes finally drifted into a deep sleep.

"Jo, your mom called again. She is worried about you. Please call her; she's going out of her mind."

Casey had been taking calls from my mum for the past six days now. I had heard Casey tell her during most of the calls that I had broken my phone and happened to be out while she was calling. She would then promise to tell me and assure her that I would call her back. I could tell that Casey was uncomfortable lying for me, but I also knew that she could sense the pain I was going through right now and knew that I wouldn't want to burden my mum with my petty men troubles so soon after losing my dad.

I was desperately trying to move on, but it was proving so much harder than I had ever anticipated. The difference between getting over Blake and Michael was that Blake was the innocent one in all of this, not me. Blake loved me, Michael didn't, and I loved Blake – uncontrollably. It proved to me that the feelings I had for Michael were more lust than love. It made getting over Blake impossible.

I had managed to get out of bed for the first three mornings, and I had met Cooper for a run each of those times. I figured that running until I struggled to breathe would make me focus more on trying to stay alive than think about Blake. But it didn't. I felt myself almost forgetting to breathe because my mind was always otherwise occupied. Cooper had noticed, but he never brought it to attention. He would try his hardest to cheer me up, even flirting with me, which he knew annoyed the life out of me; but that was Cooper, and he just couldn't help himself. I hadn't eaten much since Cooper and I had gone for lunch on Tuesday; that too was taking its toll on my body. I had nothing left inside me to burn off. By day three I was running on empty, so I decided that as much as Cooper was trying his hardest to help me, I was better off in bed. I still hadn't changed the sheets, and Blake's scent was still very much present. As much as I had tried my hardest to stick to phase two of getting over Blake, it was proving totally impossible.

I felt the bed dip, and Casey's hand brushed over my hair. "Are you going to get out of bed today?" she asked quietly.

"Probably not, no," I whispered.

"Call him," she said firmly. "It's obvious that you can't survive without him."

I didn't reply.

"He's not doing well either, Jo; Alex is worried about him."

I turned over to look at her. "He's seen him?"

Casey nodded. "He's a mess, Jo, just as you are."

I sniffed and wiped my ever-dripping tears on my sleeve.

"I did that to him," I sobbed. "He must hate me."

"He definitely doesn't hate you."

"He should hate me. I hate myself."

Casey twisted her body and lay next to me, looking at the ceiling.

"I know you want to forget him, Jo, but the more you lay here sniffing his pillow, re-reading that card, and looking at the flowers, the more you are going to drive yourself mad." She tilted her head to look at me. "And you look like shit." she observed.

"Thank you," I replied dryly.

"Get up." She sat up sharply and hopped off the bed. "Let's go out, get our hair done, maybe a facial. What do you say?"

"No," I whispered.

Casey flopped back down onto the bed. "I know you don't want to, but you need to. I need to know that I'm doing everything I can to help you; it kind of makes lying to your mom that tiny bit easier too." She gave me a lopsided grin.

"I'm sorry."

She stood up, headed towards my wardrobe, and began pulling clothes out in quick succession. "Wow, you wear a lot of black," she said with disgust.

"Matches my mood," I managed to say.

"Well get your ass out of that bed and put these on. We're going out, and I'm not taking no for an answer." She tilted her hip to the side, resting her hand just above it as she stood tapping her foot impatiently.

I let out a low growl as I scrambled out of the sheets and headed to the bathroom, hoping that as much as I didn't want to do this, it was at least a step in the right direction, and that was exactly what I needed.

Five hours later I had been completely revitalized with a facial, manicure and pedicure, and a well-needed and much-overdue haircut and colour. The hairstylist had recommended a warm chestnut – not too far from my natural colour, but it gave it a nice boost. I had asked him to take a good four inches from the length so as my bouncy curls would rest on my shoulders. He added a fringe sweeping across my brow too. I looked completely different; I loved it.

But as much as I felt brand new on the outside, my insides were still crumbling away bit by bit, a tiny piece falling away with every breath I would take. I wondered how long this would go on; would I always feel so numb? Surely sometime soon this would just be a distant memory, a learning curve that I would mold my future by.

Alex was snarling to himself in the kitchen when Casey and I returned to the apartment. We had stopped off on the way home, as Casey had insisted that I needed a touch of colour in my dark wardrobe. So with my purchases in hand, I headed off down the hallway, leaving Casey to deal with her sulking boyfriend.

"Not so fast there, Jo," he called as I stepped past the kitchen. I stopped abruptly and backed up to face him.

"What?"

He nodded through to the lounge. "You have a visitor in there waiting for you. Please tell me you haven't been fooling around with him while Blake is sat at home in pieces over you while you obviously don't give a shit."

"Alex, don't talk to her like that," Casey said, slightly embarrassed, flicking her gaze from Alex to me with concern.

"Ah, you're back." Cooper stepped into the kitchen, stopping as he reached Alex.

"Cooper, hi, what can I do for you?"

"You look amazing, Jo. Wow, look at you; you got your hair done. It looks … wow." His eyes scanned my body more than once, and I began to feel very conscious. Alex cleared his throat loudly, pulling Cooper back from wherever his mind had wandered to.

"Cooper?" I said, forcing his eyes back to mine.

"Monday," he said. "I just wanted to check your plans for Monday. Sugar with the guys, remember?"

"It's Sugar *Lounge*," Alex mumbled under his breath.

"Yes, yes, I remember. I'll be there."

"Shall I pick you up, say, eight?"

I could see that Alex was struggling to keep his mouth shut as he straightened up and crossed his arms over his chest.

"That really won't be necessary; I'll make my own way there."

"No." He shook his head firmly. "You are not getting in a cab when I am going anyway and can give you a lift."

"Really, Cooper I—"

"Stop denting a guy's pride here; just take the ride." He held his arms out wide.

I looked at Casey, who was slowly shaking her head, then at Alex, who I'm sure had steam shooting from both ears.

"A lift would be good, then, thank you."

"No problem at all, Jo. I've missed you jogging these last few days," he said.

"Just haven't felt up to it." I shrugged.

He smiled. "I understand. I'll see you Monday then." He straightened up and walked towards me. "The break-up seems to be suiting you, by the way."

Alex moved to step towards Cooper, but Casey caught his arm. Cooper closed the door firmly behind him as he left, leaving me feeling completely awkward.

"He's just a friend, Alex; he knows that there could never be anything between us." I said breaking the silence.

"Un-fucking-believable," Alex growled before storming past me towards Casey's bedroom. Casey gave me a lopsided grin and mouthed "sorry" to me.

I frowned. "He really does hate me, doesn't he?"

"You hurt his best friend, Jo; either one of us would be the same if the shoe were on the other foot," Casey said, trying her best to reassure me.

"Does he know about my past?"

"Not my story to tell, Jo." She patted my back as she too walked past and left me standing alone in the kitchen, feeling even deeper in the tunnel that was starting to form around me. The only difference was that this one had no light at the end.

I had talked myself out of going to Sugar at least one hundred times over the past few days. Marcus had invited me the day he offered me the part in *Perfect Alibi*. I, of course, had politely accepted, not realizing that almost two weeks later I would feel no less pain at what had happened between Blake and me. If anything, my feelings for Blake were growing, I felt as though the longer I was away from him, the more my love for him grew.

I had made sure that I called Mum every day since Casey had made me get out of bed, I apologized profusely for ignoring her calls and went on to tell her everything that had happened between Blake and me. She cried, I cried, and then we both cried. I had felt little relief talking to Mum about it all; the pain didn't ease one bit. Mum was doing okay. Being back at work had kept her mind occupied a lot. She sounded brighter, but her emptiness for dad was still very present and obvious. Speaking to Mum made me wonder why I was even still here in New York, but both she and Dad had insisted my life was here; I needed to at least give it another try before giving up completely and heading back home to London.

I was dressed and ready to go by seven forty-five. I had made a decent effort but felt like shit. I had put on a new dress that Casey had insisted I buy when she had dragged me from the apartment the week before. It was pale blue. I didn't do colour; I felt comfortable only in black. But as it had put me back a whopping five hundred dollars, I figured I needed at least one wear out of it.

The satin-laced bodice hugged my breasts and my waist before the chiffon skirt flowed nicely just above the knee. I paired it with my favourite strapless Jimmy Choo shoes. I looked good – better than I expected, considering it was a dress I would never have picked out myself. But looking good on the outside made no change to the feelings that were still very much present on the inside.

I could hear Casey and Alex having some sort of dispute in her bedroom. They had been doing that a lot lately, and I felt guilty that my behavior towards Blake was the prime source. I stepped into the lounge to wait for Cooper and came to an abrupt stop.

Standing at the large window looking out to Central Park West was Blake.

My heels had clicked loudly as I stepped onto the oak flooring, prompting Blake to turn and face me.

My breath caught; my heart pumped hard against my ribs. He was here, standing in my lounge, looking at me as though he were seeing me for the first time.

He let out a breath that he must have been holding and stepped forward two steps.

"Hi," I said.

"Hi," he replied quietly.

"How, um … how are you?"

"Could be better," he replied sadly. "You?"

"Same," I admitted.

"You look beautiful, Jo." his voice was full of emotion; just listening to him made me want to forget everything that had happened, walk over to him, and rip every item of clothing from his body before making mad passionate love to him all night.

Shaking my head clear of my thoughts, I looked down at my dress. "Thank you."

"Your hair too, everything is just ..."

Silence thickened the air as we stared at each other. I felt it; I could feel the electric pull that had always drawn me to Blake. I could tell he felt it too.

"I've missed you, Jo. I've missed you so much," he said as his eyes filled up with emotion.

"I've missed you too." I forced a small smile before any tears had the opportunity to squeeze their way out.

Casey and Alex's dispute spilled into the lounge as they entered from the kitchen. The whole room fell silent. To me, though, there were only two of us in that room. Standing here looking into his eyes was breaking me; having him standing so close yet knowing I couldn't just run into his arms was torture. Cooper knocking at the door broke the silence.

Blake's stance changed as Cooper entered the room. Standing straight, he seemed to focus on Cooper with venom in his eyes. Cooper walked in cocky and confident, heading straight for me and kissing me on the cheek.

"Stunning, absolutely stunning," he whispered in my ear. The guilt I felt at that moment reflected the hurt that Blake was visibly displaying. "Aren't I the lucky one this evening," Cooper chimed.

"Hey, Blake, let's get this show on the road; there are ladies out there waiting on you, man," Alex said, obviously for my benefit.

I heard Casey curse Alex, but he just laughed with amusement.

Our eyes met again, and it felt like some sort of understanding forged between Blake and me. He was telling me that there would be no ladies for him that night, and I was replying that Cooper meant nothing, no one did, only him.

"We had better head off too," Cooper said, looking at his watch before holding his hand out for me.

"It's good to see you, Blake," I said shakily.

"You too, Jo, take care," he replied with hurt.

My eyes never left Blake until he was out of sight and we were out of the apartment. This night was going to be torture. Seeing Blake crucified me completely. It made me want to crawl back into bed and cry myself to sleep yet again, but instead I was on my way out with Cooper. I would need a lot of cocktails to clear him from my mind.

The club was packed, and the music was pumping out loudly from every corner.

Cooper guided us through to the VIP area that Alex had reserved for the party; it was much less crowded, and the music was bearable.

I found Marcus first and made a beeline for him; I needed to keep mingling in order to keep my mind occupied. Marcus introduced me to every cast member that had already arrived. I recognized a few from the episodes I had sat and watched, and another few of them had appeared in other shows that I had watched back home in London. There were so many new faces that I would struggle to remember them all by name; I made a mental note to try my hardest.

"Cosmopolitan for the lady." Cooper grinned as he made his way over to me and handed me the glass.

"Thank you," I said, taking the drink and downing most of it.

Cooper smirked. "Thirsty?"

"Something like that," I replied, draining the last bit from the glass. "You want another?" I asked as I turned and headed for the bar. I was going to need many more cocktails to keep me from running off and finding Blake.

Cooper sat at the next stool while I tried to drown my sorrows. I hadn't stopped talking about Blake since I finished my first cocktail, and Cooper, being the friend he is, just sat and listened and nodded when appropriate. After my third cocktail, Blake was still the only thing I could think about, but my mind was slowly beginning to relax.

"Why couldn't I have fell in love with you," I slurred as I poked Cooper in the chest.

"Because you have no taste, that's why," he laughed as he ordered us both another drink.

"He just pulls me in. It's like he's Dynamo or something; he has this power," I said, scrunching up my eyes. "He mesmerizes me completely." I sighed. "I love him, Cooper," I said sadly. "How can I stop that? I need to just stop loving him and move on; I want to just forget about him. Can you help me forget about him?"

Cooper opened his mouth to speak a few times, but nothing came out. I could sense his awkwardness. I had sat with him all night, and all I had spoken about was Blake.

"God, Cooper, I'm sorry," I said placing my hand on his knee. No more Blake, I promise." I swept my fingers across my lips as if locking them with a key. "I need a wee," I said with a nod. "Be right back." I stumbled from the stool, holding Cooper's shoulder for leverage.

"Do you need a hand?" he asked with amusement.

"Nope," I said before making my feet move and heading through the crowd. The walls appeared to be moving towards me. I was drunk. I hadn't been drunk like this since I had experimented as a teenager. It wasn't a nice feeling, but it helped my mind to relax somewhat.

Cooper was still sat at the bar when I returned. He handed me my next drink, which I knocked back. Robin Thicke's "Blurred Lines" started pounding from the speakers. "I love this song," I said, holding my hand out to Cooper. "Dance with me." He smiled and stood as he took my hand and led us through the growing crowd that was now gathering on the dance floor. I wrapped my arms around Cooper's neck to keep me from stumbling; I was really starting to feel the effects of the cocktails as I found myself leaning into Cooper's body more and more.

Cooper un-wrapped my hands from around his neck and spun my body suddenly. My back was pressed deep against his chest, his hands wrapped around my waist, gripping me tightly as he ground against me, pushing towards him. I wrapped my arms around his neck again and started grinding against him. My head became heavy and dropped back, resting on his shoulder as we moved to each beat of the song. "What are you doing, Jo?" Cooper asked as his lips grazed my earlobe.

"Just dancing," I panted. I felt relaxed, and for the first time in two weeks, I felt my worries slowly begin to fade away. Cooper's mouth grazed my earlobe again. I didn't protest as my body was taken over by my senses. I was floating, and any inhibition I had to tell Cooper to stop had left my body and evaporated into thin air. Cooper's big hands worked their way up and down my thighs. "You feel so good, Jo," he whispered. "So fucking good."

I didn't reply; I couldn't. My body suddenly felt foreign. I felt as though I wasn't actually there, that I wasn't actually dancing with Cooper. The whole thing felt like a dream, as if I were floating above the scene that surrounded me.

"Come with me," Cooper said firmly in my ear before taking my hand and leading me through the ever-growing crowd and out into a dark hallway.

"Coop …" was all I could manage. Speech just wasn't happening right now. My eyes were blurred, my body was limp, and it took every ounce of my strength to focus on the door we were heading towards.

Cooper swung the door open with force, and the warm night air hit me, causing me to sway further into Cooper's arms.

"I've got you, baby," I heard him say as my back slammed hard against the wall. "Cooper's got you."

His mouth crashed hard against mine, his tongue forcing its way hard into my mouth. He was rough, hard, taking everything that he could get; and I was weak – too weak to resist.

"God you taste good," he growled before going in again. His kisses were bruising; the taste of blood suddenly filled my mouth.

Gripping his shirt with as much force as I could, I tried to push him away, but he was too heavy; his hard body was pressing me further and further into the wall. He had me so tight that I was struggling to take a breath, struggling to tell him no. He just carried on, taking everything that he could from me.

"Don't fight me, baby; I know you want this too."

His rough hands worked their way up my skirt, grazing hard against my thighs until he reached his destination.

Every attempt that I made to push him away was done in vain; he was too strong, too powerful for me to fight off.

"Don't fight me, baby; you want this, I know you do, don't fight me." He tugged at my knickers, and with one loud tear they were gone. He threw them to the side and took my mouth again as his fingers skimmed the top of my thigh. I tried to push my legs together, tried so hard to stop him, but his knee was pressing between both my legs, holding me firmly in place. I started to cry; I couldn't stop. I'd read about this; I'd seen it in films and on TV. I was about to be raped by one of the few people I could have called a friend just a couple of hours ago.

"Don't do this," I managed to say. "Please, Cooper, don't hurt me; please don't hurt me. I'm sorry. Please, I'm sorry!" I managed to raise my voice slightly, but it took every bit of what strength I had left; I could shout no more.

He placed his hand over my mouth to silence me. "I won't hurt you; you want this just as much as I do," he said in a hard tone, his face only inches from mine.

"Please." I shook my head as tears streamed down my cheeks.

"You are beautiful. You have no idea how long I have waited for this." I felt his fingers graze my folds, and I screamed as much as I could against his hand. But we were in the middle of a pitch-black deserted car park at the rear of the club. It was just Cooper and me; no one would hear me.

His fingers entered me roughly, pushing in and out over and over. It was so painful that it stung. Cooper placed his head on my shoulder. "Soft, so fucking soft; fucking hell, Jo." His fingers quickly left me, and his hand left my mouth as he started working on his zip.

I screamed out for help as loud as I could, but his hand quickly covered my mouth again. "Don't, Cooper, please don't; this isn't you," I cried out in a muffled tone against his hand.

"I'm sorry," He said as his hand left my mouth suddenly, "I'm so sorry."

"Get your fucking hands of her, you son of a bitch!"

Cooper stumbled back away from me "Blake," he said quietly.

Blake was pacing quickly towards Cooper, but before he stopped walking, his fist connected with Cooper's jaw, sending him crashing hard to the floor. Blake crouched down, grabbing Cooper's shirt in one hand while his other fist pounded into his face over and over again. Blood sprayed everywhere as punch after punch landed right on target.

"Blake stop, please, that's enough; you're going to kill him," I said, gasping for air to fill my lungs. Suddenly my legs gave way and I felt myself slide slowly to the ground. I heard the pounding of Blake's fist stop, and the sound of gravel crunched under his feet as he ran towards me, leaving Cooper wounded on the ground.

"Please … Blake … I …" it was becoming more and more difficult to force the words to leave my lips.

"What has he done to you?" He crouched in front of me, looking me over. "Jo … Jo, listen to me." I could feel his hands gently tapping my cheeks, but I was completely unresponsive. "What have you taken, Jo? Tell me what you have taken!"

Blake's face swayed in front of me. There were three, maybe four of Blake's beautiful faces looking back at me with the deepest concern, but I couldn't respond. I tried desperately to reach out to him, but my body had become numb, too numb to move.

I felt the world grow darker. My eyes struggled against the fight I was putting up to keep them open. Everything was closing in, and the closer it all got, the further away I felt I was lying.

The tunnel was back, and yet again there was no light.

9

My eyes felt blinded by the light that filled the room. Was this the end of the tunnel that I had been so desperate to reach recently? Had I finally made it to the end, where everything would be okay and I could finally be happy again? Was this what death actually felt like?

Forcing my eyes open again, I took note of the white walls, the beeping of machines around me. I was in hospital. My head felt as though it had been tightened in a vice. It hurt to move and it hurt to think, but I had no idea how I had ended up here.

There was only one thing that would replay in my mind as I tried desperately to recall the night's events. Blake had been there. That was all I could remember, and the more I tried to think, the more I hurt. But the one thing I did remember was Blake's face as I slowly blacked out in front of him; he was there, trying to help me.

"Blake," I said hoarsely.

I felt the warmth of his hands as they wrapped around mine tightly.

"It's okay, Jo; I'm here. Everything is going to be okay."

"What happened?" I choked out with difficulty through the pain in my throat.

I still couldn't open my eyes properly; it hurt too much. But I so wanted to see him, see his face, as he sat next to me and cared for me despite what a horrible cow I had been.

"Don't try to remember anything; let's get you better first," I heard him say gently.

"Am I going to die?" I asked nervously. I heard Blake laugh once before one of his hands started stroking the hair away from my face.

"No, beautiful; you're too pretty to die," he said gently.

I felt myself melt into his words. After everything that I had done to him, he was here; he still cared.

"Water … I need water please." I felt the warmth of his hands disappear. "Don't leave me," I pleaded.

"I'm right here." His hand took mine and placed it around the cup.

I felt the straw touch my lips, and I took a long, welcome draw from it. I finally managed to force my eyes open to see Blake leaning over me as I soothed the gravelly feeling in my throat.

"Hey you" – he smiled with clear relief – "that was quite some scare you gave me last night."

I handed the cup back to him, and he placed it on the table next to my bed.

"Can you remember anything?" he asked carefully.

I shook my head as I tried desperately to remember what had happened. "I only remember you."

He gave me a tired smile as he perched himself on the edge of the bed, taking my hand in his again. I looked down at our hands knotted together. I had missed his touch so much. I felt safe and as if I were home when he held me like this. I focused my eyes onto his knuckles; they were grazed and scratched.

"What happened to your hands?" My eyes travelled up his body, and I noticed spots of blood speckled on his shirt. "And why do you have blood on your shirt?" Fear was creeping in. something bad had happened the night before that had resulted in Blake being hurt too. "Is that something to do with me?" I asked in horror. "Did someone hurt you because of me?"

"Nobody hurt me, Jo, I swear. The only thing that hurt me last night was when I thought we were going to lose you." Blake leaned in hesitantly and placed his lips to my brow. He held his lips there for a moment before moving back just enough for our eyes to meet. "That scared me to death." His hand gently swept my hair from my face. I leaned into the warmth of his hand; I had missed it so much.

I realized I had been holding my breath when the doctor entered the room. Blake stood and greeted the doctor before standing at the foot of the bed while the doctor came to my side.

"It's good to see you awake, Miss Summers." He spoke with a

British accent; I immediately warmed to him. "I'm DR White; I've been looking after you since MR Mackenzie brought you here last night."

He placed himself where Blake had been sitting just a moment before. "How do you feel this morning?" he asked as his eyes roamed over the notes in front of him.

"Like I've gone ten rounds with Tyson and lost every single one miserably." I smiled weakly.

DR White smiled and placed his notes down beside him. "Miss Summers, your blood tests revealed a substance called gamma hydroxybutyrate, also known as GHB."

I pushed on my hands to sit straighter in bed. "What is that?"

"Miss Summers, do you have any recollection of any events last night that may have been deemed unusual?"

"I can't remember anything," I said quietly. "Why?"

"There's a high possibility that someone placed this drug in your drink; it's known commonly as a date-rape drug," he said with concern. I felt my body begin to tremor. Someone had raped me? Is that what he was saying? "Did you leave any drinks unattended last night? Or maybe did someone buy you a drink? Did you notice any strange behavior from any particular individual?"

"I'm sorry, Doctor." I shook my head as a wave of emotion ran over me. "Have I been raped?" I asked before a sob escaped. I could see Blake standing with his arms folded; his fist was gently pressing against his lips, and his eyes were full of emotion. What had he seen?

"No," he replied. "It seems your bodyguard over there got to you just in time." He nodded towards Blake.

"Thank God," I sighed with relief as my body relaxed back onto the bed.

"But the police will want to know if you can remember anything, or more importantly, who gave it to you in the first place." He smiled and stood. "You should be good to go in a couple of hours. Get some rest, and I'll be back later to see how you're feeling."

"Thank you," I said quietly as my mind fought hard to remember any tiny scraps.

The doctor stopped when he approached Blake. "Just to prepare you, word has gotten out that you're in here. You have a bit of a fan club building out on the nurses' station." He winked.

Blake laughed once. "Thanks for letting me know."

DR White left the room, and Blake again took his space on the bed with my hand in his once more.

"What did you see last night, Blake?" I asked cautiously.

Blake took a deep breath but smiled through the obvious pain.

"Do you remember who you went out with last night?"

"Of course, Cooper picked me up and we went to Sugar," I confirmed. "I only had three or four cocktails; now I know why it felt like I had drunk a hundred of them," I complained.

"Did Cooper buy a drink for you?"

I thought hard, trying desperately to recall the night's events. "I think so, yes."

"Were you with him when he bought it?" His voice was careful as he tried to help me remember.

"No, I was with Marcus."

Blake's nostrils flared with anger, but he held it back. "Did anyone else buy you a drink, or did you leave any unattended?"

"I don't remember." Suddenly it dawned on me. "You think Cooper spiked my drink?"

Blake nodded. "I think he did, yes."

"Cooper wouldn't do that; he's my friend, Blake."

"Jo, he had you pinned against the wall with his hand up your skirt," Blake said angrily before standing abruptly.

"What?"

"You were begging him to stop, but he wouldn't," he replied before turning his back to me. I could see his anger through every breath he was taking.

"Is that why you have blood on you? Did you hurt him?"

Blake turned to face me, his eyes filled with emotion.

"He almost raped the woman I love, Jo; I shouldn't have stopped until he was dead."

"Don't say that," I whispered.

"What? That I should have killed him or that I love you?"

My eyes filled with tears; I was too tired and felt too weak to try to stop them from spilling out. I turned and huddled myself into a ball, moving my eyes from his. I tried hard to focus on the few clouds that were sweeping slowly past the window.

"Don't you want me to tell you the truth?"

I shook my head slowly.

"Seeing you walk out of the apartment with him last night killed me. Right here." Lifting his hands to his chest, he pushed hard against his heart. "It killed me, Jo," he said quietly. "I couldn't bear it. I needed to see that you were okay, that you were safe. I needed to see that you wouldn't end up going home with him."

"He's just a friend, Blake; he's always only ever been a friend to me."

"Friends don't do what he did to you last night," he choked out.

"There must have been a mistake. Someone else must have put something in my drink when I went to the bathroom. I know Cooper; I know that he isn't the person you are making him out to be."

"When are you going to take off those rose-tinted glasses of yours and see what everyone else around you is seeing?"

"You need to go," I said quietly.

"I need you to take me back," he pleaded.

"I'm no good for you, Blake. Just look at what happened last night. I am no good for you," I said firmly, finally moving my gaze from the window to him. "You know that I have issues. I will pull you down, and you will regret ever meeting me."

"One thing I can stand here and say with full conviction, Jo, is that I will never, ever regret the day that you walked into my life."

"I have this ability to ruin lives. I did it to someone four years ago who only wanted to be happy, and I took that away from her and caused her pain. I've even done it to Sara, and now to you."

"Nothing that happened with Sara was your fault; when are you going to believe that?"

"I can't believe that, because it's not the truth."

"Then tell me," he said, resting once more on the bed. "Tell me everything that you are keeping from me. Let me understand why you are pushing me away. Let me help you, please, Jo; let me love you."

"It's too late," I whispered as a tear fell from my eyes.

"You are breaking me, Jo," he said sadly. "Can't you see that? You are breaking me."

"You don't know what it feels like to be broken."

"Then why do I feel like my life is over because you're not in it?"

"I want you to go," I said, swallowing past the emotion. "I need you to go. Go out and meet someone else, someone with no baggage, no issues; someone who can love you exactly how you deserve to be loved. If you want to help me, Blake, then please, just go."

Blake stood from the bed abruptly and started pacing the room. "You don't know what you are saying to me, and you are not listening to what I am saying to you," he said sharply. "I can't just fall out of love with you. I can't just go out and meet someone else when the only woman who I will ever love is you." His voice was husky and full of hurt. "You're still groggy, and you need some rest." He picked his coat up and placed it over his arm. "There is no talking to you while you're still feeling the effects of last night; you don't know what you are saying to me. I know that you always think that running from problems will somehow fix them, but you're wrong. At some point in your life, Jo, it's time to stop running."

The door opened, and Casey came rushing to my bedside. My eyes never left Blake's as he walked to the door to leave. "See you soon, Jo."

I heard the door click shut, and the dams burst. Casey threw her arms around me and held me while I cried everything that I had left inside me. Yet again I had let him go, let him walk out of my life, and the pain was back instantly – pain that I had never felt before, and I couldn't imagine it was ever going to go away.

I left the hospital later that same day feeling a little more human but no better about how I had left things with Blake.

I was beginning to see that Blake was right. At some point in life it was time to stop running, stop running and face problems head-on, solve them and continue the rest of the journey rather than run and run until you can't run any more.

He had told me that he loved me. After everything I had put him through and after how badly I had treated him, he loved me. Yet I did what I had trained myself to do since Michael; I pushed him away. How could there ever be another man on this planet that would do all that Blake had done for me when all I continued to do was push him away. I hadn't told him, but I loved him too; so much that the pain I was feeling from loving him was worse than any physical pain I had ever experienced. I couldn't tell him that I loved him, however; that would make me weak; and to keep myself strong, and to make sure that Blake moved on without me, I could never tell him just how far my love for him actually ran.

The only two people I spoke to over the next few days were Casey and my mum. I hadn't left the apartment, and I hadn't taken any calls from either Cooper or Blake. Blake stopped calling the day after my release from hospital, but Cooper was persistent. What could I say to him? What could he possibly say to me? I didn't want to believe that he had drugged me, but the more I sat and tried to remember the night's events, the more and more obvious it became that it must have been Cooper all along.

I was lying on the sofa, flicking through the channels on the TV with total disinterest, when the apartment door slammed shut, causing me to jump. Alex walked in and stood directly in front of me. His arms were folded firmly across his chest as he looked down at me with anger on his face.

"Casey's not here," I said quietly, not taking my eyes from the

TV.

"I'm not here to see Casey," he replied in a harsh tone before snatching the remote from me and tossing it to the floor.

I sighed and stood as I headed to the kitchen, knowing exactly why he was here. I opened the fridge and took out a bottle of water. When I closed the fridge door, Alex stood waiting for me, arms crossed again.

"What can I do for you, Alex?" I said in annoyance as I walked past him and went back to my position on the couch. I opened the water and took a long gulp.

"I think you know," he said harshly.

"No, I don't," I sighed.

"When are you going to stop being such a bitch and take Blake back?"

"Excuse me?" I asked in shock.

"You're sitting here miserable, he's sitting at home miserable," he snapped. "You both love each other – like, *really* love each other. He has gone out of his way to prove his feelings for you, and we all know that you're not coping without him." He sighed and perched himself on the coffee table in front of me. "Casey told me what happened to you four years ago," he said sadly.

"Oh," I replied.

"You know, I didn't realize until Casey told me that we're not too dissimilar, me and you." He smiled gently.

"How?" I answered, confused.

"When I walked into my home and found Angela – she was my fiancée before I met Casey – in bed with someone else" – he rubbed his chin roughly – "it felt as though my world had come crashing to an end. I loved her. Well, I had thought I did." He laughed once. "We were supposed to marry only a few months later. It was all booked; she had gone all out. Nothing we did was cheap; that was how she liked it. I closed myself in, wouldn't talk to anyone, I had no interest in anything except for getting my clubs up and running and on the map. I had no interest in women whatsoever.

"Then one night Casey walked into my life. Her smile, that laugh." He smiled fondly. "I fell for her instantly. I tried to fight it, but I couldn't. I fell in love with her almost immediately. I was petrified, Jo; scared to death that history would repeat itself. I had trust issues, just like you; I saw all women the same – no one could ever be trusted in my eyes."

"So how do you know when you meet that one person? The one who is different to anyone else you have ever met?"

Alex laughed once. "You just know. In here" – he tapped his head – "and in here," he said, moving his hands to cover his heart. "I had never felt so frightened in my life, Jo; I'll be honest. But now I look back and I know that Casey is the best thing that ever happened to me, and I cannot wait until that day that I place a ring on her finger and she becomes MRS Alex Taylor."

My eyes filled with tears both happy and sad.

"I know that your past relationship had a more dramatic ending, and if I hadn't known, I could never have guessed. You do a good job of hiding your emotions, which is why I know you're hiding them now too. But I know that Blake would never, ever, do anything to hurt you. Not only that, but he loves you with every single bone in his body, Jo. I have never seen him like this. He needs you, and I believe that you need him too. And if he had killed Cooper last week, I don't think he would have cared what the consequences were, as long as he knew that you were safe."

I sucked in a deep breath. "I'm so scared, Alex."

"I know," he said, softly placing his hands on my knees.

"But you have to face your fears head-on if you are ever going to get over that hurdle that has been taking away your happiness for so long."

"Do you still think I'm a bitch?" I joked as I wiped my tears.

He smiled. "No, I just needed to get you to listen to me. I think you feel alone, vulnerable, and very afraid. Let him help you get over those hurdles, Jo. Just like Casey helped me. Go tell him how much you love him, please." With that said, he stood and walked out of the apartment, leaving me alone to think about what I needed to do next.

I had been standing outside Blake's apartment for over thirty minutes. I knew he was in there; I had heard movement more than once. All I needed to do was knock at the door. Just knock at the door. But my hands felt weighed down by my sides. No matter how much my brain tried to tell me to lift them, they wouldn't budge; they wouldn't move even one inch. What if I knocked at the door and Blake slammed it in my face? What if he had got so fed up of my stupid running that he didn't even want me anymore? But what if I walked away and none of that was true?

"Just knock at the damn door, Jo," I repeated over and over to myself. "Stop being such a baby and knock at the damn door."

I knocked. Four sharp raps on the door. I waited. My heart rate picked up at the thought of seeing him again. Suddenly I realized that I hadn't thought about what I was going to say to him. Would I say hi, or would I just throw myself into his arms? I suppose I would know as soon as he was stood in front of me. It was time to let fate decide what the right thing to do was.

The door opened slowly, and standing in front of me was not who I expected.

"Hi, can I help you?" A blonde, maybe in her early thirties, stood in front of me with a smile plastered widely across her face. She was stunning. Her hair was cut into a short bob, and she had the most amazing jawline – it rivalled Blake's. She stared back at me with her big blue eyes, waiting for me to speak.

I looked down the hallway. There were no other doors; this was definitely Blake's apartment.

"I'm looking for Blake," I said. "This is his apartment, isn't it?"

"It is, yes," she said, her smile not faltering.

"Is he here?" What sort of stupid question was that? Of course he was here, and standing in front of me was the woman I had told him to go out and find; someone who could love him, look after him, and care for him. And judging by the fact that little Miss Blondie with her stupid smile stood in front of me wearing an apron with the smell of cooking floating from the kitchen, that's exactly what he had gone and done. "He's due back any minute; do you want to come in?" She held the door open for me to enter, her smile still stuck widely on her face.

She was offering me in? Did she even know who I was to Blake?

"No," I said in defeat. "No, it's okay, I'm gonna … I'm going to just go," I said as I stumbled backwards towards the lift.

"Shall I tell him who called?" she called out.

"No" was my only reply as I entered the lift and fell to the floor in tears. He had moved on; I was too late. Me and my stupid fear of getting close to someone had now caused me even more heartache than I was already experiencing. I couldn't be mad with Blake; he deserved to be happy. He deserved to be with someone who could give him everything that I couldn't, and little Miss Blondie seemed to fit the criteria perfectly. This time I had well and truly messed up, and there was nothing that I could possibly do about it.

I walked the long distance back to the apartment in a daze.

The rain was lashing down hard, bouncing on the pavements. Thunder angrily rumbled above as the sky would light up with each flash of lightning, but I didn't care. None of it mattered. My clothes clung to me, soaked right through, but it didn't matter. None of it mattered any more.

I couldn't remember crossing a single road or even looking where I was going. Maybe the pain would ease if I got hit by a car; that would at least take the focus off the feeling of the last piece of my heart breaking.

What now? What was I possibly going to do now? I had told Blake to forget me, and he had; he had moved on. I should have felt some sort of relief from seeing her standing there making him happy, cooking for him and caring for him, but I didn't. All I felt was hurt, and the crushing pain that had been slowly killing me for the past three weeks was back, only now it felt as if the lightning had struck and was slowly zapping everything out of me that I had left.

It served me right. I had pushed and pushed and pushed at him until I could push no more. I had run every time things got tough. I ran from him, and now I was paying for my mistake.

He was going to be happy now; I needed to accept that. It was what I had wanted. It was exactly what I had told him to do, and he had gone along and done it. I should have felt happy that he had finally moved on. But I didn't, and I didn't think I ever would.

By the time I arrived home, every inch of me was drenched with rain. After stripping off, I stood under the hot shower and let the water run off me as I cried the last tears that I would for Blake.

It was time to move on. New York had been good, but I couldn't stay here without Blake by my side.

I sat on my bed dressed in fresh, clean clothes and called the airline. My flight would leave in four hours. That would be the end of my time here in New York.

"I'm sorry, Daddy; I tried. I tried my hardest, but I have to go. I hope you can forgive me. I know you wanted me to stay, but there's only so many knocks I can take before I fall so hard that I'm incapable of getting back up." I smiled sadly before placing the photo of us both in my bag.

I was grateful that Casey wasn't home; I wanted to go without the hassle of anyone trying to stop me. I was weak, and I wanted to go. I was an emotional wreck, and I loved Casey like a sister; I couldn't stand hearing her begging me to stay for fear that I would cave.

I wrote her a letter along with one for Marcus and left them both on the coffee table.

Calling my mum was the last thing I needed to do before leaving for the airport. It was early evening, and I knew that Mum didn't sleep all that well; I didn't want to wake her, but I needed to hear her voice.

"Hi, Mum," I said quietly.

"Josephine, what is it? Are you okay?" The sound of her voice felt like such a comfort to me, and even though she sounded concerned, her voice soothed me immensely.

"I just needed to hear your voice, Mum," I said shakily as I scrunched my eyes shut in preparation.

"What is it, darling? What's happened?" Her voice was etched with concern.

"I'm coming home."

I heard my mum exhale a short laugh. "Don't be ridiculous, darling; you have your show coming up in a few weeks. You can't just up and leave now; what on earth will they think?"

"I need to come home, Mum; I don't care any more about work. I don't care about New York or anything that came with it. I've had enough; my life here is over. I miss you, and you're the only person who I need." I sucked in a deep breath. "Blake has moved on; he's met someone else." I swallowed hard, trying not to waste another tear. "I went over there to tell him that I love him. I never even told him that I loved him." I heard Mum sniff; was she crying? A single tear fell onto my bed. "She's beautiful, Mum. She's everything that he needs, and I can't stay here and see him with her. It's tearing me apart, and I hate myself for letting it happen. I need to come home."

"I'm so sorry, darling. But are you sure that she was his girlfriend? I can't imagine he moved on that quickly; he loved you."

"She answered the door." I wiped my tears on my sleeve. "He wasn't there, but she was cooking for him. They have been together two minutes, and she was cooking his dinner. I never even did that for him," I sobbed.

"So she introduced herself as his girlfriend?"

"She didn't have to; I know what I saw. God, Mum, it hurts so much."

The line went silent. Mum was all out of words.

"My flight leaves in ninety minutes, Mum. I need to get to the airport."

"Are you sure that you are doing the right thing?"

I nodded even though she couldn't see me. "I'll see you in about nine hours, Mum. I love you."

I turned off my phone and left it next to the letters that I had left for Casey and Marcus before writing my third and final letter, this one for Blake. I explained how sorry I was that I had waited this long to realize how much I loved him and that I would never forget him no matter how hard I tried. I took one last look around the apartment and placed my keys on the breakfast bar.

I took a deep breath and stepped out of the apartment.

"Jo."

My attention was immediately pulled to Cooper, who had just stepped out of the lift. Panicking, I stepped back into the apartment, but Cooper was there holding the door open before I had a chance to shut him out.

"Move," I said through gritted teeth.

"We need to talk," he said desperately.

"I have nothing to say to you. You either move right now or I call the police."

"Jo, please, let me explain. I didn't know what I had given you; I didn't know what would happen to you after taking it. Please, you have to listen to me," he pleaded.

"You look a mess," I said, observing the numerous cuts and bruises that graced his face.

"Yeah, well, I deserved worse; I got off lightly."

"How far would you have gone if Blake hadn't shown up?"

"I never meant to hurt you, Jo; you have to believe me. I would never, ever hurt you. Please can we talk?"

"How far?" I asked again firmly.

"I don't know what happened, Jo; I got lost in the moment. You were there grinding your ass against me; I just ... I just lost it. Look, I just need to know that we're okay. Please, Jo."

It felt appropriate that as I was leaving New York I could get some closure with Cooper before I left. I opened the door and allowed him to step in.

"One move, Cooper, and I will call the police," I said as he stepped past me and headed to the kitchen.

"I don't want you to be afraid of me, Jo; I'm not going to hurt you."

"You placed a drug in my drink, Cooper. You then dragged me

outside and pinned me to a wall, so don't you dare stand there and tell me that you wouldn't hurt me," I said shakily. "*That* hurt; believe me."

"I didn't know what it would do to you, Jo! You told me you wanted to relax, to forget about Blake. I wanted to help you to do that!"

"So what happened when you took me outside!" I yelled.

"I don't know," Cooper said sadly as he sank down onto a stool. "I really don't know. I'm so, so sorry, Jo. I am truly very sorry." I could see the pain in Cooper's eyes; I could see how sorry he was. It didn't make any of this any better, but it did help to know that he genuinely was sorry.

"Where did you get the drugs from?" I asked calmly. "Please don't tell me that you got them from someone at the club?"

"They're mine. I take them sometimes when things get a little crazy." He said this so quietly that I could barely hear him.

"You take drugs?" I asked, sitting next to him.

"Sometimes."

"Why?"

Cooper shrugged. "Sometimes I just need to forget. Forget all of the shit that surrounds me."

"What are you talking about?" I laughed once. "What shit?"

"Things that I can't tell you about," he said, meeting my eyes. "I can't believe that I almost killed you, Jo," he said, rubbing his hands over his face. "You didn't deserve that. You don't ever deserve to get hurt, not by anyone. Will you forgive me?"

I took a deep breath in as Cooper's eyes wandered to my suitcase. "Are you going somewhere?"

"I'm going home," I said simply.

"To London?" he asked, turning back to me.

"To London."

"How long for?"

I smiled slightly at Cooper before standing. "My plane leaves in just over an hour; I need to get to the airport." I stood from the stool and took the handle in my hand.

"Is this because of what I did?" he asked as his hand wrapped around my arm gently.

"No," I sighed, turning back to him, "it's not because of you." I smiled. "My life here is over. There's nothing to keep me here anymore, plus I miss my mum, so I'm going home."

"I'll miss you," Cooper said.

"I'll miss you too," I replied honestly. "Stay out of trouble, okay," I said smiling through the tears that were still very present.

"I will," he promised. "I wish things could have been different between the two of us, Jo," he sighed.

"Another place, another time, maybe there could have been another us," I admitted.

Cooper smiled slightly as he held my gaze. "Take care, Jo."

"You too."

I climbed into my last yellow cab and asked him to take me straight to the airport. Cooper had offered, but I wanted my last ride in New York to be one that I could enjoy in silence. As I watched New York pass me by, I took in every good memory that I had been lucky enough to experience.

I paid the cab driver and headed into terminal seven at JFK airport without looking back.

There were still passengers checking in their baggage for the flight, so I headed to a kiosk to check in and print off my boarding pass. Once done I placed myself into the steadily moving queue and took my passport from my bag.

I took a moment to look around at the people that surrounded me. There were businessmen, couples, and families. Everyone had a different story to tell, yet everyone looked happy, content even. I wondered whether I looked the same, whether we all hid behind a mask of some sort of heartache that we held sheltered from those looking in.

A few minutes of waiting and it was my time to check in my bag.

I stepped forward and was greeted by an overly friendly airline worker who seemed too happy for someone who was working a late shift at an airport during the weekend. She asked me the usual questions regarding my luggage, and I placed my case onto the conveyor belt before handing her my passport and boarding pass.

"Jo!" Just that one word caused me body to freeze as it echoed around the entire terminal. "Jo, stop; don't do this!"

The familiar hustle and bustle that came as standard in an airport had fallen to a dull roar with the occasional gasp and fingers pointing; following the stares from fellow passengers, I turned to see Blake running through the terminal and heading straight for me.

My mouth fell open in shock, unable to form words. I just watched as he came to an abrupt stop at the desk without making any form of eye contact with me. He reached around and removed my suitcase from the belt.

"I'm sorry," he panted to the check-in girl, "she won't be flying anywhere today."

"Blake what are you … Why are you … how?" I found it impossible to string one simple sentence together.

He was breathing hard as he captured my eyes with his, trying desperately to calm his erratic breathing.

"Don't go," he managed to say. "Please don't get on that plane."

"How do you even know?" I asked, completely dazed by the fact that he was standing right in front of me.

"That's not important right now. Getting you to stay is all that matters."

"There's nothing here for me now, Blake; I need to go."

"The girl," he breathed out. "It's not what you think."

I rolled my eyes and turned back to the check-in girl, whose mouth was so wide open I'm sure there was dribble trickling out of the corners.

"I'm sorry about this," I said, feeling slightly embarrassed. "I'd like to check my case please." I placed my hands around the handle, only for Blake to place his around mine.

The familiar pull was back; electricity sparked as our hands barely touched.

"No, she's not going anywhere," he said, taking my case back.

"Blake, stop this," I whispered. "You are causing a scene; everyone is looking at us," I said, trying not to look up as I felt every single set of eyes burning into us both.

"I don't care," he whispered.

"It's too late, Blake; it's over. Now will you please step aside and let me check my case? There are people waiting, and they are all going to end up missing their flight because of you."

Blake released my hand and stepped back slowly before turning to the watching crowd. "Hey everyone," he said loudly as he climbed upon the next available desk.

"Blake, what are you doing!" I said in a harsh whisper which he chose to ignore.

"Most of you probably know who I am," he said loudly.

I shook my head with complete humiliation before mumbling sorry to those who stood around me, but no one's attention was on me; everyone was focusing solely on Blake.

"What you don't know, however," he continued, "is that this young lady here, Miss Josephine Summers, is the woman who I am completely, utterly, and helplessly in love with."

I heard a few gasps and even a few aahs.

"Blake, please get down from there now," I said through gritted teeth.

"We have had a lot of ups and downs along the way. It's been a tough ride so far, one that has broken us both to a million pieces." He looked down from where he stood and smiled sadly at me. "And I have told her time and time again that I love her, and I know that she loves me too. But she thinks that by flying home to London, by running away from it all, that we would both be happier. She is afraid; she is petrified that by loving someone, it will cause someone else pain, that there can be no happiness without the pain. She has all this fear pent up inside her, and she just keeps on running. She would rather run than risk someone, even someone who couldn't give a shit about her. She would rather run from what she wants to save someone else's feelings. That's how selfless this beautiful woman is. But she doesn't need to be afraid. Not when I love her more than I can ever imagine loving anyone."

"Blake, people are recording you; please, come down and let's talk somewhere private." I turned to the check-in girl who was still gawping at Blake. "Do you have somewhere private that we could go, please?"

She scrambled out of her seat, but Blake ignored my request. "If you leave, you may as well cut me open right here right now and take my heart with you. I'm nothing without you, Jo; I'm just a dead man walking without you in my life."

"Don't say that," I whispered.

"Do you remember what I said to you in the hospital, Jo? About running?"

I nodded slowly. "At some point in your life it is time to stop running," I choked out.

"Now is that time, Jo."

I heard a "whoop" from one man and "so sweet" from an old lady.

"But you've moved on, Blake; I came to see you earlier, and your new girlfriend opened the door," I said, struggling to stem my emotion.

Again there were gasps from the ever-growing crowd, and even more phones were being held in the air, recording us.

Blake jumped down from the desk that he had taken over and took my hands in his. "You see that beautiful blonde girl standing over there?" I and everyone who surrounded us followed the direction of his finger to the girl who had opened the door to me only a few hours before.

"That is my sister Jasmine." He laughed once. "And that little boy she's holding?" I nodded. "That is my adorable little nephew, Fraser."

They both gave me a small wave, and I waved back, feeling totally and utterly humiliated. Of course it was his sister; she was his double. The blue eyes, the perfect jawline – it was obvious now who she was, and I was left feeling a complete fool.

"They have been keeping me company. You see, I've been a bit lonely lately."

Blake took my hands and forced my gaze to meet his. "Do you think I would just go out and find someone when the only person I have ever loved and wanted to be with is standing right here in front of me?"

"Blake," I gasped, "I don't know what to say." I shook my head in shame. "I'm so sorry."

"Say that you won't go; say that you will come home with me now and spend forever with me." He paused and took in a deep breath. Looking around, he seemed to suddenly notice that we weren't alone. He shook his head and smiled before looking back to me with the most loving eyes. "I love you. I have loved you from the first moment I laid my eyes on you, and I know that you love me too; you're just too afraid to admit it."

"I do love you," I replied. "I love you so much."

Blake let out a big breath before turning to our private audience. "Did you hear that! She loves me!"

Everyone cheered and clapped. It was complete and utter madness, but it was real, and finally I had told him how I felt. I hadn't lost him; he hadn't lost me. This was the most perfect moment of my life. I was going home – not to London, but to Blake.

"Come here," he said quietly as he turned back to face me.

Our lips crashed together, desperately, hungrily. Weeks of heartache spilled out through the way our mouths spoke for us. "I love you, Jo, and I swear I will do everything I can to protect you; I love you so much," he said as he pulled away slightly.

"I love you too, so, so much," I replied.

The crowd were going wild; it was as if the scene had fallen straight out of a film – our film, our story.

"I'm beginning to think I've just made a complete fool out of myself," he laughed, placing his brow to mine.

I slapped him playfully on the chest. "I hate attention."

"You think this is attention?" He gestured around the room. "We're gonna be going viral this time tomorrow," he said in mock horror, "believe me."

We both laughed before Blake kissed me again, and yet again the room erupted.

"We need our bubble back," I whispered.

"Anything you want, beautiful, anything you want."

I pulled back and looked at Blake, confused.

"What is it?" he asked, concerned.

"How did you know?"

A slow smile spread across his face, and he leaned in to whisper in my ear. "Your mom called me."

The shock and disbelief must have been obvious for anyone to see

"My mum?"

He nodded, smiling. "Yes, your 'mum' as you say it."

"I'm going to need to have words with her," I said.

Blake leaned down and grabbed my bag with a huge smile on his face. "Can it wait? I am in desperate need of some loving right now," he whispered.

"Won't that be a bit awkward?" I nodded to Jasmine and Fraser just as Blake took a look at his watch. "Her husband, Robert, is on his way to pick them up." He placed his hand around my waist and pulled me closer. "I need you to myself tonight; you have no idea how much I have missed you." his hand swept the hair from my face.

"I have missed you too, Blake; so much."

"No more running, okay?"

I nodded. "No more running."

Beautifully Unbroken

10

Stepping back into Blake's apartment after what had been the strangest day of my life, I was met with a whirlwind of emotions.

I was sad that I wouldn't be seeing my mum, as I had wanted. But I was happy that Blake had stopped me from going.

I was nervous about what the future now held, yet I was excited that there would be a future.

I feared that thanks to Blake's crazy show of affection at the airport, my anonymity here in New York was well and truly over, but I felt overwhelmed that he had done that, for me.

Blake placed my suitcase down on the tiled kitchen floor and turned to face me. A smile spread slowly across his face as he breathed out with what appeared to be relief. "Are you hungry?" he asked.

"No," I sighed, smiling back at him.

Slowly he approached me, wrapping his arms around my waist and pulling me as close to him as was possible. Placing my arms around his neck, I snuggled into him and breathed in the scent that I had missed immensely over the past three weeks.

"God, this feels good," Blake said, placing kisses against my temple. "You were moments from walking out of my life forever, but now you're here. I am never ever letting you go ever again; you can kick and scream as much as you're heart desires, but I am never going through this again, Jo, never."

"I don't ever want to go. I'm sorry, so sorry, Blake."

We held each other for what felt like hours, just breathing each other in as we slowly started coming back down to earth from what had been the most dramatic roller-coaster ride of emotions I had ever experienced.

Blake pulled back his head and placed his lips gently to mine. "I love you so much, and I'm going to tell you that at least a million times a day for the rest of our lives." He kissed me again, just as gently this time as the last. "And I will never let anyone hurt you or make you sad. I wasn't there for you with your father, and I will never forgive myself for that. But I'm here now, and I intend on doing everything in my power to never, ever, let you feel alone again."

"Can we talk?" I asked quietly. Blake's eyebrows knitted together with confusion. "It's time I told you everything. No more running means no more secrets; I need to tell you about my past and what happened to me."

"Only if you feel ready," he replied.

I nodded. "I'm ready."

Blake smiled lovingly and took my hand. He led me through the apartment and out onto the terrace. It was stunning. It was like his very own little country garden placed thirty floors up in the air. There were pots upon pots bursting with flowers of all colours, shapes, and sizes. There was even a lawn that was cut to perfection.

Blake led me to a large sofa and told me to sit before he disappeared back into the apartment.

I took a moment to take in my surroundings. I felt as though I were home. It was weird; this was the first time I had been in Blake's apartment, yet I felt so at home.

The switching on of twinkling lights startled me, followed by gentle music being played through some disguised speakers. It was perfect.

Blake reappeared a few moments later with two glasses and a bottle of red wine.

He poured us both a glass, handing one to me and taking the other in hand.

"I can't believe you're here," he said as he sat next to me, placing one arm around my shoulder. Leaning into him, I took a sip of wine and focused on the moon that shone brightly above us.

"Four years ago," I began, "something happened to me which took any faith I ever had in happiness and trampled all over it. It got replaced with this fear that you have seen so much in me. Fear and the need to run when things get tough. Running is the only way I have ever learnt to deal with a bad situation. When things get tough, run, and everything will be okay. That's exactly how I have lived for the past four years."

I felt Blake's fingers softly starting to graze the length of my arm. "You don't have to do this; not until you're ready." His lips met my temple, and he placed a lingering kiss there. I needed to tell him; he needed to know why I always found running the easier option.

"I had been dating Michael for just over a year. I was completely smitten with him; I thought I loved him. It's only really now …" I paused. "It's only really now that I know what love actually feels like, and mostly, what it feels like to be loved, that I've realized that the love I thought existed between us was just a figment of my imagination. It makes what happened even more painful to accept."

I swallowed past the emotion that was beginning to surface. I needed Blake to understand. I needed him to know why I was so afraid to let myself become happy.

"My dad never liked him. He played for the wrong team, according to him. That was his excuse at the beginning anyway." I let out a sad laugh.

"We became a media dream. Everyone always needed to know where we were, what we were both up to. It became a strain for me. It started affecting my work, my life, my relationship with my parents. I couldn't concentrate because every day there would be a story about us, a picture snapped of us just leaving a restaurant or a club. I started hating going out because we couldn't go anywhere without being pursued. Michael, however, loved it. He loved the attention it would bring, the publicity, the fans. He didn't care; the more, the better in his eyes. Yet he couldn't see why I hated it with a passion.

"We were snapped arguing in a bar one night. I had wanted to go home, but he was more interested in all of the attention he and his fellow players were attracting. He thrived on attention. Over the next few weeks, I refused to go out to clubs with him. We had already been the subject of one Sunday newspaper; I wasn't going to let it happen again. They didn't even know us as people, yet our pictures were plastered all over the covers, and the story to go with it was all lies – lies that they made up to help boost the sales of the damn thing.

"I spent the next few weeks miserable, avoiding public attention as much as possible and arguing with my dad over what being with Michael was doing to me. I couldn't see it, but he told me how insecure he could see I was becoming. I refused to accept that. I refused to accept anything that he told me that would paint Michael in a bad light.

"One Sunday morning I heard the front door slam shut, and my dad's voice echoed through the entire house. He never, ever, raised his voice to me apart from that morning. He was yelling for me to get downstairs right this instant. I knew something bad must have happened for him to react that way."

I took a deep breath as I still managed to keep the tears at bay, at least for now.

"He threw the newspaper at me in disgust and all he could say to me was 'I told you he would end up hurting you. When will you listen? When will you ever listen to a word I say to you?' He stormed off to the kitchen just as I unfolded the paper to see Michael on the front cover being … He was … Well, they were …" A tear finally broke through. "The pictures were graphic, disgusting. I don't even know how they got away with printing them."

"Who was she?" Blake asked gently before placing a kiss on my temple.

"Her name was Imogen. She was a dancer in the club that Michael was so obsessed with. So it kind of made sense that that's why he spent so much of his time there. Of course, he denied it all, said he was set up; she was a fan who apparently threw herself at him, and the paps just happened to be there."

Blake pulled me closer to him, holding me even tighter now.

"He begged me to forgive him for getting close enough for it to look how it did. He promised me that he wouldn't go there again and we could start over, spend more time alone, and things would change." I let out a shaky breath. "I forgave him. I took him back against everything that I believed and everything that Mum and Dad had begged me not to do. I just walked back into his arms as though nothing had happened. I was so caught up with him that I just didn't care. My dad stopped talking to me. My mum took Dad's side even though I could see that it was killing her inside just as it was me. But he was stubborn." I let out a sad laugh. "As was I."

"I'd argue the fact that you are still a stubborn lady, Miss

Summers," Blake said lightly as he placed another kiss on my temple. It made me smile; I'd say I was still stubborn too.

"Michael asked me to move in with him, so because of the strain with Mum and Dad, I packed a bag and I went. He seemed to be making an effort, too. On the very rare occasion we would go out, he would be affectionate, kissing me in public, holding my hand. I truly believed it was going to work this time and that he had stuck to his promise and changed. The media, of course, didn't buy into it; they still reported that he was sleeping around, but I shrugged it off. I knew the real Michael; they knew what would sell papers. I started to allow myself to feel happy again. I started to believe that what the papers had reported were just lies, like he said they were, that he wasn't the person they had portrayed him to be. But I realize now that they were right. Everything about him was all just for show, to save his reputation. I couldn't see any of that until it was too late. I was completely blinded by him and by what he was truly like.

"One night I had a late shoot. I was going to be out until the early hours of the morning at least. I'd told Michael that if I was going to be too late, I would stay over at Michelle's house; she was a co-star and good friend, so she understood and didn't mind me crashing there occasionally. I knew his match the next day was a vital one so didn't want to disturb his well-needed rest."

Once again Blake squeezed me gently just to make sure I knew he was there and he was listening.

"Filming went better than expected, and we managed to get away early enough for me to go home." I sighed. "I was actually exited for the first time in a couple of weeks to be going home to him. I actually felt like we were going to be okay; like we were getting through it. Mum and Dad had even begun speaking to me again – not much, but enough to show they still loved me and cared about what was going on."

My breath became shaky. Blake took my glass and placed it on the table in front of us before he pulled a blanket from the back of the sofa and placed it over me, wrapping his arms gently around me.

"The house was silent and pitch black when I walked in, so I assumed he was in bed. I started climbing the stairs, quietly so as not to disturb him. But I stopped suddenly at the sound that was coming from the bedroom. It was them. I could hear them, fucking in my bed." An angry tear rolled down my cheek which I quickly wiped away.

"I forced my legs to move and climbed the rest of the stairs. I should have turned around and walked away, but I couldn't. Something inside me wouldn't let that happen. I pushed open the door, and there they both were, Imogen and Michael, having sex in my bed." Another tear escaped at the memory of emotion that ran through me at that time.

"She looked as shocked as I felt. Michael looked like someone who had been caught with his pants down, literally. Do you know what he did?"

I turned my head up to see Blake's face. He shook his head sadly. "What?"

"He pushed her off and told her to get out." I shook my head. "Then he jumped off the bed and started grabbing her clothes, throwing them at her, yelling that she was nothing, just a mistake, and that he didn't know why he had done it. He was screaming between me and her, telling her she was nothing and then turning to me and begging me not to walk out, saying that he loved me and she meant nothing to him."

"Jo," Blake whispered before kissing my hair gently.

"I was frozen to the spot. She was shouting at me, telling me that Michael had said I was nothing to him; that he just felt sorry for me so was letting me stay there until he felt he could ask me to go. Then she would turn to Michael and shout to him that I was fat and ugly and how the fuck could he beg me to stay when he had promised her the world. Eventually she gave up, got dressed, and stormed out. But as she passed me, she stopped and turned to face me. She told me to sleep with one eye open, that this wasn't over and that she would make sure that I paid for what I had done to her."

I took another deep breath and continued. "The sad thing is, I couldn't see anything past Michael. He was my world, and I didn't care what she was saying to me; he was kicking her out and asking me to stay. It was me that he wanted, and not her. That's how naive I had become. But I couldn't bear sleeping in the bed that she had been in. I moved into the guest bedroom. He would beg me night after night to let him in there too, but I couldn't. I couldn't get the image of what I had seen him doing out of my head; but I also couldn't walk away."

The tears were flowing now as I relived the bleakest memory I held.

"He started taking his anger out on the football pitch. The once perfect and fantastic Michael Robinson got sent off two matches running, so the papers once again had a field day.

"He started going out drinking, a lot. I feared then that it would happen again, even though he promised me that he loved me. He would come home so drunk and start blaming me for it all; then he would cry and apologize and beg me to go to bed with him. Somehow I found the strength through my weakness to say no. I was so scared of catching something that I ended up having tests; it was so humiliating, and it was the final straw. Everything came back clear, and I was so relieved, but then it made me stop and think. What was I doing? Why was I letting him drag me down like this? So that night I decided it was time to move on. To get out of what was a living nightmare. Michael's team were playing in Newcastle that night, so I decided to pack my bags and go back to Mum and Dad's. I had spoken to them about everything, and they were so angry that they had let me go in the first place. It wasn't their fault, though. It was me, all me."

I sobbed.

"I went to Michael's to pack. I knew he couldn't stop me; he was the other side of the country, so there wouldn't be a better time, and I was in the right mindset for it too. It was time to close the door on the bad experience and start living again. I walked into the bedroom, and there she was, Imogen, waiting for me with a knife."

Blake's grip on me tightened.

"Seeing Sara that night brought it all back to me; Imogen looked as Sara had. Broken, hurt, angry. And she wanted revenge. She started yelling at me, telling me I was nothing, I was ugly, I was fat, and that I didn't deserve to be happy. She said that Michael had promised her everything and I had taken it all away; everything was my fault, and I was going to pay for it."

"The scar," Blake whispered.

I nodded. "She ran at me, and before I knew it there was blood everywhere. She looked down at her hands; they were covered with my blood. I don't think she had actually intended on using the knife, but she had got herself into such a state that her angry emotions had taken over. She dropped the knife and ran; left me there bleeding to death."

I heard Blake sniff back his tears. I turned in his arms and wiped his face dry with my thumbs.

"I'm so sorry, Jo. If I had known, I—" I silenced Blake by placing my finger over his mouth.

"It wouldn't have made any difference, Blake. Sara would have still come after me; she would have still hurt herself regardless of whether you knew or not. But at least she's getting help now. That's the main thing. Imogen never got any help. It turned out she was from a broken home; she didn't have any security, any love in her life. So when she fell for Michael and then he chose me over her, I took away any tiny bit of love that she was feeling."

"None of that was your fault, Jo; don't you dare blame yourself for what she did."

"If I had walked away in the first place, none of it would have happened. That's why I had to walk away from you, Blake. Do you see that now?"

"I see why you thought you had to walk away, yes, but you should never walk away from what you feel is right in your heart, Jo. It makes me sad that you would rather be unhappy to spare someone else's feelings," he said sadly.

"I'm still scared that it's not over with, Sara. When she sees what you did at the airport earlier, it's going to break her."

"She's stronger than you think, and she has love and security in her life too. I promise she will never hurt you, Jo. I will protect you from ever, ever getting hurt again, I promise."

I wanted to believe him, I really did, but it was so hard for me not to fear the future and not to fear feeling happy. I placed my head back onto Blake's chest. "The thing is, Blake, I don't want you to have to protect me; I want to be able to do that myself. I just don't think I'm strong enough."

"Says the woman who will just get into a cab with a stranger and think nothing of it," he said before placing a kiss on my temple.

"That's different."

"It's not."

"It is."

"Remind me why you don't have a car again?"

"Because New York roads frighten me; it's safer for everyone else if I don't drive on them."

"And there you go again, thinking of others before yourself," he chuckled.

"If I had thought of Imogen instead of myself, then things would be so different now."

"You don't know that, Jo."

"I do," I said honestly. "You know, Michael only visited me once in hospital. He came in, and he never even asked how I was feeling. He sat there and he begged me to tell the police that I had interrupted a burglar." I laughed sadly. "But I was done with being his puppet. I had allowed him so much control over me in our so-called relationship that enough was enough. I told the police everything – the whole truth. Imogen was arrested a few days later and charged with attempted murder. Then the guilt crept in. I felt awful. The main reason I had done it was because Michael had begged me not to. He had done wrong to both of us, not just me; he had treated Imogen like shit too."

"Is she still in prison?" Blake asked carefully.

"No," I said sadly. "She never got to prison."

"She got away with it?"

"I wish it had been that simple," I whispered. "Imogen was found dead two days before her trial began."

I heard Blake sigh before he turned us both until we were facing each other. He cupped my face in his hands and held my gaze, his eyes overflowing with emotion.

"And you blame yourself for her taking her own life," he stated. I nodded slowly. "You did nothing wrong," he said firmly. "She could have killed you, Jo."

"But I caused that, Blake; I caused her so much pain that she needed to hurt me to ease it. Don't you see that?"

Blake shook his head slowly. "No. No, I don't."

"If Sara had killed herself, that would have been my fault too," I sobbed. "Don't you see the pattern, Blake? I am responsible for other people's unhappiness."

"No," he said, holding my face closely. "No you are not. I am not going to have you think that, when it's not true. No one is responsible for another person's actions. What others choose to do, whatever path they decide to take, is theirs and theirs alone. You are not responsible for any of this, do you hear me? You are not responsible, Jo."

I nodded unconvincingly. "Can you see now why I fear happiness?"

"Yes," he sighed sadly. "Yes I can."

"Every time I feel happy, something comes along and takes it away from me. I'm so scared, Blake. I want to be happy and feel happy and not worry that something bad will come because of it, but I can't. I know I don't look it right now, but I have never felt as happy as I do now, here with you. I'm scared that feeling this happy will have consequences. So along with feeling happy, I feel so scared."

Blake released my face and wrapped me once again in the warmth of his arms. "Tell me what to do to make it all better for you."

"Just love me," I replied simply. "And if you ever meet someone else, please walk away from me and I will understand, I promise."

I felt Blake's body move as he exhaled deeply. "I know you can't see it now, Jo, but we're gonna grow old together, you and I. We're forever; I think I've told you that a million times already, but it's true. If I thought there was a chance now that you would marry me, I'd ask you."

I opened my mouth to speak, but Blake stopped me. "We're gonna have kids, lots of them. We're gonna have a nice big house out in the country. Our children will run wild in the big garden that we will have. They will want for nothing, Jo, and they will have the best mom in the world. But most of all, we're gonna have each other. Forever, Jo, because now I've finally got you, I am never letting you go."

As his words slowly sank in, I allowed myself to imagine, for the first time in a long time, that I could be happy. I believed that Blake could help me to overcome my fears and insecurities and that we could have a future, our future.

"My dad would have really loved you," I said quietly.

"And I would have loved him too, because I know that you are the same person that he was, and I already love your Mom," he chuckled before relaxing and resting his chin against my head. "She saved us; I'll never forget that."

"Do you believe in fate?" I asked.

"Yes." Blake nodded firmly. "Definitely."

"After my dad died, I wanted to stay in London. I didn't want to leave my mum; I felt that would be so selfish of me, so I called Max, told him to cancel everything I had coming up. My mum was listening to the call, and I didn't know." I smiled. "She called him and told him to ignore me and then she took your number from my phone in case I refused to come back. I was so torn. I couldn't bear leaving her, so I went to Dad's grave and asked him to help me, just to give me a sign or something. As I headed back to the car, Michael was there waiting for me. He actually asked me to take him back. I took it as a sign to come back to New York. And now, when I think about it, it's all like a jigsaw puzzle that is slowly all fitting into place. Mum had taken your number and kept it. I could have got on that plane and been in London had she not done that."

"Fate will always pull us together, Jo; we're meant to be."

"Am I meant to finally experience happiness without the pain?"

"One hundred per cent yes. I will make it my mission to prove it to you."

Just as the music faded, Blake stood and placed his hands under my thighs and picked me up. I wrapped my arms tightly around his neck and kissed him, deeply. My whole body ignited the only way it knew how to when Blake was present. Every muscle, every limb on my body was burning for him, desperate to feel his touch that it had longed for from the moment I made him walk out of my life.

He led me slowly through this apartment and into the bedroom, walked over to his large bed, and placed me gently down before his body covered mine. This time it felt different. There was no urgency, no rush; we had forever, and he was going to take his time. And I would let him. As desperate and as needy as I felt in this moment, I wanted to savor him, savor us and everything that we had together.

The sun was shining brightly through the window when I woke. I groaned and turned over to find an empty space next to me.

I could hear Blake talking on his phone. He sounded happy; his laughter filtered through to the bedroom. I couldn't bear being away from him a second longer. I grabbed his shirt and wrapped it around me before heading out of the bedroom to find him.

He had finished the call when I got to the lounge and was relaxing on the sofa, looking more beautiful than I seemed to remember. His hair was damp from the shower he must have already taken. He sat casually with a coffee in one and hand the TV remote in the other. He seemed amused by whatever it was he was watching. My attention was immediately drawn to the television to see a shaky mobile phone recording of the both of us the previous day at the airport.

"Please, no," I moaned loudly, closing my eyes and shaking my head.

Blake's head turned towards me; he was grinning. "Good morning," he said too cheerily. "Look at that," he said, pointing excitedly towards the TV. "We made *Live! with Kelly and Michael.*" It didn't seem possible to me, yet his grin was growing by the second. "Come sit with me," he said, patting the sofa before placing his empty cup on the coffee table. He was more excited than a kid at Christmas.

I dragged my feet as I approached him. "This can't be happening; tell me I'm still dreaming please," I moaned, covering my eyes with my hands as I sat next to Blake.

He laughed a happy, content laugh. "Take your hands away from your eyes and look."

"I can't," I said, refusing to move.

"They love you," he said, leaning into me.

I moved one finger and sneaked a peak at the screen, watching the moment when Blake stood tall on a desk, declaring his love for me.

Quickly my hand re-covered my eyes. "I can't watch."

"They're calling you my English rose," he murmured into my ear before placing a gentle kiss on my cheek.

I shook my head in disbelief. "Kill me; just kill me now," I moaned.

Blake's hands forced my hands away from my eyes. I quickly scrunched them shut.

"Open your eyes."

"No."

"Open your eyes or I'm going to make you open them."

"I am not opening my eyes until you turn that television off," I demanded.

Before I knew it, Blake's body was over me and his hands were attacking my ribs, causing me to scream out with laughter. "Stop! Get off me! Stop it, Blake! Aahhh!"

His weight prevented me from fighting back. He had me pinned and was not giving up.

"Will you open your eyes?" he said as he continued to tickle me over and over.

"No!" I screamed back as he continued to tickle.

"Then I'm not stopping," he teased.

"Okay, okay, I will! Please stop tickling me; I can't breathe!"

"Eyes open, Miss Summers!"

My eyes shot open and were immediately drawn to the ocean-blue eyes that looked back at me. The tickling stopped suddenly, and I fought hard to bring my breathing back to normal.

"Good morning, beautiful," he said, beaming down at me.

"Is it?" I joked, struggling to get out from his hold.

"It is from where I'm sitting," he grinned.

I smiled. "Good morning to you too then."

"Look at the TV," he demanded.

I shook my head, a huge smile breaking out across my face.

Blake let out a big sigh and smiled back.

"Wow," he said.

"What?"

"That is the first time I have seen you smile like that in such a long time; it's beautiful." He placed a quick kiss on my lips before his hand turned my head to face the TV.

"Now watch."

It was embarrassing. This time yesterday, I was completely unknown here, and only twenty-four hours later, I was the main topic of conversation on a popular morning TV show. It was complete and utter madness.

"They're calling me the new Tom Cruise," Blake laughed.

"Well, it was pretty extravagant," I admitted.

The story moved on to the weather, and Blake lifted off me, allowing me to get back up off the chair.

"Would my English rose like a cup of tea?" he asked, standing and making his way to the kitchen area.

I twisted on the sofa to watch him. "I didn't think you knew how to make a cup of tea," I asked suspiciously.

"Ah, you see, I've had a lot of time on my hands recently," he said without looking back. "Plus my sister loves the stuff, and as she spent the last few days here with me, I've turned into a pro." He shrugged playfully.

He looked up at me while he placed a teabag each into two separate cups. "See, easy." He smiled, and the smile on my face continued to grow. "Oh, and while you're smiling like that, it seems like a good enough time to tell you that we've gone viral. Alex called; we're up to four million hits on YouTube." He laughed as he turned to place the used teabags into the bin.

I let out a growl and flopped onto the sofa, covering my eyes once more while Blake continued to laugh.

I couldn't, however, wipe the smile from my face. If I had got on that plane to London yesterday, we would both be alone now, both suffering, both completely broken. But he had stopped me, although he had made a complete show of us and now we were plastered all over the television. But we had found each other again, and if it was at all possible, with every second I spent with Blake, it felt as though every part of me that had been broken before today was slowly being molded back together.

11

We sat on the terrace and drank our tea whilst eating pastries that Blake had got delivered for us fresh from his favourite bakery.

The sun was beaming down on us; it was going to be a hot day.

"What do you want to do today?" Blake asked before taking another sip from his tea.

"Hide away? Can we do that? Just hide away and not come out until everyone has forgotten who we are?"

"That's never going to happen." He stood and placed a quick kiss on my cheek before collecting the empty plates and heading back into the apartment. I followed slowly behind.

"Shouldn't you be working today?" I asked.

"Tomorrow," he said as he placed the plates next to the sink. "Today I am all yours." He walked over to me smiling like a predator about to attack his prey.

He wrapped his arms around me and kissed me gently. "However," he said carefully, "we have guests for dinner this evening."

I let out a little moan and pouted. "What about our bubble?"

Blake laughed gently. "Alex said he and Casey want to see us, so I invited them for dinner. If that isn't okay, they will understand; we will do it another night."

"It's okay," I sighed. "I'll cook."

"You don't have to do that; we can order something in."

I placed my hands on Blake's hard chest. "I want to." I nodded before letting out a little laugh.

"What's funny?" Blake asked.

I tried to stem my amusement by remembering how painful it actually felt at the time.

"When I came over and your sister answered the door. I thought she was cooking for you."

"She was cooking for me," he answered, confused.

"But I thought she was your girlfriend, cooking for you," I said quietly.

"I don't get it," Blake said with a frown.

"I cried to my mum because I had never cooked for you," I said feeling my cheeks blush with embarrassment. "Before you say anything, I know how ridiculous that has just sounded."

"No." Blake shook his head as he laughed lightly. "It isn't ridiculous; not even close. It is, however, the cutest thing you have ever told me," he teased.

I pushed him playfully on the chest, struggling to contain my smile. "So tonight, I will cook, and you will enjoy it."

He leaned in and kissed me again. "Deal."

"That is, of course, providing you have a fully stocked fridge and cupboard, because I am not going out there today." I shuddered as I pointed to the front door.

He smirked before heading back to the sink to begin loading the dishwasher. "Jasmine filled them both only yesterday; there should be plenty for you to choose from."

"Great," I said as my eyes began to roam the open-plan apartment.

"Do you know where my case is? I could do with a shower and change of clothes."

"About that," Blake said, turning to face me as he leaned against the counter. "How would you feel about leaving your case here?"

"Why would you want me to leave my case here?" I asked, confused. "I can store it back at mine; there's plenty of room."

"I mean leave it here, along with your clothes," he clarified.

"But what if I'm not here and there's something in there that I want?"

Blake couldn't hide his amusement; he laughed and walked back over to me, pulling me into him. "How is it possible for you to be *that* cute twice within a minute?" he teased, sweeping my hair away from my eyes with his fingers.

"Am I missing something here?" I was so confused and obviously missing the point.

"Move in with me."

"No," I said almost immediately.

Blake couldn't hide his obvious disappointment. "Please."

"Blake," I said, slightly frustrated. "Do you not remember everything I told you last night?"

He nodded. "Of course I do. I also remember telling you that I am going to look after you, and protect you." I opened my mouth to speak but was silenced quickly by Blake as he continued. "I also remember telling you time after time over recent weeks that we are forever, there is no end, we will grow old together" – he sucked in a deep breath – "so why wait?"

After a short while, I replied. "Because if we do have forever, and there is no end … then why rush?" I lifted up onto my toes and placed a lingering kiss on his cheek "It doesn't mean that I don't want to, because I do. I really do, Blake. Just not yet, okay?"

Blake sighed heavily. "I'm gonna ask you every day until you give in."

"And I'm going to say no until I know the time is right. It's not what you think it is living together, Blake. Things change; we would change."

"We wouldn't," he protested.

"We would," I argued back, "and I can't just up and leave Casey right now; that wouldn't be fair on her, would it?"

"You already left her yesterday," he teased as his mouth lifted into a smirk. "So technically, you are currently homeless and I am offering you a place to say."

"I am not homeless," I laughed, "but soon, I promise you, I will move in. I love you."

"I love you too."

"Now, tell me where you have hidden my case; I have a busy day of cooking ahead of me."

Blake was right; Jasmine had stocked the cupboards, refrigerator, and freezer top to bottom with food. There was enough to survive on for months if the apocalypse were to hit.

After a couple of hours of deliberation I had decided on a pot roast. I had cooked a traditional roast dinner a million times back home, so this seemed a breeze, everything just thrown in together and left to roast in the oven. Perfect.

Blake left me to it for a couple of hours and headed to the gym that he had built at the end of his penthouse. I hadn't been in there yet, but knowing Blake and how much he loved to look after himself, I didn't doubt that it would have every latest model of every piece of equipment that money could buy.

He had also told me about his mini cinema room and promised me a night at the pictures with him sometime soon. He said he would reserve us the two seats at the back; that made me smile.

I was beginning to feel so happy and content, but every now and then a feeling of dread would come over me. *There is always a price to pay for being happy.* Every time these words entered my head, I would try my hardest to push them away and think of Blake's promise to protect me and keep me safe. Surely at some point in my life, happiness could mean exactly that. Surely I could eventually have happiness without the balance of badness appearing.

I needed a distraction, so I took my iPod out of my handbag, placed it into Blake's docking station, and filled the apartment with my choice of music.

I stood and chopped the onions, carrots, and garlic before browning the meat slowly on the hob. Blake's kitchen was a dream to work in; if you didn't need it, he didn't have it, and vice versa. I began to feel exited that I was finally going to cook for the man I loved and our two closest friends.

Blake appeared an hour later freshly showered, dressed in a fitted white V-neck T-shirt and grey jogging bottoms. My mouth watered at the sight of him as he strolled over and placed his arms around my waist, watching over my shoulder as I placed everything carefully into the roasting tin ready to go into the oven.

"Are you almost done?" he asked every two minutes as I was adding the last few ingredients.

My reply would always be "One more minute."

"You're gonna need another shower, and I think it's only right that after how hard you have worked in here, I should come and scrub your back for you." His voice was so soft and teasing as his breath tickled my neck, sending all kinds of shivers all over my needy body. Yes, I would definitely need another shower.

"I just need you to switch the oven on," I said, placing the lid carefully on the pot. "I have no idea what button does what on these things and why there are so many doors; I think we must live in the Stone Age back in England. Give me a traditional stove any day of the week."

I heard Blake chuckle as he released me and headed to the oven.

"Just a low heat please; this needs to cook slowly."

"Done," he said a few moments later. "I'll go start the shower for you."

I woke feeling disorientated. It took me a few moments to realize where I was. I turned over to see Blake deep in sleep, his mouth slightly open and his arm resting over his beautiful big eyes. He looked so young and carefree, and happy.

I took a moment to just lie there and look at him, the man whom I felt so safe with, who I knew would keep his promise and protect me. And most of all, he would love me, the way that I loved him. My life felt perfect – maybe a little too perfect, but again I needed to bury that thought somewhere deep and lock the door firmly behind it. I was going to be happy.

I noticed Blake's alarm clock on his night stand. It was seven p.m.

"Shit!" I jumped out of bed quickly and started pulling clothes from my still-packed case. "Blake! Get up! Casey and Alex will be here in an hour, and we're not ready! Get up!" I threw a pillow at him, which startled him at first until a lazy grin spread across his face as he stretched his body like a lion out in the sunshine.

"We have plenty of time; come back to bed," he said, still smiling widely. His eyes were only half open, but the blue shone through like a beacon on a dark night.

I walked back to the bed, having managed only to choose my knickers and bra so far, and whipped the sheets from on top of him, leaving him lying there gloriously naked and highly amused by my outburst. "Get up!" I yelled frantically one more time. Blake was laughing as he slowly climbed out of the bed and headed into his wardrobe to pick his outfit for the evening

"You know," he yelled to me, "I've seen so many sides of you today, and I'm struggling to decide which on turns me on the most."

"Keep teasing me and I'm going to come in there and strangle that cock that you are so obsessed with using," I shouted back as I shimmied into my favourite black trousers.

"Ah, Jo, you have no idea how hard it has made me hearing you say that word so politely." He was laughing now; I could hear him chuckling away to himself, which made me chuckle too. I loved it when he was so playful; it made me feel even more happy, and I didn't think that was even possible.

"Are you done?" I shouted.

"Yep," he said as he re-entered the bedroom looking so beautiful that I debated with myself just for a second whether or not we did have time for me to strangle his cock – in a nice way, though.

"Are you drooling?" he observed.

I pulled myself together and grabbed my shoes. "No," I said firmly. "Can you go and check on the food please? I need to finish getting ready."

"For you, my beautiful, anything." He placed a quick kiss on my lips before stepping around me and leaving the bedroom.

I stood in front of the mirror, ready to do my hair and make-up. I studied my face for a short while. I was changing; I was beginning to actually look happy. I hadn't noticed before, but my face must have shown the world all of my fears before today. There were no worry lines, no frown, nothing; just happiness seeping through the pores. Even my brown eyes glistened back at me like diamonds. I was happy. I smiled and started working on my bed hair.

"Hmm, Jo?" I heard Blake shout. "We have a problem." All sorts of thoughts started running through my head as I left the bedroom and headed to where Blake was standing in front of the open oven.

"You put the food in the wrong oven," he said, holding the roasting tin in his hands.

"Don't be stupid," I laughed, but Blake's face remained impassive. "What do you mean wrong oven?" I asked as the smile faded from my lips.

"I turned on oven number one," he said, nodding to the oven farthest away. "You put the tin in oven number three." He nodded to the open one that he had removed the pan from.

"Oven one? Oven three?" I said, placing my hands on my hips. "Exactly how many ovens do you have?" I asked sarcastically.

"Three" was his simple answer.

"Why the fuck do you need three ovens!" I yelled, throwing my hands in the air.

"For occasions like this, maybe?" he answered carefully, but I could see that he was highly amused by what had happened.

"Did you not think to tell me that there were three ovens? Did you not think to say, 'Okay, Jo, my beautiful, I've switched on the oven for you, but be sure to place the pan in oven one, not two or three, as I need them for absolutely nothing.'"

Blake started to laugh, and the more he laughed, the angrier I became. The angrier I became, the more he laughed.

"This is not funny!" I yelled, throwing my arms about as I paced the kitchen floor.

"Oh my God, Jo, you have no idea just how funny this is," he laughed, placing the cold pan down on the counter before leaning back and crossing his arms over his chest. He placed one hand over his mouth to try to hide his amusement.

"I've spent all day in this fucking kitchen trying to make everything perfect for tonight, and you," I said, pointing to him, "you go and turn on the wrong fucking oven!"

"You say 'fuck' one more time and I'm going to come over there, bend you over by oven number three, and fuck you senseless until you beg me to stop," he teased.

I breathed hard through my nose, trying to stem the anger but also trying to stop the smile that I could feel trying to break through. I walked slowly over to where Blake stood and leaned my face towards him before whispering softly, "Fuck you."

I screamed as Blake reacted immediately by reaching out for my arm, which I managed to move in time, but trying to run in heels proved a disaster as I stumbled and fell to the floor. Blake's hard body landed on top of me, and we both lay there laughing full, belly hurting laughter.

I flipped over onto my back, and Blake was above me, smiling down at me. We were both breathing hard. Blake took my hands and held them above my head before taking my mouth in his and kissing me deeply, our tongues fighting to get further and further in, before he slowed and placed a trail of gentle kisses around my mouth. Pulling back, he held my gaze. "I've never felt so happy in my life," he said, and I could feel that it had come straight from his heart.

"Not even the day you had three ovens installed instead of the usual one?" I said as Blake's hands released me and went to work on opening my trousers and shirt.

"Do you remember what I told you about your witty mouth, Miss Summers?" He dragged my trousers over my shoes. "And what did I tell you I would do if you said the word 'fuck' again?" he said firmly.

"Fuck, fuck, fucking fuck," I replied with a smirk.

He growled and pulled his trousers off before getting back into position on top of me. "The shoes are staying on," he said before pounding his cock into me hard and fast.

I heard Casey and Alex arrive as I was putting the finishing touches on my make-up. Hearing Casey laugh made me feel so warm inside. What we had here, the four of us, was perfect. It was almost too good to be true. My best friend was getting married to Blake's best friend. It was as if fate had placed us altogether.

As I allowed myself to smile and feel happy, however, it happened again; the thought that with happiness comes pain came crashing into my head once more, kicking away all of the perfect thoughts that had been swimming around happily until that moment. I closed my eyes to push the negativity away, but a knock at the door brought me back into the here and now.

"Can I come in?" Casey beamed as she popped her head around the door.

I smiled. "Casey."

She entered, and immediately we held each other as if it hadn't been only two days since I last saw her.

"I've missed you," she said quietly against my shoulder.

"It's been two days," I laughed, choking back happy tears.

"You know what I mean," she said, releasing me and smiling. "You look so happy."

"I am," I agreed with a slight smile.

"Then what's wrong?"

We sat on the edge of the bed, holding hands. "I'm so happy, Casey; I'm the happiest I think I have ever been in my life."

"But?"

"But I keep having these thoughts," I said quietly. "Every time I get happy and content, something comes along and rips it away from me."

Casey sighed and gave me a sympathetic smile "I know you've had it real shitty, Jo, but this is it now; you and Blake were destined to be together. Look at how many times you have walked away only to be drawn back together again. And that video at the airport?" She sucked in a deep breath. "Wow." She loosed my hands and used them to emphasize her excitement. "I mean, it was hands-down the best thing I have ever seen! It was like something straight from a romance novel it was amazing."

"It was embarrassing," I giggled.

"I know Alex loves me; I do. But if I were ever to be asked to name someone who would truly take a bullet through the heart, allow himself to be trampled on by a herd of bulls, or jump off the highest mountain for someone? Hands down, I would say Blake. He has it bad, I tell you."

I smiled as the warm feeling slowly returned. I knew Blake loved, me and I knew what he would do to protect me, but hearing someone else say it, that they had observed it too, made it feel even more believable.

"Are you two gonna spend the night hiding out in here, or are you gonna come and have some food?" Blake asked as he stood in the doorway to the bedroom.

"We're coming," I said, still smiling at Casey. We both stood and followed Blake through to the lounge. As Blake sat down at the dining table, Casey pulled on my arm, causing me to stop and turn to face her. "It's time to move on, Jo. Forget the past, enjoy the future. Okay?"

I nodded and headed to the table to join Blake and Alex.

"Well isn't this nice?" Alex chimed. "The four of us, sitting down and enjoying a lovely meal together."

"It's the best," Blake said, grinning as he reached over and squeezed my knee, sending shockwaves through the whole of my body. I wondered how long that feeling would last. Every time Blake even looked at me, I wanted to rip his clothes off. I wondered if that feeling would ever go away. I desperately hoped not.

"I'm sorry about the takeaway; this wasn't what I had planned, but we had a bit of an oven disaster," I explained.

"What kind of an oven disaster?" Casey asked.

Blake piped up. "She put the food in the wrong oven."

"You turned the wrong oven on," I said.

"Exactly how many ovens do you have?" Casey asked, laughing.

"Three," Blake and I said in unison.

"Why do you need three ovens?"

"That's exactly what I said," I replied as Casey and I both looked to Blake for his answer.

"Tell them, Alex," Blake said as he shoved a large spoonful of rice into his mouth.

Our attention now turned to Alex.

"For occasions like this, of course," he said, waving his fork around the table.

"Of course," Blake agreed.

"Exactly," Alex replied.

"Well, if you think I'm ever going to cook using all three ovens, then you are very much mistaken, mister."

"Well, you can't even cook with one, judging by today, so I should say that's a given," he teased.

I threw a prawn biscuit at him which landed nicely in the corner of his eye. The table erupted into laughter.

"Yep!" Casey cheered. "This is perfect." She paused and then added, "So … we have some news."

Alex placed his fork down and wiped his grinning mouth on his napkin.

"You're pregnant," Blake and I both said in unison.

"No," she said, "but maybe in a couple of months if all goes well." She grinned.

"But then won't you be pregnant for the wedding?" I asked.

"We have decided that there is no point in waiting," Alex said as he grabbed Casey's hand on top of the table. The love that was oozing out of them in that moment was mesmerizing.

"We're gonna book the wedding!" Casey squealed. "We're gonna marry here in New York at Christmas."

"Oh my God, that's wonderful!" I said. Blake and I both stood and rounded the table to where they both sat. Casey and I hugged while Blake and Alex did that macho man thing where they just patted each other on the back a couple of times and acted more manly than they had since they were in high school. I never understood why men couldn't show affection to their friends the same way that women did.

"So … that's not all," Casey said. "I was hoping that my maid of honour would help me check out some venues over the next few weeks. Alex has to fly back out to Vegas for a couple of days, but we don't want to wait and miss the best place we can get." She grinned.

"I'm sure she wouldn't mind," I replied. "Have you asked her?"

"I'm kind of asking her now," Casey said, amused at my obvious ditzy reaction.

It took a few moments to sink in.

"Are you asking me to be your maid of honour?" I squealed in shock.

"She got it," Alex said.

"So cute," I heard Blake murmur.

"Of course I'm asking you, dumb-ass!"

Casey and I both screamed and started jumping up and down on the spot with excitement.

"So where do we start? And when?"

"First stop is a beautiful castle we've spotted. It's like something out of a fairy tale."

"Okay then," I said, lifting my glass to toast Casey and Alex. "Here's to what's going to be the maddest few months of your lives, but it will all be worth it."

Blake opened the door to let Casey and Alex out as I began clearing away the plates from the meal.

"Well that was a really nice evening," Blake said as he strolled slowly over to where I was loading the dishwasher.

"It was," I agreed.

"Leave the dishes; we will do it in the morning," he said,

wrapping me in his arms.

"You have work, and I have to play groom in a castle tomorrow; best to get it done now."

I laughed as Blake huffed and sulked off to continue tidying up.

"I heard you and Casey talking in the bedroom earlier." I didn't look up; he was being careful with his words. "You have nothing to be scared of now, Jo, I promise."

"I know." I nodded unconvincingly as I placed the last plate into the dishwasher, making sure not to meet his gaze.

"This is it now. Me and you and this." He gestured between us. "This is too strong for anything to break, I promise."

I nodded again before turning to face him "Is this the switch to the dishwasher, or do you have another two hidden somewhere for special occasions?" I teased.

"That's it." Blake slammed the dishcloth down onto the table and walked over to me in two long steps. He crouched down, lifted me over his shoulder, and carried me screaming into the bedroom before throwing me roughly on the bed.

He climbed over me and claimed my mouth, sucking, licking, and moaning against my lips.

"I've wanted to do that to you all night," he panted as he pulled away just for our eyes to focus.

I smiled innocently. "I've wanted you to do that all night too."

Blake's smile faded. "Are you gonna be okay tomorrow? I mean, I know that you want to go help Casey, and I think it will be fun for you both. But I know that what I did at the airport has brought a lot of attention to us, and I know that you hate attention. Will you be okay?"

I reached up and pushed Blake's hair away from his eyes "I do hate attention, yes, but I love you. And I love what you did at the airport, despite how embarrassing it was and how much attention it has caused us. But you also know *why* I hate attention."

"Sara," he stated.

"Yes, Sara," I admitted. "But I know she can't hurt me from where she is, so I think I'm gonna be okay."

12

There were a few photographers hanging around outside Blake's apartment when we drove out of the underground car park, but before anyone could see us, we had pulled onto the busy streets of New York and were heading towards my apartment building.

"Vultures," I said under my breath.

"They're just doing their job, Jo."

"They make a living by following people around, taking a random photo, and then selling it to a scumbag who will then make up a story to go with it."

"They made you see Michael for what he really was because of those photos," he said.

I didn't reply as we pulled up at my apartment block.

"I'll see you later." I leaned across and placed my lips to Blake's cheek.

"If you need me today, you call me any time. I don't care if I have to walk off set, do you hear me?"

"That really won't be necessary, but thank you," I said as I climbed out of the car and headed into the building.

"Ah, Miss Summers, how good to see you back."

I smiled. "Hello, Peter."

"I was wondering" – he cleared his throat and leaned in closer to me – "shall we be needing extra security now that you are headline news?"

Shaking my head, I laughed as I walked away. "Hopefully by tomorrow morning they will all be talking about someone else. But thank you anyway."

The lift opened, and I stepped in as Peter tipped his hat to me.

I knocked on the apartment door, and Casey opened it almost immediately. "Welcome home!" she sang.

"Thank you. I've got no keys, by the way." I walked past her and headed into the kitchen, where I flicked the kettle on.

"Everything is in your room, even the letters that you left for us all. It didn't feel right opening them once I knew you were staying. You may have told me you secretly hated me for all I know." She smirked.

"Yeah. Good thing you didn't open it," I joked back.

"It's so good to have you back." She hopped onto a stool and started spinning side to side, observing me. "Why don't you look happy to be back?"

"I am," I admitted. "I really am, it's just … Well, you know what it is. I'm scared again, aren't I? And I don't want to tell Blake, because he already thinks I can't cope without him." I rolled my eyes.

"Can you?" she asked.

"That's something that I am going to try my hardest to do," I said. "Why do I have to hold so much fear inside of me? Why can't I just be carefree and not give a shit, like you?" I forced a smile.

She smiled. "You will. In time. I just know it."

"Blake asked me to move in with him," I said as I perched myself next to Casey and took a sip of tea from my cup.

"Wow, that's … fast," she admitted.

"It is, isn't it?" I felt relieved Casey thought so too.

"What did you tell him?"

"I've told him no – not just yet anyway. Maybe when you move in with Alex it will seem the right time?"

"You aren't staying here just because you don't want to abandon me, are you? Because if so, I'll go and pack your bags for you right now," Casey replied.

"Partly, I suppose. But mainly because …"

"Because?"

"Because when I do move in with him, I worry that things will change; that we will change."

She smiled. "You are one confusing chick, Jo, you know that?"

"Anyway," I said, shrugging her off, "What time are we doing this thing today?"

"We're meeting at the castle at eleven thirty," she replied, looking at her watch.

"We're meeting who?"

Casey's shoulders sagged as she sighed heavily. "Alex told Christina; she insisted on tagging along."

"Alex's sister?"

She nodded. "The one and only."

"So why the long face? You're going to be related soon enough."

"She doesn't like me, does she? She thinks I'm after Alex for his money. I mean come on, you've only got to look at him to know that isn't the case. Channing Tatum has nothing on Alex; it certainly wasn't his wallet I was attracted to, let me tell you."

I laughed. "It will be fine, I promise. Just do what you want to do; I'm sure she must like you now if she's tagging along."

"Wants to know how much of his money I'm spending, more like."

"Well, he's loaded and he loves you. Let's go there and spend a fortune; give her something to talk about." I winked. "I'm going to take my tea, go to my room and get ready for you to drag me around a castle all day and then tell me you don't like it." Stepping off the stool, I gave Casey a quick peck to the cheek and grabbed my cup.

"I'm gonna love it; you'll see," she shouted as I headed down the hallway towards my room.

Casey was right. Everything had been left in my room, including the flowers that Blake had sent me before my audition over two weeks before. Despite the slight smell of dying flowers, a few had survived; I removed them and placed them in a vase before discarding the rest.

On my pillow were the letters that I had written, still unopened. There was also my keys, a handful of mail, and my phone.

I plugged my phone in to charge and headed to the shower.

After my shower, I wrapped a towel around my head, placed my nightgown on, and sat on my bed to catch up with any missed calls and messages I had received.

There were thirty-five missed calls, one voicemail, and fifteen texts. My phone had been switched off for just four days.

The missed calls consisted of twenty-five from Blake. Checking the call log, I found that he had called me every two minutes from when my mum contacted him until he arrived at the airport. My heart swelled with love that he had done that.

There were two missed calls from Marcus and eight from Cooper. Ten of the texts I had received were from Blake.

Don't get on that plane, I'm coming please wait!

He had sent the same message over and over again. The love in my heart grew even more. I couldn't help the smile on my face.

There was one text from Marcus:

We must do lunch, something, anything, you have no idea what you are going to have done to our ratings! I love you already. Call me!

The other four texts I had received were from Cooper.

I'm so glad you didn't go, hope we can go back to the way we were?

Call me as soon as you can.

Can I see you soon?

The final text took me by surprise. I'm not sure it was even meant for me; Cooper must have sent it to me by mistake.

You had better not be where I think you are, don't ask for my help and then betray me, I will go to the police if I need to.

After rereading that text numerous times, I came to the conclusion that it was obviously meant for someone else. But why would Cooper need to go to the police? I would ask him all about that next time I saw him.

That left just a voicemail on my phone: "Jo …" Blake sighed heavily. "Please, please, I am begging you, do not get on that plane. Do *not* get on that plane! It's not what you think; she's my sister! The girl at the door was my sister! Your mom called; she knew I wouldn't do that to you. How could you think I would do that to you?" The heavy noise of traffic filtered through, followed by Blake yelling at someone to drive quicker. "Skip the lights!" he yelled. "Change lanes!" It turned out that the person he was screaming at was his sister. I heard her tell him time and time again to calm down. It made me smile.

The message continued. "I'm coming to get you, Jo, if this motherfu—"

"Blake! Fraser is sitting right next to you!"

"Sorry, I'm sorry."

I couldn't help but laugh out loud at him.

"Jo, look. I love you, oh my God do I love you. I can't live without you, and if you get on that plane, I don't know what I am going to do. Actually yes, yes, I do know what I am going to do. I am going to get on the next flight, and I will bring you back; that's what I'll do."

He started talking again, but the voicemail was already so long that he ended up being cut off. Happy tears started to roll down my face. I was crying happy tears for the first time in months. I felt overwhelmed by the love that had poured from him when he left that message. It was raw and pure emotion.

Just as we were climbing into Alex's car, my phone rang; it was Blake.

"Hello," I answered with a smile on my face.

"Ah, good, you turned your phone back on." I heard his relief.

"I did. I also heard the adorable voicemail that you left me."

I heard Blake laugh. "I'd forgotten all about that." I could sense the smile in his voice.

"I certainly won't forget it in a hurry; it was" – I took a deep breath – "beautiful. Apart from the language you were about to use in front of Fraser, of course," I said, trying my hardest to be serious.

"Of course," he laughed.

"I miss you," I admitted.

"I miss you too, beautiful. I just wanted to check that you are okay without me."

"I'm fine," I admitted. "We're just leaving now for the castle, so I'm going to have to go."

"How are you getting there?" he said, panicked.

"Casey has Alex's car while he's away, why?"

"Because I don't want to hear that you have gotten into any more cabs, okay?"

"Yes, boss," I joked.

"I'm serious, Jo; there are some real nut jobs out there. I want you safe."

I smiled. "I'm not getting into a taxi. We are in the comfort of Alex's Audi, okay? So just relax."

"This weekend we're gonna go get you a car."

"I will get a car," I corrected him, "when I decide to."

"This weekend, no excuses. I need to get back. I love you."

"I love you too."

The castle was outstanding. Christina and I fell in love with it from the moment we stepped inside. Casey, however, didn't agree. "It's too … old," she said, scrunching up her nose.

Christina and I both laughed. "It's a castle," I said. "Castles are old, Casey. What were you expecting? The princess castle at Disney World?" Christina and I both sniggered, and Casey sighed, appearing defeated.

"I really thought I would like it here," she said, quietly disappointed.

"It's the first place we have seen; let's go look somewhere else," Christina suggested.

"Fine by me," I admitted.

"I didn't see anywhere else that I liked," she moaned. "I wanted something different, something nice."

"How about the lighthouse?" I suggested. "That's different and very nice."

"And very pricey," Christina added, prompting me and Casey to give each other a knowing look.

"Of course, the lighthouse." She smiled and winked at us. "Let's go."

"Nope." She shook her head. "It just doesn't feel …" Casey's eyes roamed the room, looking for answers. "It's too …"

"Old?" I asked.

"No."

Christina piped up. "Expensive?"

"No. I just don't feel it," she sighed. Christina appeared relieved.

"Look," I said, "let's go get some lunch, then head home, and we can sit down and go through every single venue New York has to offer and visit some more tomorrow."

"I'm sorry, you guys; I've taken up all of your time today for nothing." She frowned.

"It's not for nothing; I've enjoyed it." I gave her a quick hug.

"You want to come too, Christina?" Casey threw me a death stare but appeared relieved when Christina said that she had plans this evening so needed to go.

"Maybe we can do dinner one night?" she asked.

I smiled. "Definitely. I'll get your number from Casey and call you."

"Sounds good."

We watched Christina drive off before getting into the Audi and heading to lunch.

"See, she isn't so bad. She seemed nice and was interested in helping."

"You saw her face," Casey said, shocked. "She nearly fell through the floor when you suggested the lighthouse."

We both laughed. "It was funny, I have to admit. You should have booked it there just to see her reaction."

She frowned. "I'm never gonna find the right place, am I?"

"Of course you are. They just haven't built it yet," I joked.

We ate at our favourite bistro, and for a moment I had completely forgotten that I was the centre of a YouTube video sensation until I spotted two girls sitting not far from us pointing and whispering.

"And now it begins," I sighed as I took a sip from my latte.

"What does?" Casey asked, confused.

I nodded towards the young girls, who weren't even trying to hide the fact that they were talking about me and Blake.

"Ah sweet, you have fans," she teased.

"No. Blake has fans; I have haters," I said in frustration.

The girls decided to approach slowly, one pushing the other

forward and then retreating, and vice versa.

"I hope they have cameras in here for when forensics arrive," I said in a hushed tone.

Casey laughed, but inside me was the fear that I had done well today to forget about.

"Are you Joanne Summers?" one of the girls asked.

"Josephine," I corrected her with a nod.

Both girls giggled a little before girl number two spoke. "You are so pretty."

"Thank you," I answered in surprise.

"You and Blake will have such beautiful babies," girl number one said excitedly.

"Can we have a picture with you? No one is going to believe this without a picture," girl number two asked.

I was completely taken by surprise. "Oh, of course. Sure, um …" I pushed my chair away and stood. Before I knew it, the girls had taken up both of my sides and had handed both of their phones to Casey.

"Charming," I heard Casey say behind a laugh.

"Say cheese, everyone!" Casey chimed as she snapped the pictures on both phones.

The overexcited girls took their phones back and decided they would Facebook and tweet the pictures right away. "Thank you so much!" they both said hysterically before stumbling away and out of the bistro.

I was completely dumbfounded by it all. "What the hell just happened?" I said, shaking my head.

"They loved you," Casey laughed. "Get used to it, because that was just the beginning."

That was the kind of attention I could get used to. It was lovely that for the first time since being in New York, not only had I been recognized, but they were the sweetest girls and they actually liked me.

Granted, I wasn't going to be favoured by everyone, but it really did mean a lot when all I had ever known was fear. It was nice to feel liked, if only for just one day.

The next few days were crazy. Blake and I were like ships that passed in the night because of his busy schedule. I hated not being with him. It drove me crazy when we would go an evening without seeing each other, which only made Blake beg me more and more to move in with him. However, for me, it was still too soon. Even though it was tempting, everything still felt too fresh for me to consider it. Blake had also told me that his filming in Miami was to clash with my two recordings of *Perfect Alibi*, which couldn't be helped, but the more I let my mind wander, the more and more I convinced myself that we were going to end up slowly slipping apart. I felt my throat constrict tighter the more I thought about it, until eventually I calmed myself down by remembering how much Blake had fought for us until I had given in. That reassured me that we were tough enough to survive our time apart.

I had become Casey's personal wedding planner at some point over the past few days; the normally bubbly, outgoing, carefree Casey had turned into Bridezilla; she was struggling to find anywhere that she deemed suitable for the wedding and had even earned the name Goldilocks from Christina and me. Everywhere was either too big too small, too new too tacky, or any other excuse she could muster up. Planning the wedding was, however, helping me to forget about the time I wasn't spending with Blake and also the growing attention I was beginning to receive every time I was noticed, which was increasing every day.

I had managed to meet up with Marcus for lunch too. I think Blake was secretly making it his mission to keep me busy by asking the people he knew well to watch over me.

Marcus was so excited that Blake and I had seemed to raise the profile of his already highly popular sitcom that he even spoke about seeing whether they could write me in permanently. I told him he would regret that when things died down and I returned to being just Jo.

We ran through everything in preparation for the two weeks we would be working together. Rehearsals were due to start the day that Blake would fly out to Miami. They would take place Monday to Thursday, with the live recording being shot on the Friday evening both weeks. At least with Blake away I was going to be busy. I had my job coming up and Casey's wedding plans; I would hardly have any time to miss Blake. I hoped.

With Alex due back from Vegas the following day and Blake doing a night shoot, Casey and I had decided on a girly night in with food, wine, and as many Channing Tatum movies as we could squeeze in. I had talked Casey into inviting Christina along, and she was going to do her best to try to get along with her, forget about the perfect wedding venue for now, and have a fun night.

We made margaritas and enjoyed takeaway pizza but never got round to watching the movies. Once Christina and Casey started grilling me on my sex life with Blake, I decided it was only fair that they join in too; truth or dare it was.

No one wanted to do a dare for fear of what we would all come up with, so it was truths all round. Casey admitted that the most public place she had had sex was on a football pitch, while Christina's was on a secluded beach.

Until Blake, my sex life had been too boring for any of that. My most public place would probably have been in my first boyfriend's house while his parents were downstairs watching TV. Christina asked Casey her favourite sexual position, to which Casey scrunched her nose before replying, "You want me to tell you the best way that your brother can get me to orgasm, like multiple orgasm?"

I threw my head back, howling at Christina, who visibly shuddered from the thought.

The laughter didn't stop all night. Every question was related to sex, and it turned out that until Blake, I had been well and truly missing out.

Casey asked me how old I was when I lost my virginity. "Seventeen," I replied, which got a "whoop" from Casey.

Christina asked Casey if she had ever taken a guy's virginity. "Eeewwww, no way! That's just wrong on so many levels," was her reply.

Christina was smirking; her eyes were glazed over from the amount of alcohol she had consumed.

"Oh my God," Casey gasped. "Have you?"

Christina nodded slowly as she held her lip between her teeth. "It was sweet," she replied. "He was hot – well, still is actually." She held her hands up. "He was three years my junior, and it seemed everyone wanted a piece of him, but he gave it all to me, over and over again; he couldn't get enough," she said seductively.

Casey threw a pillow at her and told her she was a filthy cougar. We all laughed in hysterics except Christina, who was eying me suspiciously.

"Why are you looking at me like that?" I asked as I slumped into the sofa, sipping my margarita.

"Has he ever told you, Jo? Told you how wild we were and the things I taught him?"

My laughter suddenly stopped, and I heard Casey gasp as the room fell silent.

"You slept with Blake?" I asked, shocked.

"Oh yeah, popped his cherry, then taught him everything he knows," she said, wide-eyed. "And let me tell you, for a beginner, he was good. I mean, wow."

I could feel Casey's eyes burning into me; she was obviously as shocked as I was at this revelation.

"Oh, come on," Christina chimed. "It was years ago! Like fifteen years ago."

"You slept with him when he was fifteen?" I asked, shocked.

"Oh my God, that's illegal!" Casey said.

"We were both consenting. I never did anything that he didn't want to do, and believe me, he liked to do the lot. By the time I cooled things off with him, he was old enough anyway." She shrugged.

"You called it off?"

"Sure." She shrugged. "We had been … you know … at it for three years, and being twenty one with an eighteen-year-old boyfriend didn't seem so appealing once my friends and I were heading out to bars and all that; it was time I got me a real man. Mind you, I'm still actually working on that."

Casey snorted. "But being eighteen with a fifteen-year-old

boyfriend was okay, though, yeah?"

The room fell silent; all eyes were on me.

"Come on, Jo," Christina said, breaking the silence, "we're talking about fifteen years ago; he's like a brother to me now.

"I think that's probably the sickest thing I've ever heard," Casey said, pretending to heave.

"Well I think we've all drunk way too much tonight; it's bringing out too much stuff that I'm not up to hearing about. I'm going to bed." I stood and headed for my room without any further words.

"Jo, I'm sorry!" Christina shouted, "I thought you knew!"

I slammed the door behind me and fell onto my bed crying. It had been fifteen years, and even though I felt I was being ridiculous, Christina telling me that she had finished it, and not Blake, made me wonder how he had felt at the time. How long would he have carried on if she hadn't finished it? Was he in love with her back then? Did he still have feelings for her now? Did she break his heart when she finally stopped sleeping with him? I needed to know the answers to all of these questions. As ridiculous and jealous as I knew I was being, I really needed to know.

It was one thing seeing pictures of Blake with other women he had been linked with in the past, but another when one of them was his best friend's sister who not only took his virginity but carried on with him for three years and then sat in my apartment telling me all about it.

I put on some shoes, grabbed my handbag, and walked out of the apartment. Blake wouldn't be home yet, but he had given me a key and told me that the apartment was mine as much as his, although I still wouldn't move in with him officially. So I would go there and wait as long as I needed to until he returned.

I stepped out of the building and got into the first cab that stopped for me. I needed to see him; I needed to know the answers to everything that was swimming around in my head. I would sit and wait all night if I had to, but I needed to know everything as soon as he came home.

I lay on Blake's sofa watching the clock tick by. It was four a.m. and he still wasn't home.

I started having ridiculous thoughts that he wasn't actually working but instead was with someone else. The more I tried to stop myself from thinking those ridiculous thoughts, the more I imagined him having sex with Christina; the more I thought of him having sex with Christina, the angrier with him I became.

Christina was a lot like Casey – tall, slim, and tanned, with bouncy blonde hair that she seemed to enjoy flicking over her shoulder a hell of a lot.

I should have trusted Casey's instinct about her, but I hadn't. I gave her a chance, and now she had made me an emotional wreck. It wasn't even as if I could avoid her; she would be tagging along to venues with us and would obviously be part of the wedding somehow, even though Casey had said one hundred per cent that she wouldn't be a bridesmaid. It was inevitable I would see her a lot, yet every time I would see her, I would imagine her and Blake and sex.

Soft fingers brushed against my face, causing me to moan lightly.

"Jo," I heard Blake say softly. "Jo, wake up, beautiful."

I forced my eyes open, and immediately they connected with Blake's. He was smiling at me, but his smile disappeared when he noticed my obvious state.

"Have you been crying?" he asked as his brow creased with worry.

I sat up and wiped my eyes. "What time is it?"

"It's almost five," he said softly. "How long have you been here?" I stood from the chair and stepped around him.

"Jo? What's going on?" He stood and moved to approach me. I held my hands up to stop him. I couldn't even look him in the eye, as I felt the anger bubbling up inside me.

"Where have you been until five a.m.?" I asked shakily.

"You know where I've been – at work."

"And you've come straight home?"

"Of course I have; where do you think I've been?"

"Tell me about when you lost your virginity," I said shakily.

"What?" he asked with obvious confusion. "Why would you ask me about something that happened fifteen years ago? That's ridiculous," he said, shaking his head in disbelief.

"Is it?" I replied with anger. "Is it ridiculous that I had to sit in my apartment tonight listening to Christina, your best friend's sister, telling me all of the gory details about her taking your virginity, about what she taught you, how much you loved it and kept on going back for more, not forgetting how good you were, and that it went on for three whole years before she finished it with you!" I spat out. "You fucked Christina for three years, and you didn't think to tell me! Do you have even the slightest idea of how that felt, Blake? Do you!"

"Jo, calm down," Blake said softly. "I can see that you're upset."

"Upset! I'm fucking fuming! She made me feel like I should have been thanking her for teaching you what you know!" I shouted. "Everything that we have done, everything that you have done to me," I sobbed. "Did she teach you all of that? Did you do all of those things with her?"

Blake sighed heavily as he looked down to the floor.

"Answer me," I said through gritted teeth when he didn't reply.

"Jo, listen to me, please." His eyes lifted slowly to meet mine.

I was breathing hard, my whole body shaking from the emotion that had just exploded from inside me.

"Yes. I lost my virginity to Christina. And yes, we fooled around for three years. That was all; we fooled around," he said firmly.

"Did you love her?" I choked out.

Blake let out a hard laugh before shaking his head. "Of course I didn't love her, no."

"Do you ever think of her in that way now? Wonder how good she would feel beneath you while you moved inside her?"

"No," he said firmly. "I don't see her as anything other than my best friend's sister, I swear."

"Were you upset when she finished with you?" I asked, a little bit calmer.

"There was nothing to finish," he said gently.

"Has there ever been anything between you since then?"

"No," he said unconvincingly.

I straightened up. "You're lying to me."

"I'm not lying; there has never been anything since I was eighteen."

"I don't believe you," I said quietly.

Blake sighed and sat on the edge of the sofa holding his head in his hands before looking up at me. "After all of the shit with Sara when she turned up at your apartment going crazy and you told me to leave," he said carefully as I nodded. "A few days later, Christina turned up to check on me. She had been visiting Alex, and he had told her what had happened between the two of us."

I had a knot forming in the pit of my stomach; I didn't like where this was going. "Do I want to hear the rest of this?"

"I was upset, and she comforted me. She held me while I cried over you," he said firmly. "I was a mess, a complete and utter mess, Jo."

I started shaking my head in disbelief, not wanting to know the next part, but wanting to know at the same time.

"She kissed me."

A small sob escaped my throat. "And then what?"

"I didn't say no."

"I need to go," I said quietly before I turned and started walking towards the door. I had only taken a couple of steps when Blake's arms wrapped around my waist and pulled me back into his body.

"Nothing else happened, I swear," he said into my ear. "I told her that I was in love with you and I wasn't prepared to throw away any chance I had with you for a one-night stand."

I struggled out of his arms and turned to face him.

"I don't believe you."

"I swear to you, Jo; I wouldn't lie to you!"

"I need to be alone, I can't … I can't think straight around you." I headed towards the door.

"No more running, Jo. I'm not going to let you run over something as ridiculous as this," he said in a firm tone.

"You think it's ridiculous?" I said, turning back to face him. "You think I'm being ridiculous?" I puffed out a large breath of air in disbelief.

"No," he said calmly. "I don't think that *you* are being ridiculous, but we are arguing over something that happened when I was fifteen, Jo; the situation is ridiculous."

"Let me tell you something, Blake," I snapped. "I haven't felt this happy in a long time – in a very, very long time. You know me, and you know how hard I have found it to begin to trust someone again, to believe you when you tell me that I'm beautiful, to believe that you are as happy with me as I am with you, and to believe that you really do love me as much as I love you." I wiped my tears again.

"You know how much I love you. I was prepared to get on a plane and follow you to London if I hadn't gotten to you in time."

"Would you, though? Or would it have been easier to just move on? I'm sure Christina would have been waiting." Blake approached me and wrapped his arms around my waist.

"Hey," he said gently as his fingers stroked my cheek, "you know I would have come after you."

"Every time I allow myself to feel happy, Blake," I choked out. "Every single time."

"Come here." Blake pulled me to him and held me tight. Slowly, the realization dawned on me how ridiculous I really was being. What had happened in the past between Blake and Christina was exactly that, the past, and I had let my crazy jealous streak step forward again. I scrunched my eyes shut with regret before looking up into Blake's big blue eyes. He looked so tired and scared, and that was all because of me.

"I'm sorry," I whispered.

"You have nothing to apologize for," he said with relief as his thumb brushed over my lips before placing his lips there briefly.

"I overreacted. I let my defence down, and everything that I'm trying to overcome just pushed its way to the surface." I sighed before looking back up to him. "Just hearing her talk like that, it hurt."

"I know." He placed his lips to my brow and held me against him.

"I'm going to go," I said quietly.

Blake lifted my head to meet his eyes. "Don't go, please."

"You need your rest, Blake; you've been working all night, and then you come back to this."

"This," he said firmly, "is what I want to come back to every single time I walk through that door." I could see him thinking. "Well, not the tears and arguments" – he laughed softly – "but you. I want you here, Jo, with me, every second of the day that you can be."

I couldn't believe that he was still asking me to move in after the way I had just reacted to him and Christina. All of the jealousy and hurt slowly began to melt away.

"As soon as you're ready, I want you here, Jo, forever."

I lifted up onto my toes and took his mouth in mine. It wasn't frantic, or needy. Just love.

I pulled back slightly and lifted my T-shirt over my head before discarding it to the floor. Blake's eyes grew hungry as he watched me unclip my bra and let it fall carelessly to the ground. I slid my hands beneath the waistband of my trousers and let them drop to the floor before stepping out of them, his eyes on my body the whole time.

I stood in front of him wearing only my tiny knickers. Taking his mouth in mine again, I walked him backwards until he was against the back of the sofa. My hands worked on opening the buttons of his shirt, revealing his hard abs, which were moving frantically with his ragged breath. Moving to his trousers, I carefully unbuckled his belt before tugging them down to the floor.

I knelt in front of him and took his hard cock in my mouth. Looking up at him, I could see raw emotion in his eyes. There were no words; just pure, hard, raw emotion between us. Without taking my eyes from his, I guided his cock deeper into my mouth, my tongue worshipping every single inch of his hardness. He gasped as he threw his head back in pure delight. "Aah, Jo … fuck yes … aah."

I took him deep over and over, sucking with every bit of strength that my body would allow, taking him so far in I would gag. But it felt good giving him exactly what I needed him to have.

His hips moved with me gently, pushing into me with each deep suck. His hands tangled into my hair, tugging for more, taking everything he could get from me. "Ah, Jo … so good … so fucking good …" he moaned over and over.

I could feel his closeness. He began to move more frantically against me, his breath speeding up with each thrust. "I'm gonna come … I don't want to come in your mouth, Jo … let me inside you … aahhhh."

But I wanted to taste him, taste the juices of the man whom I loved more than my own life. His hands tugged hard on my head, and with one more deep, hard thrust, he stilled inside me, his warm salty liquid filling my mouth over and over again. "Fuck yes … aah, Jo … fuck, Jo … aahhhhhhhh …" Blake shouted out in pure pleasure as his juices ran smoothly down my throat.

I released him from my mouth and licked the head of his cock, removing the last bits of his juices that sat there before he pulled me up to my feet. He immediately took my mouth in his. "Let me taste it," he said against my mouth. "Let me taste what you did to me." He growled before taking my mouth harder and erratically. "Fuck, Jo, that was fucking hot." He lifted me and stepped around the settee, laying me down on my back before releasing my mouth and roughly tugging my knickers down and throwing them to the floor. His mouth was on my in an instant, sucking and licking at my folds hungrily. "Now I want you to come for me, all over my mouth, Jo. Let me taste you; give it to me." He growled before once again burying his face against me, taking everything he could get until my body exploded against him, sending me flying high above the earth with pure pleasure.

"Blake!" I screamed as my orgasm took hold of me and not only gave me the most satisfying pleasure possible but also took all of my negative thoughts and jealously that I had allowed to seep back in, and trampled all over them until they were gone. At least for now.

13

I woke alone in bed. I remembered Blake and me falling asleep on the couch; he must have carried me through to the bedroom while I lay totally exhausted from the amount of sex we had gone on to have after our first argument since getting back together.

I felt like a fool. I had worked myself up into the most ridiculous state over what Blake had done fifteen years ago. Not only that but I had also allowed myself to feel jealous of someone else when I was the one who had Blake – not Christina, not Sara. No other woman had Blake except for me.

I had even convinced myself that he was with another woman rather than working. That was how ridiculously jealous I had become.

I had showed Blake a side to me last night that I never wanted to escape from my head again. It wasn't completely my fault that I had issues controlling my jealously, and Blake was nothing like any man I had ever been with before. He really did love me, and he showed it every opportunity he got, but getting hurt as badly as I did was always going to have consequences that would arise at every opportunity.

I expected to be alone in the apartment, but Blake's sweet singing voice echoed through the rooms; he sounded happy, which made me smile. His voice sounded like velvet chocolate being poured over a fountain; smooth and silky and tempting.

Digging into my case that still hadn't made its way back to my apartment, I took my short denim skirt and a waistcoat, quickly got changed, and headed out to find Blake.

The singing had stopped by the time I found Blake; he was sitting on the terrace, reading from a newspaper.

His eyes left the page and scanned to me when he spotted me walking towards him. He folded the paper, placed it on the coffee table in front of him, and patted the seat next to him for me to join him.

I stopped in the doorway as I fiddled with my hands, feeling embarrassed.

He smiled. "Good afternoon, sleepyhead."

"Hi," I said shyly.

"What's wrong?" he asked, sitting up on his seat.

"I feel terrible," I sighed as I scratched my brow nervously.

"As in ill?" he asked, concerned.

"No." I breathed out and walked over to him. I placed my legs over his and straddled his thighs, placing my hands around his neck. "I feel terrible about last night – well, this morning. You shouldn't have come home to that. I just—"

Blake silenced me by placing his fingers to my lips. "I can see why you were upset. It's done now. Let's draw a line under it and forget it even happened. I do, however, want to know how you got here last night," he said raising his eyebrow in suspicion.

"In a cab," I replied quietly as my eyes focused on the material of Blake's T-shirt, which I was fiddling with.

"Jo," Blake said sternly, "what time was it exactly?"

I shrugged and continued fiddling with Blake's shirt.

"We're getting you a car today."

"Blake, just forget that for now. Please, I need to tell you something."

He moved his hands from my thighs and wrapped his arms around my waist. "What is it?"

"There's something I never told you, and because I acted like such an idiot last night, I need to tell you now."

"Go on," he said nervously.

"The Sunday night when we were all at Alex's birthday meal ..."

He nodded.

"I kissed Cooper," I said quickly.

Blake eyed me carefully before a smile broke out across his face. "Oh did you now?" he said teasingly as his fingers moved down to my thighs and along the hem of my shirt, which was now resting at the top of my thighs.

"It was stupid. I was upset, and I regret it," I admitted.

"And what did Cooper say when he had a taste of those lips that belong to me?" he asked as one hand moved underneath my skirt and started stroking my knickers.

My breath hitched as I struggled to concentrate. Blake's gentle strokes were so light, but the effect it was having made me want to rip his clothes off right there on the terrace and fuck him into oblivion.

"His words were," I said shakily, "'That kiss wasn't for me … it was for Blake, wasn't it?'"

Blake moved my knickers to the side and pushed two long, hard fingers inside me, causing me to gasp.

"Was he right?"

"You know he was," I managed to say softly.

"Poor bastard," Blake said quietly as he thrust his fingers over and over again inside me.

"Blake," I panted as I threw my head back in pleasure, "someone might see."

"We're on top of the world here, baby," Blake said as he tugged my head roughly to him and took my mouth. "This mouth is mine," he said roughly. "And this", he said, thrusting his fingers even deeper into me, "is mine too and always will be."

"Always," I panted. "Always yours, Blake."

His fingers left me, and before I could register what was going on, Blake had pushed his jogging pants down to the floor. With me still on top, he thrust into me deep and hard, causing me to moan out loudly.

"That's it, baby, show me. Show me what you can do to me."

I began to ride his cock hard and fast, both of us picking up a steady rhythm as we ground against each other. "I'm gonna come soon, Jo; I can't stop. I can't control myself when I'm inside of you."

In the next thrust, my whole world turned on its axis. My body shuddered as my orgasm hit every muscle and every sense, sending me flying.

Blake's head fell back as he thrust into me one more time before stilling and emptying his warm liquid into me, shouting my name over and over again until he was done. I fell forward and rested on Blake's chest as we both lay panting hard, slowly coming back to earth.

"If you moved in with me, we could do that all the time."

"*When* I move in with you, we will." I smiled, looking up at him.

"God, I love you." He smiled as he pulled out of me and shifted me from his lap.

"Where are you going?"

"I'm going to get ready for the special night we have planned," he said with excitement. "Shower?" he asked, holding his hand out for me.

Standing, I adjusted my shirt and took his hand in mine. "Where exactly are we going?" I asked.

"Tonight I am taking you to my favourite French restaurant, and then you are escorting me to a Yankees game."

"Won't Alex be offended you took your girlfriend to the game instead of him? This is a Blake–Alex thing," I stated.

"Alex is only just landing; he's gonna want the night with Casey," he said. "Which reminds me, it may be best for you to stay here again tonight, just in case you disturb them."

"Sly," I replied, "but can't we just stay here, have a night in front of the TV, eat trashy food, and fall asleep together?"

"No. I want to take you out and give you a real Yankees experience, then bring you back here and give you another great experience." He smiled, but he frowned when he noticed I didn't share his enthusiasm. "Come on, it'll be fun; you will love it. Great food followed by a great sport with great atmosphere, and your favourite man on your arm." He smiled his million-dollar winning smile. "It will also give me a chance to show you what a real sport is too," he teased.

"Okay," I said in surrender. "But I'm still not moving in."

As we entered the bathroom, we were already helping each other to undress.

I was unsure what the required dress code was for a nice meal at an exclusive French restaurant followed by an evening watching men hit a ball as far as they could before running around in a circle. So, assuming that we would be in one of the stadium's VIP boxes, I went for smart and casual by pairing up my favourite cream blouse and my favourite black trousers, along with my favourite Jimmy Choo shoes, which Blake also seemed to like.

I was happy with my choice when I walked into the lounge to see Blake wearing a black Ralph Lauren suit with a white shirt underneath that was open at the collar.

"Will this do?" I asked, holding my hands out and turning in a circle for Blake to see.

He smiled. "Perfect."

As we pulled up to the restaurant, Blake handed the keys to the valet for parking. We walked into the restaurant unnoticed, which pleased me. This was our first public appearance together since the airport last weekend, and I hoped that by now we were beginning to fade into the background. Surely now it was someone else's turn to make the headlines.

The waiter showed us to a secluded booth as Blake had requested. He then ordered us a bottle of champagne before the waiter retreated, leaving us to decide on what we wanted to eat.

"So," Blake said, "what do you normally eat when you go French?"

"Well, I've only ever eaten French once," I admitted, "so that would be whatever you brought over to my apartment that one time." I tried to work out what was what on the menu. I couldn't read or speak French; I had given up trying to learn as a child and had turned to Spanish instead; it seemed like the easier choice at the time.

"Ah, I recognize that one – le coq au vin," I said in my best French accent. "Mum used to make that, but I didn't like it." Blake had stopped looking at the menu and was watching me with a huge smile on his face. "And don't go ordering me *la cagouille* or *escargot*." I screwed my nose up. "I know they are both something to do with snails," I said in disgust.

He smirked. "Shall we try some *des cuisses de grenouille*? Or maybe some *le tete* followed by *le pied de paquets*?"

"Judging by your face, I know that you just said something totally revolting. So no. But can you speak French to me again, please" – I leaned forward so only Blake could hear me – "because that was ridiculously hot," I said seductively.

Blake let out a low moan just as the waiter returned with our champagne. "Talk about timing, right?" he laughed, gesturing to the waiter.

Blake ordered us both something in French, and even though I had no idea what it was – and I wasn't going to ask – it was definitely what we had eaten the night he had brought French food to the apartment. And it tasted delicious.

After my second glass of champagne, I decided I'd had enough alcohol when my head started to feel a bit fuzzy. I still had a Yankees game to get through, so I wanted to keep a clear head.

When we had finished our meal, Blake paid the bill and we headed outside the restaurant while the valet collected the car.

Blake pulled me into his arms and kissed me softly. "Are you ready for what happens next?" he asked, grinning.

"I assume you are referring to the Yankees and not that you are about to have your wicked way with me in the middle of a busy street," I joked.

Blake nodded, seeming to consider the latter option, causing me to slap him lightly on the chest, at which we both laughed.

"Blake! Jo! Over here!" a voice shouted from across the street. We both turned to see a photographer snapping pictures of us.

"Take no notice of him," Blake said, capturing my attention. "He's not doing anything wrong; he's only doing his job. We are happy and smiling, and the pictures will show that and only that." He held my gaze. I forced my lips into a smile.

"That's better," he said before kissing me again. I was grateful to see the valet pull up next to us. I got in the car almost before he had got the chance to get out.

"Go Yankees!" Blake said playfully as he hopped into the car and pulled away from the restaurant.

"So what's the atmosphere like up in the luxury suites?"

Blake was smirking but kept his eyes on the road. "I'm taking you for a real Yankees experience, Jo; that doesn't involve anything luxury."

"Where are we sitting, Blake?" I asked firmly.

"Well, like I said, I want to give you the real Yankees experience." He turned to me briefly before turning back to the road. "There's no real atmosphere in those boxes. I wanted you to really feel it, you know." He shrugged slightly.

"Blake," I growled, "look at how we're dressed. We can't stand down there dressed like this; we will stick out like a sore thumb!"

"I've already prepared for that," he said.

I closed my eyes and took a deep breath.

"The bag?" he said. "On the back seat?"

I twisted to see a large brown paper bag with the word "Yankees" scrawled across the front.

"What's in the bag, Blake?" I asked through gritted teeth.

"Take a look." I could see he was struggling to hide his amusement.

Throwing him one last disgusted look, I grabbed the bag and started to remove the contents.

"You want me to wear a Yankees cap?" I asked in shock as Blake pressed his lips together to stem the laughter that I could tell was bubbling up. "And a jacket? I'm going to look like an idiot!"

"You're gonna look like every other woman in the stadium," he laughed. "No one will know it's us."

"Oh and your shoes?"

"What about my shoes?" I narrowed my eyes at him.

"Under my jacket and hat in the bag."

I put my hands in once more and pulled out a pair of white Converse trainers. "Oh no." I shook my head. "No way can I wear these; I don't do flat shoes."

"Just put them on; we're almost there," he laughed.

We pulled up to the stadium and parked the car. "Well, do I look like a New Yorker?" I said, batting my eyelids at him as I adjusted my cap.

"Every single inch." He smiled before placing his sunglasses and cap on and grabbing his jacket. "Go Yankees!" he shouted again as he stepped out of the car.

Maybe this was going to be a fun night after all.

Blake kept a firm grip on me the whole time until we were seated. He formed a protective stance around me, not allowing anyone to step close enough to push into me or cause me to stumble. The stadium was packed full, and the atmosphere was amazing – nothing like I had ever experienced at a football match; it was easily multiplied by one hundred.

Once seated, Blake called over a vendor and purchased two Diet Cokes and pretzels.

"How are you even hungry?" I asked, surprised by him when he started wolfing it down immediately.

He shrugged and smiled. "I'm not. It's all part of the experience."

Picking at my pretzel, I looked around. We had blended right in; no one had noticed Blake, so no one was even remotely aware that we were sitting amongst them.

"So," I said with a smirk, "Who are you when you are at a Yankees game?"

"I'm Blake," he replied, confused.

"What I mean is, are you New York's biggest film and TV star Blake Mackenzie, or are you the son of the biggest Yankees player since Babe Ruth Blake Mackenzie?"

"Someone's been doing some research."

I smiled. "Amazing what you can find on Google."

"Amazing," he said as he laughed.

"So?"

"So what?"

"Which one?"

Sitting back, Blake placed his arms across his chest casually. "I'd like to think people see me as a bit of both," he replied.

"Show off," I said, nudging him gently.

"So tonight's game is huge," Blake said as he straightened up in his seat, ready to explain everything he thought I needed to know. "This is the Yankees' derby game, like when Manchester United play ..."

"Manchester City," I offered.

"Exactly." He nodded. "Do you know how the game works?"

"Well, I played rounders for the county in high school. From what I've seen, I don't imagine it's too different," I said over the ever-growing noise.

"Rounders." Blake nodded amused.

"Yes, there are two teams. The aim is to hit the ball as far as possible and run," I explained. "Same as this." I gestured towards the field.

"It's a lot more complex than just hitting a ball and running," he laughed.

"Okay. So there are two opposing teams," I said. "The aim of the game is to score more points than your opponents. The team earn points by completing a full circle around the bases on the baseball diamond. Games are divided into nine innings; innings are then divided into two halves. The visiting team bats at the tops of the innings, and the home team bats at the bottoms of the innings." I sucked in a deep breath before attempting to continue.

"Google?" Blake asked.

I nodded with a smirk. "Google. Shall I go on?" Just then a huge roar filled the stadium. The man seated behind Blake patted him on the shoulder a couple of times before cheering. Looking up, I noticed the big screen. The camera had stopped still, focused on Blake and me.

"Wow, the disguise certainly did the trick," I said dryly before forcing a smile for the onlookers.

Blake, being Blake, lapped it up, standing and giving everyone a curt nod, causing even more of an uproar. After a few minutes, the camera scanned, and the screen filled up with other spectators.

A man looking very official approached us in our seats. "MR Mackenzie, we had no idea you were joining us this evening," he said, taking Blake's hand in his and giving a firm shake.

Blake smiled. "Dustin, hi. This is my girlfriend, Jo."

"It's a pleasure to meet you," he said as we shook hands.

"Likewise," I replied with a smile.

"If you would both like to follow me, we have your usual seats available in the luxury suite," he said with a smile.

Blake hesitated. "I kinda wanted to give Jo the real experience, if you know what I mean," Blake said, looking determined. "But thank you, Dustin, you've been very helpful. And next time we will definitely take the suite."

Dustin smiled. "No problem. It's good to see you. And if you need anything while you're here, call me on this number and I'll be right with you." Dustin handed me a card which I placed into the pocket of my jacket.

"Thank you," I said with a smile.

"Enjoy your evening." Dustin nodded before disappearing back up the steps.

At some point during the game, play stopped and the screen lit up again, this time displaying various messages ranging from "happy birthday" to "welcome home". My heart was pounding as I waited once more for all attention to be drawn to us. Luckily the camera went to a different couple. The man then proceeded to get down on one knee and propose to his Yankee-loving girlfriend. The whole stadium roared with cheers for the happy couple.

Blake's grip tightened on my hand as I smiled with happiness for them both.

"Have you stopped breathing," Blake said with a hint of amusement as he leaned towards my ear.

"Sorry," I breathed out. "That was just … she was so happy." I smiled before I shook my head in disbelief when I realized I had just found a marriage proposal at a Yankees game romantic. "How often does that happen?" I asked.

"Almost every game," Blake laughed, "but I love how romantic you found that."

"I suppose I'm in love with the idea of love," I said, focusing back on the happy couple who were still being broadcast to the crowd. "I wonder what a world where only love existed would be like. You know?" I turned my attention to Blake. "No hate, no jealousy, no complications; just pure, undiluted love."

Blake squeezed my hand gently before leaning towards me once more. "Do you know that you've actually just described the world that I am currently living in?" he said quietly.

Smiling shyly at him, I shook my head. "How do you always know the right things to say to me?"

Blake shrugged casually. "I suppose it's all part of my plan to fix you."

The crowd erupted with cheers as the players made their way back onto the field.

"Do you want to go?" Blake asked.

"No." I shook my head. "What's a real Yankees experience if you're going to drag me away before the game finishes?" Blake's smile mirrored mine before we both turned our attention back to the field "Go Yankees!" I yelled.

The Yankees won, and everyone left the stadium on a high. Blake had made sure I got the full experience, and I had enjoyed it immensely. I found myself smiling happily to myself as we drove back to Blake's apartment.

"You haven't stopped smiling since we left the stadium," Blake said.

"I feel happy," I said simply before letting my smile drop. "I know that means there's a good chance that I'm gonna be experiencing some kind of pain soon, though, I suppose."

"Hey, stop that," Blake said quietly as he reached over and placed his hand on my knee. "Nothing is going to happen because you have had a good night, okay?"

I didn't reply. Instead I just tried to focus my mind on keeping that happy feeling that I was beginning to become so accustomed to.

Blake was talking on the phone when I emerged from the bathroom. I too had decided I could give Blake a Yankees experience to finish the night off. I had stripped down to nothing and was wearing only the Yankees jacket that Blake had made me wear and matched it with a pair of four-inch stilettos. I stepped into the lounge and leaned myself against the doorjamb, smiling at Blake as he took in my appearance.

"I'll let you know," I heard him say, his eyes not leaving my body, "but Jo starts filming next week, and I'm flying out to Miami on Monday morning, so the timings a bit off."

"I can't believe I forgot it's Dad's sixtieth," he muttered as I pushed myself from the doorway and headed over to him. Climbing onto his lap slowly, I placed my legs on either side of his. As I lowered myself onto him, I could tell he was trying desperately not to yell out from the pleasure as I rubbed my bare skin against his growing erection under the thin material of his trousers while licking every inch of the bare skin around his neck.

"Please ask Jo," I heard his mum say. "We so desperately want to meet her; we can't wait another three weeks for you to bring her here, and I'm sure she would love a break this weekend before both of your busy schedules."

I looked up at Blake and mouthed to him "This weekend?"

He nodded apologetically.

"I'll let you know," he said, looking at me for my answer.

Thinking about it for a moment, I realized that this weekend would be our last one together for a good few weeks. Blake was flying out Monday morning, and I would be heading straight for rehearsals; we then wouldn't see each other for two weeks. But then I remembered hearing Blake say it was his dad's sixtieth birthday; I felt we really shouldn't miss that. I also really wanted to meet Blake's parents, and if things really were going to go well for us both, I needed to know his family too. Blake's mum was also right, we probably both could do with a break before our busy schedules interrupted our lives.

I nodded to him and whispered, "Say yes."

"Yes?" Blake mouthed back.

"Yes."

"You sure?" he whispered as I nodded.

"Well, it looks like we will be seeing you this weekend then, Mom; Jo is nodding for me to say yes," he said, sounding slightly disappointed.

I heard his mum squeal with delight, and then she shouted to Marti to get Blake's bedroom ready for us. That made me smile.

Blake said goodbye and hung up the phone. "So you would rather spend our last weekend together for a while with my parents instead of just me, huh?" Blake flung his phone to the table and wrapped his arms around me under the jacket, his fingers brushing my skin lightly, sending goose bumps all over my skin.

"You shouldn't miss your dad's sixtieth," I said honestly.

"You're right," he said, disappointed. "Talk about timing, though."

"Isn't it you that always says we have forever, though?" I reminded him.

"We do have forever; you're right." He smiled back. "Now tell me what I can do for you, coming over here all legs and heels in your new favourite jacket," he said as his fingers gently squeezed my waist.

"I think you know what you can do for me." I smiled as I leaned forward and took his mouth in mine. My phone started to vibrate on the coffee table, but both Blake and I chose to ignore it while we were too wrapped up in each other to care. As soon as the phone rang off, however, it started again immediately.

Blake let out a low growl. "It must be important."

Sighing, I lifted myself from Blake's lap and picked up my phone from the table. It was Cooper. I was immediately filled with dread; I hadn't yet told Blake that he had been back in touch with me since that night at Sugar.

"It's Cooper," I said quietly as the phone cut off. I lifted my eyes to Blake, who was eying me with suspicion.

"Why would Cooper be calling you?" he said as he stood and took my phone from my hand.

"He's called me a few times, but I haven't spoken to him since the day I was going to go back to London, I swear," I said nervously.

Blake's eyes lifted to mine. "You spoke to him the day you were planning on going back to London? After what he almost did to you! God, Jo, no! Why would you allow him to speak to you after what he did!" I had never heard Blake raise his voice, but I knew it wasn't me he was angry with, it was Cooper. "He tried to rape you, God damn it! He would have raped you if I hadn't have turned up!"

"He feels awful about it all," I said quickly. "He didn't know what he had given me until I ended up in hospital; he's really sorry, Blake, about everything. I could tell that he meant it when he apologized."

The phone began to ring for the third time, I held my hand out to take my phone, but Blake turned away and put the phone to his ear. He didn't speak at first; I could vaguely hear Cooper saying my name.

"This isn't Jo," Blake said angrily as he turned back to face me. "Now listen to me, you sick son of a bitch, you may have somehow convinced Jo that you never intended to hurt her, but I know different; I saw the whole thing, and I know exactly what you intended to do to her. When you stepped back and started unbuckling your belt, there was only one thing you were thinking about. You would have raped her if I hadn't stopped you, and you would have killed her too! Don't you ever, *ever* call or contact her again, because if you do, I will not stop at breaking your fucking nose next time; I will break every last bone in that worthless body of yours. Do you hear me!" Blake slung my phone onto the chair and stormed into the kitchen, where he took a glass from the cupboard and filled it with whiskey before knocking it back. "You should have told me he was bothering you," Blake said without turning to face me.

"He wasn't bothering me,"

"Why are you defending him!" The sound of Blake's glass hitting the unit startled me.

"I'm not defending him, I swear," I choked out as Blake turned to face me.

"You feel guilty about Imogen, about Sara even, so you want to defend him."

"No," I said, shaking my head.

"You feel guilty that Sara is in rehab and Imogen is dead, so you're defending Cooper to keep him from prison because if he ended up in prison, you would then feel guilt for him too, when the truth is not a single one of those three are victims; it's you. *You* are the only victim in all of this, but you would rather keep someone from prison than admit it!"

"I led him on, Blake; I had been leading him on when we were dancing."

"You didn't deserve to almost die because you danced with someone." Blake grabbed his hair in both his hands. "God, Jo, when will you ever see that nothing that ever happens to you is your fault!"

We stood in silence for a long moment. "I need to go," I said quietly before turning and walking into the bedroom. Blake was right behind me as I took off my jacket and replaced it with a T-shirt.

"I'm sorry," he said desperately.

"You haven't done anything wrong," I said as I pulled up my trousers. "Don't you see, Blake? I'm not destined to ever be happy, am I? Just five minutes ago I was happy; now look at us *again!* And yet again, it is all my fault! "

"Don't leave." Blake took my arm as I headed past him. "You're going to run again; please, Jo, no more running."

"Blake, I am going to end up making you miserable. I'm already making you miserable."

"You never make me miserable, Jo. Sometimes you make me sad, but that's because you are sad too; you never cause it. I know why you think you should defend people who hurt you, I do, but it's you that needs defending, no one else. It's you that's broken; nobody else. I promised you I would fix you, and I meant it. Please, don't leave; don't you run from me again, Jo, please."

"I just want to be happy," I said as my eyes filled with tears. Blake wrapped me in his arms and held me against him. "I'm sorry Blake, I am so sorry." I whispered against his chest.

"No, I'm sorry," Blake murmured into my hair. "I'm sorry I shouted, I'm sorry I scared you, I'm sorry for everything. Going to my parents' will do you good. We can have a whole weekend of rest – no one bothering us, no one making you unhappy. Okay?"

I nodded against Blake's chest. "I'm going to miss you so much when you go away."

"I wish I didn't have to go," he said quietly. "I'm going to worry about you every minute of every day until I'm home."

"I'll be fine," I said unconvincingly, knowing that it was going to be a massive struggle without Blake to lean on. I decided in that moment, however, that it was time for me to toughen up; time I started to stand up for myself. I would begin that while Blake was away. There would be no more hiding away and no more being walked all over. Maybe Blake was right; maybe all the pain I constantly endured wasn't my fault after all.

14

Casey and I had arranged a day of shopping and spa treatments before my looming trip to meet Blake's parents. We were meeting for lunch at our favourite bistro before our shopping trip.

I hadn't seen Casey since the night Christina confessed all about her and Blake. Alex had arrived home the next day, so while Casey spent every waking hour possible with him, I hadn't moved from Blake's apartment. While he was home, we sat in our bubble; and while he was working, I spent my days mastering his three ovens and cooking for him. It was bliss. It was how I imagined my life being if I could ever be truly happy. It was everything that I wanted. But today I would head out, back into reality, back into where pain existed.

The past few days with Blake had been amazing; I had come to realize just how lucky I was having him in my life. He understood me, knew what made me happy and what made me sad, and he always knew exactly what to do to fix that, to fix me.

Walking along the busy streets of New York, I smiled happily to myself that finally my life was beginning to feel complete.

"Jo!" I heard a familiar voice shout to me. "Jo! Wait!"

I knew that voice, and I knew that it was Cooper. I felt his presence at my side as he caught up with me "Jo," he panted, "wait up."

I purposely didn't stop. I continued to walk with Cooper at my side. "You shouldn't be here, Cooper. If Blake sees you talking to me, he will kill you. You heard him on the phone the other night, and I am not prepared to lose Blake because of you."

"So you can't even talk to me now? Come on, Jo, we're friends."

"Blake can't forget what he saw you doing to me, Cooper; surely you would be the same in his position."

There was a long pause before Cooper spoke again. "I just needed to know that you're okay."

"I'm fine; why wouldn't I be?"

Cooper caught my arm and spun me to face him. "You said we could be friends, Jo; you said things could go back to how they were."

"Cooper, I was going back to London. Things were never going to be exactly the same between us. But I meant it when I told you I forgave you. I can't remember much about that night, but I do know that that wasn't the real you. I don't know what was going on in your head that you even tried it, but all Blake is trying to do is protect me; he's just doing what he feels is right."

"I worry about you," he said genuinely.

"I'm not yours to worry about, Cooper," I replied, "but I'm fine."

"Good." Cooper smiled, but it didn't reach his eyes. "I just ... I just want you to be careful, Jo. I'm happy that you're happy I really mean that, but please, keep your feet on the ground; remember your past."

"What do you know about my past?" I asked, confused.

"Enough to know that you're scared about your future."

I stood in silence, trying to remember ever saying anything to Cooper about my life before New York, but there was nothing; I couldn't remember telling him anything. He could have Googled me, but my dad had made sure that as little information as possible would be available to the public eye.

"When Blake goes away next week, I'll be here for you. If you need anything, you call me. I mean that; I want to be here for you, Jo, as your friend. I will be here for you. Okay?"

"I've got to go," I said quietly. "I'm meeting Casey, and I'm already late." I turned and started walking towards the bistro.

"See you soon, Jo," Cooper called back, but I continued to walk, not turning back to acknowledge him. It was quite possibly the weirdest conversation I had ever had with Cooper. He seemed to know something about my past, and unless I had told him while I was drugged, I had no idea how he could have known. I pushed my encounter with Cooper to the back of my mind as I crossed the last road before arriving at the bistro. Casey was browsing the menu, deep in thought, when I walked in. I headed straight to the waiter. "I need a drink, a large one."

With our day out complete, Casey and I returned to the apartment exhausted and loaded with shopping bags. Casey was most exited that I had added a lot more colour to my dark wardrobe this time instead of my usual black. She said she saw it as a good sign. That it meant I was finally becoming happy and content. That scared me almost as much as it pleased me. I hadn't told Casey about my encounter with Cooper, and I had decided that I wouldn't be telling Blake either. After what happened the other evening, I didn't want another argument with Blake, and I was pretty sure now that Cooper had got the message.

With Blake working late, I packed for our weekend. I had spent so much time at Blake's apartment recently that it felt kind of nice to be back in my own apartment, back to familiarity. I was, however, missing him like crazy, and I couldn't wait for him to pick me up the following morning for our weekend in the Hamptons.

Casey was making supper when I finished packing and headed through to the kitchen to join her.

"Glass of wine?" I asked as I removed the bottle from the fridge and grabbed two glasses.

"Definitely," she said as she filled two bowls with her specialty pasta dish and placed them over on the breakfast bar as we both sat down to eat.

"Well this is nice," Casey said as we sat side by side eating our supper and sipping wine. "Feels like ages ago since we did this."

I smiled. "Yes, it does."

"You know what, Jo? You are glowing," Casey said, beaming at me.

I shook my head with amusement.

"You are!" she squealed. "Positively glowing." She put another forkful of pasta into her mouth as she studied me. "You're having way too much sex," she said, narrowing her eyes as she pointed her fork at me.

"Casey!" I replied in shock before smirking. "We do have lots of sex," I admitted shyly. "I mean a *lot*. Does that ever slow down? At what point do we turn into a couple who only sleep together at weekends?"

Casey let out an almighty howl. "Hell no!" she screamed. "After being with Alex for almost three years" – she leaned towards me – "we're still very much hands-on, if you know what I mean."

I shook my head as I laughed. "You are insane."

"That's why you love me," Casey replied before her face turned serious. "It's so good to finally see you smiling though, Jo."

"I think things are finally looking good enough to be true," I admitted. "I do have these moments, though – moments where I convince myself that everything is going to come crashing down on me." I took a deep breath in. "But the good is definitely outweighing the bad at the moment, and every time I see Blake, he has this ability to wipe away the doubt without even realizing he is doing it."

"Have you spoken to Blake about this? About these moments?"

I nodded. "Oh, he has seen my moments, trust me," I laughed lightly. "I don't know how he puts up with my crazy ass sometimes."

"Did you just say 'crazy ass'?" Casey laughed.

"I think I did," I said, covering my eyes with my hands.

"Girl, you are getting more American and less Mary Poppins by the day," she said, feeling very pleased with herself.

We finished supper and tidied the kitchen before Casey's phone rang. It was Alex, and he was missing her. I could tell that she was disappointed every time she told him we were finishing off a special day together by discussing more wedding plans. It was obvious that deep down she would rather be with Alex. I could tell this because I would have been exactly the same in her position. Blake only had to call, and I would go running.

I had really missed him that day; it was the longest we had spent apart for a while, and I was now counting down the minutes until we would have a whole weekend together.

I eventually managed to convince Casey that I was too tired to stay up and concentrate on wedding plans, and even though I don't think she believed me, within minutes she was ready and out of the door, heading to be with Alex.

With the apartment to myself, I put on some music and ran myself a hot bath. My body felt tired, and I was aching almost everywhere. Every ache that I felt only made me think of Blake; I'm pretty sure that he was responsible for each and every one of them. I smiled at my theory. I climbed out of the bath completely beat and ready for bed. After placing my nightgown on and my hair under a towel, I headed to the kitchen to make myself a cup of tea.

My phone was flashing. Picking it up, I noticed that I had three missed calls from Blake, each less than a minute apart. I felt angry with myself that I had missed his calls and proceeded to call him back. I got voicemail all five times. Realizing he would still be working, I placed my phone in my pocket while I made the tea.

A shuffling noise startled me, drawing my attention straight to the hall. "Casey?" I called out, following the noise. There was no reply, and the front door was closed firmly. My eyes were drawn to the floor, where I noticed an unmarked envelope that had been pushed underneath.

I hesitated a moment before bending down and picking up the letter.

The envelope was plain; there was no writing, no address, no name to determine who the letter was even for – nothing.

My hands began to shake. Even though this letter didn't look like anything, after my brief encounter with Cooper earlier, my fear and insecurities were quickly beginning to resurface. I tore the back from the envelope and opened the letter.

SLUT

Nothing else graced the crisp white paper, just that one disgusting word. The letter had been typed – no handwriting, no sign as to whom it was from or even whom it was for. Was the letter even meant for me? Was it meant for Casey? There was no name or apartment number on the envelope, nothing to suggest that it had even been delivered to the correct address. But something about it had my palms sweating and my heart pounding. Surely it was a mistake. Surely it was nothing, just a letter delivered by mistake to the wrong apartment. I couldn't convince myself, yet I needed to. I knew something was off about seeing Cooper today and then receiving this letter, but nothing at all connected the two. Nothing. I wasn't a slut, that was one thing I knew for sure, and Casey was happy enough with Alex that she wouldn't be messing around with anyone either.

I folded the note and pushed it into the pocket of my nightgown before turning back to the front door and locking it securely, even putting in place the locks that Casey and I never bothered with, keeping me safe from the outside world.

Suddenly I wasn't feeling so brave any more. My need to spend a quiet night alone was quickly becoming a big mistake. I hated to be alone, I hated to be without Blake, and Blake wasn't here. I needed him, but I couldn't tell him why. This was going to be a long, lonely night.

Someone was banging on the door. I opened my eyes and realized I had nodded off to sleep on the sofa. I removed my phone from my pocket and saw that it was only ten p.m.; I must have been more tired than I had imagined. The banging started again, and my heart rate increased dramatically.

"Jo," I heard. "Are you in there?"

Relief flooded me. It was Blake; he was here. Thank God he was here.

Exhaling the breath that I had been holding, I rushed to the front door and unlocked it as quickly as I could. Upon opening the door, I didn't give Blake a chance to speak before I pushed myself into his arms and held him tight. I felt his arms wrap around me, and as if he felt my insecurities, his hold on me tightened, pulling me closer to him.

After a few moments I lifted my head to meet his gaze, trying my hardest to hide my fears. I smiled. "I've missed you."

"I can see that." He smiled, but he was watching me; he knew something wasn't right. "Are you going to let me in, or do you want me to stand out here all night?" he asked.

"Sorry." I breathed out as I released him and stepped back to let him pass.

With Blake in the apartment, I closed the door and again made sure it was firmly locked.

"What are you doing?" I turned around to see Blake standing behind me, arms crossed firmly over his chest, watching me with concern. "You and Casey never use those locks; I wondered why the key didn't work. What's going on?"

"Nothing," I lied as I walked past him and stepped into the kitchen. "Just being on my own for the first time in ages, I kind of freaked myself out; watched one too many episodes of *The Walking Dead*. There were a lot of zombies." I took a bottle of water from the fridge and drank half of the contents.

"I think that's the idea of the show, Jo," he laughed before wrapping his arms around me. "That's why you should come live with me; I could fight off those zombies." His lips grazed my earlobe. Suddenly the fear began to evaporate; I was back in my safe place again.

"And with you going away, who would save me then?" I asked, tilting my head to the side to see him.

"That's a good point that I am going to choose to ignore," he said before frowning. "I don't even want to think about being away from you; today has been hard enough."

I turned in his arms and wrapped them tightly around his neck, smiling slightly. "The perils of being so famous."

"I would give it all up tomorrow if it meant I could spend every single second of every single day in your arms," he said.

I smiled seductively. "You know what talking like that to me does, don't you?"

"I do, yes." He smirked. "Are you all packed for tomorrow?"

"Yes," I answered immediately.

"Are you tired?" he asked.

"No, but I would like to go to bed please," I said seductively.

"That was what I was hoping you were going to say." He nodded, looking pleased with himself as he picked me up and carried me through to my bedroom, where we proceeded to make up for not seeing each other for the previous twelve hours.

With Blake buried deep inside me, it was always so easy to forget the reality of life. It was easy to forget any fear, stress, or worry that I had allowed to creep inside of me right up until Blake had knocked at the door. All of those feelings were now gone and had been replaced by the only thing I felt when Blake was present. Love.

"Hi," Blake whispered as he lay panting above me as we slowly came back down to earth after our third orgasm.

"Hi yourself," I whispered as I reached up and brushed the hair away from his eyes. "Can I ask you something?"

"Of course," he said, placing his lips to the palm of my hand and kissing gently over and over again.

"How long do you think this will last?"

Blake stopped kissing me and looked at me with a concerned expression. "What do you mean?"

"You know, the whole can't keep our hands to ourselves, can't touch each other without it ending with sex over and over again, missing each other when we're only apart for a few hours ... how long do you think that will last?"

Blake looked into my eyes, seeing that fear that I was displaying to him. "I'm gonna go with forever," he said honestly.

"Forever?" I smiled.

He nodded. "Forever."

"So," I said quietly as my fingers trailed circles around his pecs, "your mum and dad are still going through that phase then?"

I failed to hide my own amusement as Blake's face changed. He scrunched his eyes shut and shook his head. "I can't believe you just put that image into my head while I'm lying here still hard as a rock and buried deep inside you," he said in disgust, which only caused me to laugh even more.

"I'm sorry," I said, trying to hide my laughter beneath my hand.

"You have just totally killed the moment," he said in a firm tone laced with amusement, climbing off me. "No more sex for you tonight, lady."

"Where are you going?" I whined.

"I now need a shower to rid me of those thoughts." He shuddered.

I shuffled to the edge of the bed and wrapped my legs around him, pulling him back onto me. "I hope they're quiet when we visit this weekend," I teased.

"No no no! Let me go!" he demanded.

"Mmm, Marti, that's it; harder, faster, ah yes!" I said, continuing to tease him as I held him tight with my legs.

"Fuck me, your legs are strong," he said, struggling against me.

"Aahhh, Marti, I'm gonna … I'm gonna …"

Blake's fingers squeezed my ribs as he started tickling me, knowing how much I hated it. I let my legs flop to the side in an effort to stop him, but he continued his assault.

"Are you done now or do I need to continue?" he panted.

"Yes, yes, I'm done! I'm sorry! Stop, please!" I screamed.

"Promise?" he asked, holding his fingers against my ribs.

Keeping my mouth closed firmly, I nodded. Blake leaned down and kissed me once before jumping off the bed.

I couldn't resist one more tease. "Ah, Julia, yes!"

Blake's body was once again above me, ticking me everywhere he could. "Do you surrender?"

"I do! I'm sorry! Please stop!" I screamed.

Blake's grip on me loosened and his expression softened. "I love you so much."

"I love you too. Forever."

I stood in the kitchen window and watched as our children played happily in the garden. Our two boys were climbing the large trees while our daughter sat with her nanny in the middle of the large lawn, brushing her dolly's hair whilst singing happily.

Blake and My dad were busy fixing the swing that hung from one of the large trees at the bottom of the garden, which he had made for me as a child. The ropes had become frayed and broken off as a result of overuse over the years.

I smiled happily, feeling content that I had finally gotten everything that I had always dreamed of: the perfect house, a loving family around me, and the man that I loved by my side. I feared nothing anymore; no one could ever hurt me again.

Warm hands wrapped around me, cradling my ever-expanding stomach. Baby number four was due to arrive any day now, and everything was perfect.

Leaning back into the warmth, I continued to watch everyone that I loved. Suddenly the sunny sky blackened. Thunder rumbled somewhere in the distance, but no one except me seemed to notice. The image of my dad standing next to the ladder that Blake stood on started to fade as he turned towards the storm and began walking towards it. I snapped my attention to the lawn. My mum was gone too, leaving only our daughter playing and singing to herself, oblivious that she was no longer playing with her nanny but instead was alone. I scanned to the trees; the boys were nowhere to be found. Then my eyes went back to the lawn. My little girl was gone too; only her dolly lay where she had sat only moments before. Then a clatter of lightning lit up the sky before I heard an almighty crash. Snapping my head to the right, I saw Blake lying on the ground, motionless. The ladder that he had been standing high on had given way, sending him crashing to the floor.

I tried to move, but the hands that were wrapped around my waist pulled me back, the grip tightening with force. I fought so hard, shouting out to Blake over and over again. I shouted to him that I was coming, but I couldn't move. A hand against my mouth silenced me. I was screaming, screaming so loudly, but no words would escape. "I did warn you, didn't I?" a voice hissed in my ear. "I told you not to walk away from me. Look at what you have caused, Jo, because you *just* ... *didn't* ... *listen*." The harsh tone of his voice made me shudder. The more he spoke, the harder I tried to escape; the harder I tried to escape, the more he gripped me, pulling me away – far, far away – from Blake and everyone that I loved.

My breathing accelerated. I felt sick in the pit of my stomach. "You are mine now, Jo, all mine; you remember that."

I screamed, but no one could hear me. I called out to my dad to come back, to help me, but he kept on walking; he wouldn't come back. I tried to call out to Blake, but the blood that now surrounded him told me that he wouldn't be coming back to me either.

My body wriggled and squirmed as I continued to scream. I was screaming as loud as I could, yet it felt as though the noise was muted.

"Shh, it's okay. I'm here; it's okay. Jo, stop fighting me; I'm here."

My eyes shot open and my body bolted upright. Sweat was pouring from me, and I couldn't breathe through the panting. It took a moment to realize my surroundings. I was home; I was safe. Blake was next to me, soothing me, calming me. "It was just a dream," he said calmly. "Just a dream, it's okay."

"I think I'm gonna be sick." I shot out of bed quickly and ran to the bathroom. Crouching over the toilet, my body convulsed as I emptied my stomach of its entire contents. I felt Blake's presence as he knelt down next to me and took my hair from my face.

"I'm okay," I panted. "I don't want you to see me like this, Blake. Please, I'm okay."

"I'm not leaving you," he said gently as he held my hair in one hand and dampened a washcloth with the other. Gently he held the washcloth against my already drenched skin and soothed me.

"It's okay," he continued to say over and over to me. "I'm here."

Once my stomach was empty and the heaving stopped, I took the cloth from Blake and stood shakily. Blake took my elbow and guided me to the sink, where I cleaned myself up.

"Did you have a nightmare?" Blake asked carefully. I nodded.

"Do you want to talk about it?"

I shook my head and refused to look up at him although I could see him watching me through the bathroom mirror. I took my toothbrush from the cupboard, squirted it with toothpaste, and started brushing my teeth.

Tears stung my eyes as the nightmare replayed over and over in my mind. Seeing my dad there had felt nice until I realized it was a nightmare. It hurt so much. I had been thinking about my dad a lot recently, about how happy he would be to see me being loved so much by someone whom I could see my future with.

I had wanted to dream about my dad so much since he left us, to know that he was okay and that we were all going to be okay too. I had desperately wanted him to tell me so. Why did he have to be in one dream that I wanted to forget desperately?

I put my toothbrush back into the cup and wiped my mouth clean. Holding the towel against my face, I allowed a small sob to escape – a tiny bit of release from the first nightmare I had experienced since six months after Imogen had been found dead. Blake was at my side instantly, holding me, once more telling me over and over that everything was going to be okay.

"Come back to bed," he said smoothly. "I will hold you; I will make sure that it doesn't happen again."

"No." I shook my head. "I can't face going back to bed yet." I stepped past Blake and walked through to the lounge. I then sat on the sofa, pulling my knees to my chest, gently rocking as the thoughts of the nightmare played over and over in my mind.

Blake returned moments later with pillows and blankets and laid me down, making sure I was as comfortable as I could be. After making sure I was okay, Blake turned on the TV and started scanning the channels. After finding nothing that suited, he then opened the TV unit and began looking through the DVDs. He emerged a couple of moments later holding up his choice. "*Grown Ups*?" he suggested.

I nodded, watching how much he loved caring for me. He didn't deserve any secrets to be kept from him. "Blake?" I said through the tears.

"What is it?" He paused the DVD and sat next to me.

"If I tell you something, will you promise me – and I mean really promise me – that you won't fly off the handle and start shouting?"

"What's happened?" he asked without making any promises.

"I saw Cooper today." I swallowed hard.

"What? Where?"

"I was on my way to meet Casey, and he caught me up in the street."

"Did he touch you, hurt you? What did he do?" Blake asked frantically.

"Nothing," I wept. "He just said he wanted to know that I was okay and to watch my step, whatever that means."

"What!" Blake adjusted in his seat and turned to face me.

"Then, tonight, I found this. It was pushed under the door before you got here." I took the note from my pocket and showed it to Blake.

"'Slut'?" he said, confused. "Well they're obviously not talking about you, are they?"

"Do you think it has something to do with Cooper?"

Blake studied the note intently. "I'm not sure. Were you too afraid to tell me because of the other night?" His eyes lifted from the note to me.

"Yes. I'm sorry. I just … I don't want you to go after him. Not because I want to protect him, because I don't, but I just don't want this, any of it."

Blake sighed. "Come here."

I shuffled over into his arms while he comforted me. "Don't do anything stupid, Blake, okay?"

"I won't." He placed his lips to my head. "Did Cooper in any way threaten you?"

"No," I said quickly. "He was friendly; the letter may just be a coincidence."

"Maybe," he said. "Don't keep anything like this to yourself again, Jo. I know you want to be strong, but I need to know you're safe. That means telling me everything, okay?"

"Okay," I replied.

Blake made us both a cup of tea before we started the DVD, hoping to wipe the nightmare from my mind. I could tell he was thinking about Cooper and the letter, and I hoped that he wouldn't do anything irrational until we knew whether the note was even connected.

Watching him as he sat gently rubbing the soles of my feet, I imagined that my nightmare could one day become reality, losing everyone that I have ever loved and having no one to pick up my pieces when I fall apart. It frightened me so much. Blake had no idea what my nightmare was even about, but he was caring for me, helping me to overcome whatever demons were present at that time. I needed this. I needed him and his balance of calm to tackle my fear. I realized at that moment that not only did I love Blake unconditionally, but that I also really couldn't imagine my life without him in it.

When I woke, the sun was shining through the apartment. I felt much calmer and happier than I had only a few hours before. I had drifted off at some point during the film, while Blake had moved his attention from my feet and legs up to my head and neck. I felt surprisingly refreshed as I stood and went to look for him.

I found him in the kitchen, making breakfast. His back was to me, and he was talking quietly to someone on the phone.

"It's important to me that you do this and you do it right, do you understand?" I heard him say.

I slowly retreated so I could listen to Blake without him knowing that I was there.

"I don't know how you plan on doing it, but you make it as discreet as possible. I need her safe while I'm away, but I do not want you mentioning any of this to her or anything that you are doing for me, do you understand?" Blake said firmly. "I don't want Jo finding out about this until I have to tell her. She's under a lot of stress at the moment, and with me going away on Monday she's pretending that she is going to be fine, but I know her, and I know that underneath she really isn't okay."

I didn't know what he was doing, but I did know that whatever it was, he was doing it to protect me while he wasn't able to.

The floor beneath me creaked, and the noise vibrated through the apartment.

"Look, I gotta go," Blake said quietly. "Send me the details when you have them, okay? And make it quick."

I rounded the corner and stepped into the kitchen as though I hadn't just heard everything that had been said. Blake looked breathtaking, but seeing him standing there making me breakfast only brought back the memories of the nightmare that I had experienced the previous night.

"Good morning, beautiful." Blake placed the hot pan back onto the stove before walking over to me and wrapping me in the warmth of his arms.

"Hi," I managed to say.

"How are you feeling?"

"Okay."

"Do you want me to call my parents and rearrange?"

"No," I said quickly. "No. We need this; I need this. Is that okay?" I snuggled up to him.

"Of course." I felt him smile. "I was gonna make these wraps to go," he said, gesturing to the stove. "I didn't know how you would be feeling about food this morning."

"I feel hungry," I said, surprised by myself. One time I was never hungry was breakfast time.

"You're hungry for breakfast?" Blake asked, shocked. "Sit yourself down, then; I'll plate it up and bring you some tea. I am not gonna miss this opportunity." As he left me, my eyes welled and tears starting streaming down my face. I let out a small sob.

"Hey." Blake was back by my side within seconds, comforting me. "It's okay; it was just a bad dream, that's all. Whatever it was is never going to happen, I promise you," he said, kissing me gently on my head.

"You were dead." I said this so quietly I wasn't sure whether Blake heard me. "It had started off so nice, a really nice dream. We had children; they were playing in the garden. We were happy; everyone was so happy. Even my mum and dad were there. I remember feeling happy, standing there watching everyone feeling so much happiness." I sobbed as my voice rose with the panic. "Then a storm came, a real violent storm, but only I seemed to notice it. Then everyone disappeared, everyone except for me and you, but then you fell. You fell, and you were bleeding, and I couldn't get to you because I was being held back," I cried.

"He wouldn't lose me. He kept on telling me that it was all my fault; that because I ran from him I deserved all of it. I tried to get to you, I really did, but he held me so hard that I couldn't move," I sobbed.

"Shh, it's okay, come on." Blake's smooth voice was barely audible through the loud sobs that just kept on coming. I couldn't stop; nothing Blake said could help me stop.

"I can't live without you, Blake, I can't," I sobbed. "If something happens to you …"

"Hey." Blake placed his fingers under my chin and lifted my face to meet his gaze. "Nothing", he said, "is going to happen to either me or you; how many times do I have to tell you that we are going to grow old together?" A small smile met his lips before he placed his lips to mine, his kiss lingering as my tears slowly subsided and calmness overcame me.

"I love you so much," I said.

"We are going to get through this next two weeks just fine. It's going to be hard on the both of us, but we're gonna be okay," he said firmly.

"Blake?" I asked quietly.

"Hm?" Blake replied as he gently wiped the remaining tears away from my face.

"Can I move in with you when you get back from Miami?"

Relief flooded Blake's face instantly. "There is nothing that I want any more than for you to come live with me; you know that." He smiled before kissing me so hard it took my breath away. "Thank you."

15

The drive to Blake's parents took just under two and a half hours.

As soon as the madness of New York was behind us, I finally felt myself begin to relax.

It had been only three weeks since Blake had stopped me from getting on the plane to London, and in that three weeks I had felt my life change considerably. I was happy that Blake had turned up, and when I thought about it now, had I got on that plane, my life would be so different now; different and miserable and worthless. In two weeks I was going to be moving in with Blake, and we would be starting a new life together. I had everything to look forward to, and with Blake by my side, I was finally beginning to believe that I could be happy without the pain.

"You're quiet over there," Blake said as we entered the small village that was home to Blake's parents.

"Just thinking." I smiled as I turned to face him.

"You nervous?" he asked.

"A little," I admitted. "I'm just glad to be out of New York. I feel relaxed already."

"Good," he said, reaching over and squeezing my knee. "This is it." Blake nodded to the house as we approached from the long driveway.

"It's beautiful," I said in awe. It reminded me a lot of the house that I had grown up in. It was very traditional and oozed family and love, and that was just what I could see from the outside. The garden at the front was surrounded by majestic white pines and every seasonal flower that was imaginable; I imagined that Blake's parents would spend a lot of time out here keeping it just perfect.

Julia and Marti were standing at the doorway waiting for us as we climbed out of Blake's Range Rover.

"Here they are," Julia said with a huge smile as she walked down the steps to greet us. Bypassing Blake, she headed straight for me and wrapped me into her arms tightly. "It's so good to finally meet you, Jo," she said, releasing me and holding me at arm's length. "We've heard so much about you."

"It's lovely to meet you too, MRS Mackenzie."

"Please," she said, "you call me Julia. I can't be doing with being called missus; makes me feel old." She winked.

"Okay." I nodded nervously. "It's nice to meet you, Julia."

"And this is Marti," she said, gesturing to Blake's dad. "Isn't she beautiful, Marti?" Julia grinned.

"Stunning," he said in his gravelly voice. "Good to meet ya." He took my hand before pulling me in for a bear hug.

Marti was exactly how I imagined Blake would look in thirty years. He had aged well, and he still looked like he kept in shape. His hair was glossy and silver, which made his blue eyes shine out just as Blake's always did.

Julia was very glamorous; her blonde hair sat in an immaculate bob, and she wore her make-up subtly. Her clothes were modern, and I could see that she spent a lot of time looking after her appearance. Her eyes were a deep brown, and they were big, just like Blake's. I could also see that he had inherited his dazzling smile from his mum.

"Okay, Dad, don't suffocate the guest," Blake teased.

"Protective of the girlfriend," Marti said, releasing me, "I like that." He winked.

"Let's get you both inside," Julia said excitedly. "Follow me, Jo." She started walking, and I followed quickly behind. "Marti, help Blake with the bags," she yelled back as she led me up the steps and into the house.

"Yes, boss," Marti teased, giving Julia a small salute as he headed to the boot with Blake to retrieve our bags.

I loved them both already; they were exactly as I had imagined, and I could tell that we were going to get along just fine. I could see why Blake was such a loving, caring person; it oozed from every single pore on Julia and Marti's bodies.

Julia and I entered the large foyer first; I took a moment to take in my surroundings. The staircase sat in the middle of the room with the first floor visible above us. It was like something out of a film; it was breathtaking. The floors were solid oak and very well looked after. The walls were filled with hundreds of photos and portraits of each family member, as well as people I was yet to meet but were obviously related to Blake, as they all had that same look – piercing blue eyes and a jawline to die for.

"I have a pot roast cooking for dinner." Julia smiled, but her smile turned to a frown as she realized something. "You're not a vegetarian, are you, dear?" she asked in horror.

I smiled. "No. I'm not a vegetarian, and pot roast sounds perfect."

"Jo actually cooked us one a few weeks back," Blake teased as he entered the house carrying the bags with Marti close behind, "didn't you, Jo?" He set the bags down and placed his arm around me, kissing my cheek.

"Lets' just say I had a go." I smiled as I turned my head and threw Blake a death stare.

"Well that's a relief," she sighed with a smile. "I never even thought to ask whether or not you eat meat," she said, shaking her head at herself. "Now," she said, smiling again, "why don't you both go get freshened up, and then we can enjoy a drink out in the sunshine before dinner is ready, and we can really get to know this lovely young lady."

Blake's bedroom wasn't anything that I had imagined it to be. There were no sports posters or topless women gracing the walls, just bumper-to-bumper film posters – horror films, thrillers, and action films filled every inch, along with a life-size cardboard cut-out of Arnold Schwarzenegger as the Terminator which sat in the corner of the room.

"So you always knew you wouldn't follow your dad's footsteps then," I said, nodding to the walls as Blake placed our bags down onto the bed and sat next to them.

Blake laughed as he recalled. "I was hopeless at baseball – all sports, in fact. My dad was horrified when I told him I wanted to go to drama school." He shook his head, amused. "He sat me down one day not long after and actually asked me if I was gay."

I couldn't help the laughter that erupted from me. "You couldn't be any less gay," I admitted.

"I know, right?" He laughed. "He knew I was hopeless at sports, but once he knew what I wanted to do, he made it his mission to train me. I was a hopeless cause, yet he would have me out in that yard every second of every day teaching me, but I just couldn't hit a ball. Catch? No problem. But hitting the damn thing – I just couldn't do it. Finally he gave up, so I got my way and started studying drama. That's where I met Marcus. He was as driven as me, really wanted to be a successful actor. We spent a lot of time together, became really close friends. Then, when I told him who my father was, he would ask me every weekend if he could come home with me and meet the legend that was Marti Mackenzie. You know where this is going, right?"

"Marcus is gay," I stated, shaking my head.

"I couldn't help myself," he said, amused. "I brought Marcus here to meet Mom and Dad. You should have seen Dad's face."

"That's cruel," I said, shaking my head.

"Obviously, Marcus being as gay as he is, it was too easy to resist," Blake said defensively.

"Poor Marcus." I shook my head but couldn't help being amused as I started unloading the bags. "And your poor dad, too."

"Yeah well, it taught him a lesson," he laughed.

I started to unpack the bags as Blake sat and watched every move I made.

"You doing okay?" Blake asked.

I nodded. "Yes."

"Sure?"

"I'm fine. Now get up and start helping me with these things."

"In a minute," he said huskily. "Come here." He tugged at my arm, and my body fell on top of his. "Blake, no," I said, trying to release myself from his grip. "Your parents could walk in at any moment," I scolded.

"Don't you want me now we're here?" he teased.

"I do, yes," I said, kissing the corner of his mouth. "Just not right now; we've only just got here," I said, still trying to release myself from his grip. "And if one of your parents were to walk in right now, you would be putting these bags back into the car and taking me back to New York," I said firmly.

"I love it when you get angry," Blake teased as I continued to squirm.

"You will see angry if you don't let me go," I said before he leaned up and took my mouth in his. His hand worked its way up my T-shirt and under my bra. He took my breast and started squeezing and rubbing.

"Blake," I gasped against his mouth, wanting so much for him to do it but feeling how wrong it was at the same time, "we shouldn't; someone could walk in."

But he continued, and I made no attempt to stop him. Lifting my skirt to my waist he pressed his thigh between my legs and started to rub, slowly relieving some of the pressure that I could feel building. Needing more from him, I started rubbing against the pressure. It felt so good. His denim rubbing roughly against the thin material of my knickers was hot; it would take only seconds before I would come all over him.

"Can I come in?" A gentle tap at the door was like a bucket of ice-cold water being poured over us both. Blake released me quickly as we both jumped off the bed frantically. My clothes were a mess, and I could feel how flushed my skin had become from my arousal. I pushed my skirt down quickly and grabbed my toiletries bag before rushing into the en-suite bathroom while Blake attempted to look as though he were taking clothes out of the bag while hiding the obvious erection that was pressing against his jeans.

"Your father is useless," I heard Julia say as she walked into the room. "I gave him one job, just one job, and he couldn't even do that," she muttered.

I re-entered the room and tried my hardest to look as though I hadn't just almost come while Blake and I dry humped on his teenage bed.

"Here are some fresh towels for you both," Julia said. "Sorry they weren't in here when you arrived. Men."

"That's no problem at all." I took the towels from Julia. "Thank you."

"I'll let you two carry on doing what you're doing." I heard Blake cough as laughter erupted from him. "Don't be too long, though." She winked before heading out of the room.

I exhaled the huge breath that I had been holding the whole time while Blake laughed.

"Wow," Blake breathed out. "I was about two minutes away from having to pack these bags back into the car and take you back to New York." He laughed as he flopped down onto the bed.

"And that is why it won't be happening again," I replied. "It's not funny."

"It was kind of funny," Blake said casually.

"Your mum walking into this room and finding me dry humping her son two minutes after we met is not my idea of fun."

"Come on, she didn't see anything. You have got to see the funny side," he laughed.

"I most certainly do not see the funny side," I said feeling frustrated.

"You are so British." He shook his head in amusement.

"And you're an arse," I replied.

"Someone's feeling frustrated," he said as he lay back, placed his hands behind his head, and studied me. "Need me to sort something out for you?"

I threw the dress I was holding at him and walked off to freshen up. The truth was, I was feeling frustrated, and yes, I really wanted Blake to sort it out for me, but Blake's mum walking in and catching us was enough to drown my libido for now.

I stood at Blake's window looking out to the huge garden beneath me while Blake sang to himself in the bathroom after finally giving up trying to seduce me and agreeing to get ready for dinner.

I loved Blake's parents' house and adored the garden even more. There was a large kidney-shaped swimming pool with sun loungers and sun umbrellas, with a volleyball net in the middle. To the right of the pool was a full-size tennis court that made Centre Court at Wimbledon look amateurish.

Before the pool and tennis court was a large pristine lawn and a decking area which I imagined was great for entertaining, judging by the size of the gas barbecue that was also present.

This was what I wanted: a home that oozed family and love, somewhere private that we could bring up our children in peace.

Shaking my head, I smiled at myself for allowing those thoughts to enter my mind.

So far I was still adamant that with happiness there came a price, Blake was still trying to prove my theory wrong, but as yet I was right; and I always would be, as far as I was concerned. Maybe dreaming of that future was a nice option, but at what cost would it come?

Blake's phone began to vibrate on the bedside table. I left the window and headed over to answer it but stalled when I saw that it was Christina.

Why was Christina calling Blake? What could she possibly have to say to Blake that would be of interest? The phone stopped vibrating but started again immediately.

"Christina," I said casually, "what can we do for you?"

I heard Christina gasp with shock at the sound of my voice. "Jo, hi, how are you?"

"Fine. What can I do for you?" I said in a clipped tone.

"Is Blake there? I need to speak to him."

"He's kind of indisposed at the moment. I'm sure I can help you."

"Can you ask him to call me, please?"

"Is Alex ok?"

"Of course, why?"

"I'm just trying to work out why it's so important for you to speak to Blake while were away, that's all."

"I just …. Please, could you just ask him to call me? It's important that I speak with him."

"Sure," I sighed.

"Oh, and Jo? About that night and everything I told you … I—"

"Forget it," I said, cutting her off. "I have."

"Well, I am sorry, and I hope that it didn't cause any bad feelings between the two of you."

"Goodbye, Christina," I said before hanging up the phone and placing it back on the bedside table.

Blake emerged from the bathroom and placed his phone into his pocket. "Ready?"

Deciding not to tell him at that moment that Christina had called, and not wanting yet another argument about why she was even calling Blake, I nodded and followed him out of the bedroom and down to the kitchen, where Julia and Marti were preparing dinner.

"Well, you two took your time," Marti said dryly. "We will have drinks outside later. Dinner is almost ready." He smiled. "Sit yourselves down," he said, gesturing to the well-laid-out table.

"Marti, get Jo a glass of wine, will you darling."

Rolling his eyes, Marti placed the pot roast in the centre of the table and headed to the fridge, from which he pulled a bottle of crisp white wine.

"One thing I can tell you about the Mackenzie men, Jo, is that you need to keep them on a tight leash," she teased before thanking Marti for his help with a kiss on his cheek.

"I'm beginning to realize that," I said in a low tone, unsure if anyone had heard me.

Blake's smile faded as his eyebrows knitted together in confusion.

I threw him a quick smile before picking up my glass and taking a large needed gulp of wine. I was wishing now that I had told him about the call. Since leaving the bedroom only a few moments ago, I had allowed myself to imagine all sorts of scenarios. Why would she need to talk to Blake all of a sudden? Was there something going on that I knew nothing about? But surely Blake wouldn't lie to me? Keep anything from me? *He loves me ... I know he loves me ... I'm pretty sure that he loves me.*

During dinner my stomach continued to knot up at the thought of Blake and Christina. I had allowed the sordid thoughts back into my head, and the longer I sat there, the more and more I convinced myself that something must be going on between them.

"You're not eating much," Blake said as he leaned in to whisper against my ear.

"I'm not very hungry," I replied quietly as I looked down at the food I was pushing around my plate.

"Do you still feel ill?"

"No."

"Then what?"

"Nothing," I replied firmly.

"What are you two lovebirds whispering about over there?" Marti asked.

"Nothing for you to worry about, Dad." Blake smiled and got back to eating his dinner. His eyes turned to me every now and then, but I didn't return the glances.

"If something is bothering you, then tell me, please," he said, leaning into me once more.

"I'm fine," I lied.

I stiffened when Blake's hand touched my knee, but he didn't move it away; instead he kept on watching me, his eyes burning into me. I had got myself into a complete state over one stupid call that was probably innocent.

"So Jo, I can't believe you're gonna be in *Perfect Alibi*; that's fantastic. I don't know if Blake's told you, but that is my all-time favourite sitcom," Marti said excitedly.

"No," I said, looking up to Marti and trying my best to look happy, "Blake hasn't told me that; must have slipped his mind." I threw Blake a quick look before turning my attention back to Marti.

"You should both come along on Friday; both Fridays, in fact. I'll speak to Marcus about getting you in to watch us record if you like?" I said enthusiastically.

"Well, I would love that," he replied excitedly. "She is definitely my favourite," he said to Julia as he pointed his fork in my direction before winking at me.

"Marti!" Julia said as she tapped his arm playfully. "What he meant to say, dear," she said, turning her attention to me, "is thank you."

"Yeah, thank you, Jo; I'm looking forward to it already."

"No problem." I smiled as I felt Blake squeeze my knee gently with appreciation.

"I've got to ask," Marti said before wiping his mouth with his napkin. "Your mother" – he placed his elbows on the table as he studied me – "is she *the* Diana Summers, the one who was in one of the Carry On movies?"

I nodded and smiled as I swallowed the small bite of food I had managed to eat. "She was in three."

"Well I'll be damned," Marti said, sitting back in his seat. "I knew I could see a resemblance. I love those movies."

"Marti won't admit it in front of you, dear, but when those films came to the cinemas; he had a massive crush on your mother."

My eyes widened in surprise.

"She was a real beauty," he said in defence. "An English rose" – he smiled – "just like our girl Jo, here."

"Thank you," I replied shyly.

"Okay, that's enough embarrassing the guest," Blake said.

"I'm not embarrassed," I said, turning to face him. "It's a compliment. You saw it as a compliment when I was called an English rose on national TV, so why not from your dad?"

Blake eyed me suspiciously for a moment before replying, "I do." He forced a smile. "I just know that you get embarrassed sometimes; my apologies." He focused back on his dinner, and conversation began again.

"Is that your phone I can hear, Blake?" the vibrating had started again, and my heart rate picked up once more.

Blake reached into his pocket and checked the screen before putting it back into his pocket.

"Who is it?" I asked calmly.

"Just Alex; I'll call him back after dinner."

Like the previous time the phone had rang, it started vibrating again straight after it had cut off. "He's obviously calling you for a reason," I said. "Answer it."

"We're in the middle of dinner," he said, moving his eyes between the three of us at the table. "I'll call him later."

I sat looking at Blake knowing that, one, that wasn't Alex calling, it was Christina; and two, he had been lying to me when we had agreed to no more lies and no more secrets.

Blake and I barley spoke for the rest of the meal. Julia went on to tell us the plans for the following day, which was Marti's birthday. It was forecast to be a red-hot day, so it was decided that we would spend the most part at the beach, where we would meet up with Blake's sister Jasmine again along with her husband Robert and little Fraser. Then it would be back here for one of Marti's famous barbecues in the evening. It all sounded lovely, and I tried to feel enthusiastic about it; I just needed to know first what the hell was going on between Blake and Christina.

We were just finishing dessert when Blake's phone started vibrating again. "I'm gonna have to take it this time," he sighed before standing and leaving the table. He headed out through the patio doors onto the decking area. He was just out of reach for me to hear the call, so excusing myself, I headed upstairs. I had been standing at the open window just a couple of hours ago, and it was directly above where Blake was now standing.

"What part of 'Don't call me over the weekend' was so hard to understand?" I heard him say. "Jo is already suspicious; she's been acting weird during dinner and is going to start asking questions if I have to keep lying to her. She knows that something is going on." My breathing quickened, and a sick feeling filled my body. "Tell her not to call me again, okay? I will call her on Monday when I have left for the airport."

My mind went into overdrive. Why would he need to call her Monday on his way to the airport? What exactly was going on between them that he couldn't tell me about? There was only one explanation: he obviously still had something going with her that he just couldn't seem to let go of.

Nothing made sense: how much he claimed to love me, how he couldn't go on without me, how much he needed to protect me and prove to me that you can be happy without paying a price. Here he was having secret phone calls with the woman who took his virginity and, according to her, taught him everything he knew, the woman that I couldn't bear to be around anymore since the night that she took my happiness and ripped it from me.

I couldn't bear to hear any more. I would see the night out for Julia and Marti's sake, and then I would confront Blake before I got on a bus or whatever I could manage and went home. I was sick of fighting for happiness, sick of constantly trying to trust someone only to get burnt over and over again, sick of trying to make myself feel happy when inside. I was dying a slow and painful death.

I could hear no more. I turned and headed back downstairs just as Blake re-entered the kitchen. His eyes met mine, and he could see that something was wrong. I refused to cry. I'd cried too many tears as it was lately; I couldn't do it anymore, so I took a deep breath, plastered on a smile that physically hurt, and walked to the table to help Marti and Julia to clear away.

Blake's body pressed against my back as I reached for the glasses on the table. "Something is wrong, and you are going to tell me what it is," he said into my ear. Slipping away from him, I carried the glasses to the kitchen, where Julia was loading the dishwasher. Blake followed closely behind.

"Ah, Blake, now you're back, you and your father can continue to clear away while I spend some quality time with your lovely girl. It's time us girls got to know each other, don't you agree?" she asked with a smile.

I felt relieved at Julia's offer; getting away from Blake right now was just what I needed. "Definitely," I replied.

"Come on, I've got some lovely albums of Blake to show you." She winked, and I forced a smile before following her out of the kitchen and through to the sitting room.

I felt Blake's eyes watching me as we left the room. Was he really so clueless that he had no idea what was wrong with me?

Julia and I had been gone for just ten minutes when Blake appeared in the lounge, concern still etched on his face. Refusing to show any emotion in front of Julia, I kept my eyes firmly on the photo album that she had placed into my lap, which was filled with photos of Blake as a baby – a beautiful baby, in fact. For a moment I allowed my mind to wonder whether our babies would look as beautiful as he did as a baby. That obviously would never happen now I knew he was lying to me about the woman I had now decided that I hated.

Julia didn't give him a chance to sit down, however; she ordered him and Marti to "go watch some sport or whatever you men enjoy doing."

I could tell he tried desperately to get my eyes to meet his before he left the room, but I wasn't going to give him anything, not in front of his parents.

"I've never seen him so happy as he is now, dear," Julia said before polishing off her glass of wine and refilling it. "I hope you don't mind" – she paused before resting back down on the sofa – "but Blake told me what happened to you," she said sympathetically.

"Oh," I replied.

"Blake will look after you now," she said, patting my thigh as I continued to look at the photos. "He is very protective over you."

"Do you think I can trust him?" I asked suddenly.

"What do you mean?" she asked defensively.

"I just find it so hard to believe I can finally be happy, you know?" I asked as I closed the book and turned to face Julia. "He's beautiful, inside and out, and even now I find it hard to believe that we can be happy and have a future. How do I know that he will never do the same to me that Michael did?"

Julia smiled, not knowing the right words to say.

"I suppose you just have to trust him," she said simply.

"Have you always trusted Marti?"

She thought for a moment before replying, "Not always, no." She turned to face me. "When he was at his peak in the game, he wasn't just a sport star; he was quickly turning into a global superstar."

I nodded. I had been there with Michael.

"He thought he was God." She snorted. "And like you, our lives were put under the microscope a lot. I couldn't trust that he wasn't up to no good when he was away from me. There would be pictures of him and his team players out in clubs, and even though there was nothing sinister about the pictures, I often wondered whether that was the life he would prefer. The children were only young; I felt like a mess. I even had to stop working at the hospital, and I loved that job so much; but because people knew who I was, it was impossible to lead a normal life. He was living his dream, and even though I had everything I'd always dreamed of, I always felt like I was put on the back burner while he swanned around like the God he thought he was. That's partly why we brought this house. It was our escape, a place that we could just be Julia and Marti, not what the press wanted us to be. In a way I think it saved us." Her voice had become very quiet as she remembered the good that came from the bad. I felt my eyes fill up with sadness for her, as it was as though she were describing my life, only twenty years before.

"Look at me getting all sentimental." She wiped her own tears and took a deep breath. "Let's blame the wine," she laughed sadly.

"I feel like you just described me," I said.

"Blake will never hurt you," she said reassuringly. "That much I can promise you." She smiled, and I so wanted to believe her.

"Do you mind if I go to bed?" I asked. "I'm exhausted."

"Of course, dear. I'm sorry; I can talk for the US."

"No," I said quickly. "It's been lovely to sit and get to know you; it really has." I placed a quick kiss on Julia's cheek before standing. "I'll see you in the morning."

"See you tomorrow, dear," Julia replied.

I couldn't see Blake as I bypassed the kitchen, but I could hear him and Marti discussing their plans for the following day. I hurried past quietly and headed upstairs to the bedroom.

I heard Blake enter the bedroom while I was brushing my teeth. My stomach knotted with anticipation.

"Here you are," he said as he stood in the doorway to the en-suite. "Why didn't you say you were coming to bed?" he asked carefully.

I shrugged as I spat out the toothpaste and wiped my mouth. "I didn't know I needed your permission." I walked past him and back into the bedroom, where I started to undress.

"Am I missing something here, because I'll be damned if I have a single idea of what the hell has happened in the last couple of hours to change your mood to this," he said defensively.

"What did Alex want?" I spat out as I slipped my nightgown on and walked over to the bedside table to remove my jewelry

"When?" he said, confused.

"Alex," I said strongly as I caught his gaze in the mirror, "he called you tonight, remember? What did he want?"

"Oh," he mumbled, "nothing particular." He shrugged.

"Well, for someone who wanted nothing, he was very persistent," I snapped.

"You know what Alex is like," he said, laughing once.

"I do, yes," I said, turning to face him, "and I also know what Christina is like. So why has she been calling you?"

"I was talking to Alex."

My heart rate increased, and anger began boiling to the surface. "Why are you lying to me?" I asked quietly.

"Jo, I'm not lying to you; why would I lie to you? Give me one reason why I would ever need to lie to you?"

"Because I know that you are lying to me now!" My voice rose, but I was careful not to let Julia and Marti hear us arguing. "I'm going to ask you one last time; you either tell me the truth, or I walk out of her right now and out of your life for good," I choked out. "I am sick and tired of being someone's go-to, Blake – someone to go to when you need some comfort and stability away from the cameras and the media, when you feel like you need some normality in your life, something to make you look good, raise your profile some. I've been there before, Blake; you know that. You know the fear that I have held on to since then. I don't want to believe it; God, I really do not want to believe it … but is that really what happened the night you stepped foot into the airport? Because at the time, I really didn't think so; but now …" I shrugged as I tried to swallow back the emotion that was building. "Now you are standing here lying to me about the one woman I can't bear to think of you being with.

"I've had enough of being treated like a fool, Blake," I said with pure emotion. "I've had enough." I sighed as I walked over to the wardrobe and took my case, throwing it onto the bed. I grabbed anything I could see that belonged to me and started throwing it into the case. Blake appeared quickly and placed his hands firmly on my arms, preventing me from carrying on with what I was doing.

"The call that I got during dinner was from Alex," he said firmly. "I swear."

I looked into his eyes deeply; I wanted to believe him so much, but my heart was preventing me from seeing any truth when my head was seeing only lies.

"When you were in the bathroom before dinner, Christina rang you. I took the call."

"Why didn't you say something?" Blake sighed.

"What like? 'By the way, Blake, the woman you are sleeping with behind my back called you earlier; be sure to return the call!'"

"You think I'm sleeping with Christina behind your back? How could you ever even think that?" His eyes roamed my face, his breathing heavy. "I love you, Jo; I love you so much, and all I am trying to do is protect you."

"Protect me from finding out?" I replied angrily.

"No," he said quietly. "To protect you when I know that I will be too far away from you to be there if you need me."

Nothing Blake was saying was making sense. I pushed out of his hold and headed back to the bed, placing more items into my case.

"Alex called me during dinner because I hadn't answered any of Christina's calls," he said, standing behind me.

"That's nice of him. Remind me to thank him when I see him next."

"Jo," Blake exhaled, "Christina runs a very successful, highly reputable security firm in New York."

"Good for her," I replied sarcastically.

"I have employed her to watch over you while I'm away," he said carefully. "That's why she has been calling me – no other reason than to look after you when I know that I can't."

Slamming my case shut, I turned my head to face Blake. "You employed your ex-girlfriend to look after me while you're away?" I asked, shocked.

"I am not sleeping with her, or anyone else for that matter," he said. "I just needed to know that you were gonna be safe while I was away, because no matter what you believe, Jo, I do love you. I love you so much that it scares the life out of me to think that I'm not going to be around to protect you for the next two weeks."

"So you employed Christina?" I asked, unable to hide the shock. "You employed your ex-fuck of three years to look after me?"

"I'm not sleeping with her, Jo; isn't that what the problem was? You thought I was sleeping with her behind your back?" He sounded as confused as I felt.

"Oh, that was the problem, yes," I said, shaking my head in disbelief. "That was a big problem! But here's a new one!" I said. "You employed Christina to look after me? To keep me safe? For God's sake! What am I, twelve years old? Incapable of taking care of myself so I need someone else to do it? I don't know what's worse – the fact that I thought you were sleeping with her, or the fact that you trust her to look after me more than you think I can look after myself!"

"It's not like that and you know it," he said firmly.

"Oh, it's crystal clear that its like that from where I'm standing," I puffed out as I stopped pacing and placed my hands firmly on my hips.

"How could you? You know how I feel about her. How could you ask her to look after me and expect me to be happy about it?"

"You weren't supposed to find out."

I laughed hard at his reply. I couldn't believe what I was hearing "That just makes it so much worse," I said, shaking my head.

"Jo, listen to me." Blake stood before me and took my hands in his. "Christina runs the best security firm in New York."

"Like I said, good for her," I replied sarcastically.

Blake let out a small laugh. "It wasn't going to be Christina who would actually be looking after you; it would have been one of her employees." I looked down to the floor, but Blake pulled my gaze back up to meet his, placing his fingers under my chin. "I worry about you. Is that a crime? For a man to worry about his girlfriend when he's unable to keep her safe because he's hundreds of miles away at the other end of the country? Is it?"

"I can look after myself, Blake. I've managed since I arrived in New York, so what's different now?" I looked into his eyes.

"You weren't mine until now," he said softly. I couldn't help the smile that tugged at my lips. I was so angry with him, but somehow he always knew how to make it better. Placing my arms around his neck, I lifted up onto my toes and kissed him.

"Please call Christina. Tell her you don't need her now. Tell her what you like, in fact, but I don't want to be babysat by that … that cougar."

Blake laughed once. "You really have no idea how cute you are, do you?"

"Just call her," I pleaded. "I've spent the whole night thinking you were sleeping with her; do you know how much that hurts?"

"I do," he admitted firmly. "That's how I felt the night of the party."

My heart sank for him because he had replied with such sadness. "So you will call her then?"

Blake hesitated. He really wasn't happy calling her to tell her I didn't need her protection. But I was adamant that I would not be babysat by her, or anyone else for that matter.

"Blake," I said, "call her." I removed my hands from around his neck and waited.

Blake sighed heavily before taking his phone from his pocket and finding Christina's number. He held the phone almost to his ear so as I could listen. She answered on the first ring.

"Hello Blake," she said in surprise. "I didn't expect to hear from you again until Monday."

"Christina, hi. I no longer require your help," he said firmly, his eyes not leaving mine the whole time. "Jo knows that I have employed you, and let's just say that she's not happy about it."

"Is this because of what I told her?" she said in an annoyed tone. I took the phone from Blake's hand and walked towards the window.

"Hello, Christina."

"Jo, hi," she replied nervously.

"Just to let you know, as sweet and loving as it is that Blake asked you to look out for me while he's away; I have decided that I am old enough and wise enough to look after myself. So thank you for owning the most successful security firm in New York; I assume that that is the one and only reason that Blake came to you in the first place." I looked to Blake, who was masking a smile behind his fist as he stood cross-armed in front of me. "But I won't be requiring anyone's protection, especially yours. And yes, to answer your question, this most certainly is something to do with what you told me the other night. It was hurtful, and you purposely wanted to stir up some sort of shit. But unfortunately for you, it didn't work, and you have now lost work because of it. Do not even think about calling Blake again to set something up behind my back, because he knows now that not telling me is most certainly not an option."

I cut off the phone and tossed it onto the bed.

"Better?" Blake asked, slightly amused.

"Don't ever lie to me or put me in that situation again, Blake," I said quietly.

Blake walked over and wrapped his arms around my waist. I

rested my hands on his firm biceps.

"I'm sorry." His lips brushed the side of my mouth. "I'm gonna worry so much about you now."

"I am going to be fine, Blake," I said reassuringly. "Trust me."

Blake sighed and pulled me to him, holding me close. "Can we empty the case, or do you want to go home?" he asked against my neck.

"I just want to get into bed and go to sleep," I admitted.

Blake took a deep breath and straightened up, his hands cupping my face. "Never underestimate how much I love you, Jo; I would do anything, and I mean anything, to keep you safe."

"I'm sorry about what I said."

Blake's lips curled up into a half smile. "You were angry; it's okay."

"But it's not okay, Blake. Even here, away from it all, we're arguing. Is this what our lives will be like now, forever?"

"We argue because we love each other," he stated.

"That makes no sense whatsoever."

Blake wasn't in bed when I woke the next morning. I could, however, hear him and Marti chatting happily outside as they sorted out the garden for the barbecue. They were debating a small game of baseball on the beach, and Marti was telling Blake that he would be a field player or pitcher only, as it would be a waste of time giving him a bat. Blake was protesting like a little boy desperate to prove his worth to his dad. Their banter reminded me of happier times when I was a child. Dad and me playing penalty shoot-outs in the garden – but I was only allowed to shoot, as I was a hopeless goal keeper.

A gentle breeze was blowing in through the open window, and the sound of the birds singing their morning song filled the room. It was bliss. I felt relaxed for the first time in so long.

I closed my eyes and absorbed the sounds of nature, the sounds that were so hard to hear in the middle of a bustling city. My mind wandered back to the previous night's events and how Blake and I had argued yet again. It was becoming tiring. Blake and I were arguing constantly lately, and although I didn't think I had overreacted last night to the calls from Christina, I did believe that I would begin to push Blake away if my constant jealous outbursts and lack of trust towards him continued for much longer.

I felt the bed dip as a soft hand swept the length of my arm.

Turning over, I opened my eyes to find Blake beaming down on me.

"Good morning, beautiful," he said with a smile.

I smiled back. "What time is it?"

"Almost ten," he said as he lay next to me, continuing to stroke my arm.

"Wow, I knew I was tired, but that's ridiculous," I said, shocked. "I was listening to you and your dad." I smiled. "Do you think he may lift your batting ban?" I teased.

"He thinks I'll end up whacking someone with the bat."

I snorted and quickly covered my mouth with my hand. "Sorry." I laughed as Blake threw me a wounded look.

"You seem happier this morning," he said, moving his hand up to my face.

"I don't want us to fight any more Blake," I admitted.

"You had reason to last night; I'm sorry I tried to keep it from you."

The birds continued to sing; it was mesmerizing. "I miss that sound."

"What sound?" Blake said, trying to figure out what I was talking about.

"The birds," I said quietly. "So relaxing, it's mesmerizing. I forgot how nice it was waking up to those sounds. I miss it."

"You miss London?" he asked, concern etched on his face.

"Sometimes," I admitted. "It's not so much London I miss."

"Then what is it?" he asked, getting comfy next to me. "Your mom?"

"Definitely my mum, but so many other things too," I said, turning onto my back and focusing on the ceiling. "I miss the countryside a lot. The house that we lived in was so much like this one – without the pool and tennis courts, though." I twisted my head to Blake with a smile. "Ours was more a tree house and a swing with a couple of football nets thrown in for good measure."

We both smiled. "I miss my mum's Sunday lunches. Every Sunday without fail we would have all of the family around so there would be me, Mum and Dad, my uncle and aunt, and my cousin Jemma. Mum would go all out; every single week there was enough food to feed a small army, but she loved how much everyone loved it. I miss that.

"I miss getting snowed in during the winter. Mum and I would be toasting marshmallows in front of the open wood fire while Dad would be outside trying in vain to dig his way out so he could get to work.

"Real fish and chips," I said excitedly. "Friday night was fish-and-chips night, and we would sit in front of the TV and eat them from the paper. It's silly things like that that gave me so many happy memories." I smiled at Blake again, and a happy tear strolled down the side of my face. "I don't want my children to have a life any different to the one that I had up until everything went so wrong," I said sadly. "I want the house in the country, I want to get snowed in and toast marshmallows in front of the fire, I want fish and chips on a Friday, eating them from the paper while we all sit down and watch a film or something. Oh, and a dog, every family should have a dog. Do you think all of that is possible?"

Blake wiped the lone tear from my face. "I know that it's possible."

"I really miss my dad, Blake," I whispered. "Every single day I miss him. Just being here and hearing you and your dad talk, it gets me, right here." I placed my hand firmly against my chest.

Blake didn't reply. He folded me in his arms and held me against him, comforted me, and made me believe that everything was going to be okay.

Blake finally left me to get changed for our day at the beach once he had been back downstairs and brought me breakfast in bed, of which I enjoyed every single mouthful. I was really beginning to enjoy breakfast for the first time in my life. I put it down to all of the sex that Blake and I were having, it was a great way to build up an appetite. My slowly expanding waistline, however, wasn't going unnoticed by me. With Blake away for the next two weeks, I would work on getting that back to normal, though. I wouldn't need breakfast without Blake here to help me burn off the calories.

My phone rang as I was heading out of the bedroom. Noticing it was Casey; I sat on the edge of the bed and answered the phone.

"Hey, Jo, how's the in-laws?" she joked.

"Don't call them that," I laughed back, "but they're great, by the way."

"Good, good," she said quickly. "I have gossip," she said, sounding sneaky.

I rolled my eyes at her. "If it's someone else's downfall, it's not really gossip, Casey; you know how I feel about gossip."

"Oh, you are going to love this gossip," she said excitedly.

"Go on then, give it to me; what's the gossip?" I said, sounding uninterested.

"Someone beat the shit out of Cooper last night. He's in a bad way; apparently he's lucky to be alive."

I felt my eyes widen with shock as I shot off the bed and walked over to the window. Blake was back out there with Marti; they were now hanging twinkly lights around the gazebo, still laughing and teasing each other. "Is he going to be okay?" I asked with obvious concern.

"Dunno," Casey said unsympathetically. "Serves him right though if you ask me."

"Casey, don't say that."

"Jo, look at what he did to you; don't you dare have any sympathy for him," she said firmly. "He's obviously tried it on with some unsuspected female again, only this time he hasn't gotten away with it."

"Do they know who did it?" I asked as my eyes watched Blake carefully.

"Nope. No CCTV, nothing. Sounds like whoever did it knew what they were doing."

I sighed, not knowing what to say.

"You still there Jo?"

"Yes, yes, I'm still here," I replied, watching Blake as he started to climb a ladder to fix even more lights to the gazebo. Remembering my nightmare, I stepped away from the window, rubbing the back of my neck frantically. Even though I didn't want to believe it, I highly suspected that Blake had something to do with Cooper's attack. He had wanted someone to be following me around while he was away, but I had refused and made him call Christina in front of me. We had then spent the night in bed together, but had he somehow arranged this in order to keep him away from me while Blake was in Miami? He had said to me time and time again that he would kill Cooper; was that his intention? To kill him? I felt sick to my stomach at the thought of him arranging it.

"Anyway," Casey chimed, "There's also another reason that I rang."

"Go on," I replied cautiously.

"What time are you at rehearsals on Monday?"

"Noon, why?" I sat back down on the edge of the bed, feeling the nausea working its way to the surface rapidly.

"I've found the perfect venue." She let out a little squeal

"Of course you have," I joked.

"Seriously, Jo, I love it. Will you come with me Monday morning pleeeeeaaassseeee," she begged.

"Is Alex still not available for these events?"

"He's happy with whatever I choose. Anyway, we have fun together and I value your opinion, plus wedding talk seems to bring Alex out in hives at the moment," she laughed.

"As long as I'm at the studio by twelve, of course I will come with you for you to decide that you don't actually like it," I joked.

"Mwaaaa!" she said loudly down the phone. "I love you I love you I love you! And this time, I know this is the place, I promise you."

"I love you too," I said with a smile. "And we will see. See you Monday, okay?"

I hung up the phone and sat on the bed, letting my mind wander to the conversation I had heard Blake have in the kitchen the previous morning.

"Ready to go?" Blake asked as he appeared in the doorway, startling me.

I nodded. "Sure."

"Everything okay?" he asked, walking into the room and closing the door behind him.

"That was Casey," I said, lifting my phone. "Cooper was attacked last night; he's lucky to be alive, apparently," I said watching Blake carefully.

"Well that's a shame," he said, walking over and sitting next to me on the bed. "A shame that he's still alive, I mean; not that he got attacked."

"Blake," I said, shaking my head and turning to face him, "How can you be so cold towards someone like that."

"Only to him," he said, correcting me. "He makes my blood boil like no other; I fucking hate him."

"I really hate to ask you this," I said as I took a deep breath, "and I don't want us to argue, but I also don't want you to lie to me, okay?"

Blake nodded. "What is it?"

"Please tell me that you didn't have anything to do with it."

Blake let out a hard laugh and shook his head. "You think I was responsible?"

"No," I said. "Well, not really. You were here and he was there and ..."

I started rambling, and Blake took my hand, capturing my gaze.

"I would never ask someone else to do my dirty work, if that's what you're thinking."

"Good," I breathed with relief.

"I would want the pleasure of seeing him with my own eyes while he begged for mercy as I kicked the last breath out of him," he said simply, smiling slightly. "I wouldn't give someone else the pleasure of that."

"Don't talk like that," I said, shaking my head.

"It's the truth," he said simply. "He deserves everything he gets after what he did to you. You could have died, Jo. So if someone has intentionally hurt him, meaning to kill the bastard, it serves him right. But I had nothing to do with it. I swear to you."

"I'm sorry I had to ask," I said.

"Well don't be. If he's in the hospital, I don't have to worry about him harassing you while I'm away, now do I?" he smiled.

"There's a silver lining?"

"Every cloud, my beautiful. Every cloud."

16

It was only a short drive to the beach, but because of the amount of luggage needed by Blake's parents for one afternoon there, Blake and I took his car while Marti and Julia took theirs.

The beach wasn't as busy as I had anticipated; which pleased me. But I was sure that as soon as word got out that Blake was here, that would probably change.

We took up a large section of the beach near a fairly secluded area. I helped Julia set up the chairs and umbrellas while Marti and Blake decided on the best part of the area in which to set up the baseball court.

Sitting back in the lounger, I let myself relax and take in the noise of the waves and the gentle sound of the breeze bringing the waves in and out gently. I hadn't yet been brave enough to remove my sundress; there were too many eyes around, and my scar was visible for those who looked too closely.

"Coming in for a swim?" Blake's body hovered above me, blocking the sun from my view. He was dripping wet from the sea; the water glistened as the sun rested on his broad shoulders.

"I don't swim in the sea, Blake," I laughed, shaking my head.

"What? Why not?" he asked shocked.

I shuddered. "Because there are things in there."

"Like?"

"Sharks," I said matter-of-factly.

Blake laughed. "We don't get sharks here."

"They said the same in Cornwall until some turned up."

"Walk with me then," he said, holding his hand out to me. I took it, and he helped me to stand.

"Don't you think you should wear your hat?" I asked as we

started walking.

"I have sunblock on."

"It's not the sun that worries me." I nodded to a large gang of girls that were watching us as we approached where they sat.

"You're not jealous again, are you?" Blake teased as he placed both hands around my waist and lifted me into the air.

I let out a small scream as he carried me to the water's edge before slowly releasing me.

The waves felt warm as the water lapped against our feet gently.

"You know I can't help but get jealous when someone looks at you," I said, pouting.

"So, so cute," he said before scooping me up into his arms and carrying me out to sea until the water splashed against my bum.

"Blake, don't please," I pleaded. "Take me back." I gripped his arms so tightly they changed colour.

Blake stopped walking when the water level was above his shorts. "Can you swim?" he teased.

"Do not put me down in this water," I warned.

"Or what?" he teased.

"You'll see," I said desperately.

Blake's grip loosened but then tightened as he pretended to drop me. I gasped in horror.

"You know," he said, nipping my ear, "no one can see what goes on below this water; we could have some fun." He smiled wickedly.

I slapped him on the chest playfully, unable to hide my smile. "I'm about to stamp on that thought for you right now."

"Never," he said, shaking his head.

"Your sister just arrived," I said, nodding over to where Jasmine, Robert, and Fraser had just arrived at Marti and Julia.

Blake let out a small growl of frustration before looking over his shoulder. "Maybe next time." He shrugged smugly.

"Maybe," I replied with a smile.

Blake walked us back to the shore, releasing me as we left the water and taking my hand.

"Uncle Bakey, Uncle Bakey!" Fraser's voice carried the whole of the way to us as he came running at full speed towards Blake.

"Here's my favourite boy," Blake said, holding his arms out to Fraser, who hit him at full force when he finally got to Blake. Blake lifted him and spun him in circles, causing Fraser to giggle hysterically.

A warm feeling filled my chest. Watching Blake so carefree and loving with Fraser was humbling. My mind wandered briefly to Blake spinning our child like that, our child giggling hysterically with joy. I didn't even notice that I was daydreaming until Blake called my name and waved his hand in front of my face.

"You in there, Jo?" he asked.

"Yes," I said quickly. "Sorry, I was just thinking."

"Say hi to Aunty Jo, Fraser," Blake said, holding Fraser in his arms.

"Hi."

I smiled. "Hello, Fraser."

"I like your glasses," he said.

Thank you. Do you want to try them on?" Fraser nodded enthusiastically as I took my glasses off and placed them over his eyes, covering the majority of his face. He struggled out of Blake's arms and headed back to jasmine, showing her his new glasses.

"He likes you," Blake said, placing his arm around my waist.

"He liked my glasses." I smiled as we started walking back to the party.

"I know what you were thinking back there, you know."

"Oh you do, do you?"

"I can't wait for us to have children either," he said as we rejoined the family. Before I had a chance to reply, he had loosed me and grabbed a towel from the bag and started drying himself off.

"Jo, it's lovely to see you again," Jasmine said as she shimmied out of her denim shorts before holding out her hand, which I shook firmly.

I smiled shyly. "Hello, Jasmine. I'm sorry about the last time we met; I feel like such a fool for thinking that you were ..." I gestured to Blake and back to Jasmine.

She laughed and waved me off. "I can imagine how it looked. I'm sorry it never clicked who you were, I knew about you; Blake had told me enough times." She rolled her eyes in his direction. "I just didn't think," she said apologetically.

"It all turned out well in the end," Blake said, placing his arm over my shoulder and planting a rough kiss on the side of my head. "This here is my brother-in-law, Robert."

"Hello, Jo, how do you do?" he said in his best British accent, which got everyone laughing in his direction.

"Robert, I told you not to do that," Jasmine said behind her smile.

"No you didn't," he argued. "You told me not to do my Dick Van Dyke impression. 'Why, it's Mary Poppins!'" Everyone laughed except for Fraser, who started looking around frantically. "Where Daddy?"

"Now look what you have done," Jasmine said.

"It's lovely to meet you, Robert," I said, shaking his hand.

"You too," he replied with a smile. He then turned to face Blake. "Blake, remind me I have your keys; everything is as per your request." He patted Blake firmly on the back.

"Thank you, I appreciate it," Blake replied, throwing the towel onto one of the chairs before turning to see my confusion. Jasmine had noticed too.

"My lazy brother asked us to go pack his case, Jo," she said. "That way you two can have a peaceful evening before he jets off on Monday." She smiled.

"You had your sister drive down from Boston to pack for you?" I shook my head in disbelief.

"Yes, well, we get more time together, and Jasmine doesn't mind. Do you, Jasmine?" Blake said.

"Of course not." She waved me off again. "Anything for my superstar baby brother." she smiled.

Marti started clapping his hands firmly to get everyone's attention.

"Well, here we go," Julia said under her breath.

Marti ran through the few rules that he had invented for beach baseball. Everyone would be playing, including little Fraser, who apparently had his grandpa's catch already.

It was decided that I would bat first with Jasmine pitching. As good as I was at rounders back in high school, I had never batted a ball on a public beach before in front of my film star boyfriend and his family, one of whom happened to be the most famous baseball player in the world.

I dug my toes into the sand and prepared for the looming humiliation.

"You have no idea what thoughts are going through my mind right now from this angle."

"Stop trying to put me off," I said innocently before giving Blake a little wiggle of my behind just as Jasmine stepped up to throw the ball. I heard Blake's low growl bubble up from inside him.

Jasmine threw the ball and I whacked it. I whacked it so hard, in fact, that it skipped past all of the fielders and landed nicely in the sea. Dropping the bat, I ran and managed a full circle before Robert reappeared wet from the sea, holding the ball above his head.

"Impressive." Marti nodded with a smile. "You certainly make up where Blake lacks, let me tell you." Everyone laughed except for Blake.

"I'm batting next," he said in frustration. "I'll show you I can hit the damn ball."

"Blake!" Julia said.

"Give me the bat."

"If you insist," Marti said, amused by Blake. Robert threw Marti the ball as everyone took their places.

Because of the speed at which Marti was able to throw the ball, Robert took on the role of catcher, and I stood in the outfield with Jasmine.

Quite a crowd had now gathered to watch. Word had obviously got around that Blake and Marti were here. But as much as I hated attention, especially if I was the centre of it, today it felt good. Since arriving at the beach, I had felt relaxed, even though I felt a pang of jealousy when a group of girls had been drooling over Blake. He had shrugged off the attention and given all of his attention to me. I really believed that he was doing what he had promised all along. He was fixing me.

Blake narrowed his eyes at Marti as he took his position to bat. Marti approached, throwing the ball into the air over and over as they stared at each other with determination.

I heard Jasmine snort to the left of me, causing me to turn my head to meet her. "Sorry," she laughed, "but this is hilarious; look at them both."

Glancing their way quickly, I too burst into laughter. "Are they always so competitive?"

"Oh God yes," she replied. "This one time, when Blake was eight or nine—"

"Jo!" I heard Marti call out. "Jo, the ball! It's yours! Catch the ball!"

Everything happened in slow motion. I could hear the calls from Marti, and I could see that Blake had dropped his bat and was heading for first base. What I didn't see was the ball – not until it hit me straight in the face, knocking me off my feet as I stumbled back and fell to the sand beneath me.

Everyone gasped. "I'm okay!" I yelled as I scrambled back to my feet, slightly embarrassed. "I'm okay. No harm done."

"Your nose is bleeding," I heard Julia gasp as everyone gathered around me.

"Oh my God," Blake said, mortified. "I'm so sorry."

"It's okay," I said calmly. "It's just a bit of blood; I'm fine. Stop fussing."

I heard Marti laugh, and everyone turned their attention to him. He stopped laughing instantly. "What?" he asked, shrugging his shoulders.

"She could have broken her nose; for God's sake, Dad, she's filming next week," Jasmine said as she tilted my head until we got to a towel.

"I'm fine. I know it's not broken; I can move it, see?" I said, wiggling my nose before placing the beach towel against it.

Marti started laughing again.

"Will you stop laughing, Dad; look at her," Blake said this time.

"I'm sorry," he said before looking to me. "Jo, I'm sorry. But the first time in thirty years that Blake here hits a ball; he goes and whacks it straight at his girlfriend's nose. You've got to admit, it's kind of funny."

One by one we all started to laugh – all of us except Blake. "Come on, Blake, stop being such a moody pants," Marti laughed as a small smile lifted Blake's lips.

"That was one hell of a shot too, damn it," Blake said before crouching down in front of me.

"Certainly was a good shot," I said.

"You sure you're okay?"

"I'm fine," I assured him.

"Okay. But we're going home," he said, standing and grabbing his T-shirt.

"Why?" I asked, disappointed.

"You shouldn't be out in this heat with your nose like that," he said.

"So you want to go back to New York?" I asked, confused.

"Can you all see why I love this lady as much as I do?" Blake asked everyone. "Back home as in to my parent's house."

"Oh," I replied, feeling a fool before standing. I slipped into my sandals, but before I got a chance to walk, Blake had scooped me up into his arms.

"Blake, my nose is bleeding; my legs haven't stopped working," I teased.

"Jo," he said with a lopsided smile, "even your sandals have heels, I've already bent your nose; I'm not risking you falling and breaking your neck to go with it."

The crowd that had gathered all began to cheer as we headed back to the car.

"Do you think we will top eight million hits with this one?" Blake laughed, nodding towards a spectator holding up his phone, recording us.

"Oh God," I whined as I buried my head into Blake's chest and closed my eyes tightly.

Blake fussed over me for the rest of the day. He told me over and over again about how sorry he was that the first time he managed to hit the ball in thirty years, it had headed straight for me, leaving me with an almighty headache and two slightly blackened eyes.

Marti, however, still found it hilarious, much to Julia and Blake's annoyance.

The garden party was in full swing when Blake and I headed outside to the garden. Blake introduced me to the guests who I didn't know before I settled next to Jasmine as she sat on a lounger around the pool while she watched Fraser splashing around with Robert.

"How's the nose?" she asked as I sat next to her.

I smiled. "A little tender, but better than I expected."

"Here you go, ladies." Blake handed us each a cocktail before kissing me quickly and disappearing over to where Marti was starting up the barbecue.

"I've never seen Blake so happy. You know, he really loves you."

"I really love him too," I replied shyly.

"I saw your face when he was holding Fraser." I turned to see Jasmine smiling at me. "You want children?"

I nodded. "Eventually, yes. Blake would make a brilliant dad."

"He would," Jasmine agreed before squealing as Robert splashed her with water. "Blake is a lot more mature than Robert; that's for sure." We both laughed. "He was such a mess when you broke up, you know?" I could see she was eying me suspiciously.

"We both were," I admitted. "I was going through a lot at the time, and I had a really shitty past; everything just became too much. I shouldn't have pushed him away; I regret that now." My eyes roamed to Blake, who was laughing with Marti.

"Don't have regrets, Jo. Everything that happens moulds who we are today. I see a future for you both; do you?"

"I didn't. Not for a while. But this past week? I can really see it." I smiled.

I had taken numerous calls over the remainder of the weekend from my mum, Casey, and even Marcus; each one of them needed convincing that I was okay. Marcus was more concerned about me sporting panda eyes on set for the recording of *Perfect Alibi* that Friday than the fact that I was injured, but I couldn't say that I didn't share his concern.

Casey was more concerned that I was going to look like a battered housewife while accompanying her around venues and told me that sunglasses would be a necessity to be seen out in public.

My mum, being my mum, was solely concerned about me. She knew that Blake would look after me, but for the first time since I came to New York, she told me that she wished I were going back home for her to look after while Blake was away in Miami.

We left the Hamptons mid-afternoon on Sunday to travel back to New York, where we would spend our last night together for two long, lonely weeks. I did not allow myself to appear sad in front of Blake as we spent the journey home discussing my busy schedule for the duration of Blake's absence.

I had planned so much in my mind that I hoped it would give me only a small window of opportunity to miss him. Even though I would spend my evenings at my own apartment, I planned to slowly move myself into Blake's penthouse so we could start our new life together when he returned. There was a happy future awaiting us. That made the coming two weeks feel so much more bearable.

We pulled into the underground parking at Blake's building just before seven pm. I couldn't help but notice Blake's growing smile as we pulled up in his usual space.

"Why are you so happy to be home?" I asked suspiciously.

"I have something for you." He turned off the ignition and started fiddling with the keys. "Don't be mad, okay?" he said. "I have been asking you for weeks now to no avail, so I took it upon myself to do this for you. I would have felt guiltier for doing it without your permission had I not almost broken your nose and caused us to become yet another YouTube sensation. So this kind of softens the blow a little. A gift to show you how sorry I am for the bad things we have faced, but also to tell you how much I love you and for the good things we're yet to face."

"What did you do?" I asked cautiously.

"Open your hand," he said nervously.

Reluctantly I opened my hand. Blake placed a key to the Range Rover in my palm.

"You're giving me a key to your car?" I asked, surprised. "Aren't you scared I might scratch it or something? I mean, I'm sure your love for this car is on par with your love for me sometimes," I joked.

"You're right; I am petrified that you will scratch my car," he joked before his face turned serious. "Press the key."

I took the key out of my palm and pressed the button with confusion. Two loud beeps that echoed through the car park pulled my attention to the left.

"Now keep your head there and press it again."

Again two loud beeps echoed, but this time I could see where it had come from. "Oh my God, please tell me that that white Range Rover is responding to this key."

"That white Range Rover over there" – he said, pointing to the shiny brand-new car to my left – "is responding to your key. It's all yours, beautiful," he said simply.

"You brought me a car?!" I squealed before unbuckling my belt and climbing onto Blake's lap, planting kisses all over his face excitedly before pulling back to focus on his face. "I can't believe you did that," I said, in awe of him.

"If I had waited for you to do it, I would have waited forever; and besides, I love you and I want to spoil you. If that means buying you a new car so I don't have to worry about you getting murdered on the streets of New York, then so be it."

I smiled. "You're so over the top; but I can't believe you did this," I said, opening the car door and climbing out before running the short distance to my car and climbing in. Blake hopped into the passenger side.

Gripping the wheel tightly, I took in everything around me. It was top-of-the-range, with every added extra that Blake's car possessed.

"It's like a cockpit in here," I squealed. "I love it; I really, really love it. But you shouldn't have done this." I turned to face him. "What could I ever give to you now that could even come close to this?"

"You get the car and I get you," he said simply. "I love you so much, Jo. And I know that we argue and we fight, but nothing – nothing – will ever spoil us. We're over the worst possible hurdles we could have faced now, and we're on the home run – excuse the pun." We both laughed, but both of us were filled with emotion. "I love nothing more than seeing you smile. You haven't been smiling enough lately, and that makes me sad. You have the most beautiful smile I have ever seen, and I want to see it every minute of every day for the rest of our lives."

"I'm gonna miss you so much, Blake," I said as my eyes filled with tears. I climbed over and straddled his lap, taking his mouth in mine carefully. The pain in my nose was still very present, but I didn't care.

"I'm gonna miss you too, Jo. But when I get back, we begin our new chapter. And I know that it's going to be the best one yet."

17

I had made Blake promise me the night before that he wouldn't wake me before he left this morning. Even though I knew how much I was going to miss Blake, the thought of saying goodbye to him face to face was too painful to bear. At four forty-five a.m., I had heard Blake climb out of bed, shower, and leave for the airport. I had held my eyes tightly closed together when he came into the room one last time and left a lingering kiss to my cheek before telling me to be safe and dream of him every night until he came home. It had taken every ounce of my strength to keep my eyes shut and not pull him back to bed, never letting him leave until I knew he had missed his flight. I allowed myself to cry as he stepped out of the apartment.

There was a note waiting for me on the coffee table when I entered the lounge telling me that he missed me already and would call me when he landed in Miami.

The apartment felt big and lonely without him, but it was only fourteen sleeps until we would be back here and it would be my apartment too. With that in mind I planned on starting my big move at some point over the next few days between rehearsals and wedding planning. Keeping my mind busy was going to be the best way to see the next two weeks through with as few tears as possible.

I told Casey that I would be driving to what she described as her "perfect venue" and to meet me in the building's car park. Watching her standing at Blake's black Range Rover waiting for me was amusing. If I hadn't had work at noon, I'd have sat and watched her fiddle with her hair, then her phone, then her clothes for hours. But, not wanting to set a bad impression on my first day, we needed to get to the chosen venue, wait an hour or so for Casey to decide it wasn't suitable, let her whine about it for another hour, and then go to work with a banging head.

Giving in to the temptation of teasing her, I rolled down the window and called her over. She scurried over, wide-eyed, and climbed into my shiny new car. "Please tell me you didn't hot-wire this on my behalf," she teased.

"Please tell me that you haven't plastered your legs in fake tan this morning; this oxford leather cost more than a new suite for our apartment," I joked as I put the car into reverse and made my way to the exit.

"Nice cover-up with the make-up by the way; you can barely see your two black eyes," Casey teased. "Did Blake buy you a car because he almost broke your nose?" she said, laughing.

"Yep," I said simply. "He had it waiting for me last night when we got back from his parents'. I had no idea until we parked up and he gave me the key."

Casey let out a low whistle between her teeth. "He's got it bad," she sang.

I nodded. "Good, because so have I. Now tell me where we're going so I can tell this bad boy to get us there ASAP."

Casey spent the whole journey trying to convince us both that this place was the one. I spent the journey asking her where we would be visiting the following day after she decided that this place was either too big, too small, too old, too new, or just not right.

We pulled up at the lake house forty-five minutes later. It was a lot like some of the venues that we had already visited, but straight away it seemed a lot more intimate and definitely more Casey.

With my mind wandering to whether Blake had landed yet, I followed Casey as she was guided around every corner of the building, not noticing whether or not she appeared interested or whether it was the same old story again. The guide eventually showed us to a room where Casey could look over the packages in private without feeling any pressure from staff.

"I love it!" she yelled as the door closed behind us.

"Really?" I asked, unable to hide my complete shock.

"This is it, Jo; this is the place that I will become MRS Alex Taylor," she said dreamily.

"I think I'm going to pass out," I said sarcastically. "You're sure? It's not too old or too new or there isn't one step less to climb for the bridal suite than you had anticipated?"

An amused smile tugged at Casey's lips. "Everything about it is just perfect. I'm gonna go and get Kelly, tell her to get us booked in."

Casey did a little victory dance before leaving the room on the hunt for our guide, Kelly.

My phone began to ring, and relief flooded me when I noticed it was Blake.

"Hi," I said happily.

"Hello, beautiful." I could sense his smile.

"You're there, then?" I asked.

"Yep, just unpacking and getting straight to work. I miss you already," he said sadly.

"I miss you too. It's so good to hear your voice," I said quietly.

"Are you at work yet?" he asked.

"No, but you will love this. Casey has only gone and found the perfect venue."

"No way."

"I know. We're here now booking it."

"That's great news," he said.

"Yes, it is. Will you call me again later, as soon as you can?"

"Just try stopping me," he said. "I love you."

"I love you too."

Casey re-entered with Kelly, who was carrying a large diary and smiling widely at something Casey had just told her. Sitting down on the plush leather seats, Kelly opened the folder and asked Casey what dates she had in mind. "I'm sorry," she said sympathetically. "The boathouse gets booked up very well in advance. If you insist on a winter wedding, we could fit you in Christmas two thousand sixteen," she said, looking from her diary to Casey.

"That's over two years away," Casey moaned.

"How about if you forgot Christmas and did it spring or summer?" I suggested. "That's only a couple of months' difference." I looked to Kelly, whose face had become even more sympathetic. "When

I say we get booked up very well in advance, I mean exactly that. We are completely booked here for the next two years."

Casey slumped back into her seat. "This is the only place I have seen that even feels right." Sitting forward, she focused on Kelly. "You have absolutely nothing for the next two years?" Her disappointment was obvious; I felt sad for her.

Kelly smiled slightly as she flicked through her diary. "We have had one cancellation just this morning actually. It doesn't happen very often, but when it does, they soon get snapped up."

"I'll take it," Casey said instantly.

"You don't even know when it is yet," I said, shocked.

"I don't care. I want to get married here, so I will take what I can get," she said before turning back to Kelly. "When is the cancellation for?"

"It is September twenty-seventh," she said, concentrating on her diary.

"Well, that's good; that gives us just over twelve months to get everything organized," I said, but Casey still seemed defeated.

"Sorry," Kelly replied, "I think you misunderstood what I said. When I say September twenty-seventh, I don't mean next year. I mean *this* September twenty-seventh. In less than four weeks."

I burst out laughing. "Well, that's ridiculous; who can organize a wedding from scratch in just four weeks."

"We can," Casey said straight away, stemming my laughter.

"Are you kidding me?" I asked.

"It's like it was meant to be, Jo!" she said excitedly.

"We will never be done in time," I said, "and you really should speak to Alex before making such a big decision."

"We will be ready, and Alex will be just as excited as I am," she said, as if it were the simplest thing in the world. "Book me in please, Kelly. In four weeks' time, I want to be walking down that aisle."

I found Marcus in the canteen, laughing amongst a small group of cast members. Immediately I was called over and made to feel like one of the team. They all introduced themselves to me once more; it had been a while since we had been to Sugar Lounge, and I'm pretty sure everyone was aware that I was out of it last time. As embarrassing as that was, given that only Blake knew about me being drugged, I pushed it to the back of my mind and pulled out the chair next to Marcus.

"A nice cup of tea for the lady," I looked over my shoulder to see Cooper standing there smiling at me. My expression must have been somewhat obvious when my mouth fell open and I was unable to string two words together.

"Hi," he said simply as he pulled out the chair next to me and sat down slowly after placing my cup in front of me; he was in obvious pain.

"Cooper," I managed to say, "what are you doing here?"

He smiled. "Hello to you too. I had a meeting this morning so thought I'd drop by and see you guys; it's been a while since I caught up with Marcus, so …" He shrugged as he sat back and placed his arm carefully over the back of his seat. "There's no need to look so worried, Jo; I'm not here to cause anything. It's not like I'm in a position to cause trouble, is it," he said quietly.

"It's just … you look awful, Cooper," I said as I took in the sights of his many cuts and bruises. "Casey said you were lucky to be alive."

He smiled. "That's a bit of an over exaggeration."

"Do you know who did this to you?"

"I got on the wrong side of someone. They taught me a lesson."

"Some lesson."

He smiled. "Yeah, well, you live and learn, I suppose."

"Look, I shouldn't really be talking to you."

"You're worried what Blake may say," he stated. "I'm here to see Marcus, Jo, not you."

I smiled. "Okay." I could live with that; there was nothing going on that could worry Blake. I couldn't stop Cooper from seeing Marcus, and I couldn't avoid Cooper completely anyway, so I would just keep my head down and get on with work.

Marcus showed me to my dressing room, which was huge and very homely. There were cards placed on the dresser along with a huge bouquet of flowers from Blake. I opened the card immediately.

> *'I wish so much I could be there to support you this next two weeks, but I know how amazing you are already. I miss you and I love you and I can't wait to see you again. I would tell you to break a leg, but knowing you, that's already a possibility. So instead, shine like the star that I know you are ... Blake xxxx'*

I smiled through the happy tears that had fallen, before taking my phone from my bag to call him. I knew he would be filming, so I left him a voicemail.

"Hello, you," I said, trying hard not to show any emotion through my voice. "I just wanted to say thank you for the flowers; they are beautiful. And I will try not to break a leg" – I chuckled – "especially as you're not here to fix it for me." I swallowed past the huge lump in my throat. "I love you so much, Blake; I can't wait until you're home, back to our home. Call me later. I love you."

I felt a pang of guilt as I hung up the phone; there was no reason to tell Blake that I had bumped into Cooper, but not telling him felt like I was betraying him in some way, even though I knew that I wasn't. Damn Cooper for turning up. Even though he said he had a meeting, I found it quite the coincidence that he was here today, of all days.

Cooper hung around like a bad smell through the whole of rehearsals. He had heard Marcus mention us all going out to dinner when we were done and had invited himself along. As much as he had said he wasn't there for me, something felt off. He had told me he was going to look out for me while Blake was away – was that was he was doing? Had he taken it upon himself to do that when I didn't want him to? Or was he actually being genuine and trying to right the wrongs that he had done by me? Either way, I tried to get out of dinner by telling Marcus I had stuff to do at home, which wasn't entirely untrue. I wanted to make a start on moving my stuff into Blake's apartment for one, and then there was Casey, who needed my help with all of the wedding prep.

But Marcus was having none of it, insisting that I would need to eat dinner regardless and asking what better there was than the small Italian restaurant that the cast used regularly.

By the end of the day, I was shattered. But I was also very hungry, so after grabbing my things, I headed outside to wait for everyone else.

A small group of people was gathered around my car as I started to approach.

"Is this your car, ma'am?" The car park attendant asked as he approached me slowly.

"Yes why?" My eyes roamed to the car to see that every tyre had been slashed.

"What the hell has happened?" I asked as I bypassed the security guard and walked around the car. "It's been keyed too!" I said in disbelief. "You have this on camera though, right? You can see who has done this?"

"What's going on?" I turned to see Marcus and Cooper exiting the building and walking quickly over to me.

"Someone has slashed my tyres and keyed my car," I said angrily. My eyes roamed to Cooper, who appeared as shocked as everyone else.

"Who did this?" Marcus asked the attendant.

"I'm afraid I don't know, sir," he drawled. "I may have been taking my break at the time."

"Well check the CCTV then," I said. "I'm calling the police."

"I'm afraid the CCTV has been out of action now for quite some time, ma'am."

"What!" I yelled at him. "So you just leave the car park unattended so you can go feed your face? Who employs these imbeciles?" I asked in anger.

"It's okay, Jo. Calm down; it's just a car." Cooper's hand rested on my shoulder, causing my body to shudder.

I shrugged his hand off me and turned to face him, scowling. "It is not just a car, and someone has done this to me on purpose," I said shakily.

"We will find out who did it," Cooper said firmly.

"How?"

"I don't know yet, but we will, I promise."

Marcus began giving the attendant a piece of his mind.

I watched Cooper as he walked slowly around the car, weighing up the damage. Anger flared inside me as I took the few long strides to him that separated us.

"You did this," I said angrily, trying to keep my voice low as I poked at Cooper's chest. "You had no reason to be here today, and yet you stayed all day so as this wouldn't look like it had anything to do with you. But I know you, I know what you are capable of, and I know that you did this." My whole body was shaking with anger. I so wanted Blake right now. I wanted him to hold me and tell me that everything was going to be okay. Cooper took my arm and guided me away from the onlookers.

"Jo, I know what you think, but I swear to you, hand on my heart I swear, this has nothing to do with me."

"Bullshit," I spat out.

"Why would I do this? Huh? Why would I want to hurt you? I have no reason to hurt you, Jo. I want us to be friends. I *need* us to be friends. I swear to you, on my mother's life, I had nothing to do with your car being vandalized. I haven't been out of sight all day; you know that."

"So you got someone to do it for you," I replied.

"No," Cooper said quietly. "Come on, Jo, please," he said quietly as his hand took mine. I pulled my hand away and walked back to Marcus.

"I'm so sorry, Jo; this should never have happened. Turns out idiot here was taking a break; someone was obviously watching and waiting for the window of opportunity."

"But why me? Why my car?"

"I'm sorry," Marcus said again. "Look, I can have someone pick this up for you, on me. I'll get it repaired and delivered back to you."

"You don't have to do that; it's not your fault," I said, rubbing my brow frantically.

"I'm supposed to be watching out for you; Blake isn't gonna be very happy when he finds out."

"Don't tell him," I said quickly. Marcus looked up at me in surprise. "I don't want to worry him when there's nothing he can do."

"I don't like lying to him, Jo," he said, unsure.

"Look, I'll tell him when he gets home, but if I tell him now, he will worry about something that he has no control over. Please."

Marcus took a deep breath. "You tell him when he gets home – no excuses."

"Thank you," I said gratefully.

"Still up for dinner?"

"No." I smiled sadly. "I just want to go home."

"Sure." Marcus took his phone from his pocket and started calling someone; I assumed it was someone to come and take the car away.

"I'll give you a ride," Cooper said from behind me.

"No," I said, shaking my head. "I'll be fine, but thank you."

"What would Blake rather you do? Walk or get in a cab?"

"Probably, if the third option involved you, yes." I nodded.

"I'm trying to help, Jo. I really just want to make things right between us. All I'm doing is offering you a ride home, nothing more. Just please get in the car," he said as he opened the passenger door for me.

Wanting desperately to say no, but knowing that if someone had damaged my car they may want to damage me, I allowed myself to give in and climbed into Cooper's Audi.

We didn't speak as we drove the short distance back to the

apartment. I was already weighed down with guilt for allowing myself to get into the car with him. He had been right when he asked if Blake would prefer me to get a cab or walk home, but he would have also rather I got a lift with anyone except Cooper.

"Thanks for the lift," I said as I unbuckled my seat belt. "And I'm sorry for what I said to you too."

Cooper smiled. "No problem. I meant what I said, though; I want to make things right between us. I understand that Blake doesn't want you around me; I'd be the same. But I would never hurt you intentionally, Jo. I miss you; I miss what we had, and if I can ever just get a tiny bit of that back, I'll take it."

"Bye, Cooper." I smiled as I climbed out of the car and headed into the building. Day one done, only thirteen left to go.

Casey bounced into the apartment the next morning at seven thirty a.m.

"Tell me you have a couple of spare hours, please," she begged, clasping her hands together.

I rolled my eyes and placed my empty cup into the dishwasher

"Don't tell me you changed your mind about the boathouse."

"Nope, all systems are a go on that front, but we need to sort dresses, and I think I may have found the perfect place that can do them at short notice. Well, your dress that is; no one will get their eyes on mine until exactly three weeks and four days, not that I'm counting."

"Give me an hour and I'm all yours." I headed past Casey towards the hallway. "Oh," I said, turning back to face her. "I have a flat tyre; can you drive?" Keeping what had happened from everyone was going to be tough, but if I told Casey, she would tell Alex; if she told Alex, he would tell Blake. I hated that I was lying, but keeping it to myself would be the best option for now.

"You have had that car five minutes," she replied in disbelief.

"I know, drove over some glass or something," I lied. "So Alex took the news about the speedy wedding okay then?" I said, diverting her attention back to the wedding.

Casey shrugged and gave me a nervous smile. "He seems okay with it. He wasn't as excited as I had hoped, but he has a lot going on with the new club so …" She shrugged and looked down to the floor.

"Men," I joked, but Casey's smile only saddened. "He told me all about Angela, you know." Casey's eyes shot up to me in surprise. "The night he came over here and told me off about Blake. I suppose he's just nervous, scared of history repeating itself," I said, knowing exactly how that felt.

"Suppose so," Casey said quietly.

"Right," I said breaking the awkwardness that had suddenly appeared. "Let's get this show on the road." I smiled as I headed down the hallway. I felt sympathy for Alex even though I loved Casey dearly. I could definitely imagine that being sprung with the news of his own wedding in less than four weeks after what had happened to him with Angela would only bring up all of the bad memories that he held. Maybe I would have to pay him a visit and repay the pep talk that he had given me when I was being stubborn about Blake. I, for one, could definitely relate to how he was feeling.

There was nothing quite like the feeling I got every time Blake's name lit up my phone screen. But that feeling was bittersweet. I looked forward to every time I spoke to Blake, but mixed with that was the guilt I felt for not telling him about the car being vandalized and the fact that Cooper had then brought me home. I hated lying to Blake, and I knew how I would feel if it were Blake lying to me, but the truth was, I didn't want Blake worrying about me when there was nothing he could do from Miami to help me. I also felt stupid. Had I not been such a child over him hiring Christina, maybe my car wouldn't have been damaged and I wouldn't have ended up going home with Cooper. I just hoped that that was the only thing I would have to tell him when he returned and found that the damage was just the result of mistaken identity. After all, I had only just been given the car; there was no way that it was common knowledge already that I had it.

The deep breaths I took repeatedly during his calls only partly stemmed the emotion that tried so hard to spill out. I hated lying, and I hated myself for doing it, but I knew it was all for the right reasons and that Blake would understand once I told him the truth.

Two hours after we had arrived at Annabelle's boutique, Casey was still undecided on both the material and the design of the dresses. She seemed too distracted to even think about what to choose. "Had I stuck with the winter wedding as Alex wanted, I would have picked the colours and designs no problem. But no" – she sighed – "I had to jump the gun, didn't I." She shook her head whilst flipping through the samples for the hundredth time.

"What do you recommend, Annabelle?" I asked, hoping to take a bit of the stress from Casey.

"Well," Annabelle replied carefully, "do you have a colour theme? Flowers, invitations, the groomsmen's ties perhaps?"

"Oh God," Casey said, burying her head in her hands. "I've rushed into this way too quickly, haven't I? I haven't even given a thought to any of those things. This wedding is going to be one big, fat disaster, and it will serve me right, won't it?"

I stepped over to Casey and crouched before her. "We can do this," I said firmly.

"How?" Casey asked, deflated.

"I'm going to ask you a question, and you say the first answer that you think of, okay?" I stated.

"This isn't a game, Jo," Casey said, slightly annoyed.

I smiled. "Trust me."

"Okay," she sighed.

"Straps or strapless?"

"Strapless," she said straight away.

"Knee length or to the floor?"

"Floor."

"Chiffon or silk?"

"Chiffon."

"Your favourite flower."

"Roses."

I sat back, smiling and feeling very pleased with myself. "Okay, Annabelle, we want a red floor-length strapless chiffon gown please."

Casey's face lit up for the first time since that morning. "How did you just do that?"

I winked as Annabelle stood and headed off to fetch the suitable material. We had made progress.

"I'm telling you, that tape measure must be wrong; it looked as old as Annabelle, so obviously isn't the same as what we use these days," I moaned as we pulled out of the boutique's car park.

"All tape measures are the same, Jo," Casey laughed.

"Well I have never been a twenty-six inch waist before, never," I said, horrified. "It's Blake's fault, force feeding me bloody breakfast every morning. I knew this would happen; I'm getting fat. He is going to go off me, and I'm going to end up big, fat and alone," I whined.

"Stop being such a drama queen," Casey laughed. "You're just content now, that's all."

"I am not content with being fat," I said in horror. "From now I am eating healthy and exercising."

Casey snorted. "Anyone would think you were the one getting married."

I frowned. "I just don't want Blake to go off me."

"That is never gonna happen," Casey laughed.

I made it to the rehearsal just in time. A black SUV that had followed me the distance from the boutique to work hadn't gone unnoticed. Knowing that Blake had hired someone else without my knowledge to look after me while he was away was comforting. Even though I had made him call Christina to cancel the job he had employed her to do, I was glad he had employed someone else regardless. As I stepped out of the car on the studio's car park, I noticed the black SUV slowing at the gates before driving off.

"Do you want me to pick you up later?" Casey asked.

"No, thank you," I said firmly. "I shall start as I mean to go on; these legs need some exercise." I smiled. "See you later." I closed the door and watched as Casey drove away.

We were well ahead of target to be ready for Friday's live show, so Marcus decided to call it a day early, and we all left by six. Marcus informed me that my car would be back at my apartment when I got home. He really was looking out for me as he had promised Blake he would. I struggled at convincing him that I wanted to walk home, and even though he put up a good fight, I won over in the end and walked the short distance home in less than an hour.

By the time I stepped into the apartment, my feet were sore and my head hurt. Walking home in heels and not eating all day wasn't the best decision I had ever made.

"You look peaky," Casey observed. "You not feeling well?"

"I didn't realize walking was such a challenge," I said as I flopped down onto the sofa and removed my shoes to discover the numerous blisters that had appeared.

Casey squirmed. "Ouch. You need to have a long, hot soak in the bath and get some decent food inside you. Shall I order us a pizza?"

"Pizza sounds great; I'm starving. Can you ask for extra jalapeños on mine please?" I said as I dragged myself from the sofa.

Casey smirked at me as I headed past her. "The diet starts tomorrow, right?"

"You've got it," I replied.

Blake called while I was soaking in the bath. It was great to hear his voice; I hadn't spoken to him since that morning, and it had been a good day, so I didn't feel as though I was betraying him in any way. I didn't, however, mention that I had walked home; he would want to know why, and then I would have to explain the car to him. He told me that they were working flat out to be finished in time, as they hadn't had a very good day of filming. As long as it didn't mean he would be later arriving home than planned, I didn't mind.

By the time Friday's live show came around, I had got myself into a routine. I was jogging to work on a morning and walking home after rehearsals. The car was back and looking brand new again, but to prevent any further accidents and to stick to my get-fit plan, I left it parked in the underground car park. The only use it was getting from me at the moment was every evening, when I would take more of my things over to Blake's apartment for when he returned home.

I never imagined that I would be grateful for the Converse that Blake had made me wear at the Yankees game, but they were proving quite handy right now. I wasn't going to make the mistake of walking in heels to or from work ever again. With my next dress fitting due the following week, I was doing all I could to ensure I would be back down to my original twenty-three-inch waist by then. Since starting my new regime, I had felt weak and dizzy quite often, so I made sure I ate on a morning and then snacked on fruit during the day before going home and cooking myself something healthy on the evening. Forcing food down me when I wasn't hungry was proving a challenge; my breakfast even made a re-appearance one morning because I just wasn't hungry enough to eat.

I hadn't seen Casey much over the past few days, so getting my own routine seemed to prove easy. I had, however, noticed the black SUV again on a couple of occasions. It began to feel comforting that I was being taken care of by Blake. Even though he was still in Miami, he was still making sure I was safe, just as he had always promised, so being followed wasn't as bad as I had originally anticipated; at least I knew I couldn't come to any harm. Cooper had texted me a couple of times just to make sure I was okay, and he had asked if I needed anything. As much as I knew Blake wouldn't approve of me talking to Cooper, it felt comforting knowing that he was also watching out for me. I could now see how hard Cooper was working to right all of the wrongs that he had done recently, and for that he deserved a little compassion from me. It had been a good week in the end. What had started off as disastrous had turned out to be a better week than I had at first anticipated. And now there was only ten days until I would see Blake again.

I arrived at the studio in good time to prepare for the live recording. Butterflies were doing a very happy dance in my stomach, but it was a nice feeling.

I walked into my dressing room to yet another beautiful bouquet of red roses sitting on my dressing table. I knew immediately who they were from.

> *'To my beautiful English rose ... I wish so much that I could be there with you tonight for the live show. I know that you are going to be amazing, because you are amazing. I know that you will shine, because you are the brightest star in my sky. I gather that you didn't break a leg, so I won't curse you by saying it again tonight. I miss you and I love you; I can't wait to see you. Yours forever, Blake xxxx'*

I laughed and cried happy tears at the same time. His note just made me miss him more and more; I couldn't wait for him to be home.

"I love you too," I whispered, rubbing my thumb over the words on the note.

A knock on my door startled me. Placing the note next to the flowers, I opened the door.

"Here she is!" Marti stood on the other side of the door, beaming at me.

"Marti," I said before hugging him, "come on in." I opened the door wide and let him past.

"Wow, that is one big bunch of flowers," he observed. "Blake, I presume?"

I smiled. "Yes, aren't they gorgeous?"

"They certainly are; he's an old romantic at heart," he said with a smile. "Anyway, I wanted to come and say hi now, because I'm gonna be heading straight home after the show."

"Oh that's a shame; I was hoping you would come to dinner," I said, disappointed.

"Julia hasn't been feeling well; I don't want to leave her any longer than necessary," he said with an edge of concern.

"Nothing serious, I hope?"

He smiled. "She will be right as rain; just need to get her to rest up more often. So good luck," he said, placing a kiss to my cheek before heading to the door. "And um, break a leg, as they say, or don't break a leg, but, you know; good luck." I smiled at his words. He was so much like Blake it was unreal.

As Marti opened the door to leave, I could hear the noise filtering in from the audience. Nerves slowly began to seep into my veins; I had been so preoccupied recently that I had managed to forget about the live studio audience that I would be performing to. But with those nerves came excitement; I had been waiting for a moment like this for years, and finally that day had arrived.

I was practically bouncing off the walls when I returned to my dressing room five hours later. The recording had gone amazingly well, the audience had been fantastic, and Marcus had been the best actor I had ever worked with. I made a vow not to tell Blake that, but he had made me feel so welcome and at home, and helped to ease any nerves that appeared without notice. I couldn't wait until the following Friday already. If I could do this as a job for the rest of my career, I would jump at it; recording in front of an audience that got involved and made me feel good was a million times better than any film or TV series I had worked on before. Anything from now on would always feel mediocre in comparison.

I stood and re-read Blake's note with a huge smile on my face; I know that he would have been proud of me.

I headed to the bathroom to freshen up before heading out to dinner. Looking at myself in the mirror, I could see my own happiness shining back at me for the first time in years. I was glowing. Gone was the sad, pale-faced girl who had arrived in New York full of anxiety and dread. I had grown. I could see my growth through my eyes, and finally I was in a happy place, with the hurdles getting pushed further and further into the distance every day.

The Italian restaurant that Marcus always ate at was packed full of cast and crew from the show. The whole place was filled with laughter and excitement at how the show had gone earlier. I missed Blake more in that moment than I had all week. I felt he should be there celebrating with me. I felt guilty that I was even trying to have a good time without him.

"Penny for your thoughts?" Cooper placed his glass down on the table before pulling out the next seat to mine.

"Just missing Blake, that's all." I shrugged as I watched the champagne swirl around the bottom of the glass that I was twiddling with.

"He would have been so proud of you tonight; you were amazing, Jo." I looked up to Cooper in surprise. "What," he asked, appearing wounded, "I can't give you a compliment now?"

"Sorry," I sighed, "it's just—"

"Blake wouldn't like me sitting here talking to you. Or being in the same room as you even," he stated.

"He's just doing what any other man in his position would do," I said defensively.

"I don't blame Blake for hating me, you know," he said quietly. "I just want to make things right, that's all."

"I know," I replied. "You're looking better, by the way," I observed.

"Feeling it too," he said. "Had enough beatings to last me a lifetime recently," he said carefully.

"Maybe you need to behave better," I joked.

"Maybe I do," he said, swigging the rest of his champagne from the glass.

"I think I'm going to call it a night." I stood and grabbed my handbag from the table.

"How are you getting home?"

I hadn't even given that a thought; I had been so caught up in getting fit and losing some weight that I hadn't even thought about what time I would be getting home. "I'll just get a cab."

"You will do no such thing," Cooper said, laughing hard. "Come on, I'll take you."

"Cooper, no. You know that's not a good idea."

"And getting in a cab in the middle of New York on a Friday

evening is?" he shrugged into his jacket and took his keys from his pocket. "I'm not gonna bite, Jo," he joked.

"Okay," I sighed, hating myself for allowing Cooper to get even closer than he should. Blake hated Cooper, that was a given, but he also hated me getting into cabs at every opportunity. Surely Cooper giving me a lift home instead would be easier for Blake to accept than if I got into a cab.

"Do you want me to see you upstairs?" Cooper asked with a hint of amusement.

"Hmm, no," I said firmly. "Thank you for the lift, but I think I'll be okay from here."

Cooper smiled slightly. "It's good to have you back, Jo."

"I'm not sure the same will apply once Blake returns, he means everything to me, Cooper, I can't lose him." I said carefully.

"I know." He nodded, turning his attention to the front window. "But it's nice to think I'm kind of protecting you in Blake's absence," he said quietly as his focus remained away from me.

I smiled, shaking my head. "I don't need protecting."

"I'm sure Blake would disagree," he said, turning to face me. "Especially if he knew about your car being vandalized."

"I think Blake already has someone watching over me."

"Who?"

"I don't know. But I keep seeing the same black SUV everywhere I go. Can't be a coincidence, surely. I told Blake before he went away that I didn't want anyone following me, but I think he went ahead and did it anyway."

Cooper straightened in his seat. "So you've seen who is driving the SUV then?"

"No, they're never quite close enough. But it's obvious, isn't it?" I asked, confused.

"Sounds that way," Cooper replied. "Just be careful, okay?"

"Of course I will." I laughed, but Cooper's expression remained impassive.

"I'm serious, Jo. Protection or no protection, just be careful." He lifted his mouth into a small smile. "See you soon."

"Bye, Cooper," I replied as I got out of the car. It seemed with Cooper that every time I felt he was back to his old self, his behaviour left me feeling confused as hell.

18

I could hear Casey sobbing when I entered the apartment. I found her sitting on the sofa next to an empty bottle of wine while she cried into the remaining wine in her glass.

I rushed over to the sofa and wrapped my arms around her immediately. "What the hell has happened?" I asked, confused.

"The wedding," she sobbed. "It's off." She buried her head into my neck and cried uncontrollably.

"Why?"

"He said it's too soon, that he isn't ready, that we should have waited," she sobbed. "I thought he loved me, but he doesn't; he doesn't love me, because he doesn't want to marry me."

"Casey," I sighed, holding her closer, "shall I talk to him?"

"No," she said firmly. "There's no point. If he doesn't want to get married, then we can't be together. I can't be with him knowing that he doesn't want to marry me," Casey cried.

I did the only thing I knew how; I just held her tight and let her cry all she needed to cry.

I had seen this coming. I knew Alex and I knew his fears; I shared them. When Casey had booked the wedding on such short notice, I knew that Alex would crumble. I would have been the same in his position. But it was still gut wrenching seeing my best friend cry so many tears over the whole situation.

It had been a long, tiring night; the only time I had managed to release myself from Casey's grip was when she had finally nodded off just as the sun started to rise.

I hadn't even managed to speak to Blake properly the night before, as Casey had been so hysterical that I could barely hear him. The small conversation that I had managed to have with Blake had yet again been filled with the guilt I felt over the time I had again spent with Cooper unbeknown to Blake. It hurt so much that I was keeping it from him that I decided I would avoid Cooper at all costs from now on. Blake was far more important to me than a friendship with Cooper, so last night would be the last time I would allow myself to be around him.

Blake always rang me like clockwork every morning at eight a.m., but by six thirty I couldn't wait any longer and called him instead.

"Hi," I said, choking back the emotion.

"Hey, what's wrong?" he said with concern.

"I just wanted to hear your voice," I said quietly. "I miss you."

I heard Blake sigh heavily. "I miss you too, so much. How's Casey?"

"She's only just nodded off; it's been one hell of a long night."

"I'll call Alex."

"Okay," I whispered.

"Is everything else okay?"

I sucked in a deep breath. "Everything else is fine," I lied, scrunching my eyes shut as guilt crept in.

"Dad said you were amazing last night." I could hear the smile in his voice.

"The whole thing was amazing," I said, remembering the buzz I felt after the show. "I just wish you could have been there."

"Me too, beautiful."

"Can you call me again later? Any time, I just want to hear you as much as possible."

"You sure you're okay?"

"I'm just tired," I lied. " I love you."

"I love you too."

The whole weekend was consumed by me running from Casey to Alex and back again, trying my hardest to make them both see sense.

I understood Alex's insecurities; I had been there. I could also understand how Casey must be feeling knowing he didn't want to marry her yet. But somehow I needed them both to see that they loved each other too much to throw everything away. I was desperate to find some common ground between the two.

I was physically and mentally drained. I had ended Friday's show on such a high, but then arriving home to find Casey upset had taken everything from me. I needed Blake right now; I needed to be in his arms and to know that everything was going to be okay. But I couldn't tell him that; I wouldn't tell him. He would only worry too much and end up being stuck in Miami longer than planned if he couldn't concentrate on his job.

It was just one week until he would be home; I knew I could do this. I had struggled through the last week, so I could do it again.

I had noticed the black SUV following me again a couple of times over the weekend. I had been out jogging on one occasion when the car had crawled slowly past me a couple of times. I had tried to approach the vehicle on two separate occasions, after the way Cooper reacted when I told him about the SUV spurred on my curiosity. I actually did want to know who Blake had following me, but before I would even get a chance to get close enough to see, they would speed away, leaving me confused and angry.

I was literally running on empty. I was hardly sleeping, because Casey would choose every evening to get drunk and sob over Alex. I was hardly eating, because I felt constantly sick from all of the stress that was building inside of me. I felt as though the walls were slowly caving in and any minute now I was going to surrender. Every day was getting to be like Groundhog Day; I would wake to Casey sobbing and do my best to comfort her before going out for a jog just to escape the crying for a while. I would then spot the black SUV and approach it only for it to drive off. I would then receive a text from Cooper offering me a lift to or from rehearsals, which I would ignore. I would then return home to yet more tears from Casey. I was becoming pissed off and very annoyed at how my time away from Blake was panning out.

"So you are still alive then?" Cooper stood outside my dressing room with his arms folded over his chest and a big grin on his face.

"Cooper," I said as I stalked past him in a huff.

"Have I done something?" he asked in confusion as he caught up to me.

"I don't know, Cooper; you tell me," I said as I stopped and turned to face him.

"What?" he asked shocked.

"I have just spent the past two hours cleaning up after someone has been into my dressing room, snapped every single head from every single flower, trampled them into the carpet, tore up my clothes, and then used my lipstick to write 'slut' on my mirror," I choked out.

"Are you serious?"

"Do I look like I'm joking?"

"Who would do that?" he asked as my eyes widened towards him. "You think it was me?" he asked in surprise.

"Well, you've done worse than this to me before," I snapped before turning and heading towards the back door. "And look, here you are again! Every time something happens to me, there you are!"

"Jo," Cooper said calmly, walking beside me. "I have nothing to do with any of the shit that is happening to you. I swear." His hands rested on my shoulders as he spun me to face him, his eyes fixed onto mine. "I swear," he said again.

"Then who is?" I said quietly.

Cooper's arms wrapped around me, and for a brief moment I allowed myself to rest my head to his chest. "I'm here for you, Jo, okay? We will get you through this, I promise."

Lifting my head sharply from Cooper's chest, I shook my head frantically. "No. No, this is all wrong. I shouldn't be letting you comfort me. You shouldn't even be here, for Christ's sake!"

"It's a good thing that I am," he said.

"No. No it's not." Shaking my head, I turned and continued to exit the building.

"Where are you going?" Cooper yelled back.

"Home," I replied without turning my head.

Cooper caught up to me once I swung open the door and stepped out onto the car park. "Get in the car; it's obviously not safe for you to be walking."

"No way," I laughed.

"Jo, you can't walk home; it's too dangerous. Come back with me, and I'll take you home."

Ignoring him, I shook my head in disbelief. "Was that all part of the plan? To get me into your car so you can finish me off?"

"No! God, Jo, just listen to me." I continued to walk and stepped out of the gates and onto the hot streets of New York. Cooper trailed behind.

"Can you stop following me?"

"I'm not following you; I'm making sure you're okay."

"You are following me. Now stop following me and go. Goodbye, Cooper." I stood and waited to cross the road, noticing the black SUV crawling slowly towards me.

"Jo, don't go any further; please stop. Stop where you are." Choosing to ignore Cooper, I stepped off the curb. The roar of an engine seemed to close in on me along with a screeching noise from tyres as they spun on the hot tarmac.

"Jo!" Cooper yelled again, but I chose to ignore him and continued to walk. The SUV sped up suddenly and was heading towards me at speed. My feet stopped working as my entire body froze. I stood unable to move in the middle of the otherwise deserted road as I watched the car that had been following me for the past week and a half quickly approaching me. The car that I had seen so many times, thinking that they were watching me, that they were protecting me, was about to knock me down and leave me to die. They were not here to protect me after all; they were here to kill me. I was unable to move my body; they would hit their target head-on. This was how my life was going to end.

Suddenly my body was moving. Cooper's arms wrapped tightly around me as he charged me out of the road, my feet dragging across the floor. We crashed to the floor with force as we made it to the other side of the road just as the SUV skimmed past us both, somehow managing to miss us.

I lay on the floor, my body shaking vigorously. We were both breathing hard as we watched the car continue down the road until it was out of sight.

Cooper had saved my life; he had risked himself and saved my life. After everything that I had said to him, everything I had accused him of, he had just stopped someone from knocking me down and leaving me for dead, risking his own life in the process.

"Are you okay?" he panted shakily.

"They tried to kill me," I said quietly. "They actually tried to kill me." I rested my head down onto Cooper's arm that was still cradled around me as tears streamed from my eyes. "You saved me," I whispered, closing my eyes tightly. "Thank you."

"Did you get the licence plate?" Cooper asked.

"No. It all happened too quick."

"Let's get you home," Cooper said as he struggled to his feet. "This time I will not take no for an answer."

I turned my head to Cooper as he parked the car. "I'm so sorry that I blamed you for everything."

"It's okay," he said, turning to face me.

"No, it isn't okay, Cooper; all you have been doing is trying to help me, and I've been so horrible to you."

Cooper smiled. "Yeah, well, you kinda have your reasons for not trusting me."

"I'm glad you followed me now," I joked.

"I'm glad I followed you too," he laughed. "I'm gonna walk you upstairs. I'm not taking no for an answer, and there is no ulterior motive; I just want to make sure you get into the apartment okay."

"I'm not going to argue with you on that one. Thank you."

"Do you think Blake will be okay about this?"

"I think Blake will be as grateful as I am. You saved my life, Cooper. But I don't want him to know about anything that has happened until he's home."

"You didn't tell him about the car being vandalized?"

"No. He can't do anything from there except worry. I haven't told him anything."

"Jo," Cooper sighed.

"I know what I am doing, Cooper. He will understand."

"Are you going to call the police?"

"I have nothing to go on – no licence plate, no suspects, nothing."

"Is there anyone that you think could have done this?"

I thought for a moment before replying. "Sara," I said quietly before turning to Cooper. "Could you do a check on her? Is there any way you could check that she is where she is supposed to be? I mean, it sounds crazy, I know, and it's been a while. I don't know why she would want to hurt me now after all this time. But she is that only person I think would want to hurt me after how she behaved that night in my apartment. Could you do that?"

"Of course I will. Leave it with me," he promised.

The apartment was quiet for the first time in almost a week when we entered.

I hoped that by now both Casey and Alex had seen sense and were back on track. I had heard enough of Casey's crying this week to last me a lifetime, and it wasn't as if I weren't going through enough myself as it was.

Cooper told me to wait in the hallway while he did a sweep of the apartment. He returned a couple of minutes later with a smile on his face. "All clear; there's just Casey passed out drunk on the sofa."

"Ah what?" I said, not hiding my annoyance as I headed past Cooper and into the lounge.

I grabbed the empty wine bottle and glass from the table before turning to Casey.

My body shuddered with instant panic when I noticed the bottle of pills that she was clutching in her hand. Dropping the bottle and glass, I grabbed Casey and shook her. "Casey! Casey, wake up! What have you done? What the hell have you done?!"

"What is it?" Cooper asked as he entered the room.

Slapping her face was doing nothing to bring her out of her comatose state. "She's taken some pills and drained that bottle," I said shakily. "Casey, please talk to me!" I begged as I shook her.

Cooper checked her pulse. "It's still strong," he said. "We must have gotten here just in time. Call 911," he demanded.

"Don't you die! Don't you dare die on me!" I cried as I grabbed my phone and dialled for the paramedics.

Everything seemed to happen in slow motion. It felt like an eternity until the paramedics arrived. While we waited, I begged Casey over and over again to acknowledge that I was there, but she was so limp, so weak, so out of it. The paramedics asked us many questions, but I didn't know any of the answers; I had no idea how many pills she had taken or how much she had drunk. I felt guilty that I hadn't even been there when it happened.

I rode in the ambulance alongside Casey to the hospital. Cooper insisted on following behind to make sure that I was okay as well as Casey. I tried Alex's number over and over again, but to no avail. *He should be the one here with Casey, not me*, I thought. He was being stubborn, and it was now truly beginning to piss me off.

It felt like the longest night of my life waiting for news on my best friend. What if I had got to her too late? What if the person who was trying to take my life had succeeded? Casey would have been left by herself; she would have died. A million different thoughts were running through my mind as we waited in the cold waiting room.

"She's going to be okay, Jo," Cooper said, bringing my attention back to the here and now.

"What if we hadn't got to her in time, Cooper? What if I had been hit by that car? We could both be dead now."

"But you're not," he stated firmly.

"But we could have been."

"Are you always a cup-half-empty kind of girl?" Cooper asked, smiling slightly.

"At the moment, my cup is completely empty," I sighed. "I just want to be happy, Cooper. But every time I'm happy, this happens: pain, fear, heartache, everything. All I want is to be happy. Is that too much to ask?"

Cooper watched me carefully as he considered what I had just told him "No. It's not too much to ask at all, Jo," he said sadly. "Look, I need to make a call. I'll be right back." He stood and headed to the door.

"Cooper?" He turned back to look at me. "Thank you," I said.

His mouth lifted into a genuine smile. "That's what friends are for, Jo."

The relief that flooded me when the doctor told me that Casey was going to be fine was like the biggest weight being lifted from my shoulders. I had been allowed in to see her briefly, but she needed plenty of rest. I asked Cooper to stop off at the club on the way home, knowing that that was where I would find Alex.

It was eerily quiet as I stepped into the club. Cleaners went about their work, mopping up spilt drinks and the smell of sweaty bodies that had filled the room only a couple of hours ago. I headed with purpose to Alex's office. I didn't knock before I entered to find him sitting at his desk, sipping whiskey and working at his laptop.

"I wondered when you would show up to give me a pep talk," he slurred without lifting his eyes to me.

"Do you have any idea where I have been for the past six hours?" I asked angrily.

His eyes lifted to me slowly before he sat back in his chair and folded his arms across his chest.

"Enlighten me; where have you been?" he said.

"I have just spent the past six hours sitting in a waiting room while doctors did everything they could to stop my best friend from dying from a booze and pills overdose," I said as angry tears stung my eyes.

Alex shot out of his chair. "What!"

"She tried to kill herself, Alex. Because of you!" I yelled. "Because you were too much of a bastard to commit to the woman who loves you and who you love because you are so stuck in the past that you would rather you both suffer than face your fears."

"Is she going to be okay?" he said, frantically reaching for his jacket from the back of his chair.

"She's lucky," I replied quietly. "The doctor said that I found her in time."

"I need to be with her," Alex said, grabbing his keys and heading for the door.

"You need to do the right thing, Alex; stop living in the past and do what's right for now."

Alex turned to me and nodded once; a silent understanding passed between us. Only a couple of weeks ago, he had stood in front of me and practically told me the same thing.

"Thank you," he said before walking out and heading to the hospital.

It took us four hours and thirty-five minutes to film my final episode of *Perfect Alibi*. The audience was again amazing, as was Marcus. He thanked me on stage for being a great co-star, and the audience cheered along. It made me feel amazing but also emotional.

I had enjoyed my two weeks there; despite how challenging it had been on the outside, this had been my favourite job in my entire career. It was a shame that it had been tarred with so much stress outside of the studio. But I was beginning to see that this was what my life was meant to be like. There were always going to be challenges and upsets; I was just going to have to learn to deal with them head-on, as that was always the better way. Running solved nothing. I was learning that now.

"You joining us for dinner this evening?" Marcus asked as we stepped off stage and headed down the corridor towards our dressing rooms.

"Absolutely," I replied.

"Great. I'll come knock for you in twenty minutes." He smiled, bumping his shoulder into mine before disappearing into his dressing room.

Yes, I was really going to miss this. It had been the perfect escape for me while Blake was away, despite that someone had tried to kill me. I smiled to myself as I thought about the saying "You could write a book about it"; that's how crazy my life had been over the past two weeks.

I opened the door to my dressing room and stepped inside. My heart pounded hard and my body shook at the sight that awaited me.

"Hello, beautiful."

I gasped in surprise. Every ounce of fear and dread and hurt that had been building up inside me for the past eleven days evaporated like vapour into the air.

"Blake," I said with relief. "Oh my God!" Happy tears burst the dams. Closing the distance between us, I took two quick steps and jumped into his open arms, wrapping my legs tightly around his waist.

Immediately the warmth from his body gripped me as his arms folded tightly around my waist. He was here, in front of me, and I was as close in his arms as I could possibly manage, but I needed to get closer.

"When did you? ... how did you? ..." My fingers grazed the short stubble of his chin as I took in the sight of him. "I can't believe you're here," I said in disbelief. "Am I dreaming, or are you really here?" I laughed.

"I'm really here, beautiful. We finished earlier than expected, and I wanted to surprise you," he said with a gleam in his smile. "You were fantastic out there, really. Wow."

My mouth claimed his. God I had missed him, more than I could ever have imagined. There was so much he didn't know that I would need to talk to him about, but right now I would enjoy the fact that he was here, in my dressing room, holding me in his arms, in my safe place.

"You have no idea how happy I am right now," I said as I pulled away briefly. "I love you so much."

"I love you too," Blake said as he squeezed my backside, pulling me closer to him.

A sharp knock at the door distracted us both. My body slid out of Blake's hold. We were both panting hard. I took a moment to steady my breathing, resting my head against Blake's chest.

"Don't move," I said quietly.

Blake smiled. "I'm never going anywhere again, beautiful. Not without you."

I walked over to the door, feeling slightly nervous. The last thing I wanted now was to find Cooper standing on the other side of the door, waiting to look after me as he had been doing since Blake had been away.

"Ready to go?" Marcus asked.

"I think I'm going to take a rain check, I'm afraid." I opened the door wider and nodded to Blake.

"Hey, you're back," Marcus said, stepping around me and heading to Blake. "How was Miami?"

He nodded. "It was good, but I couldn't wait to get back." Blake's eyes burnt into me with hunger. Sensing our anticipation to be with each other, Marcus excused himself after making plans with Blake and me for dinner the following week.

"Please tell me you moved all of your things into my apartment while I was away," Blake said as I closed the door behind Marcus.

"About that," I said carefully as I walked back to where Blake stood. "I've been really busy with Casey and Alex and work, and—"

Blake's mouth was on mine instantly, silencing me. "You're not backing out, I hope," he said against my mouth.

"Not a chance," I panted. "I only have a few things left to move. Take me home, and I will get the rest of my things tomorrow; but for now I want to go home and spend the next twenty-four hours making up for lost time."

"Don't you have a bridesmaid fitting early tomorrow?"

A small groan escaped my lips. "Okay, I want to spend the next twelve hours making up for lost time, and then forever after that."

"Forever, huh?"

I nodded. "Forever."

19

I was back in the safeness that I had become so accustomed to before Blake had gone to work in Miami. He sang happily in the kitchen as I lay in bed waking from a fairly sleepless night, but one that I hadn't minded whatsoever.

Having Blake home had eased all of my concern; I had no need to worry about anything now that Blake was back by my side.

I realized, however, that I wasn't as strong as I had hoped I could be alone, but that no longer mattered, not now Blake was back to protect me. I realized that at some point that day, there was so much that I needed to tell him. I wasn't sure how he was going to take the news that I had spent so much time with Cooper against his wishes, but I was sure that as soon as he knew that Cooper had saved my life, he would understand and be as grateful to him as I was.

Blake came strolling into the bedroom wearing only a pair of pyjama bottoms and carrying a tray full of food.

"Good morning, my beautiful," he said, placing the tray on the bedside table before kissing me briefly. "I hope you're hungry."

"Only for you," I said, wrapping my hand around his neck and pulling him to me. He kissed me again before pulling back. "We have all the time in the world for that," he said with a chuckle, "but this morning isn't that time."

I pouted, crossing my arms over my chest.

"And stop pouting," he said, tugging my lip with his teeth. "Casey and Alex will be here in thirty minutes; Alex and I have been given instructions," Blake said, wide-eyed in horror. "He's all hands-on now with this wedding, you know." Blake brushed the hair from my face with his fingers. "And from what I've heard, that's all thanks to you," he said, kissing me again. I grinned widely, knowing that somehow, through all of the shit that had happened that week, I had managed to achieve some good.

"Now eat and get dressed," he said, climbing off the bed and heading to the bathroom. The truth was that I felt starving, but today was my dress fitting and I was hoping that I had shed the excess weight I had gained as a result of Blake and his persistence to make me eat. I took a couple of bites from one of the pastries to keep me going while I got myself ready for the day ahead.

"How?" I asked in frustration. "How the hell are my measurements the same when I've barely eaten and have exercised as much as I have?" Casey's giggling only made me more frustrated. "It's not funny," I moaned.

"Come on, Jo, so you gained a little weight. You can't even tell; you don't have an ounce of fat on you," she said, wrapping her arm around me as we walked from the boutique and headed for the florist to check last-minute details.

While Casey chatted with the florist, I stepped outside to listen to the voicemail that Cooper had left on my mobile a couple of hours before: "Hey, Jo. I hear that Blake got back last night. I hope he's okay with my being your bodyguard while he's been away." I heard the amusement in his voice. "I just wanted to let you know that everything with Sara still checks out. She is still very much in rehab and receiving all of the help that she needs. I hope that eases your mind somewhat. Although I imagine it's still confusing as to who would ever try to hurt you." His voice grew quiet towards the end, as though his mind were elsewhere. "Anyway, I hope I can see you soon. Maybe. Let me know."

I decided to return Cooper's call to thank him for everything he had done for me. His phone went straight to voicemail, so I left him a message.

"Hi, Cooper, it's me, Jo." I rolled my eyes at myself; of course he would know it was me. "I just wanted to thank you for everything that you have done for me while Blake has been away. I'm glad we were able to get back the friendship that we had before … Well, before everything. You have been amazing to me, Cooper, thank you. And as for Sara still being where she is, thank you for looking into that for me. It's still a mystery who wanted to hurt me, but now Blake is back, I have a feeling I'm going to be okay." I smiled. "Oh, and just one more thing, Cooper. Thank you for saving my life. I'll see you soon."

Blake was talking on his phone when I walked into the apartment. I dropped my keys and handbag on the dining table before taking a bottle of water from the fridge. I watched as Blake approached me after finishing the call. He looked confused, hurt even.

"That was Marcus," he said, tossing his phone onto the table before leaning back against the counter, crossing his arms against his chest. "Anything you want to tell me?" he asked calmly.

"What about?" I asked nervously.

"Oh, I don't know." He shrugged. "The car being vandalized, your dressing room being trashed …Cooper?"

"What did Marcus say?" I asked shakily.

"That doesn't matter. It's what you have to say that I'm more interested in hearing."

"I was going to tell you everything once you got back, Blake, I swear."

"I got back last night, Jo, and yet you haven't told me anything."

"I was so happy to see you last night; you have no idea just how much." I stepped over to Blake and placed my hands on his chest. His arms stayed crossed. "I didn't want to spoil that. I swear I was going to tell you everything today." My voice became panicked. I was beginning to regret not telling him anything.

"Has someone been trying to hurt you while I haven't been here?"

"Yes," I replied simply. "It seems that way."

"And you didn't think to tell me? I told you I wanted to protect you. I arranged for someone to look after you while I was gone. But you said no, Jo. *You* said *no*," he said as he shrugged me from him and began pacing the kitchen. "I should never have listened to you, never. Do you know how I feel now because I listened to you? Because I chose to do what you wanted rather than what you needed? I shouldn't have listened to you. I should have gone behind your back, just like you have been doing to me for the past two weeks."

"It wasn't like that," I said quietly.

"Then tell me, Jo. What was it like, huh? What made you turn to Cooper and not me? What made you want to hide everything from me like I mean nothing? Cooper tried to rape you, for God's sake, and you turn to him when someone is trying to hurt you!"

"I wanted for once to stand on my own two feet, Blake. That is why I didn't tell you. I am sick and tired of having someone watching over me, looking after me like I can't look after myself. I am sick of it!"

"So you turned to Cooper?"

"No. I didn't, I swear. He was just there, Blake; he just happened to be there," I stated.

"What a coincidence," Blake snapped.

"He saved my life, Blake!"

"What!"

"He saved my life!" I tried to remain calm, although I felt as though my insides were slowly crumbling. "I didn't ask him to, but he did. He pushed me from the road when a car that had been following me for the past two weeks tried to run me down. The only reason I didn't tell you anything was because I knew you couldn't do anything from Miami. What could you have possibly done to help me?"

"I should have been the one who saved your life, not him."

"But you weren't here! You should be grateful to him, for Christ's sake; if it wasn't for him, I wouldn't be standing here now arguing with you!"

"Wow," Blake said, shaking his head in disbelief, "He really has gotten to you, hasn't he?"

"What?"

"Why can't you see him for what he really is, Jo?"

"He saved my life," I said again.

"Only a couple of weeks ago, he almost had your death on his hands, Jo," he spat out. "So forgive me if I don't see what there is to thank him for in all of this."

"I can't believe you are behaving like this," I said quietly.

"And you would behave differently, would you? If it were, say … Christina?" He shrugged.

"That is different and you know it," I choked out.

"Is it? You have been lying to me for almost two weeks about something that I should have known about. And then keeping the fact that you have been spending time with Cooper from me just makes this a whole lot worse," he spat back. "Do you know what your problem is, Jo?" I lifted my eyes to meet his gaze. "You forgive too easily. People hurt you, and you forget about it when they begin to show you one ounce of goodness. You only ever see the good in people."

"And that's a bad thing?" I choked out.

"Not always, no," He shook his head slowly. "But that is why you always end up getting hurt."

Blake's words cut into me like a knife. I got that he was angry, but he was actually standing there telling me that everything that happened to me was always my fault.

"Maybe I was too forgiving with you too, then," I replied.

Suddenly I realized that I had been right all along. How could I ever be happy? True happiness definitely didn't exist. Whatever had made me actually believe that there was such a thing as happiness without pain had always just been a figment of my imagination, because from the view of the world that I had right now, happiness definitely only existed in fairy tales. I loved Blake more than I ever knew was even possible, but was that enough? Was love strong enough to get us through all of the shit that was constantly being thrown at us? I took a deep breath and prepared to do the only thing I was only ever capable of doing successfully. Picking up my handbag, I headed for the door.

"What are you doing?" Blake asked in a panic.

With my hand on the door handle, I took a deep breath and turned back to face Blake.

"I'm running." I swallowed. "I'm running, Blake, and this time I am not coming back." I opened the door and ran for the lift, refusing to look back, refusing to allow myself to stay. Blake called out to me, but I ran as fast as my legs could take me. As the lift closed, I saw Blake turn the corner.

"Jo, please don't do this! I'm sorry!" his eyes caught mine as the doors closed and the lift began to make its descent. Falling to the floor, I sobbed uncontrollably. I had been foolish enough to believe I could be happy, and this just confirmed that was never going to be possible, so I did the only thing that I had ever been good at and ran.

I climbed into the car and started the engine. My visibility was poor from the amount of tears that were streaming down my face, but I needed to get away. Away from Blake, away from everything that had just destroyed the tiniest bit of happiness that I had allowed myself to regain.

I sped out onto the busy streets of New York with no idea of where I was heading or what I would do next, but I needed to get as far away from Blake as possible. The sky clouded over, and rain began to fall, clouding my visibility even more. The car echoed as my phone began to ring. The screen told me that it was Blake calling, but I would not answer. I would not let him talk me into turning the car around and going. We were done.

I had no idea where I was or where I was heading, but I knew that the more I drove, the further from the heartache I was getting, so keeping my foot firmly to the ground, I drove as fast as I could and as far away as possible.

Blake was persistent, however; every time the phone would ring off, he would redial. "Stop calling me," I repeated over and over to myself. My tears were now full-on sobs. Using my arm to clear my eyes was doing nothing to help my visibility. The car jolted forward suddenly; looking into my rear-view mirror, I spotted the black SUV on my tail. "Shit, no!" I cried as panic struck. I was being followed. I didn't know for how long, but I did know that it was the same car that for the past two weeks had followed practically every move that I had made. The same car that had tried to knock me down and kill me was following me now. My body began to shake; my eyes flickered from the road ahead to the car behind. Trying to shake them off, I took corners without warning, only for them to do the same. This was it. This was how I was going to succumb to them; this time they would catch up with me, and this would be how I would die.

I felt the car shudder again. Checking my mirror, I saw they were on my tail, bumping me over and over, trying to run me from the road. With each bump I would scream out. Fear filled my body. I had no idea how I was going to get out of this, but for now I needed to keep going, keep trying, keep hoping. I tried desperately to see who was driving the car, who wanted me hurt so badly. But my tears, mixed with the rain that was now lashing down, made the visibility almost impossible.

My phone rang again, and this time I answered. As much as Blake had hurt me with his accusations, I needed him right now. Regardless of any words that had been said in anger, I needed him to help me. He was the only person that I wanted; the only person that I had ever needed in my life. I needed Blake. This time, running had been the biggest mistake I could have made.

"Blake," I cried out.

"Jo, thank God, please come home, please. I'm sorry; I'm so sorry. We can work this out, can't we? Can we please work this out?"

"Blake!" I shouted through the sobs. "I'm being followed. It's the same car again. It's a black SUV. They're going to kill me, Blake, and I'm so scared, I'm so scared!" I sobbed just as the car bumped me again, causing me to scream out. "They're trying to run me off the road, Blake! Help me, please, help me!"

"Where are you," he said firmly. "Tell me where you are!"

"I don't know," I replied, looking around frantically, "I just kept on driving. Blake, please, they're going to kill me!"

"God, Jo, I'm so sorry, so fucking sorry. I'm going to help you, Jo, I promise. Tell me what you see; tell me any signs that you see." Blake was trying to remain calm but I could sense the fear in his voice.

Again I looked around, desperate for something to show me where I was, but my mind was so preoccupied that I didn't see the red light that I ran. Spotting an oncoming vehicle, I swerved the car in desperation to avoid hurting anyone else. "Blake!" I screamed just as I hit the curb. Noticing pedestrians I swerved again pressing my foot hard onto the brake pedal. The tyres screeched against the wetness of the road, the car skidding as it veered uncontrollably towards the wall of a small row of shops. In that moment, everything appeared to slow down, my life flashed in front of me as I clung tightly to the wheel, praying for everything to be ok. I screamed out just as the car hit the wall. The phone line went dead.

20

The airbag had inflated and deflated before I had a chance to notice. It took me a moment to realize that I was still alive. I lifted my shaky arms above the bag that had just saved my life and looked around me. I was alive, I wasn't hurting anywhere except for my ribs that were most likely bruised from the impact of the bag, but I was alive, that was all that mattered. The car was immediately surrounded by passers-by who tried to help me. It was mayhem as people shouted and called to me but all I could think about was how the hell I had managed to survive yet another ordeal from someone who tried to take my life.

The paramedics checked me over but still insisted that I get checked out at the hospital; no amount of pleading that I did would convince them that I was fine.

I was seen immediately by DR Green, who had looked after me the night I was drugged.

It was kind of nice to see a familiar face, even if it was a doctor who was treating me yet again. I sat impatiently on the edge of the bed, waiting for him to return and tell me that I was well enough to go home.

When the doctor entered the room, he was smiling happily. "You have been a very lucky lady, Miss Summers."

I smiled. "Again."

"Indeed." He nodded as he looked down to the clipboard he was holding. "Your ribs will feel a bit sore for a while but should heal in a couple of days. There are no broken bones, just quite a bit of bruising. Those bags can have quite an impact."

"Thank you. Can I go now?"

"Miss Summers," he said, moving his eyes from the clipboard to me. Panic set in, as his eyes seemed to fill with concern.

"About the blood tests that we ran when you arrived,"

"Yes?" I asked, panic stricken.

"Are you aware that you are pregnant?"

The whole world stopped turning at that precise moment. I must have been hallucinating, surely? How could I be pregnant? It was impossible.

"I'm … what?" I asked, frozen.

"That's what I thought." He smiled. "One of the routine bloods that we ran showed a very high level of HCG, confirming that you are indeed with child. You will, of course, need to book in for an ultrasound to determine the gestation, seeing as you are unaware." He smiled.

"But I'm on the pill. This is impossible; are you sure?"

"Have you maybe been ill? Or late taking your pills? Any of these factors can contribute in the pill being inefficient."

"I'm not … I'm, um … I don't know."

"I have some leaflets here for you to take home," he said with a smile. "They should help you with any questions that may arise. For now, however, you will need to stop taking the pill."

"Could it have harmed the baby? That I've still been taking the pill? I've even been drinking on occasion." I felt nausea burn my throat.

"Try not to worry, Miss Summers. There has never been any conclusive evidence to suggest that problems occur from taking the pill while in the early stages of pregnancy. Some people have been known to carry full term without even knowing that they are pregnant." He smiled.

"I'm pregnant?" I asked again in disbelief as I took the leaflets from him.

"Congratulations, Miss Summers." He smiled. "I'm sure it will sink in soon."

"But the crash? Won't the crash have caused any damage either?"

"Babies are very resilient to the kind of impact you endured. If, however, you experience any pain or spotting, it is recommended that you get checked out as soon as possible."

"I'm pregnant," I stated in complete disbelief.

"You are free to go as soon as you are ready; you just need to sign some papers at reception." He turned and headed out of the room.

"I'm pregnant," I said again, trying to process the news. I wasn't sure how I felt about the news. I loved kids, and I knew Blake did too; he had commented at his parents' that he couldn't wait for us to have children, but would he feel that this was too soon? We had left things in such a way that I wasn't sure he would share that kind of enthusiasm any more.

Looking down to my stomach I felt a small smile tug at my lips through the heartache. "So you're the reason for my twenty-six inch waist then?" I placed my hand to my stomach and immediately felt some sort of protection over the tiny bean that was floating around in there.

I placed the leaflets in my bag and climbed off the bed just as the door flung open and Blake came running towards me. "Thank God," he said, wrapping his arms around me tightly. "God, thank God you are okay."

"Ouch," I moaned, "my ribs."

"Sorry," he said, releasing me and looking me over. "I'm so sorry, Jo; I am so, so sorry," he said desperately.

"So am I," I sighed. "I'm sorry I ran, and I'm sorry I didn't tell you everything when I should have. You know that I would never go to anyone over you; you know that." I cupped Blake's chin in my hand, my fingers rubbing small circles across his stubble that I adored so much.

"I know you wouldn't have. I just hate myself for not being there for you when you really needed me. And I hate that it was Cooper who saved you. Even though I do feel grateful to him, I just hate that bastard. But he saved you; I shouldn't have said what I did, and I'm sorry that I shouted at you," he said before holding me again, this time carefully.

"I'm free to go now; I just need to sign some papers."

"So you're fine? Nothing to worry about?"

I looked into Blake's eyes. "Just take me home," I said, dodging the question. I wasn't sure yet whether he would see my news as worrying.

Blake nodded and took my hand in his. At some point I needed to tell him he was going to be a daddy, but for now I just wanted to get home and lie in his arms until I knew everything was going to be okay.

The police arrived at the apartment shortly after we arrived home from the hospital. They took a statement of everything that had happened to me that evening, and also everything that had happened to me over the past two weeks. Blake sat at the table next to me holding my hand firmly in his as I revealed every detail of what I had been through since Blake had gone to work in Miami. Occasionally I would look up at him. His smile was sad, his eyes full of emotion. Each time we were left alone for a moment while the police interacted with someone back in the office, he would turn to me and apologize over and over again for not being here, for the argument we had had earlier, and most of all for allowing me to run again. What Blake didn't understand was that nothing that had happened to me was his fault; nothing that ever happened to me was anyone's fault, except my own.

The police were interacting with officers back at the station to establish the car owner's identity. They had caught sight of the car on CCTV right here in our apartment building. They were running the checks as we spoke.

"Well, I think we pretty much have everything that we need from you for now, Miss Summers." The officer who had been speaking to us stood and gathered all of his belongings together. "If there is anything else, or something that you have missed out, don't hesitate to call us; but for now, I'm sure that you could do with some rest." He smiled. "The only thing I would suggest is that you stay put. Do not leave this building until we give you the go-ahead, understood?"

I nodded.

"Don't worry, officer; she won't be going anywhere," Blake said.

"We will be in touch." The officer smiled sympathetically before Blake showed him and his fellow officers to the door.

As the door closed, I was overcome with emotion. Placing my head into my hands as I sat at the table, I cried. I cried for everything that had happened to me during the past two weeks, I cried for how easily I had run again only a few hours ago, and I cried for the baby. I needed to tell Blake now that he was going to be a daddy, but everything else that had happened today made me too scared. Blake would either be happy or mad. If he was mad, I'm not sure how we would deal with it; if he was happy, I would be happy, but then I would be afraid of the pain that always coincided with that feeling. After holding me tightly while I cried as much as I could, Blake prepared us dinner. I wasn't hungry in the least, but I didn't have only myself to consider any more. I had a baby to look after now. After dinner Blake ran me a bath and climbed in gently behind me, his arms building a cradle around my body. No word, just actions. Just having his arms around me was more comforting than any words could ever be.

"Blake," I said eventually, breaking the silence.

"Hmm?"

"Are we going to be okay?" A small sob escaped my lips.

I heard Blake sigh heavily as he pulled me closer to him. He pressed his lips firmly against my neck.

"Of course we are," he said quietly.

"No matter what happens?"

"No matter what," he answered.

"I swear I will never keep anything from you again. I promise," I said as I turned in his arms. Water lapped over the sides as I nestled as close as I could get to him.

"Every time I think of how you must have felt, it kills me," he said. "Don't ever keep anything from me again, Jo," he said sadly. I looked up into his eyes; they were saddened. "I thought you were dead," he said. "When I heard you scream and the phone cut off …" He scrunched his eyes tight as he remembered the pain. When they reopened, they were full of unshed tears. "I thought you were gone. Just like the night at the club. I have mentally lost you twice now, Jo, and I can't even explain to you how that feels. But it's made me sure of one thing."

"What?"

"I am never, ever, going to lose you again. After everything that has happened today, the past two weeks, since I first met you even, I never, ever, want to experience life without you in it again."

I sat up and straddled his lap, taking his face into my hands. "I am so sorry," I said before kissing him. "So, so sorry." Our mouths clashed as all of the anger, hurt, and love that we both shared came spilling out at once. His hands tightened on my waist as his erection started to press against me.

A loud knock at the door startled us both. "That's going to be the police," Blake said, watching me carefully. "Everything is going to be fine, Jo. I promise." Blake climbed out of the bath and hurried through to the bedroom to change. I climbed out slowly a few moments later. I still hadn't managed to tell Blake about the baby. I had tried, I really had wanted to tell him, but the words found it impossible to leave my lips. I made myself a promise that no matter what, once the police were gone this time, I would tell Blake about the baby.

My body was already shaking before the police had even told us anything. Once dressed, I headed to the kitchen, where Blake, Detective Grayson (who was leading the investigation), and two different officers that had been at my apartment earlier were all seated around the dining table.

"Miss Summers," Detective Grayson greeted me. "How are you feeling?"

I nodded. "Okay. Have you found something?"

Detective Grayson looked from me to Blake before focusing his attention back to me.

"Miss Summers, I'm not sure exactly how to tell you this."

"What is it?" I asked nervously. Blake immediately took my hand as he sat next to me.

"In your statement," he said as he opened the folder and began reading through the text, "you mentioned a Cooper Henderson?" I nodded in response. "You say he was with you and pulled you from the road as the car approached you at speed."

"Yes, he saved me," I answered, confused. "Why?"

"We ran a check on the car that has been pursuing you. The car was rented out two weeks ago from a hire company right here in New York."

"Okay," I said, "so you have the name of the person that hired the car from them then," I stated.

"Yes, Miss Summers, we do. I'm afraid that the person who hired that car two weeks ago was Cooper Henderson."

"What?" I laughed. "You must be mistaken. Or there must be another Cooper Henderson here in New York. I mean, that's possible, isn't it? It can't be the Cooper I know; how could it be? If he wanted me dead, he wouldn't have saved me from the car." I looked from Detective Grayson to Blake. "He wouldn't have done that; I know him!" I said loudly as everyone else remained quiet.

"Miss Summers. We have a match on MR Henderson's identity. But I'm afraid there is more. MR Henderson wasn't working alone. It seems that he has been working alongside somebody else, who wanted you dead.

"That bastard!" Blake slammed his fist to the table. "I should have killed him when I had the fucking chance."

"We've seen this before. Cooper would befriend you; find out what you're doing, where you're going, etc. But the whole time, he would be reporting back to whoever else was responsible, planning their next move."

"He saved my life," I said quietly as tears started rolling down my face. "He was my friend; he saved my life."

I felt Blake's grip tighten on me. "Have you arrested him?"

"Shortly after we discovered that MR Henderson had hired the car, some of our officers went to his apartment to arrest him. He wasn't there. They did a sweep of his apartment and found numerous pieces of evidence that suggest he had been working alongside a female. Immediately, calls were put out to every officer in the area to keep an eye out for either the black SUV or indeed Cooper's own vehicle."

"So you haven't gotten him yet?" Blake asked angrily. "He is still out there?"

"Please, MR Mackenzie, let me finish. Cooper was spotted shortly after, heading southbound on Route 33. There were two people in the car, so our officers gave chase."

"Thank God," I said, feeling the relief that they had obviously found him before he could hurt me again.

"MR Henderson continued to drive, at speed. He had no intention of surrendering to us."

"So he got away," Blake said bluntly.

"MR Henderson lost control of his vehicle. He spun off the road at speed and hit a tree."

"Is he okay?" I asked quietly.

"I'm afraid MR Henderson died instantly from the impact."

I gasped. My whole body shuddered with shock. Cooper, who had saved my life only a few days ago, the man who had been one of the closest friends that I had made since arriving in New York, the person who had made me feel safe in Blake's absence, had been the person who wanted me dead. Feeling the bile rising rapidly in my throat I scraped my chair back from underneath me and ran to the bathroom. My stomach emptied its entire contents into the toilet until all I could do was heave, and even then I didn't feel finished. Cooper was dead. I couldn't accept that he had died while being chased by the police for attempting to murder me. It must have all somehow been a mistake. They must have had the wrong person, the wrong car, the wrong Cooper. He had saved me. Cooper had saved my life.

I felt Blake's warm hands on my shoulders as I finished washing my face. Immediately I turned in his arms and buried my head into his chest.

"He didn't deserve to die," I whispered.

"He tried to kill you, Jo," he said gently. I shook my head against his chest. "Why would he save me if he wanted me dead? It doesn't make any sense."

"I know." Blake placed his lips to my head and inhaled a deep breath. "Detective Grayson said he has something else he needs to talk to you about."

"What else could he possibly have to say to me?"

"The other person. They have her under protective custody in the hospital."

"Are you ready to go back out?" I nodded even though I wasn't ready to go back out to face Detective Grayson and his team. I wanted to curl up in a ball and hide from the world for the rest of my life.

"Blake held my hand as we rejoined the officers at the dining table.

"Miss Summers, I understand this is a massive shock for you. I'm sorry."

I forced a smile. "It's okay. Can you tell me about the other person? Do I know her too?"

Again Detective Grayson looked from Blake to me. "You do know her, Miss Summers, yes."

My mind went into overdrive wondering at whose name he was going to pull out. Everything up until now had been so unbelievable, so this would certainly come as no shock what so ever but deep down, I knew exactly who this was. I had asked Cooper to look into Sara for me, to find out her whereabouts and what she had been up to. He had told me that she was still in rehab, still getting all of the help that she needed to get better. That help was obviously coming from Cooper.

"It's Sara McDonnell, isn't it?"

"I'm afraid so, Miss Summers, yes." I felt the anger boil inside me for allowing myself to become such an easy target for her. "Was she ever in rehab? Was she ever getting help? Or was she after me the whole time?"

Detective Grayson flicked through the notes he held in front of him. "Miss McDonnell was admitted to Greenfields Clinic July nineteenth. She discharged herself only two days later. Her mom hasn't seen or heard from her since that day. On raiding MR Henderson's apartment, we found substantial evidence that she had resided with him since discharging herself from the clinic."

I placed my hand over my mouth in disbelief. "He knew all along that she wanted me dead, didn't he? He knew and he helped her."

"I'm so sorry," Detective Grayson replied. "There is one more thing."

I sighed heavily. "What?"

"We have Miss McDonnell in protective custody in hospital. *If* she recovers, she will be going away for a hell of a long time."

"Good," Blake said sharply.

"She has asked if you would see her."

"No way," Blake yelled as he stood from the table and ran his fingers through his hair. "Jo has been through enough; there is no way she is stepping foot anywhere near that crazy bitch."

"Miss Summers?"

I looked up at Blake before turning my attention back to Detective Grayson. "I never got to speak to the last person who tried to kill me. She committed suicide two days before she was due to start her trial."

"I'm sorry to hear that, ma'am."

"I want to see her. I want to see Sara."

"No," Blake said firmly before sitting back down next to me. "She is dangerous, Jo. Please don't do this," he pleaded.

"I need to. I need to know why, what made her want to actually kill me. I need to know. I could have asked Cooper, only he's dead now." I shrugged. "When can I see her?" I asked.

"I'll call forward now, see what we can do."

"Thank you," I whispered before standing and walking through to the bedroom. I could hear Blake talking to the officers as I closed the door behind me and sat on the edge of the bed. My mind went to Cooper, my friend who had died at the hands of Sara. I wouldn't, however, allow myself to grieve for him. Everything that he had said and done to me had been a complete lie. The one thing that I could sit here and allow myself, though, was pride. I had lived the past four and a half years scared and running. I had always associated happiness with pain. Yet out of everyone who had ever tried to hurt me, I was the one that was seated here now with a future ahead of me. They had tried and failed to ruin me. I always believed that running would save me. I had run from London to New York only to experience it all again. I had tried to run from New York, but Blake hadn't allowed it. I had been left alone for almost two weeks while Blake worked away. I had been in the presence of those who wanted me dead, yet I had survived. I had been forced to face my fears without even realizing it, and Cooper had died and Sara was under protection in hospital. I had won. Every single battle

I had been faced with, I had won. Suddenly I had no fear any more. Nothing and no one could ever hurt me again. With that in mind, I pulled myself off the bed and headed to the wardrobe. I had a few things I needed to tell Sara, and I wouldn't be holding back.

21

Blake had tried to talk me out of seeing Sara right up until the moment that we stood outside of her hospital room door, but I was not going to give in this time. This was something that I needed to do; I had questions that needed answers – answers that only she held the key to.

Blake had wanted to come in with me; he was afraid that I would crumble if I tackled this alone. But this was for me; I needed this. I needed to see how badly she was suffering because of the pain that she had caused to so many people.

Seeing Sara lying there fighting for her life while her body was wired up to so many different machines reminded me so much of when I lost my dad. The beeping of one machine echoed from the pumping of another. I was unsure whether my nausea came from the memory of losing my dad only three months prior, or from the baby that I was now looking after inside of me that Blake was yet to know about. But there was one thing that I did know for sure: the only difference between my dad and Sara was that my dad never deserved to die.

"What are her chances of pulling through?" I asked the nurse that was currently topping up a drip that was being driven straight into Sara's arm. The nurse looked to Sara, who nodded painfully before her eyes rested back on me.

"She has internal bleeding that we are finding very difficult to control. The next twenty-four hours are crucial. I nodded and stepped forward to Sara's bedside as the nurse left the room.

"Why did you call me here?" I said bluntly "So I can see how shit you look and feel guilty for the rest of my life? What?"

"I needed to tell you that I'm sorry." Her voice was strained; the pain was evident in her body with every breath that she took. But in this moment; I didn't care. "Cooper begged me not to hurt you. Once he knew what I was doing, he asked me to leave you alone; I swear he had nothing to do with this. I used him. Just to get to you, I used him." Even her sobs sounded painful. "I'm so sorry, Jo."

"Are you sorry that Cooper died, or that I survived?"

"I never meant for any of this to happen. It got out of control. I got out of control, and now …" she cried.

"And now Cooper is dead," I spat out. "He is dead because of you." Charging forward, I had to stop myself from hurting her. My hands clung tightly to the sheets on her bed. "How do you feel knowing that you are responsible for the death of the only person who was willing to put up with your shit? You killed him!" I yelled. My body shook from the adrenalin that was running through my veins. If I could have got away with it, I would have put my hands around her neck and choked the last bit of life right from her. But she didn't deserve to die. She didn't deserve an easy way out of this.

"Why did you do this?" I whispered. "Why did you want to hurt me? I have never done anything to hurt you; why did you want to hurt me?"

Sara took a deep, shaky breath. "Because you're everything that I wanted to be," she said quietly.

"Don't patronize me! I have had a lifetime of being scared of people like you, feeling intimidated by people like you! I have run, over and over again. I run because that is the only way I could ever learn to deal with people like you. Not anymore. I deserve to be happy. I deserve a good life! I don't deserve to feel as though I am the one who is in the wrong when I never have been! This ends, and it ends right now."

"If I could go back," Sara said, "If I could have seen just how out of control I was, I swear to you I would have stopped before it was too late, I never wanted anyone to die, I swear to you Jo, you have to believe me, I just wanted someone to love me, to show me how much they cared; just how Cooper and Blake both loved and cared for you." I leaned towards Sara, my face only inches from hers.

"Do you have any idea what you have put me through? Can you even imagine how Cooper's family is feeling right now?"

"I'm sorry Jo, I am so so sorry. Please … please, forgive me."

"Never," I shot back, "I will never ever forgive you or Cooper for any of this, and you know what? I hope you don't die. Death would be too good for you. Instead I want you to survive this; I want you to get better and go to trial for everything that you put me through and for killing Cooper. I want you to rot in a tiny prison cell for the rest of your life. That is what I want, but one thing I will never ever do, is forgive you."

Sara's eyes focused on me, and I could see the fear in them. I could see that she was more scared about living than of her body giving up on her right now. "I am going to go. I am going to walk out of this room with my head held high, knowing that no matter what, I didn't choose the path that you took. You did that all by yourself. Goodbye, Sara." I didn't look back as I left the room and walked straight into Blake's arms. Now I was finally ready to begin my happy ever after.

Blake didn't ask what words passed between Sara and me in the hospital room, but I sensed that he could see the satisfaction that I felt from seeing her. I could even see it myself when I stood and looked at myself in the bathroom mirror; it was as though years of heartache and fear had evaporated from my body. It was either that or what I had read to be a pregnancy glow. But I felt different too. I finally felt free to feel happy without guilt or fear. It had taken almost five years and the deaths of both Imogen and Cooper for me to realize that none of it had ever been my fault. I would always remember this from that day forward. We all choose our own paths in life; no one but you is responsible for that choice.

I sat at the dining table watching Blake as he plated up lasagna that he had made for us both. I was the luckiest woman alive to have Blake. Not only that, but I was also carrying his child. My life was finally about to begin.

"Did you use all three ovens for this or just the one?" I said as Blake placed our plates in front of us. He smiled in what seemed to be relief before kissing me quickly and sitting down.

"You doing okay?" he asked carefully.

"Ribs are still a bit sore, but other than that … yes, I'm doing okay."

"Good." Blake smiled as he leaned forward and opened the bottle of wine that he had placed on the table. I watched as he began filling his glass, knowing that now was the time to tell him about the baby. I placed my hand over the top on my glass just as he turned to me.

"I'd better not have any," I said nervously.

Blake placed the bottle down. "You okay?"

"There's something I need to tell you. I should have told you when we got back from hospital, but everything went kind of crazy. Then I was going to tell you in the bath last night, but we got interrupted by the police—"

"What is it?" Blake asked.

I took a deep breath and turned in my seat to face Blake. "At the hospital, they did some routine blood tests."

"Oh my God, are you ill?" Blake said, taking my hands in his.

"No. I'm not ill," I replied quickly. "Blake, I didn't mean this to happen; it just did. And whatever you decide we do, then that is fine by me. I don't want to do anything that you're not happy with, okay? I want to do what is right for us – for you and me and for our future. Because I can see it now; I can finally see our future, Blake, and it doesn't scare me anymore." I smiled, but tears also filled my eyes.

"Tell me what they found, Jo, please," he asked nervously.

Taking a deep breath, in I replied in a whisper, "A baby, Blake. They found a baby."

I wasn't quite sure, but it looked as though Blake had stopped functioning completely as he processed the news.

"A baby?"

I nodded. "They don't know how far or anything else yet; I need to book in for an ultrasound," I replied as I watched him carefully.

"I'm going to be a daddy?" his mouth lifted into a genuine happy smile.

"You're going to be a daddy," I choked out.

"I'm going to be a daddy," he repeated. "We're having a baby?"

"Yes." I smiled as I took his hand and placed it to my stomach. "We are having a baby." Blake's arms instantly wrapped around me as he lifted me from my seat and spun me around in excitement.

"We're having a baby!" he yelled at the top of his voice before he stopped spinning me and placed me back to the ground on shaky legs. "I love you so much," he said as his hands cupped my face. "I love you I love you I love you I love you!" His lips crashed against mine as he kissed me over and over again, telling me he loved me between each kiss. "Marry me," he said suddenly as he pulled away from my mouth.

"What?"

"Marry me," he said again with conviction.

"No," I replied with a giggle.

"Why not?" he asked, sounding wounded "We're having a baby, Jo; let's make it a complete family. Marry me."

"You're asking me because I'm pregnant."

"Am not."

"Am so." I smiled. "Would you have asked me tonight if I hadn't told you I was pregnant?" I teased.

Blake appeared to think for a while before replying, "I told you I wanted to marry you weeks ago, so technically I have already asked you."

"You know that we will get married," I said as my fingers trailed the line of his shirt collar. "Ask me properly one day, and I will say yes." I smiled.

"You are one stubborn lady," Blake said as he pulled me closer to him, "and I love you more than I could ever tell you. We're having a baby. Wow."

Blake didn't stop fidgeting the whole time we sat in the waiting room to DR Greene's office. We were about to have the first scan of our pregnancy, and for once I was the calm one. It was highly amusing watching Blake as he paced the floor, wearing the carpet visibly thin before stopping in front of a poster and reading it quickly before pacing again. When he eventually sat down, he flicked through magazine after magazine before tossing them back onto the messy pile on the table. His nervous eyes caught mine as he saw me smiling with humour at him. "What?" he asked.

"I love you," I said simply.

"I love you too," he said, finally starting to relax.

"Miss Summers, DR Greene will see you now." Blake was up and following the doctor's assistant before I had chance to struggle out of the uncomfortable seat.

"Miss Summers, hello," DR Greene greeted me as I entered the room.

I smiled as I shook her hand. "Please, call me Jo."

"Jo," she said with a smile, "it's lovely to meet you. Please take a seat. And Blake, it's lovely to see you. You have grown a lot since I saw you last," she joked. DR Greene was an old work colleague of Blake's mum's from when she had worked at this hospital while Blake was growing up.

Blake smiled as he shook her hand and sat next to me.

"He's very nervous," I pointed out.

DR Greene laughed. "You would be surprised how many of the fathers I see are more nervous than the mommies. Everything will be just fine." She smiled. "So this is your first pregnancy, is that correct?"

I nodded. "Yes."

"Have you suffered any nausea?"

"I've been sick a couple of times, but I'm not sure either was baby related," I said, starting to panic. "Does that mean there's a problem?"

"Not at all, no," she said, smiling. "Every pregnancy is different. Some women have no sickness whatsoever; others can suffer right up to forty weeks."

I felt Blake's hand wrap around mine; he was shaking. "When do we get to see the baby?" he asked nervously.

She smiled. "In a few moments. Now, as we are unsure of the gestation, we shall perform a transvaginal ultrasound scan. Have you heard of these before?"

"No," I answered, shaking my head. DR Greene stood and headed behind a curtain to the bed where the scan would take place.

"We shall perform the scan by inserting this probe here into your vagina. You won't feel any pain but may experience a little discomfort. This will give us a good idea of how many weeks pregnant you are, and we should also be able to pick up baby's heartbeat." She smiled.

"Wow," Blake gasped.

"When you're ready, Miss Summers, if you would like to remove your trousers and underwear and hop up onto the bed for me, covering yourself with the sheets provided."

Once I was in position, DR Greene appeared with Blake, who was immediately at my side with his hand firmly gripping mine.

"Okay," she said gently. "Just relax for me." I felt slight discomfort as the probe entered, but the thought of what I was about to see outweighed that by miles.

"Okay," she said, "here we go." Blake and I watched DR Greene as she pushed various buttons on the screen and studied different parts of it for what felt like an eternity.

"Is there a problem?" Blake asked impatiently.

DR Greene turned to face us; my body immediately filled with dread. "Do either of you have multiple births anywhere in the family?"

"My father was a twin." I replied knowing what was coming.

DR Greene turned the monitor to face us. "Do you see this here?" She pointed to something, and we both replied yes, but I'm pretty sure that Blake was equally as confused as I was. "And this right here?" She moved across to another little dot that looked like a blob.

"Is something wrong?" I asked.

She smiled. "Not at all, Jo. You are having twins. Here is baby one, and here is baby two," she said, grinning.

"Two babies?" Blake asked in shock before turning to face me. "We're having two babies," he said, smiling in disbelief just as the sound of two tiny heartbeats filled the quiet room.

It was the most magical sound I had ever heard. My two tiny babies' hearts were beating inside of me. How could anything ever compare to that feeling?

"Congratulations to you both," DR Greene said. "Everything looks fantastic, sounds fantastic. There are no visible problems, and they're both growing beautifully. According to this, you are ten weeks and four days gone, making your due date" – she hesitated – "April seventeenth."

"Oh my God," I gasped. "And you are sure that both babies are okay?"

She smiled. "Definitely. I'm going to leave you two alone for a moment; when you're ready, I'll see you both back at my desk."

"I'm so proud of you," Blake said, placing a kiss to my lips just after DR Greene left us.

"I haven't done anything yet," I laughed.

"You're growing two babies in there. Oh my God, two babies." He shook his head, smiling. "We made them," he said in awe. "Isn't that just the craziest thing ever?"

"Yes it is," I answered truthfully. "Maybe pushing them both out will prove a little more crazy though," I said as we both laughed.

"You know what it means that I've been carrying these babies for almost eleven weeks?"

Blake nodded. "You fell pregnant that first weekend we were together."

I shook my head in disbelief. "I can't believe that I didn't adjust the time of my pill to match the time difference between London and New York."

"Yeah, well, I'm glad you didn't." Blake smiled.

"So am I."

"So do you think you can handle living with three boys?" he mocked.

"Are you kidding me? You are going to be living with three screaming, hormonal ladies MR Mackenzie." I smiled. "I hope you can cope with that." I gave Blake a lopsided grin.

"I think we're both capable of coping with absolutely anything after the crazy couple of months we have had." His face grew serious. "Are you happy," he asked me carefully.

"I have never felt so happy in the whole of my life," I said,

Beautifully Unbroken

meaning every single word of it.

22

"For the two millionth time, Casey, nothing is going to go wrong. Everything is exactly how it should be; there is absolutely nothing for you to worry about," I said again as Casey paced the hotel room fully dressed and ready to make her vows to Alex.

"Please, I just have this feeling," Casey said, placing her hand around her neck in panic. "Please just go and check that Alex is where he should be, please."

"Can't I just call Blake?"

"No. No, he could lie for him. I want to know that you see him, physically see him, and know he's going to be there."

"He will be there," I said calmly.

"Please, Jo," she begged.

"Okay, I am going," I said in defeat. "Just take some deep breaths and calm down; you are going to hyperventilate."

Casey took two deep breaths, but her panic was still visible. "Okay. I am going to check on Alex; just keep calm. Please."

Blake opened the door semi dressed in his tux. Just lately I only had to look at him and I wanted to jump on him and tear his clothes off. I had read about this in pregnancy magazines. It was caused by the change in hormones. With me it was that plus the fact that Blake was by far the sexiest man on the planet.

His eyes took in my appearance, roaming up and down my body a couple of times before he smiled. "Wow, you look beautiful," he said, wrapping his arms around my waist and pulling me to him.

"I look fat," I said, pouting.

"You are not fat," Blake said, kissing the tip of my nose. "You're just keeping our babies warm."

A warm feeling came over me. "How do you always know the right thing to say?"

"Because I always speak the truth." He smiled before leaning in for a lingering kiss.

"Who is it?" Alex shouted from somewhere inside the room. Blake growled and pulled his mouth from mine.

I peeked around Blake's body. "Hello. Me again." I smiled.

"For the last time, I am not gonna do a runner," he said, frustrated as he tried in vain to fasten his bow tie.

"Good. Blake, keep eyes on him at all times," I said in a mocking tone.

"I am not going to run, jeez."

"Okay," I said simply. "Casey just has the crazy idea that something is going to go horribly wrong," I said, rolling my eyes.

Alex finished fastening his tie and turned to face me. "Tell Casey from me that I love her, I cannot wait to be her husband, and I will see her in thirty minutes."

I smiled. "Okay. See you both in a bit, then," I said excitedly before heading out into the hall.

"Jo," Blake called back, "can you help me with this thing?" he said, holding up his tie. I took it from his hand and placed it around his neck. His mouth lowered and he started trailing kisses along my neck.

"Blake, stop," I said, swatting him away.

"I can't; you know what these sexy curves are doing to me," he said as he continued.

"And you know how horny this pregnancy is making me. Now stop until we can actually—" Blake stopped instantly and looked down at me. "Why do you seem shorter? Don't tell me pregnancy shrinks you too?"

"Don't tell Casey," I said, looking around him to make sure Alex wasn't listening before lifting the hem of my dress and revealing to him the white Converse that he had bought me for the Yankees game.

Blake snorted. "Oh my God."

"Don't laugh," I said. "I still have twenty-six weeks to go

carrying two humans inside of me. I'm showing already and can't wear my heels without feeling like my feet and back are both breaking." I pouted. "I'm going to look like a barrel by the time spring arrives."

"But you will be my barrel," Blake teased, causing me to swat him again.

"I love you," I said.

He smiled. "I love you too. All three of you."

"Can I take this dance, ma'am?" Blake held his hand out to me; I took it instantly before he led me to the dance floor. The wedding had been beautiful. There were no catastrophes, as Casey had imagined, and there wasn't a dry eye in the house when they said their vows. It had been magical. All of the guests had waved them off for their honeymoon just half an hour before. My feet were throbbing, and I was desperate to call it a day, but Blake still had a duty as best man to make sure the night finished well.

I leaned into him as we swayed to Ellie Goulding singing "How Long Will I Love You."

"This song was playing in your apartment that first night that we—"

"Conceived these babies?" I sniggered.

"Yeah," Blake laughed.

"Feels like a lifetime ago now," I said against his chest. "It's been a truly magical day."

"It has," he said, kissing briefly into my hair.

"Can we call it a night soon?" I asked.

"Sure." Blake stopped dancing and looked down to me. "There's just something I want to show you first though." He smiled. "Follow me." He took my hand and led me out of the ballroom, through reception, and out towards the boathouse, where a member of staff stood waiting for us.

Looking down I noticed a gondola lit up by what must have been one hundred candles affixed around the perimeter of the boat.

"I am not getting in that thing, Blake," I said, shaking my head.

"Come on, it'll be fun." He smiled as he climbed down into the gondola and held his arms out for me to join him.

"What if I tip the boat?" I said, reluctant to give him my hands.

"We're not gonna tip; just get in the boat," he said, amused.

I let out a little squeal as my feet left the ground for a moment before I was safely in the boat and sitting opposite Blake.

My fingers gripped the seat as I forced myself to sit as still as possible.

Blake nodded. "Thank you, Eric."

"Is he not coming with us?" I said, panicked.

"Don't you trust me?" Blake asked.

"You don't want the answer to that right now."

Blake shook his head and laughed as he took the oar in his hands and started rowing us towards the middle of the lake.

"See," he said. "Who needs Eric?"

Slowly I began to relax. It turned out I could trust Blake in the pitch black on a lake in the middle of New York after all.

Blake stopped rowing, and we sat as the boat bobbed gently up and down. There was still a warm breeze blowing in the air, and there must have been a million stars twinkling above us.

"This is amazing," I said, looking around at the stars, which seemed to be getting brighter and more clustered. I gasped as a shooting star sped across the night sky "Did you just see that?"

"I did," Blake said, but I could tell that his eyes were only on me. "Make a wish," he said.

Closing my eyes, I couldn't hide the smile that graced my lips. "Done," I said. I opened my eyes and looked to Blake.

"What did you wish for?" he asked, sitting forward and studying me.

I smirked. "Now, if I tell you that, it won't come true will it?"

Blake sighed and shook his head. "Do you have any idea how much I love you?" he said in his deep, raspy voice.

I swallowed past the emotion that had appeared. "I do, yes," I replied.

"Good," Blake replied before placing his hand in the inside of his jacket and pulling out a tiny black velvet box. My hands shot to my mouth as I gasped in shock. Before I knew it, Blake was on one knee in the middle of the boat, opening the small box, revealing the most beautiful diamond cluster ring that I had ever seen.

My eyes clouded with tears. Blake cleared his throat; his emotions were clearly visible.

"From the first moment that I met you, I knew that you were the woman who I would spend my forever with. You captured me with you beauty, your innocence, and definitely your stubbornness." We both laughed through the happy tears that we were both shedding. "The first time you spoke to me, I wanted to shut you up by taking your mouth in mine and never letting you go. You gave me feelings that I only believed happened in movies and in books. I couldn't see how anyone could love somebody that much until I met you. And now I know that true love does exist, because mine is sitting opposite me right now. You made me believe that each one of us has a soul mate, and when you find that person, you know that you will be happy for the rest of your life. There are mountains to climb and stumbling blocks placed in your path, but you fight it. You know that this is the one fight that it is worth using every ounce of your strength to win. And you never give up. Just as we didn't give up. When I met you, you were broken. I promised you that I would fix you, and when I look at you now, I don't see broken any more. I see you – all of you. And I see that finally, you are happy. I'd like to think I'm responsible for that in some small way."

"You are," I choked out quietly.

"Do you remember when I bought you the car and you asked me what you could possibly give me to repay me?"

I nodded.

"Well, you have. Everything that I have ever needed or wanted is here in this boat with me right now. You have given me your heart, your soul, and your trust. Money can't buy that." He smiled. "But most of all, you have given me you, not forgetting those two tiny little babies in there that we made."

I smiled through the tears as I placed my hands to my tiny bump and cradled our children.

"And they are going to love you. God, they will love you so much. Just as much as I do. And they will need you, just as much as I always will. What say we close the old book and start writing a new one? This has been by far the best adventure that I have ever taken; I don't ever want it to stop." He smiled. "There is, however, just one thing that I want to change."

"What's that?" I asked, feeling my eyebrows knitting together in confusion.

"Your last name." He smiled. "Josephine Summers, will you marry me?"

"Yes, yes I will marry you," I choked out.

"She said yes!" Blake's voice echoed around the quiet lake before he took the ring from the box and placed it carefully onto my finger.

"Thank you for letting me love you," he said as his fingers knotted with mine.

"Thank you for showing me what real love is," I said before leaning forward and claiming Blake's mouth with mine.

"I will love you forever and more," Blake said as his lips left mine and his brow pressed to mine. "All three of you."

Epilogue

Three months later

"Wakey wakey, birthday girl." Blake's voice sounded as chirpy as the birds that I had spent most of the morning listening to whilst drifting in and out of an uncomfortable sleep. Groaning, I turned myself towards him and forced my eyes to open against their will.

"What time is it?" I grumbled.

"It's just past noon," he said before he leaned in and kissed me on the nose. "You didn't sleep much at all, did you?"

"These babies have built an alliance against me," I moaned, rolling onto my back, gently rubbing my bulging belly. Blake's hand covered mine just as baby one gave out an almighty kick.

"I don't think so, mister; if you wanna be a sports star, it will have to be anything but football," Blake said with a grin just as baby two joined in.

"See, I told you, they're in there working together." I smiled, feeling absolutely exhausted but completely and utterly content.

"I'm still totally amazed that there are two tiny babies in there," Blake said in awe.

"Well, they don't feel tiny," I moaned. "I feel like I'm carrying a herd of elephants." Blake took my hand and helped me up off the bed.

"Only twelve weeks to go, beautiful."

"Yay," I said with little enthusiasm. "And then they will be ganging up on us for real," I said in horror as Blake chuckled behind me.

"I'm gonna get back to the kitchen and give your mom a hand; I have been given the job of head table layer," he said proudly.

"Blake, that's because you will be getting under Mum's feet in the kitchen and no one else is around to do it." I smiled.

"Ouch," he said, as if I had hurt his feelings. "Anyway, everyone will be arriving shortly, and then you can have your present. But not until after lunch." He was like an exited child at Christmas.

"Okay." I smiled as he kissed my cheek before heading out of the bedroom and downstairs to help with lunch.

Since arriving in London a week prior to spend Christmas with my mum, Blake had insisted on fulfilling a lot of the memories that I had once told him I missed about London.

So far we had woken in time to hear the birds singing every morning, which was always my favourite memory. We had eaten fish and chips out of the paper on Friday night whilst seated in front of the TV watching a DVD. Blake had also insisted on taking me out for drives through the countryside every single day. And every single time, we had managed to get lost. It had been fifteen years since I had lived out in the sticks, and all the roads had come to look like one. Blake always found it hilarious that we were lost, though, and I loved nothing more than seeing him happy.

Later that day, the memory would consist of the big family Sunday lunch. The only person missing from the table would be my dad. It was going to be tough, but I knew that Blake would help me through it. The one thing I truly loved about Blake was that I never needed to tell him how I felt for him to know what to say to me. We were like yin and yang; one couldn't exist without the other. And that was the truth for me and Blake.

Once dressed and ready for lunch, I headed downstairs to the beautiful aroma of Mum's cooking and the sound of happiness filtering from the lounge.

"Here's the birthday girl." Uncle Anthony stood and headed over to me, and he placed a kiss on my cheek. "Look at you," he said, placing his hand to my belly. "You look amazing."

"I feel like a heffalump," I joked.

Aunt Elizabeth was next to greet me just as Jemma and Tim arrived. "Happy birthday, darling." Jemma looked as harassed as I felt. She was due to give birth any day now and was becoming frustrated with the wait. Tim was fussing over her constantly, which seemed only to make her more frustrated, as she swatted him away constantly. They were such a beautiful couple; I had envied them both until Blake had walked into my life. I loved watching how Tim would go out of his way to show Jemma his affection and not care about who was watching. Jemma wouldn't notice a lot of the time, probably because he did it at every opportunity, but it was easy to spot as an outsider looking in.

Blake and Tim had spent a lot of time getting to know each other over the past week; they were similar in a lot of ways, especially how they fussed over Jemma and me. But they looked completely different. Blake was happy lounging in jogging bottoms and a T-shirt, whereas I never saw Tim without a suit. He had earned the nickname James Bond from my uncle Anthony because even to go to a football match he would be all suited up. That, plus the fact that he was a dead ringer for Daniel Craig.

"Any signs yet?" I asked as we sat at the dining table while Blake carved the huge goose that Mum had spent most of the day roasting.

"A few pains here and there," she said, scrunching up her nose. "I just want this thing out of me now."

Uncle Anthony butted in. "It's a baby, not a thing."

"Well, a baby isn't capable of some of the tricks she keeps pulling."

"Tell me about it. Think of that and times it by two," I said, rubbing my bump. "And they take it in turns as well. One sleeps while the other plays footy with my bladder, and then vice versa."

"Wow, I'm stressing over one, and you're going to have it twice as bad." Jemma shuddered.

"Double trouble," Blake said.

"Triple if you include Jo," Tim teased.

Blake laughed. "So true. I'm just grateful one of the babies is a boy – even the load."

"You found out what you're having then?" Jemma asked excitedly.

"A boy and a girl," Blake answered immediately as he finished carving and pulled out the seat next to me and sat down.

"Wow, well that in itself is worth a celebration," Tim said, lifting his glass. "Congratulations to you both."

I shrugged. "At least this way we will only have to do it the once."

"I thought we were going to have more than two kids?" Blake said.

"Can I get these two out of me first before we make that kind of decision?" I replied defensively.

Blake smirked. "I suppose so."

"It's a shame that our babies won't grow up together like we did," I said sadly.

"Have you chosen names?" Aunty Elizabeth asked.

Blake and I looked to each other and smiled. "We're not one hundred per cent on a girl's name yet, but our son will be named after Jo's father." He placed his hand in mine and squeezed gently.

"Well, John seems like an older name, so we're toying with Johnny at the moment," I added.

"Perfect," Uncle Anthony said. "Just what we all called him as a nipper."

"He would be so proud of you, Jo," Aunty Elizabeth said before I felt Mum place her lips to my temple as she filled my glass with orange juice.

"He certainly would," Mum said before heading to the top of the table, where Dad always used to sit. She lifted her glass, and the table fell silent. I could see that she was struggling to stem her emotion as she started to speak. "This past year has been the most horrific of my life. nothing can ever prepare you for losing the man that you have loved for the most part of your life, and even though I can now deal with the fact that John is no longer by my side, each day is still as hard as the day before."

I felt Blake's thumb gently stroking my hand, assuring me that he was there for me.

"The worst part of it all is that if he were here now, and he could see what we have accomplished around this table, there would be no prouder man alive than my John." Mum sucked in a deep breath. "Oh dear, look at me getting all emotional; I told myself not to do this," she said, reaching for her napkin and wiping her eyes gracefully. "Anyway, if you are watching down on us all now, John," – she raised her glass and her gaze above us all – "I just want you to know that I love you, and to thank you for everything that I will ever need, and that is everything that I have before me around this table."

"To Johnny Boy," Uncle Anthony said, lifting his glass with a wink.

"To Dad," I said, quietly trying to bite back the tears.

"And to my beautiful daughter, Jo," Mum said. "I would never have believed even a year ago that we would be sitting here now with my daughter, her fiancé, and my two very longed-for grandchildren on the way. Happy birthday, darling, I love you." She then took a sip of her wine.

"I love you too, Mum."

"So," Mum said chirpily, "Who's hungry?"

"Do I get my present now?" I asked Blake as we were all finishing off dessert.

"Patience," he said, teasing. "You need to make your speech first."

"What? I am not making a speech," I said, shaking my head.

"Speech!" Tim shouted before Uncle Anthony started tapping his glass with a knife.

"Come on, Jo, just say … anything." Blake shrugged. "And then you can have your present."

"Promise?" I asked.

"Promise."

Reluctantly I stood to my feet and took my orange juice in hand as everyone whooped and whistled. Shaking my head with embarrassment, I began. "Dinner was lovely, Mum, thank you," I started. She nodded happily. "Well, what can I say? It certainly has been a year full of emotions. I miss Dad more than I could ever express; he was the first man that I ever loved and will always hold that part of my heart no matter what. I wish so, so much that he were here today. I know he would love Blake, and I know how much he would have loved these two little terrors," I said, cradling my stomach. "And I know that they would have adored him so, so much too." I felt my eyes well with tears. "This pregnancy has made me an emotional wreck," I said wiping my eyes.

"You have always been an emotional wreck," Blake said cheekily as he took my hand in his.

"Anyway," I said, taking a deep breath, "I love each and every one of you; you are the people who have made me the person that I am today." I drew my eyebrows together in confusion. "Hopefully that's a good thing." Everyone laughed.

"So—" I was about to raise my glass just as something warm and furry tickled my legs. "Holy shit! What the fuck is that!" I screamed as I jumped up onto my chair.

Jemma's scream echoed mine as she too hopped up onto her chair. Everyone else stayed rooted to their chairs, laughing, except for Mum, who was trying her hardest to stifle her amusement. "You, young lady, have been living away from home too long; those babies can hear you, you know."

Blake bent down to retrieve something from under the table. When he reappeared, he was holding a puppy.

"Say hi to Jasper," he said.

"What?" I asked as Jemma and I climbed carefully down from our chairs.

"Well, he is a small part of your present. He should have been in the kitchen until it was time to bring him out." He looked at the Jasper. "You little rascal," he said as he rubbed his nose against his.

"He's beautiful," I said, taking him from Blake. He looked at me with his big, sad eyes. He reminded me of Charlie, the cocker spaniel that we had had when I was a child. "Oh my God he's adorable!" I said as he licked my face over and over "How are we going to get him home?" I asked.

"Well, that is why he needed to stay hidden. Is it okay if we leave now so I can give Jo her present?" Blake asked.

"Yes, yes. The suspense is killing me," Uncle Anthony said. Mum took Jasper from me and kissed my cheek. "I can't wait to hear how you reacted to this one," she whispered.

"Come with us," I suggested.

"No, no dear. This is all for you," she said, smiling before disappearing into the kitchen with Jasper.

"Oh no," Jemma cried. "I think my water just broke!"

"What!" Tim yelled as he pushed his chair away and started pacing the room. "We haven't brought your bag. How long until she comes out? Are you in pain?"

"Aarrgghhhh." Jemma cradled her stomach as a contraction hit. She started puffing out quick, short breaths. "Jesus that hurt."

"Okay, dear, keep calm," Aunty Elizabeth said, rushing to her side. "The baby isn't going to arrive just yet, but we need to get you to the hospital."

I watched everyone fuss around Jemma. Mum had returned and sat one side of her while Aunt Elizabeth talked calmly to her, and Blake was reassuring Tim, trying to calm him while Uncle Anthony got on the phone to the hospital. I was rooted to the spot, unable to move myself or to speak even; I just sat and watched as Jemma cried out over and over in pain.

"She's gonna be fine, Jo," Uncle Anthony said, squeezing my shoulder before heading around to help Jemma out of the seat.

"Oh my God, the contractions are close," she screamed as she stood. "This baby is coming!"

Everyone followed her and Tim out of the house and helped to get her into the car. I knew that labour had to be painful – I had watched quite a few shows about it recently – but seeing it first-hand opposite me was the most horrifying thing I had ever witnessed.

"She's gonna have the baby," I said in a hushed tone. "She's going to have that baby, now." I began to panic; my breathing became ragged.

"Okay, calm down," Blake whispered. "She's going to be fine."

"She was in pain."

"Well, that's kind of what happens during labour."

I looked down at my stomach and realized that before I knew it; that would be me.

"I'm not gonna be able to do it." My breathing became heavy, but Blake just laughed.

"God, I love you more and more every day," he said, holding his hand out to me. I stood on shaky feet.

"What if I can't do it? How will they get these babies out if I can't do it?"

"Jo," Blake said, holding my shoulders and meeting my eyes, "you are the strongest woman I have ever met. You may not think so, but I know so. You are going to be fine."

Uncle Anthony and Aunt Elizabeth reappeared, looking nervous but elated.

"You will call me, right? As soon as you hear anything?"

"Of course we will," Mum said. "Now go; the suspense is killing me."

We were somewhere out in the countryside; this time Blake had programmed the satnav to tell us where to go, but he was still refusing to tell me anything until we got there.

I checked my phone over and over for news on Jemma, but there was nothing as yet.

"We're here," Blake said as we pulled into a narrow country lane. I looked around frantically but could see only trees ahead and around us. Until finally it came into sight. We were approaching the house that I had grown up in; Blake was taking me there for my final memory.

We got out of the car and stood before the home that I had loved so much as a child. The house that had given me the best memories that were so dear to me.

Noticing that the house looked empty, my eyes scanned to the "Sold" sign that was pinned to the side of the garage.

"I hope whoever has brought this house is as happy as we were here," I said, not taking my eyes from it. "It looks exactly how I remember." I smiled. "Thank you for showing it to me," I said, turning to Blake. He placed his arm around my waist and pulled me closer to him.

"I'm sure that the new family is going to have their happiest memories made right here in this house too. Just like you," he said, kissing my temple. I hugged him briefly. "Do you want your present now?" Blake asked.

"Finally," I said, releasing Blake and turning to head back to the car.

"Where are you going?" Blake asked.

"But I thought—"

"Just come here a moment."

Feeling confused, I walked back to Blake and stood at his side, waiting. Blake moved behind me and put his hand into his pocket. "Close your eyes," he whispered into my ear.

Even more confused, I closed my eyes.

"Hold out your hand."

I lifted my hand and tried desperately not to peek as I felt the coolness of something metal touch my palm.

"Now open your eyes," he said, placing his hands onto my shoulders.

When I opened my eyes, my attention was immediately drawn to the key that Blake had placed in my hand.

"This isn't a car key," I said quietly.

"No. No it isn't," Blake murmured into my ear.

"Blake?" I turned to face him, wanting desperately for my feeling about the key to be true.

"Happy birthday, Jo," he said, nodding to the house.

My whole body filled instantly with the most mixed array of emotions that I have ever felt.

"You didn't," I said, shaking my head.

"Oh, I did," he said happily.

"No," I said, unable to believe what was happening.

"Yes," he replied with a sparkle in his eye. "And if you look just over there," he said, pointing just above the roof.

I tried to focus in on the area he was pointing to but was unable to make out anything other than the clouds that were forming.

"Can you see the bubble that I had built especially for you?"

"Our bubble." I smiled. Blake took my hand and started leading me to the house.

"How? I mean … when? How did you?"

"When we found out you were pregnant." He smiled as he took the key from me and opened the door before gesturing for me to go in.

"But how?" I asked again.

"I contacted your uncle and asked him to keep checking for houses in the area you grew up in." He smiled as he closed the door behind us. Immediately I headed through to the huge kitchen and looked out to the back garden. "When he rang me and told me that this house had come up, it was like everything that was meant to be was being handed to me on a plate. I couldn't believe it."

"I don't know what to say," I said as happy tears started to fall. "It's perfect. It's the most perfect gift, the most perfect house, I just …" lost for words, I wrapped my arms around his neck and kissed him. "I am the luckiest girl in the world, do you know that? What did I ever do to deserve you?" I asked.

"It's me that's the lucky one, Jo. My life before you was nothing, meaningless. I am the lucky one."

I smiled. "We're going to have to agree to disagree on that one."

"Do you know what we are going to do in this house? We are going to bring our children up here, then our other children." I laughed against Blake's neck as happy tears rolled down my face. "Our grandchildren," he continued. "Our great-grandchildren. And this is where we will grow old together."

"What about the penthouse?"

"We will keep the penthouse." He shrugged as if it were the most normal thing in the world. "We will commute," he laughed.

"Commute?" I shook my head in amusement.

"Sure," he said, as if it were the simplest thing in the world. "But this will be our home. This is where our children will grow up," he said.

"What about your parents?"

"We will still see them just as often. Probably more once the babies arrive."

I rested my head down on his chest. "I love you so much."

"I love you too, Jo. So much that it hurts. I want to make you happy every minute of every single day."

"You do, Blake; you really do." I lifted my head and kissed him again.

"The tree swing is still out there," I said, looking over his shoulder.

"Do you want me to take it down?"

I thought for a second before answering. "No, just make sure it's secure."

"Sure." He smiled knowingly. "Come with me," he said, taking my hand. He walked us into the lounge, where an open fire was roaring. Placed in front were bags of marshmallows and two roasting sticks.

He shrugged. "I know we're not snowed in."

"But it's perfect," I whispered.

We sat in front of the fire and toasted marshmallows and talked about our new house. Blake and Uncle Anthony had modernized it immensely, but it was still the exact same house that I remember so well. It was perfection.

After stuffing myself with marshmallows, I lay on the rug with my head in Blake's lap and watched the flames as they flickered happily against the wood. Blake's fingers gently stroked my hair with the sound of just the crackling wood surrounding us.

I didn't realize I had drifted off to sleep until my phone rang. Jemma had given birth to a healthy six-pound baby girl. The day continued to get even more perfect.

After I placed my phone back in my bag, Blake arrived carrying two steaming mugs of hot chocolate before sitting next to me as we lapped up the warmth of the fire.

"Uncle Anthony and Aunt Elizabeth are staying with Mum for a while longer; apparently it's quite a clean-up job when your waters break all over an antique dining set." We both laughed.

"It's starting to snow out there," Blake said, nodding to the large window that looked out on the garden. I pushed myself from the floor, walked over, and watched as the snow began to come down thick and fast. Huge snowflakes started sticking to every possible surface; it wouldn't be long before I could get out there and make an honorary snowman for my dad.

"Do you want to go now before we end up getting stuck?" Blake said as he stood behind me and wrapped his arms around my waist.

"Can we stay?" I asked.

"Tomorrow is Christmas Eve, Jo; what if we can't get out?"

I turned in Blake's arms and cupped his face in my hands.

"Then we spend our first Christmas here in our new house."

"Are you happy?" Blake asked as he swept my hair from my face.

"I am the happiest that I have ever been. And do you know what makes it even better?"

"What's that?"

"I no longer fear anything. The only fear I have now is getting these two monkeys out of my body," I laughed. "Other than that"—I shrugged—"I no longer believe that there is ever a price to pay for being happy, and I know now that happiness isn't always followed by pain. You did what you always promised me that you would do Blake; you fixed me, thank you."

About the Author

D. M. Brittle had been interested in writing a novel for a few years but had never managed to put pen to paper until just over twelve months ago. She loves romance novels and is in love with the idea of love, which made writing Jo and Blake's story her passion. Her writing stalled last summer when her dad became ill. Unfortunately her dad passed away just before Christmas. Starting the New Year, she decided to get back into writing the story, knowing that her dad would be more than proud of her for achieving something that she had dreamed about for so long.

D M Brittle currently lives in the West Midlands, England, with her husband of fourteen years and her two girls, who are nine and five.

Acknowledgments

There are so many people that I would like to thank individually but there simply isn't enough paper!

First and foremost, thank you to each and every single one of my readers who took a chance on a brand new author and read Beautifully Unbroken, I never expected the response that I have received so thank you, each and every one of you. Thank you for the amazing reviews and for persuading me that we haven't had enough of Blake and Jo yet; their story will continue soon in Beautiful Perfection.

Thank you from the bottom of my heart to the only 2 people that I allowed to read Beautifully Unbroken before it was published. Samantha Gough and Jemma Ross, thank you for telling me what you liked and what you wanted to see more of in the book, I love how much you loved the story and how involved you both got when getting the book out there, I look forward to doing it all again with you for book 2!

And finally and most importantly, to my family and friends, especially my husband and children who put up with me and my mood swings while I tried and tried to get the book perfect, thank you for loving me and supporting me, I love you all so much.

47396015R00197

Printed in Poland
by Amazon Fulfillment
Poland Sp. z o.o., Wrocław